A

CRIMINAL

DEFENSE

A
CRIMINAL
DEFENSE

A LEGAL THRILLER

WILLIAM L. MYERS, JR.

THOMAS & MERCER

Text copyright © 2017 by William L. Myers, Jr.

Published by Thomas & Mercer, Seattle

www.apub.com

Amazon, the Amazon logo, and Thomas & Mercer are trademarks of Amazon.com, Inc., or its affiliates.

ISBN-13: 9781503943421
ISBN-10: 1503943429

Cover design by Faceout Studio

Printed in the United States of America

This book is dedicated to my parents, Bill and Evelyn Myers, the two most selfless people I've ever had the privilege of knowing. You devoted yourselves to each other and to your children, teaching us through your own example the value of hard work and a soft voice.

I miss you.

1

Thursday, May 31

It's eight o'clock in the morning and I'm parking my car in front of Celine Bauer's sad row house. The exterior of the three-story structure is beat-up brick. The house has a wooden porch, its green paint dirty and starting to peel. Flowerpots adorn the porch and the top step, but the plants are dead. Half a dozen newspapers, still in their plastic wrappers, are scattered about. Celine Bauer has clearly stopped caring about her home, something I've seen before in the parents and spouses of the imprisoned. As hope drains from their hearts, everything else becomes pointless.

Two years ago I agreed to take on the case of Celine's son, Justin, charged with second-degree murder in the beating death of a University of Pennsylvania undergraduate. Justin and two of his friends were tried together, and all three were found guilty. Celine sat through the trial convinced that her son's lawyer was incompetent. Justin had been a straight-A student at West Philly High, had never gotten into trouble before. According to his mother, Justin had not been with his friends when they beat the other boy to death but had joined up with them shortly afterward, not knowing what they'd done.

Celine sent me a heartfelt letter, asking for my help. She knew about me because I had recently won the release of a young man wrongly convicted on evidence manufactured by a rogue police detective. I agreed to review Justin's trial transcript, and, when I did, I saw immediately that Celine was right: Justin's trial counsel had completely botched the defense. I took the case pro bono and filed a petition for writ of habeas corpus on the grounds of ineffective assistance of counsel, which the trial judge promptly rejected. I then appealed to the Superior Court. We lost. Finally, I filed a petition for allowance of appeal to the Pennsylvania Supreme Court, the criminal law equivalent of a Hail Mary pass. But miracles do happen, and earlier this week I'd received the court's order granting my appeal.

I'd phoned Justin's mother three times in as many days but never heard back. I wanted Celine to hear the news, and her failure to return my calls told me she needed to.

Celine opens the door on the fourth knock. Her eyes are flat. I smell alcohol on her breath. We stare at each other until she backs away from the door, leaving it open for me to follow her inside. The living room looks much like the porch. Dead and dying plants. Mail in a pile on the floor. Plates crusted with food on the coffee table. Celine flops down on the sofa, lights a cigarette, waits for me to tell her the bad news.

I lower myself onto a worn chair on the other side of the coffee table. I take a deep breath. "It's good news, Celine," I say. She grunts. "No, really. The Supreme Court has granted us an appeal. They wouldn't do that unless they felt there were real grounds to hear the case. There's a strong chance we'll get a new trial. And if we do, I feel that we can win it."

Celine stares at me for a long time. Then she puts her cigarette out in the chipped glass ashtray on the coffee table. "When will the judges decide? When can I tell Justin he'll get a second chance? It's killing him in there. He gets beat up all the time. He's telling me he's gonna join a gang, for protection. He needs hope."

I nod. "It'll probably take about six months."

Celine sighs. "A long time."

"It's something for Justin to hang on to." I lean over, pick up the bourbon, and stand. "You don't need this." I walk the glass into the kitchen and empty it into the sink. When I come back, Celine is on her feet. "You're a strong woman, Celine. And you have to be the strongest you've ever been. For your son."

Celine's back stiffens. Her eyes harden. I nod again, hoping the fire I see in her will survive the coming months.

I walk to the car and start it, look at my own eyes in the rearview mirror. "You'll get that woman's boy out of prison," I say. "You will." And I mean it.

People like Celine and Justin are the reason I left the DA's office to become a defense attorney. The reason I often violate the sacred rule of lawyering: don't get personally involved. When I care about the client, it's always personal for me. But not all clients are like the Bauers. Many of my clients are guilty of everything they're charged with, and then some. They don't hire me to get justice but to avoid it at all costs. Find loopholes, get the evidence excluded, spin the jurors' heads with clever cross-examinations, and break their hearts with hard-luck stories—it doesn't matter how, just get them outta there. And the worst among them are the entitled executives who play shell games with other people's money, the white-collar defendants who drive to my office in Bentleys and ask my secretary if she can validate their parking. I care about those clients about as much as they care about everyone else—I'm only in it for the money.

An hour after I get back to my office, I'm set to meet one of them. Phillip Baldwin. Philadelphia's own homegrown mini-Madoff, Baldwin turned his family's hundred-year-old private-investment firm into a Ponzi scheme.

Since the day of his indictment by a federal grand jury, Phillip Baldwin has sworn his innocence and vowed to fight the charges all the way to the United States Supreme Court. Baldwin's trial is set to begin in three weeks, and my law partner, Susan Klein, and I are counting on the fees the case will bring in to pay our overhead.

At 9:45, I join Susan outside her office, and we walk down the lushly carpeted hall toward one of our conference rooms. The feel of our office is sleek and modern: a marble-floored lobby with tiger-wood receptionist desk, recessed lighting throughout, white walls adorned with original paintings of iconic Philadelphia city scenes—Boathouse Row, the art museum, Independence Hall.

We enter the conference room, and Baldwin stands to greet us. I'd read that Baldwin wore $10,000 William Fioravanti suits. The deep-blue double-breasted number he has on now certainly looks like it could go for that much. He paid much more for his Patek Philippe watch and sapphire cuff links. Baldwin even has a rich man's hair—thick, silver-gray, and sculpted atop his chiseled, fifty-five-year-old face.

We all sit down, and Baldwin begins. "Mick, Susan, thank you for agreeing to meet with us at the last minute. Some things have happened, and Kimberly and I felt it important to see you right away." He nods toward his thirty-year-old second wife, who is model-tall and thin with superbly highlighted brunette hair and blazing blue eyes. Kimberly Baldwin is one of the finest-looking Miss Pennsylvanias our commonwealth has ever turned out.

"What's happened?" asks Susan.

"Kimberly and I have talked it over, and I want to plead."

"I don't understand," my partner says.

"They're going to kill us," Kimberly says, her eyes filling with tears. "And Phillip's children."

"More death threats?" Susan asks.

Kimberly nods. "But these are serious." She reaches into her Louis Vuitton handbag, pulls out an envelope, and slides it across the table. Susan and I take turns reviewing its contents.

"Pictures of Kimberly leaving the gym," says Baldwin. "And of my twin daughters, taken at college. They're only twenty years old, for God's sake." As he speaks, Baldwin's handsome face contorts, overpowering the Botox that normally keeps him wrinkle-free. "And this," he says, handing me a note with letters cut out of magazines, the kind kidnappers write in movies.

It reads: *You rot in jail or they rot in boxes.*

"You've had death threats before," I reiterate.

"But now they're threatening *me*," says Kimberly, forgetting Baldwin's children. "And so are those government lawyers."

I see Baldwin stiffen at the mention of the US Attorneys' Office.

"The feds are threatening you?" Susan asks.

"They say they just want to talk . . . ," Kimberly begins. "God, I'm so confused."

"*Confused?*" Baldwin's face turns scarlet. "What's there to be confused about? The government is the enemy. You're my wife. You don't talk with them. Ever!"

"Let's everyone take a breath," Susan says.

"Just call the feds and get me a deal, Mick," says Baldwin.

"You realize the least you'd be facing is ten years."

Baldwin stiffens again. "Just get the best deal you can. Maybe in one of those places like they sent Martha Stewart or Michael Milken."

"Federal prison isn't the country club everyone thinks it is," says Susan.

But it's no use. The meeting drags on for another hour, until just after eleven, Baldwin refusing to change his mind.

Susan and I escort the Baldwins to the lobby, telling them they should sleep on it, then walk together to Susan's office. Susan flops down into her beige leather chair. I sink into one of the visitors' seats on the other side of the expensive glass-top worktable Susan uses as her desk. She takes off her artsy black-framed glasses and fastens her long ash-blonde locks with a hair tie. Her strong jaw and aquiline nose appear sharper without her hair hanging down to soften them.

"If my math is correct," I say, "half a million dollars just walked out the door."

"It's not the death threats Baldwin's afraid of, you know."

I raise my eyebrows.

"He's afraid of *her*. Kimberly. That she'll turn state's evidence against him."

"You think she knew about the scam?"

"Sweet little trophy wife is smarter than she looks."

I consider what Susan said. "Why would the feds even bother with her? They have more than enough to convict him. What else could she tell them?"

Susan gives me a rueful smile. "She could tell them where he's hidden the money."

I nod. Thieves like Baldwin always squirrel away a chunk of their ill-gotten loot in case the government ever comes knocking on their door.

Susan sinks back in her chair and sighs. "How much do we have in the operating account?"

"Not much," I say. "About eighty thousand."

Running a small law firm is a lot like being the bunny on a greyhound track. The greyhounds represent all your overhead: payroll, rent, electric, insurance premiums, phone and Internet, advertising, postage, plane fare, mileage, paper costs. The partners who own the law firm are the rabbit: always running as fast as they can, trying to stay ahead of the dogs.

"We should have paid the line down last year, when we got the money from the Lynch case." Susan's talking about the fee we received on a defective-product case we referred out to another firm. Though we'd talked about exactly that, in the end we decided to take the money as a distribution. I'd used part of my share to build a pool behind my house. Susan used hers to remodel the kitchen in her condo. The rest we spent upgrading our offices.

With the Baldwin case coming to trial, Susan and I had put most of our other cases on the back burner. That would have to change.

"Everyone'll have to start burning the midnight oil on our other cases," I say. For a second, I question whether taking on the Justin Bauer case was a good idea. But only for a second. The Phillip Baldwins of the world may be *how* we keep the doors open, but the Justin Bauers are *why*.

Susan shakes her head, looks up at the ceiling. "Not a good day for McFarland and Klein."

I walk to my office, sit for a minute, then turn my chair to look out the window, toward City Hall and, in the distance, the Delaware River. The clock at City Hall reads 11:40 when I sense a presence behind me in the doorway.

"Hey."

I turn around. It's the firm's lead investigator, my younger brother, Tommy. At five ten, Tommy is the same height as I am, but his broad shoulders and thick chest make him a far more powerful physical presence. The buzz-cut hair and prison tats peeking above his shirt collar imply a roughness not disguised by his expensive sport coat and precisely creased slacks.

Tommy walks in and takes a seat across the desk from me.

"What's up?" I say without enthusiasm.

Tommy raises his eyebrows. "What's eating you?"

I shake my head, wave him off. Tommy holds my gaze for a moment, and I am amazed, as always, that I can stare straight into his flat brown eyes and have no more sense as to what's behind them than if he were wearing *Blues Brothers* sunglasses.

I'm about to say something when Angie buzzes me on my speaker. "There's a call for you. She says she needs to talk to you right away."

"Who is it?" I ask, glancing at my watch. 11:45.

"It's that reporter, Jennifer Yamura."

Yamura recently broke an enormous police-corruption story, disclosing that the district attorney's office was running a grand-jury investigation into a well-organized ring of cops conspiring with local drug dealers to sell heroin and cocaine. The grand jury proceedings were, of course, meant to be confidential. In fact, the grand jury's very existence was supposed to be secret. And it was, until the young Channel 6 reporter divulged the proceedings on the six o'clock news. She claimed to have learned about the investigation from unnamed sources who were both privy to the investigation and somehow involved in the ring.

As details of the investigation emerged, it turned out that the story's timing couldn't have been worse. The police and DA's office had been finalizing plans to conduct a major sting that supposedly would have uncovered additional key players as yet unknown to the authorities. When the grand jury came to light, the cop ring shut itself down, and its members crawled back under their rocks.

The prosecutor in charge of the grand jury, Devlin Walker, is now fit to be tied. He's subpoenaed Yamura to appear before the grand jury to find out her source and what else she might know.

I tell Angie I'll take the call. As I pick up the receiver, I tell Tommy, "Whoever Yamura's sources are, they're in deep shit." I put the receiver to my ear.

Yamura introduces herself and tells me that, given the subpoena she's received, she wants to hire her own defense attorney. Channel 6 and ABC already have a squad of lawyers assigned to the case, but she doesn't trust them.

"I can see you tomorrow at four," I say as I type the appointment into my computer. I hang up and look at Tommy.

"When does she have to go before the grand jury?" Tommy asks.

"Monday." Four days from now. "Subpoena says to bring all of her notes and her laptop as well."

"She may as well bring her own frying pan, too."

"It's almost noon. You up for some lunch?"

"Can't today," he says, jumping up. "Gotta see a man about a horse."

I watch Tommy leave, wondering why he came into the office at all. My glum demeanor might have turned him away just now, but more often it's Tommy who's in a bad mood. My brother's a testy, unpredictable person, but I give him a lot of leeway considering all he's been through. Susan is less tolerant of him, and we've gotten into it a couple of times about Tommy's continued employment at the firm. But he's proven invaluable in a number of cases, and I've won the argument so far.

When Tommy's gone, I reach for the *Inquirer* on my desk. The front page features a story about David Hanson, an old friend of mine from law school. David is general counsel at Hanson World Industries, a Fortune 500 company headquartered in Philadelphia. HWI has never gone public. Its shares are owned by the direct lineal heirs of its founders, those heirs being David himself; his half brother, Edwin, who's the CEO; and two- or three-score cousins, aunts, and uncles. Today's article is all about a complex business arrangement that David has put together between HWI and a collection of companies in China and Japan. If the deal goes through, it will bring hundreds of jobs and millions of dollars to Philadelphia. The article paints a shining picture of my old friend. Then again, I've never known any account to portray David in less than glowing terms.

My phone rings and I see that, somehow, it's already 12:30. Angie's at lunch, so calls coming in for me ring directly to my line. I pick up the receiver. It's Jennifer Yamura again. She wants to move up our meeting.

We agree on a time, then I hang up and finish reading the feature about David Hanson. I toss the newspaper back onto my desk, stand, and look out the window.

About forty-five minutes later, I'm walking east on Walnut Street, Rittenhouse Square behind me to the west. Overhead, the sky is a brilliant blue, the temperature an even eighty degrees with low humidity and a light breeze. The people I pass on the sidewalk seem upbeat, happy. I wish I could say the same for myself.

That's when I see her. Half a block down Walnut, walking toward me. My wife. Piper is five foot six with a lithe runner's body and well-toned calves. Even carrying a large shopping bag, she glides almost weightlessly on the pavement. A blonde-haired, blue-eyed beauty turning men's heads on the street.

Piper spots me and her eyes flash with surprise, then flatten as she forces a smile. We approach each other and stop. Despite the weather, the air between us feels frigid.

"What are you doing in town?" I ask. "I thought you were going to spend the day at the mall, have lunch with one of your girlfriends." That's what she'd told me this morning.

"It's too nice to spend the day inside a mall. So I thought I'd drive into Center City, check out the shops." Piper nods to the stuffed Lululemon bag.

"I wish I'd have bought stock in that company," I say.

"My parents have Gabby for the night," she says, referring to our six-year-old daughter. "She loves the new car, by the way."

Over the weekend, Piper bought a BMW convertible without telling me.

"Did you set up the automatic pay thing through the bank account? The first payment's due the middle of next month, I think."

Livid with Piper, I pause before answering. I'm an expert at masking my emotions, but it's all I can do to restrain myself. I smile, jaw tight. "It's all arranged."

A moment later, Piper and I part ways. I turn to watch her, my heart rent with fury and sorrow.

Back in the office, I sit at my desk and try to will the day's difficulties into their own compartments. I'm a savant when it comes to compartmentalizing. I can store something away in my mind for hours, days, weeks. Sometimes forever.

I start checking my e-mails but quit halfway through. I pick up the phone to return an important call but hang up after it rings once on the other end. There's a draft of an appellate brief on my desk, and I pick it up, start to edit it, but toss it aside after a page or two. I'm just too distracted to work. My insides are roiling.

I close my eyes, open them, take five deep breaths, then five more. It doesn't help, so I decide to go for a run. I rip off my work clothes, throw them onto my desk in a heap, and put on the running clothes I always bring with me to work. I'm flying the instant I leave the building.

My normal run is a ten-mile loop along the Schuylkill River. Today, I take it way too fast and am wiped out when I get back to the office. I dry myself off with paper towels in the bathroom, change back into my work clothes, and try to get some work done.

My mind is still spinning, and I realize it's hopeless. I leave the office, get my car, and head home. Passing 30th Street Station, I call Piper. I can't reach her at home, so I call her on her cell. She says she decided to go to the mall after all and that she'll get home about the same time I do. I tell her I'll pick up something for dinner at Whole Foods . . . not that I'll be able to eat anything.

Piper and I live with our daughter, Gabrielle, about fifteen miles west of Philadelphia. Our house is a sixty-year-old stone Cape Cod on three-quarters of an acre on a quiet, tree-lined street. Piper fell in love with the house instantly when she first laid eyes on it four years ago. "It's absolutely perfect," she told me when we put in our bid. Then, the minute we took possession, she set out to change everything about it. In order of attack, Piper replaced all the wallpaper and lighting, tore up the carpeting and laid new hardwood floors, put in a new kitchen and upstairs and downstairs bathrooms, and finished the basement. The only things she hasn't replaced are the windows and roof.

I pull my car up to the three-car garage built into our house and walk in the back door. I'm immediately set upon by Franklin, our two-hundred-pound Bernese mountain dog, the Main Line beast *du jour*. I place the Whole Foods bag on the granite counter and give Franklin the hugs and treats he's come to expect when I get home from work. Turning back to the counter and the grocery bag, I notice a business card stapled to an invoice of some sort. I pick it up and see that it's an estimate for a new cedar-shake roof: $30,000.

Jesus Christ.

Piper enters the kitchen. Her face is drawn, her eyes and nose are red. "I don't feel well," she says. "I'm not going to eat." With that she passes by me, walks down the hall, and goes up the stairs.

I turn away from her. Given how I feel right now, it suits me that we're not having dinner. I wander into the family room and sit numbly in front of the television. Reruns of *Law and Order* play themselves out on the tube, but I can barely see the images on the screen through the fog that envelops my mind. The eleven o'clock news comes on, then Jimmy Fallon, then *Late Night with Seth Meyers*. I sit zombielike on the couch until Carson Daly comes on at 1:30, then will myself off the sofa and make my way upstairs.

I pause and stand at the doorway of Gabrielle's room. Her empty bed evokes a hollow ache inside me. I can feel her absence outside myself as well, an unnatural stillness that pervades the air, the walls, the floors—as though the whole house misses her. One of my favorite things is to read Gabby to sleep at night, then sit and watch her breathe. *A Sick Day for Amos McGee* is one of Gabby's current favorites, as is *The Day the Crayons Quit.* The book I most enjoy reading to her is one I saved from my own childhood, the Dr. Seuss classic *Green Eggs and Ham.* Too often, I come home from work so late that Gabby is already asleep. When that's the case, I read to her anyway. Piper's always thought it odd, but I like to think that, even asleep, some part of Gabby's mind can hear me and knows I'm with her.

I feel a presence at my side and look down to see Franklin standing next to me. He stares through the doorway to Gabby's bed, then looks up at me. I lean down and pat his head. "Don't worry, boy. She'll be back tomorrow."

Unlike some parents' daughters.

Franklin and I turn and walk down the hall to the master bedroom. I follow him in and watch him curl up on the faux-fur rug at the foot of our bed. I brush my teeth, then undress in front of the bed, watching Piper the whole time. She's curled up in a fetal position on her side of the California king she bought a few months earlier. She's covered from head to toe, so I cannot see her face.

For the next hour and a half, I toss restlessly in a futile attempt to fall asleep. Across the bed, Piper shifts position as often as I do. She doesn't answer when I ask if she's awake, but I know the rhythms of her breathing and can tell she's no more asleep than I.

Then the phone rings. The neon-blue light of the alarm clock reads 3:15.

Gabby! is all I can think.

I snatch up the phone and listen to the panicked voice on the other end of the line. "Slow down," I tell the caller. But he can't. After a few minutes, I interrupt. "All right, listen. I'll be there as fast as I can. Just don't say anything to the police. Anything at all."

I hang up the phone and sit up on the edge of the bed, trying to process what I've just learned. Through the darkness, I hear Piper ask me who it was.

"It was David Hanson," I say. "He's been arrested for murder."

I feel Piper stiffen. I turn to face her. She stares at me, her mouth open. I wait for her to ask the obvious question, and when she doesn't, I answer anyway. "The victim is Jennifer Yamura. The reporter."

2

Friday, June 1

It's 5:15 a.m. when I walk into the police department's Ninth District headquarters on the corner of Twenty-First and Hamilton Streets. The building is a squat three-story structure with a tan brick facade and a concrete fascia just below the roof line.

"Hey, Mick. Heard you were coming." It's Ted Brennan. He was a rookie officer when I left the district attorney's office. Good kid. His dad, also a cop, out of the Sixth District, has about five years until retirement.

"How's my guy?"

"Hanson? Sweating bullets." He shrugs almost apologetically. "We got him dead to rights."

Ted proceeds to tell me the circumstances of David's arrest. "The 911 operator gets a call about 11:30. The caller says there's shouting and loud noises in a house on the seventeen hundred block of Addison Street, near Rittenhouse Square. Dispatch sends a squad car with two officers to the scene. The lights are on so they know someone's at home. They knock, but no one answers. They keep on knocking and ringing the bell. Still no answer, so one of the patrolmen stays at the front door while the second runs around back to Waverly, which is the alley between the houses on Addison and Pine. He finds your man running out the back of the house, tackles him, cuffs him. Partner comes around and walks into the house, where he finds—ta da!—one dead reporter."

I inhale. "Weapon?"

"Basement stairs. Your client pushed her down, and she bashed her head in."

I think for a minute. "Who's been with him?"

"Tredesco and Cook." Brennan smiles. "I'm sure they're doing their best to make him feel at home."

I've never met Cook, but I know John Tredesco. He's cunning. He'd probably gone at David from eight different angles already, trying to catch him in a lie.

"Can I see him now?"

"Sure, but it'll take a miracle worker to get this guy off."

Brennan escorts me to the interrogation room. I pause in the hallway, look through the window. David is slouched in a seat behind a gray metal table, rubbing his forehead with his hand. His thick chestnut hair is a tangled mess. He taps his right foot nervously under the table. When the door opens and he sees me, David slowly lifts his athletic six-foot-three frame from the chair. The energy that normally powers his movement has been drained from him. His broad smile is long gone from his face, his blue eyes bloodshot.

"Four hours. That's how long they made me wait to call you. And another two hours for you to show. I'm going out of my mind!"

I motion for David to sit back down. "Did they offer you a nonwaiver of rights? It's a form that says you don't want to speak to the police or waive your right to an attorney."

"Yes. And I signed it. And I told them you were my lawyer and I wanted to speak to you. And they still made me wait four hours."

"Did you say anything to them—anything at all?"

"Just that I wanted to call my lawyer. You. And I kept on saying it, and they ignored me and made me sit here in this room. Tried to trick me into answering questions."

"Who tried to trick you? How did they do that?"

"Two of them. They told me their names, but I don't remember them. They tried to play nice with me. Ask me how I was feeling. Did I want any coffee? Talked about the Phillies. What am I, some idiot who's going to fall for that?"

I let David vent some more, then ask him a third time, "Before you signed the nonwaiver of rights, did you say anything else to the police?"

"Nothing. I was at work all afternoon—that's what I told them. Then I told them I wanted to call you."

"That's not nothing." I give David a hard look. "*Were* you at work all afternoon? *All* afternoon?"

David stares at me for a moment, then closes his eyes, lowers his head.

"Great," I say. "Now you're on record as having lied to the police."

His eyes still closed, David says, "Please, just get me out of here."

I spend an hour with David and then drive to my office, getting in by about seven o'clock. I'm the only one there, and I will be until Susan arrives in an hour or so. My mind is spinning, my heart pounding like a hammer. My thoughts drift back to the times I spent with my law-school classmate and partner in crime, David Hanson. Long hours studying late into the night for finals. Good hours spent at Phillies and Eagles games. Wild hours spent at parties and bars. Mild but happy hours spent in restaurants after graduation. Outings with our wives. I jump forward and think about David now, the David I haven't seen in a while. David the cheater. The cliché husband who can't keep his dick in his pants. Finally, I think ahead, to David the accused. I know what's ahead for my old friend. And I know that I will be the one holding his hand through all of it. It'll have to be me if this is going to turn out well—for everyone.

◆ ◆ ◆

David's preliminary arraignment is scheduled to be held at 11:00 a.m., which is pretty prompt for Philadelphia, where the arrest-to-arraignment time can be as long as twenty-four hours. The arraignment procedure is a two-headed hydra. David would remain at the station house while the assistant district attorney and I appear before the arraignment court magistrate about a mile away in the preliminary arraignment room in the basement of the Criminal Justice Center. We would see David, and he would see us, only via closed-circuit television.

The hearing room is actually a suite of two rooms. The first, a gray waiting room, has the feel of a bunker. Its front is a glass wall through which you can see the goings-on in the courtroom proper. The courtroom rules, posted on a piece of white paper taped to the window, announce that there will be no talking, no children, no eating or drinking, no chewing gum, and no reading of newspapers or books. Cell phones, of course, must be off.

The courtroom itself has just enough room for the judge's bench and two counsel tables. Each of the counsel tables is crowded with a phone, a flat-screen monitor, and a keyboard. Boxes are junk-stacked in front of the right side of the judge's bench, which is topped with its own computer screen and vertical file folders jammed with manila envelopes. The courtroom is better lit than the waiting room, which serves only to highlight the clutter.

The assistant district attorney sitting in the waiting area looks young enough to be carded at bars. He stands when I walk in. We introduce ourselves, and I ask him for a copy of the complaint. He shifts on his feet and tells me he's going to have to delay the arraignment for a couple of hours while the complaint is tinkered with.

"Tinkered with?" The DA's charging unit, which works all night, should have finalized the complaint long before the arraignment. "What are the charges going to be?"

"Third-degree murder, obstruction of justice, and tampering with evidence, the last I saw."

I expected the low-level homicide charge. It would be too early in the investigation to charge anything higher. The obstruction and tampering charges pique my interest, but I don't press the ADA for details, knowing it's better to wait for the complaint. I tell the young prosecutor I'll see him shortly and walk back to the office.

I told our staff about David's arrest before heading to court, saying I didn't know much, only that the police had caught David Hanson running from Jennifer Yamura's house late the night before. And that Yamura herself was found dead inside the house, apparently from wounds to the back of her head caused by a fall down the basement steps.

"This'll be an important case for our firm," I told them. "A headline grabber, and I want everyone steeled for battle from the get-go."

When I enter our lobby, my secretary, Angie, looks up at me. "No news," I tell her. "The DA is massaging the charges, so I'll have to go back."

I head for my office, where Susan joins me a few minutes later. "You okay?" she asks. "You don't seem yourself."

"Yeah, yeah. This one's close to home, that's all."

Susan considers this. "Given your friendship with David, maybe I should handle the case. Or maybe we should steer him to another firm."

I tell Susan I'll consider it.

But there is no way I'm letting this case out of my hands.

I call Tommy as I walk back to the courthouse. My call goes to voice mail, so I leave him a message to call me right away. On the bench this morning is Delia Smick, who was a bail commissioner until her title was changed to arraignment court magistrate. A tough cookie in her midforties, Delia has graying black hair and the raspy cigarette voice of a Melrose Diner waitress. She's wearing a black shirt with white polka dots that goes well with her hair and the black-framed glasses perched at the end of her nose.

The magistrate recognizes me and sighs when I walk into the courtroom. That's because my presence means the perp in her next case will be represented by private counsel rather than a public defender. Private attorneys, especially those hired by wealthy clients, can be pesky. The judge lowers her gaze to the computer and begins to read the complaint. Her eyes widen when she sees who the defendant is. Once or twice while reading she looks up at me, then back down at her screen.

A couple of minutes pass. The young ADA who was there that morning is nowhere to be seen. Her Honor asks me if I know where he is, but before I answer, I see her eyes grow wide again, and she says to someone behind me, "To what do we owe the honor?"

Turning around to follow the magistrate's gaze, I am shocked when I see Devlin Walker, the first assistant district attorney. Only in the rarest cases would a senior DA show up at a preliminary arraignment. That the first assistant himself would appear is unheard of.

Walker is wearing a double-breasted black suit with a silver-and-black striped tie over a blazing-white, crisply starched shirt with French cuffs held shut by gleaming onyx cuff links. Devlin walks directly over to me and extends his hand. I can see he's measuring the level of my surprise—one small factor to add to the calculus that will become our contest in this case.

Devlin Walker is an imposing presence. A former star basketball player for Central High, he stands six four and weighs an easy 215, not an ounce of which is fat. Devlin has a large head, square jaw, and wide-set eyes. His forty-four years have just begun to salt his hair, which he keeps short and perfectly combed. Devlin composes his face as a study in seriousness—an acknowledgment of the enormous responsibility the people have placed on him, and his pledge that he will not let them down. The same sense of responsibility carries over to Devlin's role as a pillar of the African American community. City employees are required to live within city limits, so, unlike many prominent black officials who reside in Chestnut Hill or some other upscale section of the city, Devlin keeps his home on the Penn campus in West Philadelphia, just a mile from the row houses in which he was raised. Within his neighborhood, Devlin is an icon. He's a deacon in the Rock of Ages Baptist Church, a Big Brother, and a Boy Scout leader. It is accepted wisdom in the DA's office that Devlin will succeed his boss as district attorney.

Devlin and I have a history. He was, to put it simply, my major rival at the DA's office. Devlin graduated law school two years before I did and was one of my mentors for a time. I found he was someone I could go to for both practical advice and help on issues of law. Then something happened that cooled him toward me. Devlin began taking note that, like him, I was working seven days a week and always on the hunt for bigger cases to handle. "You're on his radar," a colleague warned me. "Watch out." During the next several years, Devlin won a number of important cases and, in the flush of his victories, became more magnanimous, more indulgent toward me again. Then when *I* began trying and winning major jury cases, Devlin went back on the offensive. Criticism of how I'd prepped certain witnesses or tried a case would float into the ear of a senior ADA, who'd then happen by my office and question me about it. Or Devlin would suddenly steal away a junior ADA who was working to help me prepare for trial. "Sorry, man," Devlin would say. "Got an emergency. Have to pull rank." Then came my string of high-profile drug-trafficking victories. Devlin declared all-out war against me. I won't pretend it was a one-sided battle by then. I was incensed at what I felt to be an unprovoked attack, so I began to impede Devlin and to enlist other ADAs to help me. By the time I decided to end my career as a prosecutor, a dozen of the more ambitious attorneys had aligned themselves with me against Devlin, and vice versa. Either Devlin or I, most believed, would eventually become district attorney. So bets were placed on whose coattails to hang on to.

It shouldn't have surprised me, then, that when I announced my decision to leave for private practice, my supporters directed a great deal of anger toward me. A few did everything they could to persuade me to change my mind, fearing that Devlin would direct all the good cases to his guys and the junk cases to them.

My colleagues' worries proved to be unfounded. Devlin Walker didn't punish the attorneys who had aligned themselves with me; he didn't have to. He'd won the war. So, Devlin, ever the strategist, did what America did to the Germans and Japanese after World War II: he co-opted his former enemies, made them into his allies. The result was that my former friends continued to hate me for leaving, but they ended up loving Devlin Walker.

So, I wonder, *why is he here today?*

Devlin hands me the complaint as he looks up at the magistrate and declares, "This is a very serious matter, Your Honor. A promising young woman is dead. A young woman who had information vital to an ongoing grand-jury investigation. Information that may now be lost forever. And now she's the victim of a premeditated murder."

Magistrate Smick rolls her eyes. "Why the speech, Mr. Walker? There's no jury here. No press. Oh, wait. Is that Ms. Cassidy I see?" I glance back and see Patti Cassidy, a reporter for the *Philadelphia Inquirer.* "Now, how did you know to be here?"

I hear Judge Smick's words through a fog. Devlin's reference to premeditation has jarred me. I begin to review the complaint, knowing what I'll find. Despite what the young ADA told me, the DA's office is charging David Hanson with first-degree murder.

Scanning the complaint, I see something that grabs my attention. The DA is alleging that, before he fled the scene, David had tried to clean the house of evidence. The complaint says the dishwasher was running, the vacuum was sitting in the middle of the floor. Cleaning supplies and rags were sitting on various tables.

I lift my eyes from the complaint to the small flat-screen television sitting by the judge's bench, just in front of the defense table. The image is of David sitting in a cluttered cinder-block room in the Ninth District station house. He is looking right at the camera, but his eyes are glazed. I'm not sure how much he sees or comprehends.

The magistrate asks Devlin what the Commonwealth's position is regarding bail.

Walker answers immediately. "The people vehemently oppose bail. Bail is almost never accorded in murder cases. And we need to send a message to the community that no exceptions will be made just because a defendant is rich and connected."

Magistrate Smick looks at me over her readers. "Is that your position, Mr. McFarland? That I should allow your client to be released just because he's got a lot of money?"

"Of course not, Your Honor. Mr. Hanson should be released on bail because it's called for by the guidelines. First, the primary purpose of bail is to secure a defendant's appearance at trial, and there is no chance that Mr. Hanson will fail to appear. He has close ties to the community; indeed, he is a community leader. And he is highly motivated to appear for trial in order to prove his innocence and restore his good reputation. The second purpose of bail is to ensure the safety of the community. There's no reason to believe that whoever killed Ms. Yamura has a larger plan to harm additional people. Certainly, there's no basis to believe that Mr. Hanson would perpetrate some sort of crime spree. Finally, there are facts that cast doubt on Mr. Hanson's guilt."

"For example?"

"The fact that the complaint doesn't state when Ms. Yamura was killed, let alone that it was close in time to Mr. Hanson's having been found in the house. Furthermore, the complaint alleges no specific motive for Mr. Hanson to have killed Ms. Yamura."

Devlin heatedly argues the points, conceding that although the preliminary forensics—primarily the temperature of the body—point to a time of death many hours before David was captured fleeing the house, he was caught trying to clear the house of evidence. Devlin then claims that Hanson's motive will undoubtedly become clear as additional facts are uncovered.

Magistrate Smick stops the argument and reminds Devlin and me that a preliminary arraignment is not the place to decide the merits. She sets bail at half a million dollars. I see David exhale with relief through the CCTV. It's the first sound I've heard from him throughout the proceeding.

"Will you be waiving the preliminary hearing, Mr. McFarland?"

"Yes, Your Honor." Most experienced defense attorneys will opt for a preliminary hearing to learn details of the prosecution's case. I don't want a preliminary hearing for David because the result—that the court will find sufficient evidence to bind David over for trial—is a foregone conclusion. If we hold a public hearing, the details of the young woman's death and David's flight will wind up all over the media.

After the arraignment, I approach Devlin Walker in the hallway. "Murder one?" I say. "Really?"

Devlin looks down at me, his face set in stone. "Murder one, Mick. Really."

"You can't even put him in the house at the time of death. By your own admission, it was *hours* after the crime that the police saw him leaving."

"Not leaving. Running away. After spending an undetermined amount of time trying to clean up his mess. As for his whereabouts at the time of death, if he wasn't with the victim, where was he? If he has an alibi that can be corroborated, then this is all just a big misunderstanding, and I'll drop the charges."

"Do you really think there was premeditation? That he went into the house intending to kill her?"

"I don't know whether he went there with a plan to kill her or whether he formulated that plan once he was alone with her. But you know as well as I that the period of premeditation can be very brief. That's criminal law 101." Walker pauses, then adds, "On the other hand, your client and the decedent could have gotten into a fight. He could have flown off the handle and pushed her down the stairs in a fit of rage. That would only be voluntary manslaughter. I could see that. Is your client thinking of coming clean, pleading out?"

"That would be nice, wouldn't it? Your first-degree murder charge scares my client into admitting that he killed her in the heat of passion? A quick, easy win for the prosecution, and one step closer to becoming district attorney?"

Devlin flinches at my reference to his ambition. "Let's not make this personal, Mick."

"The defendant is a close friend of mine," I answer, almost choking on the words. "I won't be serving you any silver platters here. You want this one, you're going to have to take it from us."

Devlin leans into me. "That's exactly what I'm paid to do."

With that, he turns and walks away.

It takes two hours to arrange for David's bail. We are set upon as soon as we leave the station house. Reporters surround David and me and follow us down the block like a swarm of yellow jackets. They jam microphones into our faces as we walk toward the car I have waiting outside.

"Did you kill her?"

"Were you having an affair?"

"Why did you try to hide evidence if you didn't do it?"

Once we're at the firm, I sit David in a conference room and tell Angie to get him some coffee. "I'll be back in a minute," I tell David.

I go into my office, sit behind the desk, take a breath.

But before I have time to think, Angie calls on my speakerphone. "Patti Cassidy from the *Inquirer* is on the line. She wants a quote."

I sigh, say I'll take it, and let Cassidy machine-gun questions at me. When she's spent, I count to three and say, "Okay, Patti, here's my statement. Mr. Hanson will cooperate fully with the police in the investigation into Ms. Yamura's death. He's as eager as everyone else for the real perpetrator to be apprehended and brought to justice." Before Patti can attack me with a barrage of follow-up questions, I hang up. I hope she quotes me word for word. I want to convey to the reading public—i.e., the potential jurors—that David is cooperating and that the investigation is ongoing, implying that even the police aren't sure they got the right guy. Bullshit, of course, but, hey.

I return to the conference room, tell David to go home. "We'll meet again on Monday and discuss the case in detail. In the meantime, say nothing to anyone about the charges, or your guilt or innocence. Except to Marcie, of course."

David's face turns white at the mention of his wife's name. "She's visiting her sister in Los Angeles, with the boys." He holds up his cell phone. "I just left a message with her brother-in-law. I told him to tell her I'd been arrested, but that it's all a huge mistake and that she shouldn't believe anything she hears." David looks like he's about to break. He looks down at his shoes, then back up at me. "This isn't going to just go away, is it?"

"No. The DA's going to push hard to convict you."

"But I didn't do it."

"That doesn't matter," I say. "Once the DA charges someone, the prosecutors and police stop looking for another perp and work together as a conviction machine. I've been there. I know how it works. They won't stop until they get a plea or a guilty verdict."

I walk David through the firm's reception area and watch him leave the office. "He already looks like a dead man walking," I say to Angie.

She doesn't answer me, but from the look on her face, I can tell what she's thinking: *He threw that poor girl down the steps; he deserves what he gets.*

For the next hour, I create a computer file for the Hanson case and type in everything I know about it.

Angie calls me over the speakerphone. "Detective John Tredesco is calling on the Hanson case. Want me to say you're not here?"

I think for a minute, then tell Angie I'll take the call.

"Hello, Detective."

"So I hear your client is eager to cooperate with the police," Tredesco says snidely. "When can I expect to meet with him and take his statement?"

"Funny as ever, John." Tredesco is known for having no sense of humor. At all.

There's a pause at the other end of the line. "So you're telling the press that Hanson is doing everything he can to help us out, but he's not even going to meet with us? How is that *helping our investigation*?"

I smile. "By making sure that a jury isn't bamboozled into finding Mr. Hanson guilty. He and I will, ultimately, free the police department and the DA up so you can find the real culprit."

"So I guess that means you won't agree to produce a DNA sample?"

"You'll get it when you file your motion."

"That's the way it's going to be, eh?"

"It's a murder case, John."

"That's *exactly* what it is. And your client is the murderer."

With that, the line goes dead.

I know the DA's motion to compel a DNA sample will be filed with the court by morning and granted by the afternoon. My refusal to volunteer David's spittle is pointless. But, like I said to Tredesco, this is a murder case. I'm going to make the prosecution dot every *i* and cross every *t* to get what they want.

I buzz Angie, ask whether Tommy's called me back. She says he hasn't, so I dial his cell again. It's the only phone he has. Voice mail. I'm not happy. I want to hit the ground running, but my investigator's gone AWOL.

I leave the office at 4:30. In the car on the way home, I call Piper. She asks how it went with David. I pause, then tell her the prosecution is going for murder one, and that it seems Devlin Walker himself will be handling the case. I hear Piper take a deep breath. Before I can say anything else, she tells me she's tired but that she has long-standing plans to go out with two of her girlfriends. I'm tempted to snipe that I knew nothing about those plans, but it's just as well that I'll be on my own for the evening. I need time to think. The Hanson/Yamura thing is going to be complicated. A murder case is an unruly beast under the best of circumstances. And these are not the best of circumstances.

By six o'clock, I'm sitting behind the desk in my home office, eating a Primo Italian hoagie that I picked up on my way home. On the wall across the room from me is a large flat-screen TV. I pick up the remote and turn on the local news. The dapper *Action News* anchor, Jim Snyder, leads off with the handsome millionaire's brutal slaying of a promising young reporter. The newsman begins with a brief recap of Jennifer Yamura's budding career, starting with her graduation from college, her brief stints as a field reporter in smaller markets, her jump up to Philadelphia, and her recent scoop in breaking the story about the DA's investigation into the crooked-cop ring. Then he feeds the audience with background on David Hanson. He tells them that David is forty-two years old, that he was raised along Philadelphia's Main Line, where he attended Episcopal Academy, an ostentatiously expensive private school attended by the offspring of the region's wealthiest citizens. That he graduated seventeen years ago from the University of Pennsylvania Law School. That he's an executive vice president and general counsel of Hanson World Industries, the multi-billion-dollar Philly-based conglomerate David's grandfather founded eighty years before. Then Jim moves to the juicy stuff. He says the police apprehended David as he ran from Jennifer Yamura's house, that he appeared to have been trying to clean the house of his fingerprints and hair, and that he may have been having an affair with the young reporter. As the pièce de résistance, the news show's producer flashes a photo taken of David and Jennifer standing together at a black-tie charity event. Both of them are smiling, and the teleprompter tells Jim to say that the picture was "taken in happier times for both David Hanson and Jennifer Yamura."

Being early June, it's still light out at seven, so I decide to drive over to Valley Forge Park for a quick six-mile run. A couple of hours after I get back, Piper returns. She tells me she had too much to drink at dinner and that the lobster isn't agreeing with her. She makes another early night of it.

I call Tommy's cell phone once Piper is upstairs but still can't reach him. I figure he's hiding out at his trailer near Jim Thorpe, a small town eighty miles north of Center City. He goes there to brood when he's in one of his funks. Hopefully, he'll work himself out of it by Monday. I leave a message telling him I need him on the Hanson case. He must have heard about it on the news.

Come on, Tommy. Don't disappear on me now.

3

SATURDAY, JUNE 2

The weekend passes slowly. On Saturday I play a round of golf at Aronimink, the country club Piper and I joined at the insistence of her father, Thatcher Gray. My foursome includes my next-door neighbor along with two criminal defense attorneys. They pepper me from the get-go about the Hanson case, and I deflect their questions for three or four holes until they get the hint that I'd rather not talk about it.

When I get home, Piper tells me she's handed Gabby off to her parents for the entire weekend. I'm not happy.

"I thought we agreed to take Gabby to Longwood Gardens tomorrow," I say. "She was looking forward to it."

Piper shrugs and says she's taking a day trip to New York with her friends.

"Don't you think you should have asked me before you sent our daughter away?" I ask. "You know things will heat up quickly with the Hanson case. I may not have a lot of free weekend days for a while."

Piper cocks her head. "It's really not a big deal, Mick. Just go play another round of golf."

I hear her open and close the back door on her way to the garden. Through the kitchen window, I watch her lay out a dozen or so potted flowers to plant. She arranges them three different ways before settling on a pattern. I close my eyes, shake my head.

I met Piper during my seventh year with the DA, while I was busy with a high-profile murder trial. The defendant was a young neurologist who'd killed his wife to clear the way for a relationship with his married next-door neighbor, with whom he'd been having an affair. The case garnered a lot of news coverage, largely because of the salacious details that came out in the testimony. Quickies in the kitchen. Blow job at the barbeque. It all made for quality journalism. Even Anchorman Jim's eyes sparkled as they scanned the teleprompter.

I was in the office late one night, working on the case, when District Attorney Ned Hoffman came into my office and ordered me to accompany him to a political fund-raiser at the art museum. Ned's date had canceled on him at the last minute, and he needed someone to go with him.

An hour later, Ned and I were standing together in the grand staircase discussing my trial when a tall, rail-thin man in his fifties approached us with a stunning young woman in tow. Having attended political functions before, I'd assumed the woman was a trophy wife— or an escort. Then Thatcher Gray introduced himself and his daughter, Piper.

"Thatcher is a partner at Morgenthau Harrison," Ned told me. "Tom, this is Michael McFarland, whom you've probably read about in the papers. He's trying the neurologist murder case."

Thatcher Gray nodded his approval. "That surgeon sounds like one rotten egg," he said. "I hope you get a conviction. Do you think you will?"

Before I could answer, Ned interceded. "Mick's our best trial attorney. Relentless. Precise."

"Plodding. Tedious," I interjected. Everyone but Thatcher Gray laughed. I spoke a little bit about the case, sharing some details that had not yet been disclosed at trial.

Piper's father studied me as I spoke. "You seem like a serious young man. And these days, that's exactly what we need."

I thought Piper's father was talking about fighting crime, but I would later learn his remark was referring to his daughter's dating history. Thatcher Gray believed she'd frittered away too much time on subpar men.

"Piper works right here at the museum, in the contemporary art department," her father said. "She studied fine art at Yale. Spent another year at the Sorbonne."

Piper rolled her eyes.

"Contemporary? As in Picasso?"

"And one or two others."

"You could take Mr. McFarland on a tour of the collection right now," Thatcher Gray suggested to Piper, whose smile vanished.

"That would give us a chance to talk," Ned said, taking the tall lawyer by the elbow and leading him away.

"That was smooth," I said to Piper as we took the hint and walked off. "Like they've done this before."

"I love my father, but he's a meddler."

"Does that mean you won't show me?" I asked. "The collection?"

"I'd be glad to get away from this reception," Piper answered. "I only came because my mother bowed out, as usual. She hates these things. And I could hardly claim to my father that I couldn't make it here because of work. But I'd rather not go back upstairs. Would you mind if we ducked out of the building altogether? Grab a bite in town?"

It was a pleasant fall night, and Piper and I walked the mile or so down the Ben Franklin Parkway to Center City. We decided to get something to eat at Mace's Crossing, a tiny pub right on the Parkway.

We spent the next hour feeling each other out, sharing the CliffsNotes versions of our lives. I told Piper I'd gone to college at Penn State and law school at the University of Pennsylvania; that I was raised just outside of Lancaster, a small city about sixty miles west of Philly; that both my parents were dead; and that I had a brother. I didn't tell her that Tommy was serving six years for aggravated assault at the State Correctional Institution in Fayette, Pennsylvania. Piper told me that her parents had raised her in Villanova. She'd attended elementary school at Agnes Irwin in Rosemont, then moved on to Episcopal, the same school David Hanson had attended. I already knew from Piper's father that she'd gone to Yale and then studied in France.

I asked Piper what drew her to art.

She laughed.

"What's funny?" I asked.

"Art is part of life. Asking someone what draws them to art is like asking what draws someone to air, or food. I can't imagine a life in which art doesn't play a major part."

I thought about her answer. "And why contemporary art, specifically?"

"Because it's still alive," she answered. "Still evolving, growing." Piper told me she appreciated the Old Masters, recognized their genius. "But when I look at a painting by Rembrandt or Da Vinci, it feels dead to me. Like I'm in an antique store, looking at a worn piece of furniture. That's sacrilege, I know, and some of my friends at the museum would have a fit if they heard me say it. But art has to feel alive to me for me to enjoy it." Piper talked on for a while, then she shared her secret pleasure: abstract expressionism. Artists like Jackson Pollock, Mark Rothko. Piper said she was entranced by the exuberance and frank aggression of their brushstrokes and the resulting intense imagery of their work. The nonrepresentational splashes of paint, which I'd always scoffed at, were, for Piper, liberating bursts of pure passion unconstrained by antiquated notions of form and structure.

When Piper had finished, we sat quietly for a moment. Then she asked me what drew me to law. I tipped back my second Guinness. "When I was in high school, I picked up a book about the My Lai massacre. That's where a company of American soldiers slaughtered more than three hundred civilians in a village in South Vietnam. Mostly women and children. The book told the story of the young military lawyer who prosecuted Lieutenant William Calley, the only soldier court-martialed for the massacre. It told how the lawyer fought against the high-priced civilian lawyers brought in to defend Calley. How the lawyer took the court, step-by-step, through the massacre until, by the end of the trial, he'd laid out the overwhelming case that led to Calley's conviction. When I was done reading the book, I decided that was going to be me. I was going to become a lawyer, go after the bad guys, lead my juries step-by-step through the crimes, build my cases fact upon fact, until there was no outcome possible other than a conviction."

When I was done, Piper waited a moment and asked, "What happened to that lieutenant?"

"Calley was sentenced to life in prison, but his sentence was reduced, and he served only a few months in a military jail."

Piper's jaw dropped. "That's outrageous."

I nodded.

Piper thought for a minute, then asked if I'd ever lost a big case.

"One or two," I answered. "But sometimes all you can do is fight the good fight."

"Is that how it feels to you when you're in court? Like you're fighting the good fight?"

"Most of the time. Pretty much all of the time," I said, though even then I had some doubts. "I've had a few cases where I wasn't convinced that a jail term was warranted." I'd seen many cases handled by other prosecutors where the state locked someone away it needn't have. Like Tommy.

"So, are you as serious a man as my father thinks you are?"

I had crossed my eyes and stuck out my tongue. Piper laughed.

I watch Piper now, planting her plants. One of her favorite things to do. But I see no joy in her face. Today, the gardening is just work. Sweat and toil and the passing of time. Something to keep her distracted. I sigh, then clench my teeth, my heart tossed in a crosscurrent of fury and sadness. I close my eyes and lower my head. "Oh, Piper."

4

Monday, June 4

When I finally get to the office at 2:00 p.m., Angie greets me, then hands me the Monday editions of Philly's two papers: the *Daily News* and the *Inquirer*. "The *Inquirer* is the worse of the two," she says.

I scan the front-page articles of both papers as I walk down the hall to my office. The *Daily News* article, headlined "Millionaire Murderer?," sits above a full-color picture of David Hanson. The article recounts the details of the death of Jennifer Yamura, then gets right to the meat: David's wealth. According to the article, David earns more than $1 million a year as general counsel at Hanson World Industries. His stock holdings in the company, most of which he inherited when his father died, are estimated to exceed $90 million. The article lists various properties owned by David, including his estate on the Main Line, a beachfront shore house in Stone Harbor, New Jersey, valued at $5 million, and another house in Costa Rica.

"Just wonderful," I say out loud to no one. This is the kind of reporting that makes it so difficult to select a fair jury.

The *Inquirer* article is indeed worse, though for different reasons. Written by Patti Cassidy, its headline is "The Millionaire's Mouthpiece."

It isn't as much about David as it is about David and me. It explains that David and I were classmates at Penn Law, that we lived together in an apartment with two other law students during our second and third years, that we were moot-court partners, that we both interned at the district attorney's office, and that I was a groomsman at David's wedding. The story carries over to page two, where our law-school "pig book" photos are displayed side by side. Reporter Cassidy concludes the article by mentioning that my firm represented one of David's uncles in an insider-trading case, and that I'd handled a drunk-driving matter for David's nephew. Patti calls me the Hanson family's "go-to guy" for criminal matters.

The most damning thing about the article isn't the factual history but the unwritten insinuation that David and I are somehow tied together in the crime itself. This type of accusation could irreparably poison potential jurors and ruin any chance of David's getting a fair trial. One thing I've learned in my career is that, whatever the jurors may think about a client, it is imperative that they see his lawyer as acting in good faith; that is, that the attorney believes in his client and his client's case. When that happens, the attorney wins a lot of goodwill from the jury, and that goodwill can, in a close case, carry the day. On the other hand, any hint that an attorney is knowingly working a con in the courtroom will cause jurors to despise him and his client both.

I toss the paper into the trash and call Tommy again. David Hanson is due in at three o'clock. I'd wanted Tommy to sit in on the meeting, but he's nowhere to be found. "Tommy, I really need you in the office," I tell his voice mail. "This is the fifth time I've called. What's going on?"

David arrives fifteen minutes later. I meet him in the lobby and shake his hand. His grip is tentative, and he releases his hand quickly. His face is drawn, his mouth downturned. His weekend with Marcie must have been hell.

I lead him to the conference room, where I introduce him to Susan and Vaughn Coburn, our associate. Angie has been kind enough to bring in a coffee platter. The silver tray, porcelain cups, and pastries sit in the center of the table. No one reaches for any of it.

"So, do you have any idea who you want to handle the case from this point forward?" I ask, getting ahead of Susan. "I can draw you up a list of names, though I expect you already know the defense bar's biggest players." My offer is an insincere one. I could never admit it to anyone, but I would do anything to keep David's case.

David stares at me. "You're the one I called, Mick. I want you."

I breathe a sigh of relief and prepare to move on. But Susan jumps in.

"That's not a good idea," Susan says. "If you read the *Inquirer* this morning, you already got a taste for what the press is going to do. And it's never a good idea to let a close friend handle a case this important."

"I've known Mick a long time," David says. "I know I can count on him."

My gut twists, but I say nothing, just nod my head. David and I study each other for another long moment. "All right, then, let's get to it."

I open my leather portfolio and pull out the yellow legal pad inside. Then I remove the Montblanc pen from my shirt pocket and lay it on the table. "Before I begin writing anything down," I start, looking directly at David, "I want to say something very important. If you committed the crime—"

"I didn't!" David interrupts.

"Please let me finish. If you *did* do it, and if you have any intention of going to trial rather than accepting a plea, you must not tell me or any member of the firm that you did it. Under the code of ethics, a defense counsel's ability to question his client at trial is severely circumscribed when the lawyer knows the client is guilty."

David leans forward. "I went to law school, too. I know the rules. But, please, will you just listen to me? I. Didn't. Do. It."

I nod. "I'm glad to hear that. It makes our job easier. All we have to do is tell the truth. Which means, at this point, that it is imperative that you *do* tell the truth to me and Susan and Vaughn. The truth about everything even remotely connected to the crime. What you were doing at the time of the murder. Your relationship with the victim."

"Why you were in the victim's house at 11:30 at night, trying to sterilize the place," Susan adds.

"Everything," I say. "Understand?"

"I get it," David says.

I nod again, pick up my pen. "Okay, then. Tell us what happened."

David looks around the room, at me, then Susan and Vaughn. He takes a deep breath. "Well, you know about Marcie," he says to me. "Her illness." David looks at Susan and Vaughn, sees that they don't know. "My wife, Marcie, was diagnosed with breast cancer four years ago. The doctors said all she needed was a lumpectomy and some radiation. So she had the procedure and the radiation, and that was supposed to be the end of it. Marcie plowed through it and seemed to have recovered. Her first-year exam was clear, and we breathed a sigh of relief. But at the two-year mark, the cancer was back, and the doctors told her she had to have a mastectomy. They gave her genetic testing and discovered she was at high risk for developing cancer in her reproductive system as well, so she had her uterus and ovaries removed, too. She lost her breasts, her uterus, her hair. She was sick as a dog again, from the chemo. Then she started on a drug called Tamoxifen, and it threw her into menopause. That was last September—eight months ago—and she hasn't been the same since. She was depressed all the time. She didn't sleep. Constantly snapped at the children, at me. I dreaded coming home at the end of the day. I know it sounds terrible, but it's true. It's . . . awful."

He pauses, and we all nod our understanding.

"Anyway, it all got to me. The stress. The worry. I needed to escape, somehow. I was weak. I ended up making a big mistake . . . with Jennifer."

David stops here, looks at me, at Susan, at Vaughn.

Susan glances at me, then says, "So you had an affair . . . because your wife got cancer?"

David snaps, "Don't judge me. You don't know what it's been like. I wanted to be there for Marcie. I *was* there for Marcie."

Susan closes her eyes. She's biting her tongue so hard I won't be surprised if it starts bleeding.

"I know it's wrong, what I did. I've hurt Marcie terribly. And I feel awful."

"How long," I ask, "were you seeing Jennifer Yamura?"

"Not long at all. A month, six weeks. We met at that charity event in January or February. We got together a few times after that. It was just a casual thing."

"What's a few times?"

"I don't know. A handful. Five, ten."

"Ten is two handfuls," Susan pipes in.

David pretends not to hear her.

"Where did you get together?" I ask.

"Always at her house. Never in public. And I came in the back door, through the alley, so no one would see me."

"When is the last time you saw Jennifer Yamura alive?" asks Susan.

"Maybe a week before she was killed. We got together."

"Not on Thursday, the day of the murder?" I ask. "You're certain?"

"Absolutely."

I wait a beat, then say, "I have a friend in the crime-scene unit. He said the official time of death won't be determined until the autopsy, but based on the rate of body cooling, CSU estimates that Yamura was killed sometime between one and three o'clock Thursday afternoon. So here's the sixty-four-thousand-dollar question: Where were you between one and three o'clock on Thursday?"

"I was at work all morning." David pauses here. "Then I left the office. And, well, who's to say I didn't just drive home?"

Vaughn speaks up for the first time. "Your parking card, for one."

"My parking card?"

"Your office is in the Comcast building," Vaughn says. "I'm guessing you park in the lot and that you're a monthly. There's a computer record showing every time you enter or leave the lot. So you can't claim you drove out at lunchtime unless you actually did."

Vaughn Coburn's got a great street sense, an awareness of the nuts and bolts of life in the big city. Vaughn grew up in one of Philly's toughest neighborhoods. A fair-haired kid of middling height and weight, Vaughn probably would have had a hard time except that his uncle was an ex-boxer who operated a gym where he trained up-and-coming fighters. Vaughn spent a lot of time there, working out and sparring, and he got to the point where he could handle himself anywhere. After high school, Vaughn went to Temple for both undergrad and law school. Spent two years with the public defender's office before joining the firm last year.

"I didn't say I did," David says, suddenly testy. "But isn't it the prosecution's burden of proof to show where I was when Jennifer was murdered? Rather than my burden to show where I wasn't?"

Vaughn, Susan, and I all exchange glances. "David, let me be frank," I say. "The police have you inside a young woman's house late at night for who knows how long while the woman's body lies on her basement steps. Instead of calling the police like an innocent person would do, you decide to try and erase all history of your presence in the house. Then when the police do arrive, you don't open the door for them but run out the back door and down the alley. So, prosecutor's burden of proof or not, you'd damn well better have an alibi showing that you were nowhere near Jennifer Yamura when she was murdered."

I pause to pour myself a cup of coffee.

"Remember, you already have one strike against you. On the night of your arrest, you told Detectives Tredesco and Cook that you were at work all afternoon. By now, they've already spoken to your staff and found out that's not the case. So you better have at least one witness who can place you far away from Addison Street between one and three o'clock."

David stares at me for a long minute, then looks to Susan and Vaughn almost defiantly. "There must have been hundreds of people who saw me. I was on Kelly Drive. I went for a walk."

Susan's mouth opens. Vaughn rolls his eyes.

David continues, "I left the office about 1:15. It was beautiful outside, so I thought I'd get some air. I walked to the parkway and decided to take in the Chagall exhibit. But when I reached the museum, it was so nice out I decided to keep walking toward the boathouses. I guess my mind wandered, and I ended up walking the whole way to the Falls Bridge. That's where I turned around. I walked back to Center City, made my way to Rittenhouse Square, and took in the art show. Then I walked back to my office, got in my car, and drove home. By then it was about six o'clock."

I look down at my still-blank legal pad. "I run the river drives a lot. The round trip from Center City to the Falls Bridge and back is about ten miles." I look up and give David a hard stare. "And another mile or so to Rittenhouse Square and back. All in your business suit?"

"Like I said, it was really nice out. There was no humidity. I didn't even sweat."

"And your work shoes . . . ," I add.

"I wasn't running, Mick. It's not like my feet would have gotten hurt."

"Did you run into anyone you know?" asks Susan.

David thinks. "I'm not sure. I don't think so."

"So lots of people saw you," says Susan, "but none who would remember."

"Why don't we take a break?" I say. "I need to make a couple calls."

Susan, Vaughn, and I file out of the conference room and go directly to my office. I sit behind my desk. Susan and Vaughn take the visitors' chairs.

"Am I missing something," asks Vaughn, "or is he trying to follow your advice by telling us he did it without actually saying the words?"

I look at Susan. "What do you think?"

"I'm with the Boy Wonder on this one, Batman."

The door to my office opens, and Tommy walks in. "I didn't get your messages until this morning. How you guys doing?" he says to Vaughn and Susan, who sense my irritation and leave.

"I left you five messages," I say when Tommy and I are alone, my voice thick with anger.

"Hey, don't jump all over me. I said I didn't get them."

"How can you not get my messages? I left them on your cell."

"I went camping for a couple days."

"Come on, man. I get through to you at your trailer all the time."

"I wasn't at my trailer. I just told you, I went camping. In my tent. Up at Hickory Run State Park."

"Since when do you go tent camping?"

"I don't have to tell you everything about me. You don't tell me everything."

I want to jump up out of my seat and scream at Tommy. I want to ask him what the hell he means by that. But I hold my tongue.

"Okay, forget it," I say. "Here's what I need you to do."

Tommy interrupts. "You think he's innocent?"

I take a breath. "I don't know whether he is or not. Either way, I'm going to do everything I can to keep him out of prison."

Tommy stares at me for a long moment. "What do you need from me?"

"Right now, I want you to sit in on the rest of our meeting."

"He's here? Now?"

"Is that a problem?"

"No problem. Let's go."

I buzz Angie, ask her to have Susan and Vaughn come back to the conference room.

David tenses up the minute he sees Tommy. Tommy's own eyes launch daggers.

Susan moves right back into the questioning. "We were just about to get to the night of the murder. So, it's Thursday night. What happens?"

David inhales, looks around the room—at everyone but Tommy. "I got home about seven. Took a shower. Watched some TV. Marcie and the boys were in California with her relatives, and I was alone. About 10:30, I decided I wanted to see Jennifer. So I drove into town. I parked on Seventeenth Street. I walked down Waverly Street, the alley behind Addison Street, knocked on the back door. Jennifer didn't answer, and the lights were off. I figured she was out, so I thought I would go in and wait for her. I opened the door using my key."

"She gave you a key?" Susan interrupts.

"Well, yeah. Is that bad?"

"Just surprising, since you weren't really in a relationship and only saw each other a handful of times," she answers, somewhat snidely.

David considers this, then continues. "When I got inside, I turned on the kitchen light, then started to walk to the living room. When I was in the hallway, I saw that the basement light was on, so I pushed back the bead curtain she has hanging in the doorway to the basement. I looked down and saw Jennifer. She was . . . on the steps. Flat on her back. Her eyes were open, but she wasn't moving. So I went down to her, shook her a little, said her name. Her eyes stayed open, but she didn't answer and she didn't move. And there was blood everywhere. I knew she was dead."

"Why didn't you call the police?" Vaughn asks.

"I panicked. I thought about Marcie. With all she'd gone through, it would just kill her if it came out about me and Jennifer. So I thought, 'Hey, nobody knows about us.' I never told anyone and Jennifer promised she wouldn't, either. That was part of the deal."

"Deal?" Susan raises her eyebrows.

David pauses. "Our understanding! Our—For chrissakes, Susan, it's just a word."

"Let's all take it down a notch," I say. "Keep going. What did you do next?"

David exhales. "I know it was stupid, but I decided to clean the place. Get rid of anything that could point to me. I mean, it was probably hopeless, but I had to try. At least get rid of the spare clothes I kept there. But then I figured I needed to *really* clean the place. My hair and fingerprints. DNA. So I loaded the dishes into the dishwasher, then started vacuuming and wiping everything I could think to wipe. Then I heard the knock at the door and the guy saying 'Police.' I froze. I didn't know what to do. Then they knocked again and started ringing the bell, too. Finally I responded, said to hold on a minute, like I was going to let them in. And you know the rest. They got me in the alley. Took me down. Cuffed me. Walked me to the squad car and stuffed me inside. Next thing I know the whole street was jammed with cop cars." David closes his eyes. "Christ, what a nightmare. What a fucking . . ."

Vaughn pours a glass of water for David, who drinks it empty, then acknowledges Tommy for the first time since Tommy and I sat down. Something passes between them, but I can't tell what it is.

"When I came to the station to meet with you the next morning, one of the cops told me that the patrolmen showed up at the house because a 911 caller said he heard shouting and loud noises coming from inside. But you're saying you were alone with Yamura's body."

"I was alone. There was no yelling, no loud noises. The caller was lying." David reaches for the pitcher and pours another glass of water. His hands are shaking.

We all sit quietly for a moment to allow David to compose himself. Then I broach the issue of the fee. "For a case of this seriousness, the firm is going to do a lot of work," I say. "Tommy will investigate the case to the hilt—talk to all the neighbors, Jennifer's coworkers, everyone who knew her, try to find holes in the prosecution's case, try to find someone else with a motive to kill her. Susan and Vaughn and I will put our heads together and map out a legal strategy. Lots of work, lots of hours. Even before trial. We're going to require a substantial retainer. Let's start with seventy-five thousand dollars. As we get closer to trial, we'll revisit the rate."

David stiffens. "Seventy-five thousand dollars seems like a lot up front, Mick."

Susan and I glance at each other. "We're talking about your freedom, David."

David looks at me coolly. "I'd like to start with fifty thousand. If that runs out before trial, we can talk."

I shake my head. "All right . . . ," I say slowly. "We'll start with fifty thousand. But I'm not going to hold back on doing things I think may help just to save a dime. That's not how I work, even when I'm not representing an old friend."

David considers this, then shifts gears. "First-degree murder carries a mandatory life sentence, doesn't it?"

I nod.

David closes his eyes, lowers his head. "Jesus."

"All right. I think we've done enough for now," I say. "Why don't you go home and keep working on things with Marcie."

I ask Susan, Vaughn, and Tommy to remain in the conference room while I escort David out of the office. At the door to our suite, David absently shakes my hand, glances at me only briefly before turning and walking down the hall. When I get back to the conference room, the others wait for me to sit.

"Tell me about David's temper," Susan says. "Is he a hothead?"

I think back to the time I first met David, on the first day of civil-procedure class. I was already seated, and David came in and sat beside me. He smiled, introduced himself, held out his hand. He did the same thing to the guy on the other side of him. While we waited for the professor to show up, David told some funny story that had us in stitches. In my mind's eye, I see David over the next two years, laughing at the New Deck Tavern on Sansom Street, across from the law school, picking up undergrads, laughing as he drove Cheryl Cooley and me down to Atlantic City in his Mercedes convertible, laughing during a party he and I and our two roommates threw at our apartment in West Philadelphia.

"I don't remember him that way," I say to Susan. "At all."

"People change," Vaughn says. "And the guy was under a lot of stress because of his wife."

I don't say anything. I've heard a lot of guys say, *But that's not me. That's not who I am. I was under a lot of stress.* I don't think stress makes a person "not me." I think it brings out the "me" beneath the surface.

"Why not call?" Susan says, out of nowhere.

I look at her, not understanding.

"David says he decided he wanted to see Jennifer that night, so he just drove to her house," she says. "Wouldn't he have called first? To make sure she'd be there? And that she'd want to see him?"

Vaughn picks up on Susan's line of thought. "He'd at least have called on the drive in, or when he got to the house and saw it was dark. But he didn't say anything about trying to call Jennifer."

Susan gives me a hard look. "He didn't call before he left his house because he *knew* she wouldn't answer. He didn't call once he got to the house because he already knew what he was going to find."

I look at Tommy to see what he thinks of this. But he doesn't say anything. Just purses his lips and looks away.

After a minute, I stand up. "Susan, Vaughn, let's each of us write a memo to the file. Put down everything we know, everything we think we know, and where we think it leads." I turn to Tommy. "Come on," I say. "We can talk about where you're going to start." I lead Tommy out of the conference room and down the hall to my office, where I close the door behind us.

"What was all that between you and David?" I ask as I sit behind my desk. "You looked like you wanted to tear each other's throats out when we first walked in."

"Just something I don't like about him. I guess he feels the same way about me."

"You think he did it?"

Tommy's eyes grow dark. "What do *you* think?"

"What I think is that I don't know whether David did it or not. Either way, we're going to have a real fight on our hands. Devlin Walker's handling the prosecution personally. Not just because it's high profile, but because Jennifer Yamura had just blown open a big police-corruption investigation."

"I don't know why that investigation should have anything to do with the case against Hanson." Tommy stands abruptly. "I'll talk to the neighbors. See if anybody saw anything that could help us. Then I'll put some feelers out through some badges I know. Maybe find out if the DA is planning on holding anything back from us."

"Don't forget about the call."

Tommy looks at me.

"The 911 call that led the police to the house. The guy who called said he heard yelling and loud noises. Yamura would have already been dead for hours when he called. Someone wanted the police to show up and catch David. And that means the caller knew Yamura was dead and wanted David arrested for her murder. We have to find out who that caller was and why he is out to frame David."

"I didn't start this job yesterday," Tommy says.

I watch Tommy leave the office. I think about his moodiness. His periodic disappearances. What he must be going through. I look down at the pictures on my desk. One is a picture of Piper on our wedding day. The second is of Gabrielle at five years old, dressed up for church on Easter.

The third picture is of Tommy and me and our parents. Tommy was eight and I was ten. The four of us are standing on the beach in

Ocean City. Though I viewed our parents at the time as old, I see now how impossibly young John and Penny McFarland were. Young and attractive and optimistic.

In the picture, John and Penny tower over us. Tommy and I are both wearing swimsuits and flip-flops. I'm holding a plastic shovel. And Tommy is wearing the white cowboy hat he got for his birthday that year. He wore that hat everywhere.

Wearing a white hat makes you the good guy. That's what Tommy thought. And being the good guy was a big thing to my brother. We occasionally got into fights when we played together because I wanted to be the good guy, too. But Tommy would have none of it. When we played, Tommy always had to be the cop, and I had to be the robber. He was the sheriff, and I had to be the outlaw. Only if I refused to play would Tommy relent and allow himself to be the bad guy. But then he would play halfheartedly.

My mind holds plenty of other snapshots of Tommy when we were kids. I see him as a toddler, in a playpen in the middle of our living room, throwing toys out and laughing as our mother scrambled to pick them up. I see Tommy at six riding his plastic Big Wheel down our driveway, a Band-Aid on one of his knees from an earlier mishap. I see him running down the stairs on Christmas morning, his arms out in front of him, ready to tear into the presents under the tree.

And I see Tommy on that fateful morning when he was ten and I was twelve, sitting at the breakfast table. Our mom, her blonde hair tied on top of her head with a rubber band, wearing a sleeveless white-collared shirt, khaki shorts, and low-cut sneakers, moving around in front of the stove. Dad sitting at the head of our small kitchen table, to Tommy's left, reading his Saturday-morning newspaper, wearing jeans and a green T-shirt emblazoned with the logo of the company he worked for: Manheim Newbestos. I watch my mom serve my dad his breakfast—ham-and-cheese omelet, white toast, bacon—then turn back to the stove. After a moment, she turns toward the table again, with Tommy's plate. Tommy's face brightens at the stack of pancakes. Mom smiles back at him and keeps smiling as she sits suddenly on the floor and lies back until she's flat on the linoleum. I see Tommy smiling down at her, about to laugh at the game she's playing. I hear my dad call my mother's name, first calmly, then not. I watch my dad shoot out of his chair and run around the table to my mother, who isn't moving at all. Or smiling anymore, though her eyes are still open. I hear my dad repeating Mom's name over and over. Then I hear Tommy begin to cry, and I look over at him and he's weeping uncontrollably, not really knowing what's going on but seeing how upset our dad is. Finally, through my mind's eye, I see myself sitting across the table from Tommy—not moving, not crying, just sitting there, frozen, taking everything in—until I look out the kitchen window, see a bright yellow bird, and my eyes follow it away from the house, across the field, and up and up and up.

Away.

I stayed away for a long time. I was still gone at the time of my mother's funeral. I remember my body standing next to the casket as it hovered over the grave. But I wasn't looking at the casket, wasn't paying attention to whatever it was the priest was saying. I fixed my attention on the other side of the cemetery, where a hearse led a slow procession of cars to another grave site. I watched the long black limousine and the cars behind it come to a stop. I studied the people getting out of their cars, some grim-faced, others bored. After a while, a bird's call pulled my attention to the sky, thick with gray clouds threatening to break open and shower the land with tears. But I would not cry that day. Only Tommy and our father wept, unable to escape the grief crushing their hearts like a vice.

5

WEDNESDAY, JUNE 6

Wednesday afternoon finds me on the sixth floor of the Criminal Justice Center. I'm leaving Courtroom 603 following a victory at a hearing on a prosecution motion to revoke bail for one of the firm's many repeat clients.

"Nice win, counselor."

I turn to see two cops standing in the hallway behind me. Detectives Tredesco and Cook. Tredesco is tall and fiftyish with thinning black hair and a potbelly sticking over his cracked leather belt. Cook is pudgy and looks to be in his midtwenties. His crew cut is blond, his face is wide and round, just like his watery blue eyes.

"Got a minute?" asks Tredesco.

I look at my watch, shrug, glance at Tredesco's partner.

"Ed Cook," he says, extending his hand, something Tredesco hasn't done.

"So, how's the Hanson investigation coming?" I ask, looking at Tredesco. "You figure out yet that you got the wrong guy?"

Tredesco laughs, sort of. "The investigation's going well. We got a body and your client standing over it, trying to clean up the mess."

"So what's to talk about?"

"I'm here to give your client a chance to help himself. The DA might be willing to go easy on him, let him plead down. All he has to do is turn over the victim's computer. The money and jewelry he can keep."

I look from Tredesco to Cook, then back. "I'm sure you can't wait to tell me what you're talking about."

"What, Hanson hasn't told you already? He took Yamura's laptop—the one with all her notes—when he murdered her earlier in the day. He took her money and her jewelry, too. He didn't mention any of that?"

"Wow. That's dynamite stuff. And if Hanson can find the laptop, he gets to cop a plea to what? Manslaughter?"

Tredesco glares at me. Shifts from one foot to the other. Tries another tack. "Look, Mick, you and I go way back. We worked some good cases together. Put away some real bad guys."

"And some not-so-bad guys," I interrupt. Tredesco knows who I'm talking about. The year before I left the DA's office, I'd prosecuted Derek Blackwell, a young numbers runner Tredesco had arrested for the murder of a competitor. It was only after I'd won a conviction that someone I knew heard Tredesco bragging that he'd framed Blackwell—apparently he'd been spending time with Tredesco's girlfriend. I confronted Tredesco about it as soon as I learned the truth. It became a bone of contention between us, and we never worked together again.

"Get your client to turn over the laptop. The DA figures it's where Yamura kept all her info on the grand-jury investigation. If we could look at it, we could learn who her source was and press him for more names. Take down the whole ring, not just a few of them. That's why Walker's willing to deal."

I smile, take a minute to think about what Tredesco has told me. "So, to summarize our conversation so far, you've given me evidence of at least two people other than my client with a motive to kill Jennifer Yamura. A cash-strapped *nonmillionaire* who robbed Yamura of her jewelry and money. And a snitch cop who betrayed the police department and desperately doesn't want his name disclosed. Anyone else have a motive? Oh, right—all the crooked cops who haven't been identified yet who'd love to have gotten their hands on the reporter's computer and shut her mouth permanently at the same time."

Tredesco's narrow-set, fish-pale eyes turn to ice. "Just remember: I gave you a chance to help your client."

I smile at the two detectives until they turn to walk away, but the smile's a lie. I'm worried sick.

Back in the office, I'm at my desk when Tommy walks in. Today he's dressed in jeans and a black Harley-Davidson T-shirt which, along with his buzz cut and veal-shank arms, makes him look like a thug. He takes one of the visitors' chairs. I wait for him to say something. He doesn't, so I start in myself.

"Do you have anything yet? Have you spoken with the neighbors? Anyone see anything?"

"Slow down, Kemo Sabe." Tommy's words are lighthearted, but there's an edge in his voice. He pauses, rubs his brow. "I'm on top of it, all right? I talked to the neighbors on both sides of Yamura's house. One guy works in advertising. He was in New York and didn't get home until the afternoon after the murder. So he doesn't know anything. An elderly, gay couple lives on the other side. The one guy was asleep in the afternoon. The other one says he was watching TV, so he didn't see or hear anything. They both went to bed around ten and were woken up after David was nabbed in the alley and all the cop cars showed up. I talked to some of the neighbors across the street, too, and the ones who were home during the day didn't see anyone come in or out of the house all day, not that they were looking out their window. None of 'em called 911."

Tommy pauses. While I consider what he's told me, he reaches over to my desk, lifts one of the pictures. It's the one of him and me and our parents at the beach. "I always liked this picture," he says. "Except, did you ever notice how Mom and Dad and I are all looking at the camera, but you're looking away? Like you're somewhere else."

It's a loaded comment, given our history, and I choose to ignore it. "Anything else, or is that it?"

Tommy stands and replaces the picture. He casts me a hard glance, then turns and leaves. So much of our conversations consist of what we *don't* say to each other.

After the cerebral hemorrhage took our mother, it was just Tommy, our father, and me. The first two weeks after the funeral were a whirlwind as Dad tried to keep the three of us out of the house and away from the bottomless hole created by our mother's absence. He whisked the three of us to Hershey Park, Gettysburg, a Phillies game, tractor pulls, even the firing range.

After two weeks, Dad had to go back to work at the asbestos plant, and I was charged with overseeing Tommy. Dad's rules for Tommy and me that summer were simple: we were to check in with Ms. McBreen, a neighbor who agreed to keep an eye on us, every day for lunch; I was to keep Tommy near me at all times; we were not to ride our bikes on busy streets. Finally, the nearby quarry was off limits—no swimming, no climbing. Hunger motivated us to comply with the first directive. As for the second, it wasn't totally unbearable for me to have Tommy tag along, because both of us hung with a larger group of kids from the neighborhood. So I could ignore my pesky younger brother while still keeping him within eyesight. The rules about riding our bikes on high-trafficked roads and not playing in the quarry were, of course, absurd, and Tommy and I and all our friends—whose parents had imposed the same proscriptions—broke them at will. I can remember a dozen times when my friend Mike and I, riding our Schwinn ten-speeds, led others down the highway in the baking heat of summer afternoons, cars and flatbeds and semis whizzing past us as Tommy and all the other younger brothers struggled to bring up the rear. We'd race for the quarry and the relief its cool, dangerously dark waters would bring to our scorched, shirtless backs.

Only once did Tommy and I get into real trouble with Dad that summer. It was a weekend day in late August, just before the new school year, and our whole group was taking turns swimming in the quarry and scaling its jagged rock walls. Tommy and another kid his age, Danny, were the best climbers. "Spiders," Danny's brother called them every time Tommy and Danny climbed the quarry wall, their arms and legs extended wide as they inched their way up, down, and sideways. Normally, we would all ride to the quarry together and leave together. That day, though, Mike and I had decided to go off by ourselves. Mike had heard of a place farther down in the county where some teenagers supposedly drag-raced their cars. Mike said if we rode hard, we could get there in an hour, watch some action, and still get home before dinner. I figured Tommy would be all right at the quarry without me because the other older kids were still there. But Mike and I got lost. By the time we got back, it was almost dark. I was late for dinner and was envisioning Dad scolding me while Tommy smirked. But when I entered the front door of our house, I could see instantly that Dad wasn't in a mere scolding mood. He was furious. Not because I was hours late, but because Tommy had not yet come home.

"Where is he?" our father demanded. "Where the hell is Tommy?"

Pride required that I not burst into tears, but the effort took all my strength. My mind raced for something to say that wouldn't get me into even bigger trouble than I was in already. But there was nothing to grab hold of. Finally, I blurted it out. "We were at the quarry. Mike and I left. But everyone else stayed. All the older kids. And Tommy."

"Jesus Christ!" It was hardly the only time I'd heard my father take the Lord's name in vain. But this time was different. Even at twelve, I could tell that Dad wasn't cursing out of anger but fear. "Come on!" he ordered, and the two of us hopped into his F-150 and tore for the quarry.

We found Tommy in the gathering darkness halfway up the quarry wall, sitting on a small ledge. I didn't understand why he was there. The ledge was only twenty feet above the water and an easy climb down. Then my eyes scaled the wall upward until, another twenty feet up, I saw Danny, hanging on for dear life. I knew instantly what had happened: Danny had lost his nerve. He was too terrified to move. Tommy stood guard below him, having refused to abandon his friend.

My father cursed under his breath. Then he looked down at me. "Wait here," he ordered. "Do not move." Then he made his way along the narrow dirt-and-gravel path that rimmed the quarry on one side. The path was just a foot wide, and Dad had to navigate it facing the quarry wall, holding on in places to reach the part of the wall where Tommy and Danny were perched. In the light of the rising moon, I could see that our dad's back was soaked with sweat by the time he reached Tommy. I heard the two of them talking, and I figured Tommy was giving Dad directions on how to get up to Danny, whose whimpering I could now hear clearly. Then Dad started up the wall. His climb to Danny seemed to take forever. I could see that every movement required intense effort and concentration. He paused often and wouldn't move a limb off a hold until he tested all three other limbs for solid purchase. He was sucking wind by the time he was halfway up. But he continued, talking to Danny, reassuring him the whole way. Finally, he managed to reach Danny, got him to hang on his back, and began the long, torturous climb back down, Danny's choking arms wrapped around his throat the entire time.

Only when Dad and Danny reached the ground did Tommy begin his own descent. It was effortless and took him less than a minute.

I stood at the entrance to the quarry as Dad, my brother, and Danny made their way toward me. The four of us stood for a minute. Danny continued to whimper while Dad huffed and puffed. Tommy stood still with his feet apart, glaring at me.

"Everyone left us. And you left us first. You fucker."

I looked over at our father. Instead of scolding Tommy, he merely looked back at me. I could see in his eyes exactly the same thought Tommy had just uttered: *You fucker.*

It's Friday and I'm home early, just before six o'clock. Gabby runs out to meet me in the garage. I bend down and grab her, then swing her in the air and cradle her in my right arm. I use my left to bend down and pet Franklin, who has ambled up behind his human sister. Gabby immediately starts in on a story about the dog chasing a rabbit in the yard. Her enthusiasm and energy make me smile, and I stand for a few minutes as Gabby recounts her tale. Then I carry her through the hallway and into the kitchen where, having finished her story, she impatiently wiggles out of my arms and runs off to another adventure.

Piper is in the kitchen, blending herself a smoothie. She doesn't turn to face me as she begins anew our now-ongoing fight about the roof. I reiterate to Piper's back that we cannot afford a new $30,000 cedar-shake roof right now. "The only money we have coming in is David's retainer," I say. "And that isn't going to go far. Especially since he cheaped me down on the amount."

Piper turns to cast me a harsh look, then looks back at the blender and jams a banana into it. She closes the lid and turns on the mixer, drowning me out.

I leave Piper and walk into my home office, sit behind the desk. One of the photographs on my desk is of Piper on our wedding day. She is standing on the lawn after our ceremony, radiant in her white gown, a broad smile on her face. I remember the picture being taken, and I remember exactly what I was thinking: *I can't believe I just married this beautiful woman.*

Piper and I were married in May, fifteen months after we met. We had discussed having a small ceremony and were thinking about Washington Chapel in Valley Forge Park. Thatcher Gray had other ideas. His only daughter, he insisted, was going to have an appropriately sized wedding at a proper venue. So Piper and I ended up getting married at the Church of the Holy Trinity on Rittenhouse Square in a ceremony that included seven groomsmen, seven bridesmaids, the bishop, and three hundred guests including key partners at Thatcher Gray's law firm, some industry executives, and local politicians. On our wedding night, I joked to Piper that I'd had to spend most of the reception being introduced to my own guests. Paid for almost entirely by Thatcher Gray, the reception itself was an ostentatious affair at the Rittenhouse Hotel.

The first year and a half of our marriage was the happiest time in my life. I sold my tiny condo downtown, and Piper and I used the money to buy a small twin in Chestnut Hill. I continued to work hard, riding herd on the city's bad guys while Piper stayed on at the art museum. When I wasn't on trial, I made it home around eight, about the same time as Piper, and the two of us would prepare dinner together as we talked and laughed about our days. On the weekends, we went out with other young couples—assistant DAs and their spouses, Piper's friends from work, and some law-school classmates of mine who'd decided to practice in Philly—including David Hanson and Marcie. Piper and I saw ourselves as young and hip and happy, on the fast track to fantastic lives.

The only fly in the ointment was Tommy. Piper admitted to me early on that she, to some extent, and her parents were uncomfortable with the fact that my brother was doing hard time for a violent crime. I tried to explain to Piper and her parents that despite his criminal record, Tommy was not a bad guy, that he'd had a tough time of it growing up because of what had happened with our parents. Thatcher answered with the old chestnut that I, too, had suffered the deaths of my parents and I'd turned out fine. I replied that Tommy had been much closer to what happened with my father because he was still living at home while I was away at school. Piper and her mother, Helen, tried to understand, but Thatcher Gray was having none of it. To him, the line between Tommy and me was as clear as the demarcation between good and evil.

About four months after we were married, I decided it was time for Piper to meet my brother. I drove her to the state prison outside Harrisburg, where he was locked up. At that point, he wasn't scheduled to be released for a couple of more years, but I wanted to begin breaking the ice between him and Piper sooner rather than later. I even dreamed that they might eventually strike up a true friendship, that Piper would welcome Tommy into our family once he was released.

Piper fidgeted the whole way. Her father had clearly terrorized her with overblown notions about the danger of prisons and convicts. The security procedures necessary to gain entry only added to Piper's anxiety. And when Tommy finally entered the visiting room and I saw Piper's eyes, I knew I'd made a mistake. He strode into the room like a bull. He must have weighed 220 pounds, all of it muscle. His head was shaved. His neck revealed a fresh—and infected—blue-green prison tattoo. The knuckles on his hands were black and swollen. His eyes were flat, his lips tightly pursed. Halfway through his prison term, my little brother had successfully erased all outward appearances of humanity.

Tommy reluctantly allowed me to give him a brotherly side-hug. Then Piper stepped around him and tried to put her arms around him, too, which didn't go well at all.

The next hour was an exercise in awkwardness. I tried to start up a dialogue, but Tommy limited himself to clipped answers to my questions. For her part, Piper prattled on and on and on—about the weather, the war, politics, the ride up, her parents. Everything but the three of us. In the end, no one reached anyone.

The drive home was interminable. Piper regretted having let me bring her to see Tommy, and she was angry at herself for "botching it." She fell silent for a long time. Then she looked over at me and said, "Those poor men. Forced to live like animals in that awful place."

I glanced over and saw a tear running down the left side of her face. I remember wondering at that moment whether she had changed her views about what I did for a living.

The TV in my office grabs my attention when it flashes the photographs of three police officers. The big story on the six o'clock news—based on the reporting of the late Jennifer Yamura—is the disclosure of the names of three of the cops who allegedly participated in the drug ring and were given immunity to testify before the grand jury. I'm surprised that Yamura was able to obtain such confidential information. Everyone involved in the grand-jury process is made to swear an oath of secrecy. The penalties for violating that oath are severe and include imprisonment. Why would anyone take the enormous risk of telling her?

In the wake of Yamura's death, the station and its lawyers supposedly struggled over whether to make the information public. "In the end," says Anchorman Jim, "Channel Six had to attach paramount importance to the public's right to know." With that, Jim reads off the names of the policemen: "Officers Terrance Johnson and Stanley Lipinski, and Lieutenant Lawrence Washington."

The last name shocks me. I had worked with Lawrence on a dozen cases while I was with the DA. He was a good cop, hardworking and honest. Lawrence was never the type to plant evidence or press for inflated charges against a defendant. He wasn't rough with the perps, either. He treated everyone with respect. He was a gentleman.

I stare at Lawrence Washington's police photograph. He looks older than when I last saw him five years ago. He's lost some hair. His jowls are looser. And there's something in the eyes that I haven't seen before.

What is it? A guilty conscience? Sorrow? Or was he simply tired the day they took the picture? I shake my head.

"Lawrence."

I say his name aloud, feeling suddenly sad for him, close to him.

I take my eyes away from his photograph and scan the other two. Lipinski I know but wish I didn't. A bad actor. I've never met Terrance Johnson, who appears to be much younger than the other two. I wonder what bad break or twist of fate motivated him and Lawrence to betray themselves, their families, the police force. What surprise did life spring on them at exactly the right moment to make two good men go bad?

6

Monday, June 11

The following Monday, the prosecution's case materials arrive in my office. The documents include the incident reports, a compilation report, the arrest memo, and the property receipts of the items that were taken from David on his arrest, along with the CSU log. Because David's case is so high profile, it has been rushed through the system, which means that I also receive the crime-scene photos, autopsy report, and photographs—they usually take more time. Still, it will be a while before I get the fingerprint and DNA analysis.

I go right to the crime-scene photos. I quickly scan the shots of Jennifer Yamura's house: outside, front and back, and the first and second floors. Then I focus my attention on the photographs of the basement steps and her body. My heart quickens as I look at her face, eyes open, seeming to stare up at me. I spot the blood spill on the sixth and fifth steps from the bottom, the steps her head must have struck when she fell. I study the massive pool of blood on the concrete block at the bottom of the steps, where her head is lying. And it strikes me that this is wrong.

Her head should be higher on the steps. And there are fresh abrasions on both of her knees. She's lying on her back, but her knees are bloodied.

This isn't making sense.

I grab the police reports, which make mention of the head wounds, the knee injuries, and some lighter abrasions to the palms of her hands—all injuries that the investigating officers would have been able to see with their own eyes. Deeply confused, I reach for the autopsy report and learn that the cause of Jennifer's death was exsanguination from a ruptured artery in the back of her head resulting from blunt-force trauma caused when her head collided with the steps. Going back to the police reports, I read that the basement floor had been scrubbed with a cleaning agent but that luminol testing revealed trace amounts of latent blood.

There can only be one explanation for all of this, and it hits me like a bolt of lightning: Yamura must have survived the fall down the stairs!

She made it off the steps, crawled along the basement's rough concrete floor, scraping up her knees and her hands. Someone—whomever she was crawling away from—then took her back to the stairs and kept her there until she bled out.

"Jesus Christ." I spring from my chair, close the door to my office. I pace and think. Then pace some more. A million questions flood my brain. I sit down at my desk again, study the crime-scene photos, the police reports, the autopsy report, over and over. "Jesus Christ," I repeat. "Jesus fucking Christ."

After lunch, and after I've spent several hours reviewing and summarizing the prosecution's evidence, I receive a call that I've been expecting from Devlin Walker. He offers the kind of deal that Detective

Tredesco suggested he might: David pleads to first-degree manslaughter, "Man One," and Devlin will urge the Court to impose the minimum sentence. "But," Devlin is quick to add, "any plea agreement has to include producing that laptop. No laptop, no deal."

I chuckle. "David plead? Are you serious? I've just finished reading all the police reports, and I found more than enough to make reasonable doubt a lock."

"Like what?"

"Like the stolen computer you just mentioned. Along with stolen jewelry and cash. So, what, you're going to argue that my millionaire client emptied Ms. Yamura's wallet, then took her laptop and jewelry so he could pawn it, because he needed the money to buy that double-wide he'd always dreamed of owning?"

"Please. Your client's a smart man. He took the computer and the money and jewelry as a smoke screen to make it look like a robbery gone bad."

I let his theory hang in the air for a moment. "Why are you involved in this case at all, Devlin? You haven't tried a murder case in years."

"That's easy. I'm running the grand jury looking into the police drug syndicate. The decedent had information critical to the investigation. I had a vested interest in getting Ms. Yamura in front of my grand jury and questioning her. Her murder prevented me from doing that."

"It's that simple?"

"It's that simple." Devlin waits a beat. "Hanson killed that young woman, Mick. Something obviously went wrong with their affair. He got pissed, pushed her down the stairs. Then when it was clear she wasn't going to die, he made sure she did. That's cold. And a jury will crucify him for it. He'll rot in prison forever. But he can avoid all that by pleading to Man One. *If* he produces the laptop. And it better not have been opened. Not a single document read. Our forensics guys will know it if Hanson or anyone else has even *looked* at the files. Please make that very clear to your client."

Not long after I hang up with Devlin, Angie buzzes to tell me that David has shown up at the firm and wants to see me. I have her bring him back to my office. David appears haggard and tired. Still not as bad as he looked the morning after his arrest, but close.

"How are things with Marcie?"

"Hell," he says. "Half the time, she's screaming at me. Half the time, she's giving me the silent treatment. Stomping around the house, slamming doors, ignoring me. The boys know something's wrong between us. I don't know what to tell them." David pauses here, looks past me out the window. "Her family hates me. Her sister called me on my cell phone the other night for the sole purpose of telling me what a piece of shit I am."

David's looking at me now. "My own family's hardly on speaking terms with me, either. Except Edwin, of course. He has plenty to say."

Eighteen years David's senior, his half brother, Edwin, is the CEO of Hanson World Industries. Groomed from an early age to take control of the family business, Edwin is reputed to be both brilliant and ruthless.

"Such as?"

"He just told me to take a leave of absence from the company. It was all I could do not to hit him in the mouth. I came here instead, to blow off steam."

"Are you going to do as he says?"

"What choice do I have? Edwin runs the show."

I think about this. "A leave of absence isn't a bad idea, actually, so long as it looks like it's your idea. You need to issue a statement that although you're innocent, you're taking some time off for the sake of your family, and also for the good of the company and its many employees. It'll look selfless and high-minded of you. It'll also tell potential jurors that you're already suffering as a result of the charges brought against you."

I call Vaughn, explain the situation, and ask him to draft something.

David asks if there've been any developments in the case. I tell him that, as a matter of fact, I'd just that morning received the prosecution's materials. I tell David about Jennifer's head injuries, her scraped knees, the blood traces on the basement floor where someone tried to clean up. David's eyes never leave me as I explain it all. He doesn't move a muscle.

After I finish, David waits for moment, then says, "But I didn't clean the basement. I never went the whole way down."

Which makes me wonder, *If David didn't put her back on the steps, then who did?*

7

Wednesday, June 20

The following week, on Wednesday, Susan and I are in the conference room talking about firm finances when Tommy and Vaughn come in together. We say our hellos, and I ask Tommy if he has anything new on the Hanson case. He lets me know that a cop he's friends with in the Ninth District has confided to him that in the weeks before Jennifer Yamura's murder, her neighborhood had been struck by a small crime wave of break-ins and burglaries.

"That could be pretty helpful to us at trial, right?" Tommy asks. "Supports the theory that she was killed during a burglary gone bad? It'd jibe with her computer and jewelry and cash being gone."

"Absolutely," I say. "I'll have Vaughn serve a subpoena on the police department asking for all reports of break-ins and burglaries in that neighborhood during the six months before the murder—and since. We'll see what we can flush out. Good work. Anything else? How about those three cops?" I ask, referring to the three cooperating police officers who had been named two weeks earlier.

"Word on the street," Tommy answers, "is that Terrance Johnson is holed up in a hotel room downtown, being guarded by some cops assigned to the DA's office. Lipinski's spending his days drinking himself blind at a North Philly cop bar, daring *them* to come and get him."

"And Lawrence Washington?" I ask.

"Off the radar. He's the smart one."

Susan looks at Tommy. "You really think the bad cops will actually try to kill those three?"

Tommy nods. "A message for anyone else thinking about turning state's evidence. And three dead cops floating facedown in the Schuylkill River would be a pretty loud message."

We talk a little more, then they leave me alone in my office. I think about the robberies in Yamura's neighborhood and ponder whether I could persuade a jury to believe that Yamura was merely another random victim in Philly's endless stream of murders. That David didn't scrub the house because he'd killed Jennifer, but because he found her already dead and freaked out about being identified as her lover. But why would a home invader drag Jennifer back to the steps to wait for her to bleed out and die rather than simply run away?

Whatever tack I take, I'll have to deal with the fact that David had no problem casually traipsing around the house one flight above the murdered corpse of his lover, perhaps for hours. Not something you'd expect a person to be able to stomach.

Unless he was a sociopath.

I'll have to carefully plan my portrayal of David to the jury and craft a story to fit it. Reciprocally, I'll need to figure out how to cast Jennifer Yamura herself.

I had met Yamura twice. The first time was at a black-tie charity gala sponsored by Project Home to raise money for the homeless. I was standing with Jack Lafferty, a chief inspector and one of only a handful of cops I could still count as friends after I'd left the DA's office. Jennifer Yamura was petite, thin, and no taller than five two. She had slender arms, highlighted by her sleeveless blue-sequined dress, and tiny, well-manicured hands. Her face was round, with almond eyes tilted slightly upward at the ends. Jennifer Yamura's white teeth were flawlessly aligned, and the overall effect of her face was so striking that she could've been featured in one of those Korean Air TV commercials—except that her ancestry was Japanese.

She had planted herself in front of us and greeted Jack. "How have you been?"

"Well enough," Jack answered coolly.

"And you're Mr. McFarland, one of the rising stars of the criminal-defense bar." Yamura said this with just enough irony to make it more cutting than complimentary.

"I've tried a few cases," I said.

"Bet you have some good stories." She smiled.

"Is that why you're here?" I asked. "Looking for a story?"

"I'm here to support the cause. But, of course, I'm always looking for a story. You have one you want to share?"

I tried to think of something glib but fell flat.

Yamura persisted, asking questions about my practice. The inquiries seemed innocuous enough, but I got the distinct impression I was being studied, probed. Evaluated for my potential usefulness.

Jack turned to me after Jennifer Yamura had walked away. "That one's radioactive," he said. "She glows real pretty. Just don't get too close." He then proceeded to tell me all he knew about her. Jennifer Yamura was socially ubiquitous. She frequented cop bars as often as she attended high-end social events. She went to Flyers, Phillies, Sixers, and Eagles games. She attended all the city's ethnic parades. She participated in and reported from the Broad Street Run in May and the Distance Run in September. And, of course, she attended all the political rallies, press conferences, and contentious city-council meetings.

"She seems to be everywhere, all the time," Jack said. "On the hunt, trying to bag the big scoop that will land her in an anchor's chair."

I looked across the room to see Jennifer Yamura talking to the mayor. She touched his wrist, laughing at something he said.

"She seems enthralled," I told Jack.

"I'm sure that's exactly what she wants him to think."

I shelve the memory and remind myself that Jennifer Yamura was someone's daughter. That, somewhere, her parents are shattered by her loss.

This grim thought sends me back to the birth of my own daughter. I see Piper on the birthing table, squeezing my hand so hard I thought she'd break it, until the obstetrician lifted our tiny, purple baby into the air.

"Oh my God," I had whispered, my heart awash in joy. I looked down at Piper, who was crying, and it was my turn to squeeze her hand.

We took Gabrielle home with us the next morning, after Piper's parents stopped by the hospital to see the baby. As I drove our precious new cargo through the city streets, I felt an unfamiliar sense of fear—the first of many moments of new-baby terror I would experience over the next month. Gabrielle was so tiny and looked so fragile to me that I held my breath the first fifty times I held her. Piper laughed at my obvious trepidation.

"You're not going to break her," she'd say.

"Of course not," I would agree, but I continued to handle Gabby like a pack of nitroglycerin.

During the early days of Gabby's life, Piper and I spent hours next to Gabby's crib, watching the gentle rhythm of her breathing, overwhelmed by the new life we'd created.

I remember one afternoon, sitting there, stroking her thick black hair and letting my mind carry us both into the future where Gabrielle's life would unfold. I envisioned her as a toddler, crawling along the floor looking for new things to touch and lift and put into her mouth. I saw her walking between Piper and me, looking up at us, holding our hands as we escorted her to the bus stop for her first day of kindergarten. I saw Gabby sitting in fifth grade, drawing hearts and writing the name of some boy she had a crush on over and over again inside the cover of her notebook. I saw her, gawky and long-legged, crying on her bed as a teenager. I saw her walking next to me down the aisle as I steeled myself to hand her off to a better man. And I saw her in a hospital bed, cradling her own firstborn child.

Jennifer Yamura's father must have had the same experience with his own daughter, the same hopes and visions for her future. A future that ended in a pool of blood in a dark basement. Thinking this cuts me to the bone.

8

Tuesday, July 10; Friday, July 20; Thursday, July 26; Wednesday, August 1

Three weeks pass. The Hanson case is pushed off the front pages by other, equally sad stories: a local congressman faces corruption charges while his son is convicted on twenty-two counts of bank and tax fraud; a local man is on trial for allegedly shooting his stepdaughter and then videotaping himself having sex with her corpse.

On a Tuesday in the second week of July, I get to argue the Justin Bauer case before the state supreme court. It's been said of Pennsylvania that it's made up of Pittsburgh on the west end, Philadelphia on the east, and Alabama in the middle. Geographically, most of the state is populated by staunch conservatives who hold a dim view of the rights of criminal defendants, a view historically well represented by the justices elected to our state's supreme court. The panel that faces me now, however, gives me reason for optimism. Last year, two of our Republican justices were forced off the bench when the state attorney general released copies of pornographic and misogynistic e-mails exchanged by the justices and members of law enforcement. They were replaced by two Democrats who both began their careers as criminal-defense attorneys.

From the get-go, the court's questioning makes clear that most of the justices are as convinced as I am of the ineptitude of Justin Bauer's trial attorney. But that's not enough. I have to show that the trial attorney's ineptitude so undermined the truth-determining process that no reliable adjudication of guilt or innocence could have taken place. In other words, I have to convince the justices that, were it not for the trial attorney's blunders, there would have been a good chance Justin would not have been convicted.

It's a high hurdle.

The rules of appellate procedure do not require the defendant's presence in the courtroom during oral argument. But I have brought Justin nonetheless—and Celine as well. Not because I expect they'll understand the nuances of my legal argument, but because I want them to see the *passion* with which I present their side. Justin was let down by his former attorney, and I believe it's imperative that he and his mother witness a lawyer actually fighting like hell for them. They're owed at least that.

The argument goes as I expect. The justices are tough on both sides but more on me than the prosecution. Still, I hear in their questions an openness that I haven't come across in a long while. After the hearing, I walk Celine into the hall. She grills me on the questioning, wanting to know why the judges were pressing me so hard. I do my best to explain, wishing the law weren't so obtuse. In the end, all I can do is leave her with a sense of guarded optimism and, hopefully, the feeling that, finally, the law is hearing her and her son.

The next two weeks bring a heat wave. Day after day of high humidity and ninety-degree temperatures require me to change shirts twice a day. The heat makes me yearn for the beach. Makes me remember how, when we were first married, Piper and I used to bolt out of Center City every Friday afternoon in the summers and head to Cape May, where we'd rent a room in a bed-and-breakfast.

The first time we'd gone to the beach together was when we'd just started dating.

"Next to the museum, this is my favorite place," Piper told me as we walked the broad sand beach toward the lighthouse. "When I look out at the ocean, at all that open space, it feels like time, too, expands. That the pace of everything slows down. And if I stop and stand here facing the ocean"—Piper continued, doing so—"and take a deep breath . . . it feels like the whole world is inhaling with me. And all the pressures of the world melt away."

Piper turned to me when she said this. She smiled when she finished and, in that instant, her beauty struck me. It physically struck me. The shimmering blonde of her hair as it danced around her tiny ears in the balmy sea breeze. The sapphire of her smiling eyes. Her rose-pink lips. Her fine jawline. The way she tilted her head ever so slightly to the left.

I'm not sure how long we stood there, facing each other, but I'm sure Piper could see how I was looking at her.

"Have you ever stayed at a bed-and-breakfast?" she asked then, smiling in a very different way than before.

A couple of hours later, we lay beneath the sheets on a thick mattress on a creaky brass bed on the wood-plank second floor of a bed-and-breakfast on Gurney Street. Our lovemaking had been gentle, sweet, almost ethereal—until the passion had overtaken us. Now, in the afterglow, the pace of the world had slowed down again. Piper's head was nestled under my arm as we both lay still. In the distance, I heard the calm sea waves roll in to caress the sand. Inside, the only sounds were the rhythms of our breathing.

"And all the pressures of my world melt away," I said. But Piper didn't hear me. She was asleep. So I kissed the top of her head and told her I loved her.

Now I'm back in my office on a Friday, reading a brief on my computer. Tommy walks in and says he's gotten word that Devlin Walker is going to have Jennifer Yamura's house gone over again.

"My friend tells me they're going to search every nook and cranny of the place for hair, prints, lint—*breath molecules*—everything. Walker thinks that whoever was Yamura's source about the grand-jury investigation was probably at her house at least once, so maybe he left a DNA calling card."

I lean back in my chair and consider this. I'm about to make a suggestion when Tommy beats me to the punch. "I think we should get into that house first."

"Good idea." I call Vaughn into my office and tell him to draw up a motion for a scene inspection. I explain that the ADA is planning to scour the house soon and that I want to see it once before then.

"Should I call Hanson, tell him to be there with us when we search?"

"I don't think we'll need him there." I hang up with Vaughn and look over at Tommy. "Want to grab lunch?"

"Nah, can't today," he says, getting up.

"Gotta see a man about a horse?" I smile, but Tommy's eyes darken. "What's the matter?"

"Lot on my mind. No big deal."

"Going tent camping again?"

"Maybe." Tommy turns and walks out of my office.

I watch him go, the visual of Tommy roughing it under the stars taking me back to when we were teenagers. By the time he was in tenth grade, my brother had his life all mapped out. After graduation he was going to enlist in the military, Special Forces. He would serve our country on the most dangerous assignments. When he was discharged, he would go into law enforcement. "Big-city cop," he told me. "The front line. Down and dirty." I had no trouble even then envisioning my brother as a hard-ass cop in Philly, New York, Chicago, even Detroit.

When Tommy was in eighth grade, he began pumping iron in our basement. Then he bought a punching bag and started taking boxing lessons in a gym downtown. After a year of lifting, Tommy had gained thirty pounds and was ripped. The boxing lessons made him quick with his hands and feet. He once conned me into going a few rounds with him out in the backyard. Two minutes after we started, I was bent over, sucking wind.

In tenth grade, Tommy joined the wrestling team. Most of his teammates had already been wrestling for years, and Tommy was way behind them on technique. But he was a quick study, and it didn't take long for him to catch up. What impressed his coaches, however, wasn't the sharpness of Tommy's learning curve but his brute strength. Tommy's teammates called him "The Slab" because he was as hard as marble. Tommy was strong enough that, unlike his teammates, he didn't starve and sweat himself to wrestle in a class below his normal weight. He wrestled at 185, going up against guys who normally walked around ten to fifteen pounds heavier. And he beat them.

The summer after tenth grade, Tommy worked in the lumberyard. It was grueling, bull work under the hot sun. He loved it. Every morning, he would leave our house at six armed with two thermoses of grape Kool-Aid and a paper bag carrying his five sandwiches, chips, and carrots. He'd walk to the bus stop and catch the bus into town. Twelve hours later, he'd walk back in the door, filthy with sweat and sawdust, his hair matted, his shirt torn more often than not. And he'd be in the best mood—more energized than I was, even though I'd only put in eight hours doing light work at the local farmer's market.

Tommy was set to return to the lumberyard following eleventh grade. Then one of his friends at school told Tommy about his own job with a sporting outfit that hosted whitewater rafting tours in Jim Thorpe. Tommy accompanied his friend to the Poconos the weekend after school let out and was instantly hooked. When he got back that Monday morning, Tommy got our father's permission to leave for Jim Thorpe for the summer.

At the end of the summer, Tommy came home with a dark tan and dozens of pictures of him camping, in the raft, and with various groups. He looked like a bronze god of the river.

A wave of sadness sweeps across my chest as I sit in my office, thinking of Tommy back then. Confident, strong, tough. My brother was ready to meet the future on his own terms. Little did he know the future that was steamrolling toward him didn't look anything like he expected.

Our motion to inspect Jennifer Yamura's house is granted the week after we file it, and Tommy and I find ourselves walking from the office toward Addison Street. It's Thursday, July 26. The morning rain is gone, and the clouds are clearing, but the eighty-five-degree air is heavy with humidity, making it feel more like a hundred. Tommy carries a camera in case we want to take pictures. As we walk west on Addison, we come to the house near the end of the block. It's a three-story brick row home. The shutters are trimmed in green, as is the door. A piece of yellow crime-scene tape hangs broken in the doorway.

As Tommy and I reach the front door, it opens. A uniformed cop exits the house and descends three worn, white-marble steps to the street. Behind him, John Tredesco appears in the doorway. He isn't wearing his jacket; his sweat stains show.

"What are you doing here?" I ask. "The court's order was clear: a uniformed officer can watch us enter and leave, but we inspect the house by ourselves."

Tredesco smiles. "You know, it's funny. We all refer to this place as Yamura's house. But she didn't own it at all."

I don't know where Tredesco is going with this, but it makes me uneasy.

"Cut to the chase, John. I don't have all day."

"It wasn't easy to unravel it," Tredesco answers. "The recorder of deeds lists the owner as HD Holdings, some corporation out of Delaware. But that corporation is owned by another corporation, HDD Holdings, also of Delaware, which is owned by yet another corporation, HWD Holdings, in the Virgin Islands, which—guess what—is owned by yet another company. A huge conglomerate registered to do business in Delaware but operating almost everywhere in the world. You know, sometimes I wonder whether, when you get to the bottom of it, the whole fucking country isn't owned by a single company."

I pull out my cell phone and click a picture of Tredesco. "Unless you get out of my way in the next two seconds, I'm going to call the judge and tell him that you're interfering with a court-ordered view of the crime scene."

The detective ignores me. "When I contacted the company that owns this place, they forwarded me to their legal department. I left messages, but no one returned my calls. I figure that's because the company's legal department is shorthanded, seeing as how its general counsel is away on leave pending the results of his upcoming murder trial."

Fuck. It takes everything I have not to say it out loud. I turn abruptly and walk to the end of the street. I'm seething as I dial David's number.

"What the hell?" I say as soon as he answers. "You *own* Yamura's house?"

There's a long pause at the other end, then David tells me *he* doesn't own the house, the company does. "How'd you find out?" he asks. "And why does it matter?"

Through gritted teeth, I explain my scene inspection and all the shit that Tredesco's dishing out to me. "It matters," I say, "because with

HWI owning the property—and I assume the purchase of the house was your doing—the prosecution has a much stronger link between you and Jennifer than they had before. It matters because you told me you only saw her a handful of times, that it was just a casual thing, when, plainly, she was more to you than a mere fling." I now know why David had referred to his relationship with Jennifer as a *deal*. "It matters because you weren't honest with me."

"Oh, grow up," David snaps. "I didn't give a fuck about her. And I promise you, Jennifer wasn't the least bit emotionally involved with me. It was a business deal. I had the company buy the house and let Jennifer live there. In return, she would fuck me whenever I wanted. And I wasn't the only one she was seeing, either. Neither of us cared."

"Well, I'll just put it that way to the jury. 'Ladies and gentlemen, don't you believe for one second that my client had a motive to kill the decedent. There was no jealousy here, no motive to kill. You see, my client, my *married* client, the guy with a cancer-stricken wife, simply hired Ms. Yamura to be his concubine.'"

I hang up on David and return to the house. "You could have called me about this ahead of time," I tell Tredesco. "Instead of waiting until I was at the front door."

Tredesco smiles again. "Yeah. I know." He turns to the uniformed officer and tells him to stay outside while Tommy and I inspect the house. "Don't let them leave with anything," he adds, winking at me.

Tommy and I watch Tredesco get in his unmarked car and drive down the street. I tell Tommy what David said about not giving a damn about Jennifer, that they both saw other people. Tommy seems to accept this with as much equanimity as he did the news about David owning the house. He turns and leads me up the front steps.

The front door opens into a large living room. It's expensively outfitted with crown molding, cherrywood floors, and built-in bookshelves on either side of a black-marble fireplace. The walls are painted a muted gray. A small chandelier hangs in the center of the room. Over the fireplace is a pastel watercolor painting of two swans—very feminine. The sofa and love seat are of white fabric and sit around a chrome-and-glass coffee table. A vase with wilted flowers sits in the middle of it. Jennifer Yamura clearly had expensive tastes—good thing her keeper could afford to indulge them.

"Nice place," says Tommy. "Don't you think?"

"Yeah, nice," I say. "Let's see the back."

Tommy leads me through the living room to the kitchen, the only other room on the first floor other than the powder room. The kitchen cabinetry is all white, with light-gray marble countertops and brushed chrome hardware. The doors of the upper cabinets are faced with glass to reveal the crystal stemware and china inside. Lights mounted under the cabinets shine down on the counters. The ceiling is fitted with recessed lighting. The refrigerator is a Sub-Zero. The dishwasher is a Bosch. The oven is a six-burner gas Viking. All spanking new.

Tommy and I retrace our steps, enter the short hallway that encloses the door to the powder room and, across from it, the doorway to the basement stairs. A curtain of brightly colored glass beads covers the cellar doorway. "Her hippie side," Tommy says. He pushes aside the beads, and we both look down the steps. There are twelve—wooden, uncarpeted, old, and splintered. Obviously not part of the remodel. The bottom step rests on a concrete block about four inches high. The last four or five steps are stained with blood, and a large brown stain discolors the concrete block and the floor near it where Yamura's blood drained and pooled.

Tommy descends the steps, and I follow him. The basement is small, and the walls are cheaply paneled over rough cement. There is no finished ceiling, so I can see the wooden beams, ductwork, and wiring. Tommy walks over to a large plastic basin, turns the water on and off. I nod to the floor behind him.

"This must be where she crawled, tried to get away from her killer," I say. Tommy looks at me, nods, but says nothing. We dawdle for a few more minutes, looking around, then walk back upstairs.

"I'll check out back," I say. I walk through the kitchen and open the back door, step down onto the cement parking area behind the house. It's just big enough for one car; there's barely room beside it to get out and walk to the back door. The back wall of the house is stucco, smooth, and freshly painted in a French yellow. The glass-paned back door has a fresh coat of white paint as well.

Waverly Street, the alley that runs behind the houses on Addison, is just wide enough for a single car. Across Waverly, the houses on Pine Street come right up to the sidewalk, leaving no room for parking. Directly across from Jennifer Yamura's place there's a courtyard between the back extensions of two large homes. Empty but for trash cans, it's protected by an eight-foot, iron-barred security gate with a "No Trespassing" sign.

I stand in the alley and look up at the windows on the second and third floors of Jennifer Yamura's house. After a minute, Tommy appears in the second-floor window just above the kitchen. He looks down at me and I up at him. We hold each other's gaze for a long moment, and I see something undefinable in Tommy's eyes. He nods at me and turns away.

I cross the yard, walk up the back steps, and enter the kitchen. I meet Tommy in the living room.

"David spent a lot of money buying this house for her, fixing it up," I say. "Maybe he cared for her more than he let on."

"Or maybe he didn't buy the house for the girl," Tommy says. "Maybe he bought the girl for the house."

The following Wednesday, I'm sitting in my office at eight in the morning. David is coming in at ten to discuss his case. I'd called him again following the house inspection. Neither one of us was in a better mood during the second call that day than we had been during the first. I expect our meeting today to be stormy. Then Vaughn rushes in with news that makes me think the meeting will go even worse than I expect.

"Did you read the *Daily News* this morning?" He hands me the tabloid.

I gape at the headline above the front-page color photo of Jennifer Yamura's house. It reads: "Addison Street Geisha House?"

"My God." Someone from the police or DA's office has leaked to the newspaper the fact that David, through Hanson World Industries, owns the house in which Jennifer had been living. The theme of the article was that David had been keeping Jennifer in the house as his mistress, "like an old-fashioned geisha girl."

"This is so wrong," Vaughn says as I read. "The fact that Jennifer's ancestry was Japanese? That geisha thing? It's racist."

I sigh and look up at Vaughn. "More to the point is the fact that it makes David look like he's also a racist. And an elitist."

"And a pig," adds Susan, walking into my office, her own copy of the *Daily News* under her arm.

"Why didn't he tell us this?" Vaughn asks.

"Maybe for the same reason he won't tell us where he really was when Yamura was murdered," says Susan.

"You think he's guilty?" Vaughn asks.

"I think he has a lot to answer for," she says. "Like why he's out chasing other women while the mother of his two children is fighting cancer."

Susan and Vaughn leave me to read the article, which details the juicy family scandal from which David Hanson sprang. When Edwin was eighteen, their father divorced Edwin's mother to marry his secretary, who was then pregnant with David. It was a bitter and public divorce and caused Edwin to hate both his father and his younger half brother.

The phone on my desk buzzes behind me. It's Angie, telling me that David has arrived. I ask her to have Susan and Vaughn meet me in the conference room, and I walk down the hall to meet David in our foyer. We shake hands perfunctorily, and I lead David into the conference room, where we both sit down.

As livid as I am with David, I promise myself not to lose my cool. David is, after all, a client. And for things to work out, it is imperative that he remain so. The last thing I want is for David to fire me in a fit of anger because I can't hold my tongue.

I take a deep breath, then begin. "David, the reason I've asked you to come and meet with us today—"

David cuts me off midsentence. He, apparently, has not resolved to keep *his* cool with *me*. "I know why I'm here, Mick. Okay? You're pissed about the house thing. I should have told you about it. I fucked up. I get it."

It's Susan's turn to interrupt. "Did you see the story in the *Daily News* this morning?"

David whips his head toward Susan. "Yeah, I did. And so did my brother, who spent forty-five minutes reaming me out over the phone as I drove here this morning. He's already taken away my job. Had my security card revoked so I can't even get into the fucking building. Now he's demanding that I give him my proxy to vote my shares so I won't have any voice whatsoever in how the company is run. What's he going to ask for next? My balls on a silver platter?"

I pause a moment to let David see that I'm hearing him. I'm about to say something to calm him down, but Susan just can't hold back. "What's with the kimonos?" she demands. One of the things mentioned in the news article was that the police found seven silk Japanese kimonos in Jennifer Yamura's closet, a fact the reporter used to play up the geisha angle.

"Jesus fuck," David says. "It was a joke between the two of us. I came in one time and Jennifer was dressed in a kimono, and she pretended, *pretended*, like she was a geisha and I was her lord, or something. It was role-playing. That's all. After that, whenever I went to Japan on a business trip, I would come back with a kimono and give it to her. But she never *wore* them. That one time was the only time." David shakes his head, plainly both exasperated and exhausted.

"All right," I say before Susan has a chance to attack again. "I know you're under a great deal of stress right now," I begin. I pour a cup of coffee for David and then one for myself from the silver coffee service that Angie has set up on the conference table. Vaughn grabs a couple of croissants. Susan broods. "It's not our intent to add to it. We just want to make sure there will be no more surprises. We can deal with things, if we know about them. Put our own spin on the facts. But if the first time your legal team finds out about something that's potentially damaging is when we read it in the newspapers or see it on TV, then it's too late."

David looks at me. "All right. I get it."

"Is there *anything* else?" I ask. "Anything that might look bad if it comes out?"

David looks up at the ceiling and inhales. He's thinking. It looks like he's about to shrug his shoulders when Vaughn says, "The kimonos." David looks over at Vaughn, who continues. "You said there were seven of them. The first one, the one Jennifer already had and wore as a joke. And the other six you purchased when you went to Japan?"

"Yes?"

"How often did you *go* to Japan?" This is Susan, who has apparently figured out where Vaughn is going.

A light goes off in David's eyes, and he stiffens. I can see that he, too, gets it. "I go to Asia, including Japan, about twice a year." He directs his next comment to me. "I'd actually been seeing Jennifer for almost three years. Not just a handful of times, like I told you."

"And the house?" I asked. "When did you buy it?"

"I already owned it by then. I'd bought it for . . . someone else. Then she relocated and the house was sitting empty. After a while, I started seeing Jennifer, and eventually, I told her she could move in."

So Tommy was right when he speculated that David hadn't purchased the house for Jennifer, but the other way around. I look from Susan to David, who stares down at the table.

"So," says Susan, "playing devil's advocate here, when your case goes to trial, the prosecutor will be able to say that you purchased the house to keep *one* woman, and then after you broke up, you went out and *acquired* another woman to keep in the same house. Even before your wife got sick and things became stressful between the two of you."

David says nothing, still averting his eyes.

I take a deep breath, forge ahead. "Your alibi for when Jennifer Yamura was killed. Is there *anything* you want to add to what you already told us?"

"Anything *different*?" clarifies Susan.

David ignores Susan and looks directly at me. "I didn't go to the house the day Jennifer was killed. I only went there that night."

"Where—" Vaughn gets the one word out before David stands abruptly.

"We're done here," he says, then turns to leave.

"Sooner or later, you're going to want to tell us where you really were, what you were doing," Susan says to David's back.

David turns. "Am I, Susan? Am I going to *want* to tell you? Are you really going to *want* to know where I was and what I was doing?" This last remark he directs at me. Then he's gone.

Vaughn is the first to speak. "Did he just tell us he did it? Did he just say that we really don't want to know where he was when Jennifer was murdered because the answer is he was right there, tossing her down the stairs?"

"That's not what I heard," I say. "And it's not what you heard, either. Got it?" I turn to Susan. "You seem to have quite a hard-on for the man."

Susan gets her back up, starts to say something, but cuts herself off.

"Look," I say, "I don't much like David right now, either. But I don't want to lose him as a client. We can't afford to lose him."

Susan looks away for a long minute, then turns to face me again. "I don't get it. David went to law school with you at Penn, an Ivy League school. And wasn't he on the *Law Review*? He has to be a smart guy. A lot smarter than he's looking right now."

David *is* smart, but maybe not in the sense Susan means. And David did get himself on the *Law Review*. But it wasn't due to his grades. Instead, he had to write his way on. No easy task even for the best legal writers and research wonks—for David it would have been impossible, because of his lack of patience. David never could have planted himself in the law library long enough to lose himself in the research necessary to author a paper of sufficient depth to win a spot on the *Law Review*.

But David had a secret weapon, a carefully cultivated asset that none of his competitors possessed. He had our roommate, Kevin Kratz, the smartest guy in our class. During our first year of law school, David invited Kevin to every ball game and concert and party he went to. David made sure that Kevin was never left standing alone in the middle of a crowd, that his beer mug was always full. And David was the one who persuaded Allen Davis and me to let Kevin live with us in the apartment we rented during our second year . . . when David would have to write his paper to win a place with that publication.

I read the paper David submitted under his name to the editorial staff. It was, in a word, brilliant. Exhaustively researched, tightly reasoned. Almost literary. The work would have been a source of pride to any Supreme Court justice's law clerk. I had little doubt at the time that Kevin was proud of it, and I was certain David praised and thanked Kevin to no end for it.

And yet, at the time—and this may be a sad commentary on my own ability to judge people—I did not question at all the sincerity of David's friendship with Kevin Kratz. Even when, at the end of our second year, David persuaded Kevin to lobby for him to become editor-in-chief, when Kevin clearly, and by leaps and bounds, was the better man for the position.

I shrug. "He's definitely a smart man. Very smart."

9

Friday, August 10

It's Friday morning and I'm staring at the face of Stanley Lipinski. Of the three corrupt cops identified by the press in connection with the grand-jury investigation, Lipinski is the one who'd planted himself at the local cop bar, essentially taunting the cops he'd snitched on to come for him. The story of Lipinski's murder is playing out on the seven o'clock news on the small TV in our kitchen. My daughter and I are sitting on stools at the island in the middle of the kitchen, Gabby eating her Trix while I wait for Piper to finish frying the vegetable omelet we'll share.

I know a lot of good cops. I could name fifty I'd be shocked to hear accused of corruption. Stanley Lipinski is not one of them. Lipinski viewed himself as the police-department version of a hockey team's "enforcer." Some cops get rough with suspects because they truly believe in the good-guys-bad-guys dichotomy and think the bad guys get what they deserve. But that wasn't Stanley Lipinski. Stanley inflicted pain because he enjoyed it. Everyone—cops, perps, even prosecutors and defense attorneys—gave Stanley a wide berth.

But the bad guys, the real bad guys, will only put up with so much, so I wasn't surprised when the Thirteenth District's enforcer ended up dead. He had, after all, not only testified against his cohorts before the grand jury but also all but dared them to come and get him. Apparently, they did. Lipinski had gone down hard in a rapid-fire spray of bullets on the sidewalk just outside McCraven's Tavern in North Philly. According to eyewitnesses, so many bullets had torn through his torso that Stanley was effectively disemboweled, his guts spilling onto the pavement while he remained upright, shouting, "Fuck you!"

When the story finishes, Piper turns from the TV to me, and I see that all the color has drained from her face. "They're going after everyone who helped Jennifer Yamura with that story, aren't they?" Before I can answer, she asks, "Have you heard from Tommy?"

"Not for a few days," I say.

"Can you give him a call? Make sure he's all right."

"Why wouldn't Tommy be all right?"

Piper turns back to the omelet, which is now overdone.

I stare at her back for a moment, wondering whether Tommy and Piper are keeping things from me. After Piper recovered from the shock of her visit to Tommy in prison, the two of them became close. Piper began writing to him. At first he didn't reply, but Piper persisted, and Tommy eventually sent her a one-paragraph missive thanking her for her letters. He wrote that it made him feel good to know that someone on the outside was thinking about him. The next week, the floodgates opened. I went to the mailbox to find another letter from Tommy. The envelope was thick, and Piper told me it was ten pages long. She wouldn't tell me what Tommy had written, and I didn't press; I was overjoyed that Tommy and Piper were developing a relationship. I wanted him to become part of our family once he got out of prison, and Piper was laying the groundwork for that to happen, despite the poison her father had been feeding her about my brother. The day he was finally released, Piper came with me to pick him up at the prison.

The following week, I introduced Tommy to my now-retired partner and founder of my law firm, Lou Mastardi, who agreed to hire Tommy as our firm's investigator. Tommy lived with us for the next six weeks—Gabby was two at the time—while he reintroduced himself to freedom. The adjustment was not an easy one. He seemed to be on edge all the time, always looking over his shoulder. He would wake up in the middle of the night and walk outside to our patio. More than once I woke to find Piper gone from our bed, and spied her through the window sitting next to Tommy, talking quietly. It warmed my heart to see Piper helping my brother make his return to society. I believed that she played a critical role, both then and throughout the ensuing years, in bringing back the brother I'd last seen before our father's illness and death.

Sometimes, though, and I hate to admit this, I felt a pang of jealousy. Tommy bared his soul to Piper. I got that, to a point. Piper is a nurturer and I—Lord knows—am not. But I am Tommy's brother, and I would have thought that, even if he couldn't bring himself to open himself up fully to me, he could have shared more than he did. What came to irk me even more was my suspicion that Piper herself shared things with Tommy that she didn't tell me, her husband. Call me a dinosaur, but I think I should be her main sounding board and soul mate. I pressed Piper about this a few times, but she always shrugged it off or threw it back at me, complaining that I spent my weekends on the golf course rather than out in our garden, like Tommy often did. Needless to say, this type of response did not reassure me. But I did my best to push down my angst, securing it in one of my many mental lockboxes.

"Are you going to call Tommy or not?" Piper says, her back to me as she scrapes the omelet out of the frying pan.

"I'll call him from the car," I answer. "I'm sure he's fine."

Half an hour later, on the way to the office, I do call Tommy's cell phone. I get the usual message, and I leave my own, asking him to call me back.

Angie is on the phone when I arrive at the firm. She flags me down and tells the person on the other end to hold on because I'd just arrived. "It's Patti Cassidy," Angie says. "She wants to know if you have a comment on that dead cop." I nod and tell Angie to put the reporter through to my office.

"Patti, how are you?" I begin, using my sweetest voice.

"Sorry, Mick, but if we could just cut to the chase, I have to get my part of the article together ASAP for the website. Or someone else's name is going on it."

"Okay, here's my quote: Officer Lipinski's murder only underscores that some very bad actors are as unhappy with the people involved in the grand-jury investigation as they were with Jennifer Yamura for reporting it."

There's a pause at the other end of the line. "Is that going to be your defense in the Hanson case? That Jennifer Yamura was murdered by people connected with the police drug ring? Are you going on record with that?"

"Not a chance," I say. "You—and everyone else—will learn at trial why David Hanson couldn't have murdered Yamura."

I click off and speed-dial Tommy. Again, I get his voice mail. I hang up without leaving a message.

Stressed, I decide to go for a run. My ten-mile routine run along the Schuylkill River usually relaxes me. But today it's no help. I just can't clear my mind of the widening rift between Piper and me, and the canyon separating me from my brother.

Halfway through my run, I cross the Falls Bridge to head back to town on West River Drive. The minute I turn the corner, I see the darkness enveloping the sky to the east. The clouds already cover Center City and are heading my way. Before I get a mile down the drive, I can hear it coming. A wall of rain pounds the ground a hundred yards from me. Then fifty, then the rain is upon me. Instantly, I'm soaked. It's so thick I can barely make out the headlights of the cars approaching to my right.

When I arrive at the lobby of my building, the guard at the front desk, with whom I've exchanged greetings a hundred times, casts me a suspicious look, wondering who this street person is trespassing in his gleaming marble-and-chrome environment. I show him my access card. It's soaked, so it doesn't scan, and he has to key in the elevator for me.

In the men's room, I use paper towels in a futile effort to dry off. Eventually, I give up and return to my office.

I try again to reach Tommy and curse when I hear his voice mail. I call home. Piper tells me that she still hasn't heard from Tommy, either. I tell Piper I'm going to drive up to his trailer in Jim Thorpe. She says to be careful. I think about that. Tommy is definitely sharing things with Piper that he hasn't with me.

An hour later, I'm driving down a rough path called Lizard Creek Road. I turn into Tommy's campground and pass some big-ass RVs that cost more than most people's homes, and continue until I find the turnoff for Tommy's campsite. I see the weathered picnic table sitting next to his trailer, covered with a canvas tarp. As I pull up, a man sits down at the table, gnawing on a corncob. But that man is not Tommy. Neither Tommy nor his pickup is anywhere to be seen.

I step out of the car. The air is sweet with the smell of freshly barbequed chicken. The man sitting at the picnic table puts down the cob, wipes his hands on a paper towel, and stands. He walks toward me as I park my car and get out.

"Hello, Mick," he says, extending his hand.

"Hey, Lawrence," I say, extending my own hand. "Long time no see."

Lieutenant Lawrence Washington smiles. "Long time *nobody* see."

Lawrence is a tall, proud-shouldered African American. His hair, now almost fully gray, is cut short. He is neither light-skinned nor dark-skinned. His reserved and mannerly demeanor has always shone in sharp contrast to his chosen line of work. Let's just say I have never heard someone address Lawrence as Larry.

"Where's Tommy?"

Lawrence takes a seat, rests his arms on the table, and folds his hands. "Oh, he's around. Had to go down to the store, get some supplies."

"In the middle of dinner?"

Lawrence smiles again but doesn't answer. Tommy knew I was coming. Piper must have gotten through to him on his phone. Maybe she'd been in contact with him this whole time. Maybe she just wanted me to come up here to see him. Or, as it turns out, *not* see him until after Lawrence and I have had a little sit-down. Maybe I'm being paranoid, but I'm starting to feel that this whole thing has been orchestrated.

"So what is it we're supposed to talk about?" I ask Lawrence.

"You're a sharp one, Mick. You always were."

I'm running out of patience. "Come on, man. What are you doing here? Or, if you want, we can talk about Stanley Lipinski."

"Stanley Lipinski *is* what I'm doing here. I do not want to end up like him, which I surely would if I'd have stuck around."

"There's witness protection," I say. "Like Terrance Johnson."

Lawrence smirks. "Provided by the police. Police protecting you from the police. Not a good formula, by my math. I don't hold out much hope for young Terrance."

I nod, take a seat, and look at the big paper plate of barbequed chicken on the table. Lawrence tells me to help myself. He picks up his corn on the cob, and we eat together in silence until he's finished.

"It was because of Cecilia," he says suddenly.

"Your wife," I say. "I heard. I'm sorry." Cecilia Washington had been Lawrence's high school sweetheart. Each was a refugee from a fractured household. Coming from a war-zone neighborhood, Lawrence and Cecilia had recognized in each other the same "I am better than this" spark of self-determination and pride. They married the month

Lawrence graduated from the police academy, raised three daughters, sent them all to college, and saw them all married. This was common knowledge on the force and in the DA's office, at least among those of us who worked cases with Lawrence. Also common knowledge was that Cecilia had developed a neurological condition that slowly robbed her of her health, then her mobility, then her life. It was an awful way for someone to die. And awfully expensive as well.

"I took her to every doctor I could find," Lawrence says. "Every specialist, and everyone who claimed to be a specialist. We tried all the known therapies and drugs. Tried the experimental ones. I even flew Cecilia down to Mexico. Twice. About halfway through it all, I just plain ran out of money. Our savings were gone. Retirement account empty. Every cent of equity in the house used up. I had to find the money to go on. It was that simple. Guys I worked with knew all about it. One day, one of them came up to me. Said he knew of a way to help me out. Now, I knew that guy, and I knew that whatever he was serving up was gonna be rotten. But I didn't even blink. I looked him right in the eye and said, 'Where do I sign?'"

When Lawrence pauses, I get up and walk a few steps to a plastic Igloo cooler, pull out two bottles of beer, and bring them back to the table. Lawrence and I take turns throwing them back in the hot night air. The sun has set, and we're surrounded by the constant sounds of the crickets and cicadas. Every now and then, a twig snaps nearby, a groundhog or maybe a fox making its presence known. When Lawrence and I finish our beers, I retrieve two more.

"So," I say, handing Lawrence his bottle, "about Tommy."

Lawrence unscrews the cap, takes a long swallow, then looks at me hard. "Don't judge him, Mick. He's had a tough road."

"I know all about Tommy's problems, and I *don't* judge him."

Something flickers in Lawrence's eyes. My brother clearly has problems I don't know about, and he's going to tell me about them, at least some of them, right now.

Before he has a chance to start, I jump in. "I'm still wondering what brings you here specifically. How do you and Tommy know each other?"

Lawrence smiles. "Got a nephew—Kyle. Shit for brains. High school dropout. A rap sheet longer than your leg before he was sixteen. A mouth that got him into trouble every time he opened it. At nineteen, the fool got sent up for hard time for aggravated assault and robbery. One day in the big house, he says the wrong thing to the wrong guys. Next thing you know, everyone's playing kickball, and Kyle's the ball. In the middle of the game, a white guy walks by. Big guy. Thick as a redwood tree. Doesn't like the whole five-on-one thing and decides to break it up. Few minutes later, lots of guys lying on the floor, broken noses, cracked ribs, busted jaws. Redwood's caused some damage. But he's on the floor, too. There were five of them, after all."

Lawrence takes a long draw on his beer, then continues. "Fast-forward about three years. Shit-for-brains Kyle's on the street, one of his many short vacations from the state correctional system. My sister Catherine has prevailed upon me to take the boy under my wing, spend some time with him. So one night, I take my nephew to McCraven's in North Philly. Cop bar, you know the place."

I nod, thinking of the late Stanley Lipinski dying outside the same tavern's front door.

"We're there for a while when Kyle gets all excited, says, 'That's him!' It was the guy who saved his ass inside."

"Tommy." I recall the one time I visited my brother in the prison infirmary. Now I know what put him there.

Lawrence nods. "So Kyle and I go over to your brother. I thank him. Buy him a beer, and we get to talking. One thing leads to another, and before you know it, we're friends."

Lawrence and I sit in silence, until he says, "I owed him."

"Meaning what? You brought Tommy in on it? On the drug thing? You owed him so you thought you'd help him make some easy cash?"

"It's more complicated than that." Lawrence throws me a sharp look, stares until I look away. "You've heard of Jimmy Nutso."

It's a statement, not a question. James "Nutso" Nunzio is a powerful underboss in the Delaguardia crime family, whose turf includes all of South Jersey and Philadelphia. Every defense attorney in town—and every Philly resident who can read a newspaper—knows about Jimmy Nutso.

I nod.

"One of Jimmy's guys who makes book is a gentleman by the name of Tony Oliviella, who works out of a storefront right over on . . . well, let's just say he's not too far away from the Melrose Diner. Now Tony's own menu features the regular fare: ponies, boxing, college football, all the pro sports."

I can see where this is going. Tommy gambled more than he should have, got himself in deep hock to the mob. He needed cash to pay his tab. I say as much to Lawrence, who confirms it.

"So one day, Jimmy Nutso himself placed a call to Tommy. No threats, of course—you never know when a line is being tapped. He just said, 'Hi, Tommy. How you doin'? Maybe we can meet sometime. Or maybe there's no need for that. It's up to you.' The message was loud and clear."

"Jesus," I exhale.

"Now, Tommy always has his ear to the ground. He hears things he probably shouldn't. One of the things your brother found out about was our little escapade out of the Thirteenth. Tommy came to me one day and asked to be let in. I said no. He said I owed him, and I said I know I do, and that's why I'm not letting you anywhere near this. Then he explained why he needed the money. I cursed him up and down, just like my shit-for-brains nephew. But, of course, I knew then that I had no choice but to bring him on board, because he'd be doing the Schuylkill River face-float otherwise."

I think for a minute. "Has Tommy been inculpated, before the grand jury?"

"No, sir. And there's no way he can be. I was Tommy's only contact. My people knew I'd brought someone in to help transport the goods, but they didn't know who it was."

I lean back, exhale a breath I didn't realize I'd been holding. At the same time, I hear tires crunching over gravel behind me. I turn and see headlights approaching us from a little way down the road.

Lawrence stands. "I'll let you two alone so Tommy can finish the story himself."

"There's more?"

Lawrence smiles. Sadly, it seems to me. "There's always more."

With that he takes his paper plate and paper towels, empties and deposits them into a big plastic trash can near the end of the trailer. Then he walks up the two wooden steps leading to the door of the trailer and disappears inside.

Tommy stops his pickup behind my car, gets out, and walks up the gravel driveway. He walks past me without saying anything and goes into the trailer. He's inside with Lawrence for a good ten minutes. Then Tommy comes back outside, walks to the cooler. He pulls out two Miller Genuine Drafts and hands one to me.

"So," Tommy says.

"So." I look across the table at him. I'm feeling hurt and angry. He'd gotten himself into trouble. Again. I understand that. I can see how that would happen with Tommy. I don't like it, but I get it. But instead of turning to me to help bail him out, my brother sought out Lawrence, a dirty cop he met one night in a bar. As I mull this over, Lawrence's words come back to me: *Don't judge him.* Tommy pulls an opened pack of cigarettes from the pocket of his dark-blue T-shirt. He taps one out, puts it to his lips, and lights it with a Zippo. He inhales deeply and coughs. We look hard at each other.

"So," I repeat.

"Jennifer Yamura," Tommy says.

Here comes the rest of the story.

"You were fucking her."

"For a while, sometime back. Met her at O'Dwyer's," he says. Another cop bar. "Girl was a hard drinker. Whiskey, straight up. We had some laughs. She invited me back to her place."

"To the house on Addison Street." Now I know why Tommy suggested we get in for a scene inspection before the forensic guys came back. Somewhere in the house, there would be evidence of Tommy's presence. Hair, prints, something. Now I also understand why Tommy showed such animus toward David.

Tommy smiles. "She showed me her kimonos."

"And a whole lot more."

Tommy smiles again. At least his mouth is smiling. His eyes look tired and beaten down. I can see that he isn't getting a lot of sleep. "It's all my fault," he says. "The whole mess."

I ask him what he's talking about.

Tommy sighs. "That girl could screw," he says. "But it was more than that. I thought so anyway. We talked. About everything. Her rich brother. Her parents. The shitheads she worked with. My fucked-up life. Her wacky relationship with your friend David, that piece of shit." Tommy pauses, lights another cigarette, takes a couple of deep drags. "She had a way of pulling you in, making you feel like she was really into you. Like you could trust her. So I did. Bad move. Bad fucking move. I told her about my troubles with the mob. And how I was working to get free of them."

"You told her about the drug ring."

Tommy closes his eyes and nods. "And the grand jury. Devlin had a full head of steam by then. Lawrence had already testified."

"*You're* the source that Devlin Walker's been after. The source of Jennifer's story."

"Yes. And no. I didn't know a lot of what she wrote about in her story. Like who else besides Lawrence had testified before the grand jury."

I think about what Tommy has just told me. "So you were the springboard. Once Jennifer knew from you that there *was* a story, she went out and got her hands on someone else. Someone who knew a lot more than you did about the details of the investigation."

"Way I figure it."

"Still, if Walker finds out about you, he'll crucify you."

Tommy's eyes flatten. "He wouldn't be the only one."

"The bad guys," I say, thinking of Lipinski being disemboweled by gunfire.

"The bad guys," Tommy repeats.

Tommy and I sit at the table for a long time, neither of us saying anything. Until Tommy looks at me and asks, "So, Mick, what's your take on all of this? How does it all fit together?"

I spread my hands. "I don't know yet," I say. "There's still so much we don't know. Like who the second source was. Who mowed down Lipinski? Why did Devlin Walker act so fast to nail David for murder one? Why's Devlin so hot to get David to plead?"

"And, of course," says Tommy, "who pushed Jennifer Yamura down the stairs."

"Of course," I say as something—I'm not sure what—flashes across Tommy's eyes.

We sit there, looking at each other in silence. Then, abruptly, Tommy stands and walks into the trailer.

10

Saturday, August 11

I bolt upright in bed. My chest is pounding. I'm hyperventilating. Piper sits up next to me, grabs hold of my arm.

"Mick. Mick. Are you all right?"

I take a couple of deep breaths, tell Piper I'm okay. "Just a bad dream," I say.

Piper lies back down as I get off the bed, grab my robe. The blue neon numbers read 4:15. It's Saturday morning. I've only been asleep a couple of hours. By the time I got back from Tommy's trailer in Jim Thorpe, it was well after midnight. My head was spinning when I went to bed, and it seemed like I lay there forever before sleep reached up and pulled me down.

Downstairs, in the kitchen, I use our Keurig to make myself a cup of coffee. I take the mug onto the back patio and sit down at the table. My hand shakes as I lift the mug to my lips.

What a mess.

"What a fucking mess." I say it out loud this time. The murder, the crime ring, the grand-jury investigation. Tommy and Jennifer Yamura.

David Hanson. All of them mixed up in it now. And Piper moving away from me, maybe soon lost to me forever.

I have to find a way to make this turn out well for all of us. A lone tear slides down the right side of my face. My mouth starts to quiver. But I stop it. I stop it cold.

"No," I say. "No more."

And deep inside my head, I hear the iron gears turning, tightening the hard-closed doors of my mind's many compartments. I finish my coffee and make my way to the basement, pull some running shorts and a shirt from the dryer.

It's not even 6:30 when I return, but Piper is already up and making breakfast. The table is set for just the two of us, which means Gabby is still in bed. She's set out a large glass of orange juice for each of us. The bacon has already been cooked and is nestled in paper towels to absorb the grease. She's working on the eggs.

"How was your run?" she asks.

"Good. You're up and at 'em this morning."

Piper uses a spatula to scramble the eggs. "How was Tommy?"

I nod my head. "He's fine. They're both fine," I add. That Piper doesn't ask me who I'm talking about tells me that she knows all about Lawrence Washington. A bubble of anger rises inside me, but I push it down.

Piper stares at me for a long minute. "Is Tommy in trouble? Are they going to find out about him? The district attorney? The bad cops?"

"I don't know," I say. "They haven't found out about him so far."

"But they just searched that reporter's house again."

Jesus. She knows not only about Tommy's involvement in the drug ring, but about his affair with Jennifer Yamura as well. The anger rises again, and this time I don't try to stop it. "What the hell, Piper? I'm just finding out all this shit about Tommy, and you've known all along?"

She shrugs, maddeningly calm. "You're not his counselor."

"I'm his brother! And I'm your husband! He should confide in me. And so should you. How can I help if I don't know what's going on?"

Piper laughs. She actually laughs. "How can you *help?*"

Now I'm really stewing. I don't deserve this. But I hold my peace while Piper finishes cooking the eggs and puts them and the bacon onto my plate, lays it on the table without looking at me. Then she turns away and begins eating at the counter.

Still with her back to me, she says, "I got a second estimate on the roof. It's five thousand less than the first one."

The roof? I thought this had been settled. "It could be ten thousand less, but we still can't afford it right now."

Piper whips around. "We can't afford to have our roof blow off, either. The whole house will be destroyed."

"There's nothing wrong with our roof. It's only eight years old."

"The last windstorm tore off half the Shabses' shingles. And their roof was no older than ours."

"The Shabs? Who are they?"

"You don't pay attention to anything. If it weren't for me, you wouldn't know a single one of our neighbors!" With that, she grabs her plate and juice and leaves the kitchen.

As far as I can tell, and I've thought about this a million times, the crack in my marriage first opened five years ago, when I left the DA's office. Piper and I had first met during the infamous neurologist murder case and the flush of victory that came with the conviction. In quick succession, I won guilty verdicts in two other high-profile murder cases and was becoming one of the city's better-known crime fighters. The DA himself invited me to his home in Chestnut Hill for dinner. The mayor requested that I stand next to him on a dais and offer some remarks at a turn-in-your-handguns rally in North Philadelphia.

Those were intoxicating days, for Piper and me both. And for someone else: Piper's father, who was watching my ascent closely. Several times, Thatcher Gray referred to me in company as "our future district attorney." I laughed it off at the time. But it quickly became clear to me that my father-in-law wasn't joking. He fully expected me one day to become Philadelphia's DA. I tried to explain to him that I was one of a hundred, a small cog in a big machine. That there were many fantastic and committed prosecutors in the district attorney's office, and that, in any event, I had no political aspirations and even less political skill. Thatcher downplayed my protests, waving his hand as if shooing away so many pesky flies.

"Don't you worry about political skill," he said. "That's why campaigns hire consultants. And don't worry about the money to pay for them," he added. "I have powerful friends with deep pockets."

My father-in-law's encouragement had the opposite effect on me, cementing a decision I was already leaning toward—hanging up my prosecutor's spurs and going into private practice.

Before I made the leap, though, I tested the waters with Piper. I asked her to sit with me at our kitchen table and ran it by her.

"You mean you want to start representing the *criminals*?" she asked me.

"They're not all criminals," I answered. "Innocent people are charged, too." It was a weak argument, and I knew it. But I let the words hang in the air for a minute, then said, "The money will be a lot better. We could move to a bigger house, on the Main Line, near your parents. Your mother could help you with Gabby," I added. Our daughter was a year old and giving Piper, by then a stay-at-home mom, a real run for her money.

Piper sat for a long minute, staring at the floor. Then she looked up at me and asked, "Is this about Tommy?"

The month before, toward the end of my time off with Piper and the new baby, I had received a call from the prison that Tommy had been beaten up pretty badly. I drove up to the prison in Frackville to see him. Lying in the infirmary, Tommy could barely talk because his jaw was wired. His nose was broken. His left eye was swollen shut. Both of his hands were wrapped in bandages. When he saw me looking at his injured hands, he said between his teeth, "That's from what I did to the other guys."

I returned home shaken, more scared for my brother than I'd ever been.

"That's part of it," I answered. "The other part is . . . well . . ."

"My father. How he's pressuring you about becoming district attorney."

I nodded.

Piper looked past me, out the kitchen windows. Then she put her hand over mine, looked me in the eyes, and said, "You do what you think is right." And she meant it. Of that I'm certain, even looking back on it now. Of course, at that point, neither Piper nor I had been subjected to her father's wrath.

I broke the news to Thatcher that I was leaving the district attorney's office for a private criminal-defense practice just after I gave my notice. The four of us were having dinner one night at the Capital Grille on Broad Street. We were halfway through our first course when I announced my plans.

Thatcher dropped his spoon into his lobster bisque and turned his head toward me so deliberately that it looked like he was moving in slow motion. After a long minute, he looked to Piper and asked through his clenched jaw, "How could you let him do this?"

It was all Piper could do to maintain her composure. She always obeyed her father. I don't think I'd ever seen them exchange a cross word. I could feel her own anger rising inside her. She held her tongue at dinner, but railed to me about her father once we got home. Soon enough, though, she focused her anger on me instead.

I think about all this on Saturday night as I drive Piper and Gabby to the Grays' house for dinner. The trip from Wayne to Villanova takes only about ten minutes, but the tension between Piper and me makes the drive seem interminable.

I turn the car into a wide cobblestone driveway. The precisely manicured lawn spreads out on either side like twin emerald oceans. Annuals are arrayed in perfectly ordered rows, Prussian soldiers on a parade ground. The Grays' house is an imposing stone Normandy with crimson shutters and a dark slate roof. It's positioned squarely in the middle of their two-acre property. It was hard for me to believe that someone as joyful as Piper was when I first met her could have been raised in such a forbidding structure.

Thatcher Gray opens the door. Piper's father is dressed in a long-sleeve white shirt, dark crisply creased slacks, and polished Italian loafers. His gray hair is trimmed close to the sides and top of his narrow head. Piper leans in to kiss her father, her full, red mouth a stark contrast to her father's thin, bloodless lips. Thatcher extends his hand to me coolly.

"Mick," he says, his close-set blue eyes scrutinizing me. We shake perfunctorily before Thatcher bends to pick up Gabby. "And how's the prettiest girl in the world?" he says as he lifts her. Gabby looks back at me and rolls her eyes, clearly thinking, *Not this again.*

The four of us move through the living and dining rooms to the kitchen, where Helen Gray is preparing dinner. Helen, a petite woman wearing a green cocktail dress, turns as we enter, her eyes and mouth smiling widely. She hugs and kisses all three of us, then offers Piper and me some wine.

"From the cellar," Thatcher says about the wine, reminding us about the wine cellar he had built into his basement earlier that summer. Piper told me the construction cost almost $50,000—a steep enough price that Thatcher decided to cancel his and Helen's annual trip to Europe in the fall. According to Piper, her mother was upset by this, but, of course, didn't share that with her husband. Thatcher Gray suffers criticism poorly.

During dinner, Helen asks how soon it'll be that Gabby goes off to first grade.

"It's less than two weeks now," I tell her. "Gabby has been getting more and more excited as we get close to it." Our daughter enjoys learning new things, but what she's really looking forward to is the social component.

"School is imperative, Gabrielle," Thatcher declares, leaning toward Gabby. "You want to have a nice house when you grow up, and nice clothes and nice friends. School is where you learn the things you need to know to get them."

Gabby looks down at her plate and pushes around her vegetables as her grandfather lectures her.

"This trout almondine is superb," I tell Helen. "You've really outdone yourself."

Helen beams, but her smile fades quickly as her husband pipes in.

"I had the best trout almondine for lunch the other week," Thatcher declares. "In the city, at that restaurant on Rittenhouse Square. The one that's fitted out like a French bistro. What's it called? Parc?"

I shoot an annoyed glance at Piper as Helen takes a long draw on her wine. Piper ignores me, asks her father how he's doing.

"I'd be doing better if it weren't for the economy," he answers. "First the Chinese threaten to take down the whole world with their inflated stock market, and now those idiots in England are leaving the EEC, thanks to the millions of low-income voters who have no clue as to how the global markets work."

If the House of Lords were ever to award seats to Americans, Thatcher Gray would be the first man to get one.

"There were plenty of big-money men who voted to leave, too," I say. "They have to take some share of the blame."

Piper's father doesn't miss a beat. "Big-money men like the one you're representing? Phillip Baldwin. That SOB hurt a lot of good people. Including a number of my friends and fellow club members. And you're trying to get him off scot-free."

"Actually, he's going to plead. He's just signed the agreement. He'll probably report to prison sometime next week. It'll be in the papers, I'm sure."

Thatcher chews on this for a moment. "How long will he get?"

"The term is twenty years, though he'll likely be out in ten. A full decade behind bars."

"Ten years! For what he did? That villain should rot until the next ice age."

Helen comes to my defense. "Ten years isn't nothing, Thatcher. I'm sure prison will be pretty awful for him."

Not a man to brook dissent from his own wife, Thatcher shoots Helen a sharp look. Helen picks up her wine and looks away. Piper keeps her own counsel, not wanting to get between her parents. She's made that mistake before.

We sit uncomfortably for a few minutes, then Thatcher takes another tack. Swirling his wine, he looks over at me and says, "Baldwin going to trial would have brought in a lot of money for your firm, I imagine."

I try to feign nonchalance. "The firm's doing well, so the Baldwin thing's not a big deal."

Thatcher glances quickly at Piper. He's won the point, and we both know it. Still, he hasn't cut me deeply enough. He goes for my Achilles' heel.

"How's that brother of yours?"

Piper's father has met Tommy a handful of times. Despite Piper's best efforts to get her father to warm to Tommy, the older man has shown no interest in befriending my brother, or even acknowledging his right to exist. I smile inwardly as I recall Tommy's initial description of Thatcher Gray: "Sir Thatcher, a stick up his own ass."

Before I can answer her father, Piper chimes in. "Tommy's doing very well. He's been a great help to me in my gardens, and he's working hard with Mick on the David Hanson case."

At the mention of David's name, Thatcher winces. Like many of the city's big-firm lawyers, Thatcher isn't sure how to deal with the charges against David. On the one hand, social propriety requires that a certain distance be maintained. On the other, if David manages to escape conviction and reclaim his old job as general counsel of Hanson World Industries, he will once again control the allocation of millions of dollars in legal work.

When dinner is finished, I volunteer to help Helen with the dishes as Piper and her father repair to his study. After we're finished loading the dishwasher, Helen and I join Piper and "Sir Thatcher." When we enter the study, we find the two of them sitting on the tufted leather couch that is positioned in front of Thatcher's antique mahogany desk.

"Good news, honey!" Piper exclaims when she sees me. "Father's going to lend us the money to get the new roof!"

As soon as we've put Gabby to bed and we're in our own bedroom, I start in. "What the hell, Piper? I mean, really. What did you tell him when you were alone? That all that stuff I said about the firm doing well was just a bunch of bullshit?"

"I didn't say any such thing. I just said we needed a new roof, and money was a little tight, that's all."

I want to hit something, I'm so frustrated. "For fuck's sake. We do not need a new roof! The one we have is fine! Why aren't you hearing me?"

"Why aren't you hearing *me*? The roof is not fine. It's flimsy and it puts our house in danger."

I don't even know how to respond to this. It's just nuts. But then again, I know it's not really the roof that's tormenting Piper. My heart is beating a mile a minute as I decide to give Piper a chance to share what's really going on.

"I don't know what's happening with you," I say. "You've been moving away from me for a long time. I can see that. But these past couple months, it's like you're running away. You're always off with one of your girlfriends, in New York, or out for the night, or whatever. And when you are at home, you're either attacking me or not really here."

Piper looks over at me, her eyes incredulous. "*Me* not here? Wow, Mick. Fucking wow."

I turn away and start to leave.

"Yeah, that's it. Walk away, Mick. Go somewhere else."

"Fuck you!" I shout over my shoulder as I stomp down the stairs.

11

Monday, August 20

Finally, some good news. It's just before noon on Monday. I'm sitting in my office, having just hung up the phone with Arthur Hogarth. A-Hog, as he's been nicknamed by the bar, is the managing partner at Hogarth, Blumenthal, and Fishbein, Philly's most successful, headline-grabbing personal-injury firm.

The poorest-kept secret in the legal profession is that the easiest way to make money is to refer personal-injury cases to guys like Arthur Hogarth. Although as the referring lawyer you're still technically part of the client's legal team, the A-Hogs and their lackeys do all the work on the case and, just as important, front all the costs. The end result is that you, as the referring attorney, spend no time on the case, invest no overhead, bear no risk, but reap the rewards when someone like Arthur obtains a settlement or collects on a verdict.

This happened with one of my own clients, Candice Crenshaw, a twenty-two-year-old "performance artist" at Delilah's Den who was arrested for drug possession three years ago. I'd beaten the charges. A year after that, the young stripper was back in my office, opening her shirt to me. Candy's left breast was the most perfectly sculpted breast

I had ever seen. Her right breast was a pancake and had more stitches than a Raggedy Anne doll. As it turned out, the right-side implant had burst during augmentation surgery, bringing on a massive infection that destroyed the mammary.

An hour after Candy appeared in my office, I walked her through the doors of Hogarth, Blumenthal, and Fishbein for a meeting with Arthur. Over the course of the next two years, A-Hog navigated Candy's "broken boob" case through the legal system. He sued everyone even remotely involved in the enhancement surgery: the surgeon, the nurses, the anesthesiologist, two residents observing the surgery as part of their rotation, the hospital, the implant manufacturer. He mowed down scores of people in depositions. He identified dozens of witnesses ready to testify to what an upbeat, happy, well-balanced, good-natured, responsible, wonderful, doting, and saintly friend, daughter, sister, neighbor, convenience-store customer, mass-transit rider, and God-fearing American Candy was before she was turned into a circus freak. And what a hopeless, despairing, distraught, defeated, deflated, destitute, God-fearing American her deformity had caused her to become. Impressively, Arthur's witnesses included Leon Auerback, the big-time Hollywood agent (and, Arthur confided in me, his college roommate), who showed up at his deposition to reveal that just before Candy's surgery, she had been about to sign on for a starring role in an edgy series on HBO.

"The upshot," I tell Susan as she sits in my office, "is that the case has just settled for three and a half million."

Susan lets this sink in for a minute. "So our third of Arthur's third is . . . ?"

"Three hundred and eighty-nine thousand."

At my mention of the amount, Susan exhales. "Breathing room," she says. "Finally."

"Let's take everyone to lunch," I say.

In the wake of the unexpected ending to the Phillip Baldwin case, we'd been putting pressure on Vaughn, and our paralegals, Jill and Andrea, to file as many motions, interview as many witnesses, do as much legal research as possible in our other cases, bill as many hours as they could—to generate cash flow. Everyone is exhausted, and the pressure in the office is palpable. We all need a break.

Half an hour later, the whole firm—Susan, me, Angie, Vaughn, paralegals Andrea and Jill, even nineteen-year-old Katrina, our file clerk—are seated around the table in the center of the main dining room of the Capital Grill. As our waiter brings our appetizers, Angie asks where Tommy is.

"Still out chasing alibi witnesses for Terrell Davis." Terrell Davis's case is another murder scheduled to go to trial the month after David Hanson's—and we still hadn't found the two friends Terrell claimed he was with across town at the time of the drive-by shooting he's accused of taking part in. It's not that our client hasn't done his best to help us. So far, Terrell has given Tommy three pairs of names. But every time Tommy interviews the potential alibis, they fall apart on close questioning. "Terrell's got to find some friends who can memorize a simple story line," Tommy had complained.

I share this with the group, and we all chuckle. Then Vaughn tells a story about a call girl he once represented who went by the name of Wednesday. "So I asked her why not pick some other day of the week, say, Saturday or Monday? She looks at me like I'm dumb as wood. 'Isn't it obvious?' she says. 'Wednesday is hump day.'"

We all burst out laughing. Vaughn's punch line opens a valve, unleashing the pressure that's been building inside of us for the past few months. Susan and I take turns regaling the table with our own tales, and I realize this is what I love about practicing in a firm like ours. It is a truism among lawyers that the practice of law would be great were it not for the clients. And criminal-defense attorneys complain the loudest of all. After all, our clients are not only needy and demanding—they are also, for the most part, criminals. Some are violent criminals, sociopaths, or pathological narcissists.

But these are the worst of the lot, and the fewest. Most of our clients don't find themselves in orange jumpsuits because they harbor a truly malicious nature. They run afoul of the law because their neighborhoods and schools teem with indolence, indifference, and outright criminality. They fail not because they're unable to adapt to society's mores, but because they adapt too well to the rules of poverty and violence that govern the world in which they're raised.

Lawyers like me, firms like mine, do our best to guide these men and women through the intestines of the dragon they woke up inside. If they're lucky, we'll get them out the other end before too much more damage is done. If we're lucky, we'll get paid fairly and enjoy a few laughs along the way—to go with the tears, frustrations, and outright defeats.

Almost as though she's been reading my mind, Susan looks at me and says, "Not like being a DA, is it?"

I smile and shake my head.

"Would you ever go back?" asks Vaughn.

I don't even have to think about it. "No," I answer. Nothing more. Just no.

The waiter delivers our entrées, and the conversation lulls. We order more drinks and desserts as well. By the time we stand to leave, we are stuffed and loopy. The sun makes us squint our eyes as we leave the darkened restaurant and head back to the office for what we all know will be an afternoon of zero productivity.

After wasting an hour at my desk, I'm about ready to pack it in when Vaughn and Susan enter and turn on my TV. Devlin Walker stands behind a walnut podium, solemnly explaining that the investigating grand jury has recommended charges be brought against seventeen members of the Thirteenth and Fifteenth Districts of the Philadelphia Police Department, all of whom, he announces, were arrested at their homes in the early-morning hours. Devlin drones on about no one being above the law. Then he begins to read off the names of the officers arrested.

An hour after the press conference wraps up, Angie buzzes me. "Devlin Walker's on the phone," she says. "Line one."

I lift the headset and punch the button. "McFarland."

"You saw?"

"I saw. And?"

"It's time, Mick. Get Hanson to plead. I'll accept involuntary manslaughter. Heat of passion. But I need the laptop. More names could be on it. More bad cops."

"Hanson doesn't have the laptop. Because he didn't kill Yamura."

"Just remember, the laptop has to be pristine. I don't want a single file touched. Not a single document. You hearing me?"

"You have a nice day," I say.

"Goddamn it, Mick! I'm giving your client an easy way out."

"Easy?" It's my turn to shout. "Plead to a crime he didn't commit? Go to prison? Lose what little is left of his reputation? Produce a computer he doesn't have? Exactly which part of that is the easy part?"

"Just do your job and convey the offer. A few years for manslaughter, or the rest of his life for murder one. And don't forget about the computer. It's the only reason I'm even talking to you."

"We'll see you at trial."

I hang up the phone, lean back in my chair, and close my eyes. Devlin's obsession with Jennifer Yamura's laptop, and his insistence that it be turned over completely untouched, tells me that he knows something about the computer that I don't.

12

Tuesday, September 4

Two weeks after the indictment of the crooked cops and Devlin Walker's call, Vaughn enters my office. "Tommy was right about the robberies," he says. "The police records show that the week Jennifer Yamura was killed, there were three daylight burglaries close to her house. Two of the robberies happened before Jennifer was killed, one after."

"Police catch anyone?"

Vaughn shakes his head.

"I'll tell Tommy to get statements from the property owners. We'll list them as witnesses."

Vaughn smiles. "I'm starting to smell reasonable doubt."

"We've a long way to go."

Vaughn leaves, and I call Tommy and tell him that the cop who tipped him off to the mini crime wave was right. "We have the addresses and owners' information," I say. "I'll e-mail them to you now. Swing by and get their statements."

"Sure," Tommy says. He sounds tired.

I ask how Lawrence Washington is holding up, and tell him I'm concerned about him harboring an AWOL witness wanted by the police. The idea that Devlin Walker will find out that Lawrence has been holed up with Tommy scares the shit out of me. If Walker found out about Tommy's link to Lawrence, he might figure out that Tommy was involved in the drug ring. I like Lawrence, but I don't trust that he would go to jail to keep Tommy out. And I *won't* allow my brother to be taken back to prison.

"You don't have to worry about Lawrence," Tommy answers. "He knows how to keep a secret."

"Sure—just ask his buddies in the drug ring."

Tommy says nothing on the other end, but I can feel the tension.

"Look, if the prosecutors find out Lawrence hid your involvement, his plea deal will be voided, and he'll be staring at a long prison sentence. They'll use that to turn him against you."

"Lawrence owes me, Mick. That's the difference between me and those other cops. And a long prison term isn't in Lawrence's future—no matter what happens."

I don't get the insinuation, and I tell Tommy so.

"Lawrence has liver cancer. It's metastasized to his lungs and his brain. He wants to enjoy his freedom while he still can. I told him he can stay at the trailer as long as he wants. I'll keep going up whenever I'm able. Bring supplies, help him. Keep him company. Until . . ."

"You really want to go through this again?"

"Hey. I'm the rock. The Slab. Remember?" Tommy tries to sound lighthearted, but his voice is tinged with bitterness.

I can't recall exactly when I first became cognizant of my father's coughing. I want to say it was in tenth or eleventh grade. At first, Tommy and I made jokes about the old man's smoking. But as time went on and the hacking worsened, we got more serious with him, pressuring him to quit. He did, finally, when I was a senior in high school and Tommy a sophomore. By then it was too late, though none of us knew it. And it wouldn't have made any difference if our father had quit cigarettes years earlier—or never even started smoking. It wasn't the smokes that killed him but his job at Manheim Newbestos, the asbestos plant where he had worked for twenty years as a machinist.

When I left home after graduation, Dad was coughing as bad as ever, but he was still working and looked healthy enough to wrestle a bear. Throughout my freshman and sophomore years in college, Dad still looked pretty strong, though he often seemed to have a hard time catching his breath. I remember being home during the summer and tossing a football around with Tommy and our father in the field behind our house, and Dad going out for a long pass and then being bent over at the knees, sucking air after he'd caught the ball. Tommy and I exchanged concerned glances, but Dad shrugged it off and told us it was no big deal. When summer was over, I went back to college for my junior year. Whenever I called home, Tommy would tell me Dad seemed to be getting worse, but when I returned for Thanksgiving and Christmas and Easter, he appeared energetic enough and had a positive attitude. I'd asked him more than once when Tommy wasn't around how he was doing, and he said that, apart from the cough and the wheezing, he felt fine.

Still, I wasn't all that surprised when, after my brother graduated from high school, he told me he was putting off enlisting in the military for a while to stay home with the old man.

The summer between my junior and senior years, I stayed on campus because I had a chance to work in a local law office. Before the summer started, though, I did get a chance to go home once. It was then that I began to see a marked change in Dad's appearance. He'd lost weight and his skin didn't look right. I made a point of getting home every other weekend, and it seemed that Dad had plateaued. He didn't look great, but he didn't seem to be getting worse. I remember saying so to Tommy one night late in August after the three of us had gone out for some beers at a bar near our house. Tommy and I were sitting together on the picnic table in our small backyard. It was after midnight, and the sky was brilliant with stars.

Tommy raised his head for a long moment and looked back at me, hard. "But he *is* worse, Mick."

January of my senior year, Tommy called to tell me our father had retired and hired a lawyer. When I asked why, Tommy answered with a single word: "Asbestos." It was only then that I put two and two together and realized that our father wasn't suffering emphysema from smoking. I called one of the lawyers I had worked for in State College that summer, and he told me all about the massive asbestos litigation that had been going on around the country for years. I drove home that night and, after our father had gone to bed, pressured Tommy to tell me how bad he really was.

"Come on, Mick. Open your eyes! Or your ears. He coughs nonstop. He's lost thirty pounds. He's bad. You already know that. Stop bullshitting me—and yourself."

"I'll withdraw from school. Help you take care of him."

Tommy snorted, an angry sound. "You have one more semester. Go back to school. Finish up. Graduate. Then you can help me with Dad."

Tommy and I spoke to our father, who said he agreed with Tommy. "After you graduate, the three of us will take a road trip together," he said. "I always wanted to rent one of those big Winnebagos, go to the Grand Canyon."

So I went back to State College for my last semester. The second week of April, my phone rang at two in the morning. I leaned over in bed and picked up the receiver. The air at the other end of the line was dead for a full five seconds. "Hello? Who's there?" I asked impatiently, my eyes still closed.

"Dad's gone."

I bolted up in bed. *"What happened?"*

But Tommy had already hung up.

The next few weeks were a blur. The long drive home. My father's lifeless body in his bed. The funeral. The wake. The meetings with the lawyers. I floated through it all in zombielike numbness. The only thing I can remember with any clarity is my brother. As distant from the ordeal as I felt, Tommy seemed to me to be wholly present, wholly in control—of himself, our relatives, the attorneys, funeral directors, caterers. Me. I think it was the first time I'd ever seen my little brother as a grown-up, as a man. It startled me. I was twenty-two years old, a senior in college with three years of law school ahead of me. I was a student, and I saw myself that way. Not a child but not fully an adult yet, either. I had the body of a man, the face of a man, but hadn't even begun making my way in the world. My twenty-year-old kid brother, on the other hand, had been working for two years at the local ball-bearing plant. He'd become the caretaker of our ailing father. He paid the bills. Painted and rewired the house. Took our father to his doctor's appointments, nursed and entertained him at home. And when Dad passed, Tommy took control of the situation like an old-time party boss.

But then, a few weeks after I'd graduated and come home for the summer, Tommy fell apart. I turned in early one night. Tommy was sitting on the couch, watching TV with a beer in his hand when I went up to bed. The next morning when I came downstairs, Tommy was still sitting there. The TV was still on. Tommy wasn't holding the beer anymore, though, but an empty fifth of Jack Daniel's. Half a dozen empty beer bottles littered the coffee table. I asked Tommy if he was all right. He ignored me, kept staring at the television. I cleared the coffee table, removed the whiskey bottle from Tommy's hand, and turned off the TV. Tommy closed his eyes but otherwise didn't move a muscle.

Tommy didn't leave the house for three days. He didn't bathe or shave, either. Or change clothes. His eyes grew hollow. Because he wasn't eating, Tommy began to lose weight. His chiseled face grew gaunt, his skin turned sallow. The thing that frightened me most, though, was what I saw in his eyes. Tommy was afraid. More than afraid. And I thought I'd figured out why. After our mother died, Tommy had latched on to our father like a barnacle on a keel. Wherever Dad went, Tommy went. Whatever Dad did, Tommy was there helping him. When Dad worked on the car, Tommy handed him his tools. Tommy accompanied our father to Home Depot and Lowe's, the grocery store, beer distributors—everywhere. And it dawned on me, finally, that Tommy was hanging around our father for protection. Whatever had seized our mother and killed her before our very eyes had left our father standing. As strong as death was, Tommy had believed, our dad was stronger.

Dad's invincibility, I decided, had become a core tenet of young Tommy's belief system. But that a priori principle had just been shattered. Death had come for our father, just as it had hunted down our mother. The only thing Dad's gargantuan strength had bought him was a long, slow demise. Death couldn't knock the old man down with a single blow as it had his wife, so it picked him apart, piece by piece, pound by pound, and ate him alive. Tommy had witnessed it happen, and he was terrified. And there was something more. Tommy had stood shoulder to shoulder with my father through the whole thing, tried to fight off the old man's death himself. But he'd failed. And Tommy's failure to save our father, I decided, filled him with guilt. I could see that, too, in Tommy's eyes. Bottomless guilt.

I congratulated myself for figuring it all out, and I fed Tommy every timeworn bromide I could think of. There was nothing Tommy could have done. It was just Dad's time. Tommy had his whole life ahead of him. Dad was now with Mom, and they both wanted Tommy to be happy.

Tommy sat in perfect stillness while I counseled him. Sometimes he'd just grit his teeth and stare at the wall, the television, some spot on the ceiling. Sometimes he'd close his eyes and shake his head. And sometimes he'd glare at me, every muscle in his granite body tensed up like he was ready to spring, tear me apart. And when he got that way, I became afraid. Tommy was a physical force, like our father had been. God help any man Tommy turned against.

The summer months wore on. I spent my nights tending bar at a local pub owned by a high school classmate. When I came home from work at 2:30 or 3:00 in the morning, Tommy would still be awake. We'd exchange some small talk, then I'd go to bed while Tommy stayed downstairs, pacing the floor, drinking, watching television, occasionally crying. In early August, Tommy went back to work at the ball-bearing plant. He lasted two days before getting into a fight with his foreman and storming out of the building. Tommy told me what had happened when I got home from work, and I blew my top at him. I told him he had to pull himself together. I urged him to go down to the local recruitment office and resume his long-held plan to make it to the Special Forces.

"You're falling apart at the seams," I told him. "You need structure. And with Dad gone, there's no reason to put off your own dreams any longer. Just take the first step. Stop being self-destructive. You're beating yourself up for no reason. There's nothing you could have done."

Tommy, sitting on the couch, his head in his hands, looked up at me with red-rimmed eyes.

"You've always been smart, Mick. Real smart. But you don't know anything."

"What the hell is that supposed to mean?" I was shouting. I couldn't bear to see my brother like this. "What's with all the self-pity? I look at you the past couple months, and I ask myself who is living in my house. I don't know this guy. He looks like my brother, but he sure as hell doesn't act like him. Come on. Clean yourself up. Stand up and move forward. Man up, Tommy. Man the fuck up!"

I stormed up the stairs and slammed shut the door to my bedroom. After a few minutes, full of remorse, I walked back down to apologize to Tommy. But he was gone. The front door was wide open, and our dad's pickup had disappeared from the driveway. Tommy was back on the couch the next night when I came home from work. I tried to apologize, but Tommy brushed me off.

"It's no big deal," he said. "Leave it alone."

The following week, the money came in. By the time my father died, huge funds of money had been set aside by the courts to pay out asbestos claims. Some cases went to trial, but most were settled out of court, according to criteria that had been agreed to by the plaintiffs' attorneys and corporate defense counsel. My father's case was one that settled. A big factor, I learned, was the "dying deposition" he had given a month before he passed. Dad was videotaped lying in his bed, on oxygen, as he was questioned by his own counsel and then by three lawyers representing the asbestos companies. The ordeal went on for almost two hours, during which our dad, with Tommy sitting next to him and holding his hand, talked about his life, his marriage, his sons, and his illness—coughing, hacking, and choking all the while. I had no idea this ever took place until my father's lawyer mentioned it to me when he called to say the case had settled. After the call, I asked Tommy about it.

"It was pathetic," he answered. "Fucking pathetic. I think that was the whole point," he added bitterly. "But I guess it got the job done."

I was stunned by the amount of money the case settled for. Even after the 40 percent siphoned off by the lawyers and with the case expenses and medical liens, Tommy and I each ended up with more than $200,000. Enough to pay for law school for me. Enough, it turned out, to fuel Tommy's sudden flight from whatever demons were tormenting him.

Two weeks after I left for law school, I received a postcard from South Beach. I turned the card over and read Tommy's scribble: "Sun, sand, and blondes. It doesn't get any better." No phone number or address. Six weeks later, just before Thanksgiving, I received another postcard, from Cancún, Mexico. On the back of the card, Tommy had again scratched some vacuous contrivance intended to convince me of what a great time he was having, ending with "Happy Turkey Day, bro." I figured that was Tommy's way of saying we weren't going to get together for the holidays. It was six months before I received the next postcard. This one was from San Francisco, and it featured the zigzagging Lombard Street, billed as the crookedest street in the world. More postcards dribbled in over the next three years, from the redwood parklands in Northern California; the Grand Canyon; ski resorts in Colorado, Montana, and Wyoming; and the beaches of Fort Lauderdale and the Bahamas.

It wasn't until the summer after I'd graduated from law school that I laid eyes again on my brother. I was at our father's house, meeting with the owner of a small cleaning service I was interviewing. The housekeeper who'd kept the place up was moving, and I had to hire a replacement. The phone rang, and it was Tommy on the other end. He was at the Greyhound bus station downtown and asked if I'd pick him up.

Tommy was waiting on the curb when I pulled up, a small knapsack sitting on the pavement beside him. He was sunburned and bloated, carrying a lot of extra weight. His eyes were bloodshot. He had a week's worth of whiskers and unkempt hair. When he climbed into the passenger seat, he grinned broadly and shook my hand.

"So, how was law school?" he blurted, his words carrying a not-so-faint aroma of stale beer.

"Interesting," I replied, trying to hide the coolness I was feeling toward him. "How was . . . the Western hemisphere?"

"Fanfuckintastic."

"I guess so. Sounds like you jet-setted to the four corners."

I wanted to add something sharp about coming home on a *bus*. Tommy's share of the money from the lawsuit was, obviously, gone.

My plan had been to drive back to my apartment in Philly once I'd shored things up with the new house cleaners. With Tommy home, though, I decided to stick around for a few weeks. I lasted three days. Living with Tommy was like sharing a house with a pack of nocturnal rodents. He was up all night and was loud about it. The television and stereo blaring, shouting matches over the phone with some woman he'd left in Albuquerque, New Mexico. And in the morning, bottles and pizza boxes strewn across the coffee table and floor. Socks and sneakers and T-shirts, even his boxers, left on the furniture.

I suppressed my anger, my disgust. Half a dozen times I sat down with Tommy, described the last three years of my life—the rigors of law school, the imperious professors, my initial concerns that I wasn't smart enough for an Ivy League law school, being intimidated by the wealth and worldliness of some of my classmates, my hopes and fears about starting to work in the fall at the district attorney's office. Then I'd pause and wait for Tommy to open up to me. Nothing came out. Unless you counted some sordid story of how he'd nailed two NFL cheerleaders in Dallas. Or how he and his buddy had kicked three other guys' asses outside a bar in Detroit and spent the weekend in the pokey. Tommy shared nothing about what was going on inside him. The only nanosecond of honest emotion he betrayed was in response to my mention of our father, when a dozen dark colors flashed across his eyes.

In the early afternoon of my fourth day with Tommy, I woke him up on the couch and told him I had to get back to Philadelphia. "But you should stay here as long as you want. I'm going to call the lawyers and tell them to draft something up, to transfer my share of the house to you. I want you to own it by yourself. I have a little money left, and I'll make enough at the DA's office to pay my rent." Tommy thanked me and said he was planning to go down to the lumberyard he'd worked at when he was in high school. He said they'd given him a standing offer to come back anytime he wanted. I told him that was a great idea; then I walked out and drove away.

A month later, with the title to our dad's house now exclusively in his name, Tommy hired a real estate agent. He had her price the house for a fast sale. As had happened the year our father died, Tommy was on the road before Thanksgiving. This time, though, the first contact I had from—actually, about—Tommy didn't come in the form of a postcard, but a phone call. Early in February, I received a call at my office from Spencer Watley, a classmate of mine at Penn Law. Like me, Spencer had just begun his career as a prosecutor. Not in Philadelphia, though; he had returned to his home in Pensacola, Florida. Spencer called me to let me know he'd just been assigned a case in which the defendant had badly beaten up another man who, it turned out, was an off-duty police officer. The defendant was Tommy.

"The background check showed he was from Lancaster, Pennsylvania, and you'd talked to me about a brother named Tommy. I thought I'd call and give you a heads-up in case your brother couldn't get through to you."

I exhaled and asked where Tommy was in the process.

"Still in lockup, waiting for his arraignment. I don't think he has a public defender yet."

"What's the charge going to be?"

Spencer paused before answering. "Aggravated battery."

I froze. Aggravated battery is a felony that can carry serious jail time.

"It was a cop, Mick. And your brother beat the hell out of him."

I said nothing.

"Plus, there are all the priors."

"Priors?"

Spencer read through a long list of messes and altercations Tommy had gotten himself into during the previous three years. Most involved fistfights that were pled out on public nuisance and intoxication charges. Tommy had copped to two assault charges, however, and spent several months in jail. His carefree tour of the Americas and Mexico hadn't been so carefree, after all.

"He never told me about any of this," I said, more to myself than to Watley. "Is there anything you can do for him? Reduce the charges to simple battery?"

Spencer paused at the other end of the line. "I'll see what I can do. But even with simple battery . . . with his record, he'll still do close to a year."

I sigh. "A lot better than what he'd face for agg battery. I'll owe you one, Spencer."

"A big one."

It was almost a month before Tommy returned my many calls to his cell phone. By then he'd been out on bail and had rented an apartment in Pensacola until his plea deal was finalized.

"Why did you have to get involved?" he asked, defensive from the outset.

"You're welcome," I snapped back.

"I didn't need your help with this."

"You were facing an aggravated-battery charge."

"I could have gotten them to reduce it."

"You think so? It was a *cop*, Tommy. And the prosecutor told me about your priors. Why didn't you tell me about any of that? And what the hell is going on with you that you're getting into so much trouble?"

"It's not a big deal. A few dustups is all."

By now my head was starting to bake. "This shit isn't a joke, Tommy! You've probably already fucked up your chances of getting into Special Forces. And law enforcement isn't going to touch you now. What happened to all of your plans?"

On the other end of the phone, Tommy laughed bitterly. "My plans are dead. I guess I killed 'em."

And with that, Tommy hung up.

This is why I'm so concerned about Tommy now. As if going through an endless deathwatch with my father didn't scar him badly enough, now he seems to be planning to put himself through it all over again—for Lawrence Washington. I figure Tommy's had his act together for so long that he may not remember his long, hard fall to the bottom. I close my eyes and shake my head.

"Not again," I say quietly.

Please, God, not again.

13

WEDNESDAY, SEPTEMBER 19

It's the middle of September. I enter the firm, wave to Angie. The minute I reach my office, she buzzes to tell me our banker, Sandra Linney, is on the line. When I pick up the phone, Sandra says she's near my building, asks if she can come up and meet with me and Susan. I tell her sure and punch Susan's extension. The line goes directly to Angie.

"Where's Susan?" I ask.

"Not here," Angie answers. "Doctor's appointment."

I walk into our office kitchen, brew myself a cup of coffee on the Keurig. By the time I'm finished, Sandra's at reception and I walk her to my office. She sits across from my desk. She doesn't look happy.

"Let me guess," I say. "I'm dying." Sandra looks puzzled. "That's what your face looks like. Like a doctor about to tell a patient he has a week to live."

Sandra forces a smile. "It's not that bad. But it *is* bad." She takes a deep breath. "The bank's in trouble. We failed a federal stress test, and the government is all over us to clean ourselves up, pull in as much of our unsecured paper as possible."

I know now where this is going, and the bottom falls out of my stomach. The line of credit to our firm is unsecured. It's not backed up by real estate or cash, just my signature and Susan's. "Jesus, Sandra."

"I don't have a choice. My bosses say I have to call in the loan."

"Who can I talk to? Who can I meet with?"

Sandra shakes her head. "No one. The decision's been made. If it makes you any happier, you're not the only one I have to deliver this news to. At least you have some money coming in to cover the loan. You just settled that big case, right? What was it—Crenshaw?"

You bitch—I want to scream it at her. I know exactly why they've chosen to call in the loan now. I believe in being transparent with all the companies that do business with the firm. When I got Arthur Hogarth's call about the Crenshaw case, I e-mailed Sandra about our coming windfall. Now, almost exactly thirty days later—the normal period between a settlement and the plaintiff's receipt of the check—Sandra is in my office with her hand out.

"You've been a good customer, Mick. Moving forward, we can—"

"Moving *forward*?"

She knows we won't be moving forward. That I'll close out our accounts, move the money to another bank.

As soon as she's gone, I pull up QuickBooks on the computer. The $275,000 balance on the line of credit will eat up all but $111,000 of our share of the Crenshaw settlement. About enough to keep the firm breathing for a month. Which would be bad enough if Susan and I hadn't sucked $30,000 out of the firm the day after Hogarth's call. I couldn't wait to get home that day to tell Piper that we wouldn't have to borrow money from her father for the new roof. I took her a check for $15,000, half the cost of the roof, to use as the down payment. My taking the $15,000, of course, meant that Susan had the right to do the same, and she did so to pay for a new living-room suite for her apartment.

I close my door and tell Angie not to let any calls through. Tomorrow, I'll have to tell Vaughn and the others that our windfall is going to blow right past us and that they'll all have to send the billable-hour clock spinning again. More motions. More hours in the office. Anything that lets us withdraw money from the client-retainer accounts.

The phone rings again. I pick up the receiver, ready to ream Angie. But before I can start, she tells me it's Piper. I exhale and say I'll take it. Piper gets right down to business. The roofers are ready to start tomorrow, and they're looking for the second half of their money.

"Before they start?"

"That was for the materials," Piper explains. "The new money is to pay the workers. Is there a problem?"

"I'll bring home a check tonight," I say curtly, then hang up. Things have been especially bad between us since our blowup after we returned home from dinner with her parents. We're civil with each other, but just barely. I'm still angry at Piper's soliciting money from her father for the new roof. I'm annoyed, too, over her stinging remarks about my always leaving. As if my working hard is an excuse for her to play the bitter housewife. And all my ill feelings are just the gloss covering a black ball of rage. It's taking all my strength not to launch the nukes, put everything on the table. But it's too soon.

It's four o'clock and I'm standing at the reception desk, signing a letter for Angie to mail when two men saunter in. "My two best friends," I say. Detectives Tredesco and Cook. "Come to tell me the DA's dropping the charges against David Hanson? You've decided to look for the real killer? Maybe even dig up some actual evidence?"

Tredesco snorts. "There's that famous sense of humor I told you about," he says to his partner. "Nah, Hanson's going down. But you may be right about evidence. How about we have a chat."

I lead the detectives into the conference room. "Okay, John. So what brings you to my little kingdom?"

"It's the incriminating calls," he answers. "The calls your panicked client placed to you after he killed Jennifer Yamura."

My heart skips a beat. Tredesco is walking in the wrong direction, but I know instantly what he's getting at. Still, I play dumb. I look at Cook and say, "Your partner fall off the wagon?"

Tredesco is instantly pissed. "Fuck you, Mick. I'm seven years clean and sober. And don't act like you don't know what I'm talking about. The phone records show two calls from Jennifer Yamura's iPhone to your office. One at 11:45. And one at 12:30. I'm figuring Hanson called you just after he sent the reporter down the stairway to heaven and then a little later, just before he left the house. Or is the phone company wrong?"

Tredesco is wrong about the calls, of course. They were both from Jennifer herself. The first was to set up the appointment to see me. The second was when she moved the appointment up. Something had happened between the calls to upset her, though she didn't tell me over the phone what it was.

I smile smugly at Tredesco. "You're so far off course that part of me wants to keep my mouth shut and watch you flounder. But I'm too soft. So I'm going to help you out here. Both of those calls were placed to me *by* Jennifer Yamura. She wanted to hire me to represent her in connection with the grand-jury mess. She called once to set a time to come in, then a second time because she decided she needed to get together sooner."

Tredesco's eyes flash fury. He'd shown up thinking he was going to catch me off balance. He probably figured that, as David's attorney, I would reflexively hide behind attorney-client privilege, which would have only confirmed what he suspected—that the calls on Jennifer's cell phone had indeed come from David.

"Horseshit. All that story tells me is that you and Hanson worked out a cover for the calls. You're smart; I'll give you that. So's your client. But both of you together aren't going to think your way out of this mess." Tredesco shoots out of his seat, turns, and leaves.

Ed Cook sits for a moment, staring at me blankly, a deer in the headlights. Then he, too, stands and leaves. This time he doesn't shake my hand.

He's learning.

14

Tuesday, September 25

It's Tuesday morning, the week after the bank's decision to call in our line of credit. I've told Susan, and she's as stressed as I am about our money.

My phone buzzes. It's Angie. "It's Patti Cassidy," she sighs. "She says it's important."

I sigh back. "With Patti, it's always important," I say. "All right, I'll take it." I try never to miss a chance to talk to the press about a case, spin the story in some way favorable to my client. "Hi, Patti," I say, my voice as sunny as I can make it. Not an easy task. "How are things with you these days? I hear you're up for some journalism award."

Patti skips the pleasantries, gets right to it. "I'm calling to see if you want to comment on the second geisha house."

Silence hangs between us as I try to figure out what she's talking about.

"The brownstone, in New York?"

"I honestly don't know what you mean."

"Your client, David Hanson," she says. "Turns out the house on Addison Street isn't his only love nest. He has another one, in Manhattan. And there are, like, three Chinese girls living there."

"Jesus Christ." I say it before I can stop myself. "No! Wait."

Patti laughs. "I'd rather just quote your expletive."

I take a deep breath, try to lower my blood pressure. "Look, I'm sorry. Can you just give me a little more background?"

"Sure. About two weeks ago, we get an anonymous tip that your client's Philadelphia pied-à-terre is one of a pair. That he has a second house in New York. The caller even gives the address. So we do a little research and find out the house is held in the name of HD Holdings, the first link in a chain of companies ultimately ending with Hanson World Industries. A couple of reporters stake out the building, watch who goes in and out. They see not one but *three* young women living in the house, all young and Asian and quite beautiful. I'm sure they can't wait for their lord and master to show up."

My ears perk up. "So he hasn't been seen there? At the house?"

"Come on, Mick. A house full of Asian girls? Owned by the same corporate fronts your client used to buy the place in Philly?"

My head is bent low. My eyes closed. I'm rubbing my forehead with my left hand as I hold the receiver with my right. I'm irked at the delight Patti is obviously taking in telling me this. But my ire at the reporter is nothing compared to the rage building inside me at David Hanson. Still, I remind myself I am a professional, with a job to do. And part of that job is damage control. So I give Patti my statement: "Here it is, Patti. This latest story, undoubtedly leaked to the press by the DA's office, serves only to betray the prosecutor's mission to sidetrack the public and poison potential jurors with gossip and innuendo in the hopes of distracting everyone from the only real issue in this case: my client's actual guilt or innocence. It seems that a few sorry members of law enforcement, and the press as well, have forgotten that every citizen is innocent until proven guilty, and that an accused citizen's right to freedom from wrongful imprisonment isn't to be stolen from him for the sake of selling a few newspapers."

"Ouch. Sounds like we hit a nerve."

"More than one."

I hang up, then dial David's cell number. I leave a message, tell him to call as soon as possible. Then I dial his home number. Marcie answers on the second ring. After an awkward pause, I tell her it's me and ask for David. Marcie informs me he's not home but should be soon. "I'm going to drive out there," I say. "Something happened. Is about to happen. There's going to be another story, about David. I need to talk to him before it comes out. I should talk to you, too."

Marcie asks me to tell her over the phone. I say I'd rather not. I ask if I can bring Susan.

"The more the merrier."

I feel awful for Marcie. So much bad has happened in her life in such a short time. The cancer. The radiation and chemo. Then her husband is indicted for murder. Then comes the Philadelphia geisha-house story revealing that David's been cheating on Marcie for who knows how long. And now it's about to get even worse. David isn't just some schmuck who got caught having a fling. He's something else entirely: a man who keeps women for his enjoyment. Asian women. Marcie will want to kill him. Or herself.

I walk into Susan's office, tell her what's happening, and ask her to drive with me to David and Marcie's house. "I'll need you there for moral support when I tell Marcie about the place in New York. I'll also need you there to keep me from strangling David."

I spend the drive to the Hansons' thinking about Marcie. I first met her in the Hamptons, where she and some friends had rented a beach house for the summer. David drove me up, told me he'd found a terrific girl and wanted me to meet her. "She's the only woman I've ever met who's as competitive as I am," David confided. She was also, it turned out, striking. Tall with long, toned legs, thick raven hair, emerald-green eyes, high cheekbones, and flawless olive skin.

When they were married a couple of years later, I was a groomsman. For several years afterward, David and Marcie and Piper and I often got together for dinner. We even once spent a week vacationing on Martha's Vineyard. But over time we drifted apart, pulled away from one another by our very different social circles.

The last time I saw Marcie was a few months before David's arrest, when Piper and I had dinner with Piper's parents at the country club. We crossed paths in the lobby. Marcie was different from the tanned and smiling athlete I first met in the Hamptons. She was pale. Her once-fit limbs were bone thin. Her ample chest was gone. She had opted against reconstructive surgery after her mastectomy, and her blouse hung limply. She didn't smile once. I saw in her eyes a look that took me a while to decipher. It wasn't just pain, though that was certainly present. Rather, Marcie's eyes broadcast confusion. As though—I decided—she simply could not understand how this could have happened to her, how her body, once a powerhouse of vitality and strength, could betray her, could decide to eat itself alive.

I drive past the large stone columns framing the entrance to a quarter-mile-long cobblestone driveway leading to the front of the Hanson family compound, Blackthorn. The main house is a three-story Victorian Gothic monstrosity constructed of large, coarse limestone with two turrets framing the center entrance and reaching fifteen feet above the roofline, and squatter turrets on each of the building's four corners. Built in 1915, the house in many ways typifies the notion of luxury held by many turn-of-the-century, self-made American millionaires like Linwood Hanson.

"This place makes me feel cold just looking at it," Susan says as we walk toward the entrance.

Marcie opens the door before we knock. She doesn't look anything like the sickly, haunted creature I'd last seen. Her face is pink, her skin supple. Her eyes are bright and alert. And though I try to avoid looking directly at it, her bosom is large. She must have had the reconstructive surgery, after all.

Marcie sees me scrutinizing her and says, "I'm not quite the six-million-dollar woman, but I do feel that I've been rebuilt from the ground up."

Once we're inside, I lean in and kiss her cheek. Susan says something about how lovely the house is.

"All the warmth of a prison," Marcie answers, "which it is, literally, in a way." I already know the history but listen as Marcie explains to Susan. "David's great-grandfather bought most of the stone for the exterior from a company that had been storing it since the 1860s. The stone had been harvested from a demolished Civil War–era prison in upstate New York. Linwood Hanson thought it was charming that his house was built from prison block."

Marcie leads us to a drawing room, and we sit on facing couches. Susan and I look around as Marcie pours us coffee from an ornate silver service. The room is cavernous. The ceiling is twenty feet above the floor. Two gigantic candelabras sit on either end of a white-marble fireplace big enough to garage a Mini Cooper. The walls are fitted out in polished, dark woods. Crimson-hued Orientals overlay the parquet flooring. Susan comments again on how lovely everything is.

Marcie ignores her. "So, Mick. What is it you need to tell us?"

I exchange glances with Susan, bite my lower lip, and inhale. "There's a story that's going to come out," I start. "Not a good one. I wanted to give David a heads-up, and you."

"More women?" Marcie asks matter-of-factly.

"Uh . . ."

"It's all right. David and I have had some long talks since this all started. Some very long talks. I know what's out there. I think I do anyway."

"Okay," I say. "There's a townhouse in Manhattan . . ." I proceed to tell Marcie about the call from Patti Cassidy.

When I'm finished, Marcie smiles. "The brownstone on the Upper East Side," she says. "A *lovely* place," she adds, glancing at Susan. "And the three young girls. Yes, I've met them, and I can tell you that they're all very, very sweet."

Susan and I look at each other. We both exhale.

"So it's not some Asian love nest?" Susan says.

Marcie smiles. "Certainly not. Not now."

"Not *now*?"

"Not since David and I have begun talking. Before then, of course, it had been just that—a place where David stored his strumpets until he wanted to play with them. But the women who are there now are anything but playthings. Each is a gifted musician, here on scholarship at a top music school."

"How . . . ?"

"It was easy. David simply told the girls who had been living there to leave, and he paid them a good deal of money to do so. Then, with the help of some prominent men in Japan and the People's Republic of China, we moved in three other girls. College girls. Who, coincidentally, look almost identical to the girls who had been living there before. And although the house was bought by Hanson World Industries, the paperwork will show that it has been leased, for more than three years, to the People's Republic of China for use as a home for visiting students."

"The paperwork?" I ask.

"Backdated, naturally. Edwin will be furious when David produces the lease."

Now I'm completely lost. China? Japan? Edwin? I spread my arms. "I'm afraid all of this is going way over my head."

Marcie smiles, takes a sip of coffee, puts down her cup, and says, "Let me show you." She leads us to a door at the end of a long hallway.

She puts her thumb on a square metallic box hanging on the wall. The door unlocks and swings opens automatically. Marcie leads us into a space utterly different from the rest of the house. "David's study," she says. Though not as large as the sitting room we have just come from, the space is substantial, maybe twenty-by-twenty-five feet. Behind David's desk, the far wall is all floor-to-ceiling windows that showcase the view beyond of a lush, well-ordered garden full of flowering plants that features a pond and a wooden footbridge. "It's a Japanese garden," Marcie says, following my gaze. "David has become a student of ikebana, the art of Japanese flower arranging."

"Looks like your husband has fallen in love with all things Japanese," Susan says, looking around the room. "That sword, for example."

"It's a *katana*, a samurai sword. From the thirteenth century and signed by Masamune—Japan's greatest swordsmith. David refuses to say how he came to possess it, but I suspect a major bribe was involved."

I move closer to the glass display case. Beneath the sword is an ornamental sheath. The sheath sits on twin metal holders. The sword, however, does not appear to be mounted on anything; it just hangs in the air. I feel Marcie behind me, watching me study it. "Amazing, isn't it?" she says. "There's some kind of electromagnetic field inside the box that keeps the sword in midair like that. The display cost a quarter of a million dollars to set up."

"Yet all I'd have to do is get a bat and smash the glass, and the sword is mine."

Marcie laughs. "You'd never get out of this room. Any damage to that case causes the study door to lock automatically." She follows my eyes to the windows. "That glass is several inches thick."

Susan and I exchange glances. I wonder if she's thinking what I am. All this planning to protect a sword, but the guy's fool enough to get caught with his pants down? Stupid enough to try to clean up a murder scene?

"This is interesting," Susan says, looking at a painted kimono hanging inside another glass case mounted on a wall.

"It's an art form called *tsujigahana*. It's from the Edo period, late 1800s."

The sword and kimono are hardly the only things Asian in David's office. On the third wall hang three striking silk scrolls, each encased in glass. They depict peonies, chrysanthemums, and roses, with dark-blue butterflies hovering over rich pink petals and dark leaves. Marcie tells us they were done in the mid-1700s by Ito Jakuchu. Like the samurai sword, Marcie says, they are priceless.

The furniture also is distinctively elegant—and familiar. "Nakashima?" I ask. George Nakashima was a Japanese American woodworker and architect who became one of America's premier twentieth-century furniture makers. His original work is extravagantly expensive, when someone is willing to part with it at all.

"Nakashima," Marcie affirms. "David's father was a personal friend, and David and Edwin both visited him many times in New Hope, where he had his shop. I sometimes think that David's love affair with the Asian culture began with Nakashima's art. Which brings us, in a roundabout way, to why I decided to share this with you."

Marcie leads Susan and me back to the drawing room, and we all sit. Marcie pours more coffee, and then she resumes.

"It was never David's idea to go into law. He wanted from the outset to run Hanson World Industries. David's father, however, left that mantle to Edwin. Still, David went to work for the company right out of law school, as you know. And he's worked hard ever since to break into the operations side. For a long time, he was just beating his head against the wall. Then, about six years ago, things changed. By then David had immersed himself in the cultures of Japan and China. He was making monthly, sometimes weekly, trips to both countries, using his connections to arrange private tours of the countries' museums and archaeological sites, and to stay in the private homes of some of the most powerful men in both nations. David knew that, sooner or later, HWI would have to break in to Asia in a big way—not just to build manufacturing plants like Apple, but to open the Chinese market to HWI's products.

"It looked likely that HWI would begin selling some of its personal-care products in China, but Edwin, always a bull in a china shop, pardon the pun, offended the Chinese. So as much as he hated doing it, he had to ask David to smooth things over. David flew to China and used the networks he'd already built there to keep the deal alive. Pretty soon, the company was selling a whole range of products in China."

"Because of David, basically?"

Marcie nods. "Recently, HWI was on the verge of cementing a joint venture with powerful companies from both China and Japan. It was an unprecedented arrangement for everyone concerned, especially HWI. And David built it all on his relationships in the countries." She pauses.

"Edwin?"

Marcie nods again. "Was furious. Not just because David was the company's rising star, but because David was leveraging his Asian influence to pressure Edwin for an executive position on the operations side of the business. Worse yet, David had HWI's Japanese and Chinese partners pressuring Edwin as well. Edwin finally, grudgingly, agreed, and David was about to be named President of HWI-Asia, making him second-in-command in the company to Edwin, and Edwin's heir apparent."

Marcie takes a sip of her coffee.

"And then . . ." Her eyes darken. She puts down her cup and saucer. "And then Jennifer Yamura. David is disgraced and forced to resign as chief legal counsel at HWI. His hopes to take a seat in the company's operational pantheon are dashed. And Edwin's as happy as a pig in shit."

Susan leans forward. "Because?"

"Because Edwin and David hate each other."

I'm nodding. "It must have galled Edwin to no end to have the Japanese and Chinese business partners breathing down his neck about David."

"So," says Susan, "it's possible that Edwin leaked the story about the house in New York."

Marcie purses her lips. "I wouldn't put it past him."

I consider everything Marcie has told us. "How solid is the paper trail backing the fake lease?"

"Solid. And David's Chinese backers agreed up front to give affidavits, if necessary. Same with the girls, of course."

I smile. I'm going to make Patti Cassidy sweat for this one. I'll bring Devlin Walker into it, too.

Abruptly, Marcie stands, making clear that our business is concluded. I infer from this that David won't be coming home anytime soon, contrary to what she told me over the phone. She escorts us to the front door and opens it. Susan thanks Marcie for meeting with us, and I do, too. Then in the doorway, a thought strikes me. I turn back to face Marcie.

"Did Edwin know about the house on Addison Street before David's arrest?"

"David told me he didn't. But Edwin is enormously clever, and he micromanages the company, keeps his hands on everything, his nose in everything. So who can say?" Marcie waits a few seconds. Then she looks me in the eyes and says, "David is *not* going to be convicted."

I hesitate. "Well, of course I'll do everything in my power to—"

"You're not hearing me. David is not going to be convicted. Period. And you'll do whatever it takes to make sure of it. *Whatever* it takes. Do you understand me?"

I hold Marcie's stare, then nod slightly and turn away. I catch up to Susan at the car. We pull out of the driveway and head back into the city. As we cruise down the Schuylkill, Susan turns to me. "What the hell was all that?"

I exhale. "That was a wife doing her best to defend her husband."

After a while, Susan says, "Did you notice that she didn't ask the question?"

I don't have to ask which question Susan's is referring to. She means *the* question. Whether David is guilty. Whether he killed Jennifer Yamura.

"She didn't ask," Susan says, "because David's told her everything. Marcie knows he's guilty. And she doesn't care."

"Maybe . . . and maybe she does care, or did in the beginning, but now things are working out. Between them, I mean. To hear Marcie describe things, it almost sounds like the murder charges have brought them closer together."

"Murder as the foundation of a happy marriage . . . ," Susan intones. "I wonder what Dr. Phil would say about that."

"Not murder. Forgiveness."

Or, given that Marcie ordered me to do whatever it will take to get David off the hook, maybe something else. Like two serpents seeing each other for the first time and liking that they are of the same sort.

I wonder what would have happened with my marriage if I had been arrested instead of David. Would Piper have circled the wagons with me to fight off the attack, as Marcie seems to be doing with David? Or would she have led the lynch mob herself?

15

THURSDAY, SEPTEMBER 27

David and I sit side by side at the defense table. I look to my left, where Devlin Walker huddles with a junior ADA. They are reading the brief that we just handed them. Behind us, a crowd fills the courtroom. Vaughn has alerted the press that something big is about to happen, and the piranhas are present en masse. Among them is Patti Cassidy, whom I have subpoenaed, and who casts me an angry look. In the seats just behind David and me are Marcie Hanson and, to her left, three young Asian women. To Marcie's right is a stern-looking Chinese gentleman in his fifties, a member of the diplomatic staff of the Chinese consulate. Marcie marched her entourage into the courtroom so they could take their seats fifteen minutes ago, then promptly presented me with a cheat sheet that set forth her witnesses' names and the lies to which they're prepared to testify.

The first thing I did when I got back to the office after visiting Marcie Hanson was to tell Vaughn to call the clerk's office and request an emergency hearing. We received a call back in two hours informing us that William Henry had been assigned to the case.

Before he was elevated to the bench, William Henry served two decades in the public defender's office. He is a believer that a criminal defendant's right to a fair trial is the keystone of liberty. Judge Henry does not abide prosecutorial hijinks in any form. In his view, any effort by the government to distract attention from its high burden, or to give itself a leg up, is intolerable. His Honor, no doubt, takes an especially dim view of pretrial leaks by the district attorney.

I look back at the prosecution table and find Devlin Walker glaring at me, seething. He gets it now. I'm going to blame the DA's office for leaking the story about the second geisha house in New York to Patti Cassidy. What Devlin doesn't know yet is that the courtroom is filled with witnesses prepared to testify that the story was complete nonsense, a fact that will make Judge Henry doubly angry. Devlin slowly shakes his head no, silently telling me not to do this.

Don't you dare. Or I'll make you pay.

The door to the robing room opens. In a whoosh, Judge Henry is on the bench. His face is red, his lips pursed. He looks around the courtroom, takes everyone in. His gaze hangs for a long minute on Patti Cassidy, then he turns to Devlin Walker. The normal procedure would be for the judge to ask me to state my position first, then give the prosecutor his turn to reply. But Judge Henry skips right to the fun part. "Well?" he says to Devlin. Just one word.

Devlin is taken aback, but only for a moment. He leans forward, raises my brief above his head, and declares, "Rubbish." Then he sits.

But Bill Henry will not be assuaged. "Not so fast, Mr. Walker. What do you mean, rubbish? Are you telling me your office did *not* leak this story to the press to poison the potential jury pool? Are you telling me someone else leaked it? Who would do that, Mr. Walker? Who besides the prosecution has anything to gain by this type of leak?"

Before Devlin has a chance to answer, I leap to my feet. "Your Honor, the leak is only half the story. The other half is whether there's any truth to it. Present in this courtroom are the three young women whose reputations have been smeared by the story in the *Inquirer*. Also here, and prepared to testify, is Mr. Hsan Chan, who will, if he takes the stand, tell the court that he is a member of the Chinese Consulate General's office in New York, that he knows the three young women, that they are in this country on student visas, that all three are studying music at a prestigious school in New York City, and that they are able to do so thanks to a grant from Hanson World Industries. A grant arranged through a program designed by *Mrs.* Hanson, who is also in the courtroom and ready to testify. One more thing that all these young women will attest to is that they've never even met David Hanson, let alone engaged with him in any sort of a sordid relationship.

"Which reminds me . . ." I withdraw a civil complaint from my brief case and walk it to Patti Cassidy. "Mr. Hanson and each of the three young women are suing the *Inquirer*, and Ms. Cassidy personally, for defamation." Patti gasps as I hand her the complaint. The spectators, most of whom are Patti's fellow newsmen, fall quiet as a crypt, undoubtedly thinking, *There but for the grace of God go I.*

Now it's Devlin's turn to leap to his feet. "My office had no involvement in this!"

His outburst triggers loud murmuring throughout the courtroom; Judge Henry slams his gavel to reestablish order. He closes his eyes, rests the head of the gavel against his temple, pauses to gather himself, make sure he gets this right. Opening his eyes, the judge says matter-of-factly, "There will be no witness testimony. There is no need. I'm going to grant the defendant's request for a gag order. Neither side, from this point on, is to say or leak anything publicly about this case. And it works both ways. If something detrimental to the defense finds its way into the wind, I'll know it came from the prosecution. If something detrimental to the prosecution gets out, I'll know it came from the defense. In either case, one of you will find yourself in contempt of court. Am I understood?"

I nod and say, "Thank you, Your Honor." Devlin's nod is almost imperceptible. He thanks no one.

And the hearing is over.

I leave the courtroom to find Marcie Hanson holding her own mini press conference in the hallway. Marcie chastises the *Inquirer* for unjustly crucifying her husband by twisting a wonderful program designed to help young musicians into a "sordid and, quite frankly, racist" attack that blemished not only her husband's reputation but that of three utterly innocent young women. "I'm looking forward to the newspaper's quick and unqualified apology for this travesty," she continues. Marcie also has some choice words for the "coward" who tipped off Patti Cassidy to the New York house. "You're curled up in your hole, safe in the cloak of anonymity. You may think that what you did was clever, but all you accomplished—all that you *almost* accomplished—was to further the efforts of those who want to deny my husband his right to the fair trial at which he can clear his name. He *will* rebuild the life that has been so unjustly shattered by the false charges brought against him by the DA's office."

I smile and shake my head. One broadcast-worthy sound bite after another. All delivered with flawless grammar and the indignant tone of a woman defending the man she believes in. I am, at this point, quite frankly awed by how well—and how quickly—Marcie and David pulled this all together.

"Not bad, eh?" It's David, now standing beside me. "It's certainly taken the wind out of Patti Cassidy's sails," he adds, nodding toward the stricken reporter standing at the back of the pack, the blood drained from her face and lips.

I take David's arm and guide him down the hall a bit, away from the crowd.

"When we were out at your house yesterday, Marcie let Susan in on the enmity between you and Edwin. Susan asked if Edwin might even have been the person who tipped off Patti Cassidy, and Marcie said she wouldn't put it past him."

David looks away, watches Marcie address the reporters for a moment, then returns his gaze to me.

"Edwin." He spits out his half brother's name. "He couldn't have found out about the brownstone any more than he could have discovered the house on Addison Street, which is a whole lot closer."

I take a minute, let David's words sink in. My eyes widen. "Edwin didn't leak the New York house to the *Inquirer*. *You* did. You and Marcie. The two of you orchestrated this whole thing. To poison the well, set up Devlin, make it look to the potential jury pool like Walker's not playing by the rules, like he's out to get you any way he can, whether you did something wrong or not."

David smiles. "Most of the credit belongs to Marcie. She's quite the strategist, it turns out."

"Jesus, David. Don't you realize if the reporters dig deep enough, they'll eventually find something that leads them to the truth? If it comes out that the brownstone was originally a fuck pad after all, and that your three musicians are merely part of a massive cover-up, you might as well go ahead and stick the needle in your own arm."

David's no longer smiling. "That's why it's important to get that apology from the *Inquirer* and close out the defamation suit as soon as possible. Once the threat of a lawsuit is removed, the paper will lose its will to dig up new information to defend itself."

"You've thought this all out, have you?"

"Figuring out how to extricate myself from this clusterfuck is pretty much *all* I think about."

David and I face off for a long moment, before I say, "No more tricks. Not without running it by me first."

Fury flashes across David's eyes. But he quells it quickly and blesses me with a broad smile. Then he crosses his heart, winks, and walks away.

An hour later, I'm back in the office. It's just after noon, and the details of the hearing are all over the midday news shows. The TV reporters, happy to feast on their own, cap their recounts with the fact that I have brought a civil defamation suit against the *Inquirer* and reporter Patti Cassidy, who is shown fast-walking away from the Criminal Justice Center after the hearing.

"Now she knows how it feels," Vaughn says as we watch the story on the big flat screen in my office. "Where's Susan?"

Angie and I share a glance. "Lunch."

When I originally told Susan about the plan to bring in the phony witnesses, she fought me on the petition. After I decided to move ahead with it anyway, she refused to accompany me to the hearing. When I told her afterward that Marcie and David had leaked the story themselves, she blew up.

"This isn't ethical! You're helping David and Marcie perpetrate a fraud on the public. Worse yet, you personally misled the court."

"I didn't say anything that was untrue," I argued. "I simply filed a petition stating that a story averse to my client's right to a fair trial had been leaked and asked for a gag order. I made no representations myself."

Before she left my office, Susan stopped and told me, "For some reason, you've decided to let David and Marcie lead you down the primrose path. You can do whatever you want. Just understand, I will not walk that road with you. I'm not going to cochair this case unless you agree to play it straight. I'm not losing my ticket for anyone, let alone David Hanson and that scheming wife of his." Susan pivoted back toward the doorway and saw Angie standing there. "I'm taking an early lunch," she said as she stormed out of the office.

Now, watching the news with Vaughn and Angie, my discomfort over Susan's rebuke and my anger at David have dissipated. I am flush with victory and feeling grand.

"How about the three of us go to lunch?" I ask. "Celebrate the win."

Two hours later, Vaughn, Angie, and I return to the office, stuffed from our meals and lightheaded from our drinks. I putter around my office, open my snail mail, respond to congratulatory e-mails from some fellow defense attorneys who happened to catch the midday news.

It's just before five, and I'm about to log off my computer when Angie walks in and hands me a padded envelope.

"I forgot to give you this," she says. "Katrina gave it to me when we came back from lunch. She said an old lady dropped it off, claimed it was personal and confidential, for your eyes only."

"Let me guess," I say. "My son's in jail, and here's the evidence that proves he didn't do it."

"See you tomorrow," Angie says, and walks out.

I hold the envelope in my hand for a minute, wondering whether I should toss it in the trash or go through the pointless step of watching it first. I'm about to leave anyway, so I think, *Why not?* I tear open the envelope. Inside are an envelope and a DVD. I put the DVD into my computer, and a video appears on the screen. I recognize the scene. It's Jennifer Yamura's backyard and the back of her house. There's a date on the video screen: May 31 of this year. The day of Jennifer Yamura's murder.

Oh, Christ.

I quickly stop the video, get up, close the door to my office, then sit back down and restart it. A figure appears on the screen at time stamp 11:50 a.m. A man. He appears in the alley on the left of the screen, from the east. He walks directly to Jennifer Yamura's kitchen door, knocks.

Jennifer appears after a few seconds, opens the door for him. Before the man enters, he looks back, and I see his face.

I am thunderstruck.

By the time the video finishes, I am shaking. It's all I can do to keep from throwing up. I get off my chair, pace the office. This is a disaster. The atomic bomb.

What the fuck am I going to do?

"Think," I tell myself. Then I spy the envelope on my desk and reach for it. There's a piece of paper inside. A single sentence is scrawled:

I will contact you soon.

I realize it instantly: blackmail. That's how this is going to play out. I sit down at my desk and replay the video. I understand now. A lot of things that didn't add up before about Yamura's death now make perfect sense.

I secure the DVD in my office safe. I move to my desk, stand beside it. I lean over, my hand clutching the corner of the desk. I take deep breaths until my heart slows. Then I sit down, pull my wastebasket out from under my desk, and throw up. When I'm finished, I turn my chair around and face the window. I think back to my mother's death in our kitchen, how I envisioned myself flying out the window to escape the grief that had dragged my father to the floor. I recall my father's funeral, and how I mentally sequestered myself by fleeing to another burial, a stranger's casket on the other side of the graveyard. The two most horrific episodes of my life, and I found a way to remove myself from the pain that racked everyone else. Looking out my twentieth-floor window now, I see City Hall and, past it, the streets and buildings below Broad, leading eastward to the Delaware. I wish more than anything that I could fly where my eyes and my mind are taking me now—into New Jersey and across it, to the Atlantic Ocean beyond.

Instead, I stay at the office late into the night, mentally navigating the maze, trying to figure a way out of this for David Hanson, for everyone who matters to me. When I'm finished, I realize there is only one path to safety, a perilous route where the decisions to take the final, essential turns will have to be left up to others. A journey whose first step must be taken by someone else: David Hanson. Whatever amount the blackmailer demands, David Hanson must—absolutely must—pay it. Or all is lost.

I wonder what David will say to me when I show him the video. Will he invent some story to exonerate himself? Or will he break and admit the truth?

16

Friday, September 28

An awful night. I don't get home until after midnight. The house is dark, Piper and Gabby both long in bed. I sit behind my office desk in the dark for close to an hour, the only sounds my own breathing and the rhythmic ticking of the antique grandfather clock in the living room. I mentally relive the day, amazed and horrified at how the world can turn on a dime. I ponder the plan I've constructed to save everyone from the fallout of Jennifer Yamura's death. I analyze it, tear apart and rebuild it, over and over. What could go wrong? How can I guarantee nothing will? The answers are always the same: a million things. Or nothing.

Wearily, I make my way up the stairs, take off my clothes, climb into bed beside Piper. I toss and turn and count the hours on the alarm clock, minute by minute by minute. Sometime after 4:30, I fall asleep.

The alarm sounds at six. I grumble, reach over, and push the buttons on the top of the clock until the noise stops. I turn away and pull the covers over my head, but it's no use—I can't fall back to sleep. Moping my way to the bathroom, I relieve myself and climb directly into the shower, stand under the hot water for a long time, head bent, eyes closed.

It's close to seven when I walk into the kitchen. Piper is standing by the counter, pouring herself a cup of coffee. Gabby is sitting at the table, eating Froot Loops.

"I suppose I should say congratulations," Piper says.

I look at her, not comprehending for a moment. Then I realize she's congratulating me about my victory at the gag-order hearing—now the farthest thing from my mind.

"Thanks," I say halfheartedly, changing places with Piper at the coffee machine.

"Jeez, what's wrong with you? And why were you so late?"

I sigh. "I was at the office. I had to get something finished."

"Why didn't you just finish it here?"

My hackles go up instantly. The home-versus-office battle has been bitter ground for Piper and me for years. It's the main reason Piper built out my home office for me, insisted I have remote computer access to my work server. It was a birthday gift and, in fairness, quite a grand one. The problem, as I explained to Piper more than once, is that, as one of the owners of the firm, I have to be physically present at my office downtown to lead my troops.

"Mick. Did you hear me? I need you to take Gabby to school this morning. I'm meeting Julie for an early yoga class."

"Huh? Yeah, I heard. That's fine. I'd love to take Gabby to school," I say, mustering enthusiasm that I don't actually feel for anything right now. I wink at Gabby as I say it. She smiles perfunctorily, the regent acknowledging her serf, then returns to her cereal.

Two hours later I walk into the firm's reception area. Tommy's there, talking to Angela. I interrupt them, tell Tommy, "We have a problem.

Come on." I pass Tommy and lead him into my office. "Close the door," I say. A minute later I'm sitting behind my desk, and Tommy is across from me in one of the guest chairs.

"What's up?"

I take a breath. "There's a tape." Tommy looks at me, not understanding. "Yesterday, someone—an old woman, according to Katrina—dropped off a videotape for my eyes only. It shows the back of Jennifer Yamura's house on the day of her murder. It shows who went in and out that day."

Tommy's mouth opens, and I see his hands tighten on the arms of the chair. He looks at me, stone-faced. He waits a beat, then asks, "Is there something you want to say to me?"

"No." I'm nowhere near ready to talk about what's on the tape.

Tommy glances out the window behind me, then looks back at me. "So. Now what?"

"Now? I make damn sure David Hanson pays whoever delivered that tape whatever they want to make sure the video never sees the light of day."

"It's blackmail?"

"What else?"

Tommy doesn't answer, and we stare at each other. "I guess that's it, then." He slaps the arms of the chair, stands, and leaves without looking back.

"Close the door," I say. Tommy hesitates, then closes the door a little too hard.

I stare at the door, resigned to a fact I'd come to terms with a long time ago: that I no longer understand my brother and probably never will again.

When Tommy came home after his stint in prison for beating up the cop in Florida, he didn't seem as restless as he'd been. It was almost as though going to jail had calmed him in some way.

He'd settled back into the lumberyard job of his youth, making decent money and even dating Rachel, a nice young woman from Lancaster. For two years everything went smoothly. There was even talk of a wedding.

Then one day I was sitting behind my desk at the DA's office when I got a phone call from her. She asked if Tommy was visiting me in Philadelphia. She hadn't seen him in almost two weeks. Neither had his bosses at the lumberyard.

I drove to Lancaster, got into Tommy's apartment, and quickly determined he hadn't been home in a long while. There was little I could do but wait. Finally, Tommy turned up in jail in Camden, New Jersey. It turned out he'd painted a strip club's parking lot with the blood of two other patrons. One of the victims was the nephew of the town's mayor.

As I would only learn years later, the guys Tommy pulverized had been in the process of raping a woman in their van. Tommy passed by, heard what was going on, opened the van's side door—the creeps hadn't even bothered to lock it—and gone to town on the assailants.

Things turned out worse than they had to for Tommy. In sentencing him, the judge never took into account that Tommy had prevented a rape because Tommy never said a word about it. The rape victim ran before the police arrived and never came forward about what happened. Tommy himself never explained why he attacked the two men. He wouldn't even talk to the lawyer the court appointed to represent him. Or me, for that matter. He just sat back and let it all come crashing down on his head.

The sentence was five years. Tommy took the first plea the prosecutor shat on him. He left the courtroom as he'd entered that day, in an orange jumpsuit, leg manacles, and handcuffs. He glanced back at me only once, just before they took him out the door. It took me the whole drive back to Philadelphia to figure out the look in his eyes, but I eventually realized what it was: relief. Like he'd gotten what he deserved. I paced my apartment the rest of the day, alternately crying and raging at my brother.

"For what?" I'd shouted. "What do you think you did that you deserve this?"

I'm pulled from my thoughts by the phone. It's Angie. "Mr. Ginsberg's on line one."

Alexander Ginsberg is the most respected and feared attorney in the city, if not the state. Fortune 500 corporations, CEOs, mafia bosses, politicians—the rich and powerful of every stripe and calling—scramble to hire Ginsberg when the carpet is pulled out from under them. After the hearing over the leak to the *Inquirer* about the second geisha house, I'd hired him to sue the paper for libel, telling Ginsberg that David Hanson wasn't looking for money but for a public apology.

"I've been on the phone all morning with the *Inquirer*'s lawyer," Ginsberg tells me. "The paper is ready to print a front page mea culpa, so long as we promise not to file a lawsuit and bankrupt it."

"You mean bankrupt it *again*," I say. The *Inquirer*'s financial problems have plagued it for years, even causing the paper to seek bankruptcy protection once before. "How soon will they run the apology?"

"Their lawyer says tomorrow, if David will sign a release before then. I've already drafted something. I'll send it over, let you look at it." Ginsberg pauses, then says, "You know, the paper fired Patti Cassidy . . ."

I thank Ginsberg and do some paperwork, make some calls. After an hour, I leave my office, tell Angie on the way out that I'm heading over to the food court at Liberty Place to pick up a sandwich from Bain's Deli. "Back in a few," I say.

Leaving by the Market Street entrance, I turn right toward Sixteenth Street and see the preacher on the corner. He's there every day, railing against adultery, alcohol, Congress, the Internet, sexting, and every other form of human folly that makes its way into the media. Today, though, he's not shouting. He's engaged in conversation with an older woman. I am about to walk by them when the woman turns and looks at me. She's about five foot five. Her hair is dyed yellow, her eyes icy blue. Her face has the pallor of someone not used to the sun.

She steps aside, then walks alongside me to the corner, where we stop. "You should listen to what this man says, Mr. Lawyer," she says in a distinct accent. Russian or Eastern Bloc, I guess.

I stop and stare at her.

How does she know I'm a lawyer?

"Everybody thinking only of themselves these days. Police selling drugs, husbands cheating on their wives, people killing each other. And everyone wants to get rich," she says.

And then it hits me: she's the older woman who delivered the tape to my office yesterday.

I open my mouth, but I don't know what to say.

"I'll be in Rittenhouse Square, the center, in an hour," she says, then turns and walks across Market Street.

Half an hour later, I walk past the spot where I happened upon Piper the day of Jennifer Yamura's murder. A hundred years ago, it seems. The sidewalk is more crowded now than it was that day. I look at the faces of the people passing me in the other direction, hoping I don't recognize anyone. Entering Rittenhouse Park, I become conscious of the weather for the first time. It's warm for fall. The leaves are still green and thick on the trees. The sky is bright blue. A gentle, cooling breeze blows from the northwest. It's beautiful outside, and I think to myself how wrong it is that the weather can be so lovely on such an awful day.

I walk the diagonal path that crosses the park. The benches on either side of me are filled with people, mostly younger, eating lunch, sandwiches in opened deli paper on their laps. Talking, I suppose, about work or lovers or the latest movie. I see the old woman ahead, sitting on a concrete bench right in the center of the park. Her eyes lock on mine. The faintest trace of a smile forms on her lips. I sit down next to her. We sit silently until she decides to speak.

"You think he's crazy?"

I look at the old woman, confused.

"The preacher in front of your building—do you think he's insane? Because he stands there giving speeches that everyone ignores."

"Maybe we're all insane for ignoring him."

The old woman smiles.

"Good point." Then her smile disappears.

"The video . . . is very interesting, don't you think? Yes, I'm sure you do," she answers for me in her thick Eastern European accent. "A very interesting young woman, my neighbor. Very attractive. Very popular with the men."

So apparently the woman lives in one of the buildings across the alley from Yamura's house, on Pine Street.

"Is that why you installed the camera?"

The old woman laughs. "Hardly. No, you can thank the Philadelphia Police Department for my cameras, Mr. McFarland."

"You have me at a disadvantage," I say, causing the woman to chuckle again.

"Yes, I guess so. Big disadvantage."

"I mean that you know my name, and I don't know yours. Will you share that with me?"

The old woman looks up at me. "Anna Biernacki. Anna Groszek, ever since I married my worthless ex-husband. We both came from Poland. His idea, my genius husband, that we come here, to America. He tells me, 'We go to the United States, we work hard, we get rich, we come home, live the good life.' I say okay. So we come to America, and *I* work hard while he gets drunk. Ten years later, Solidarity brings democracy to Poland, and my husband decides it's a good time to return home—by himself. I don't hear anything from him for months, but a friend calls me from my city of Poznan. She says Emeryk told everybody I am dead. Married Agneszka Walczak. Six years older than Emeryk and the face of a cow. But her father is wealthy and old. My husband, he's done well for himself." Anna pauses, then spits out his name. "Emeryk."

I let her stew for a minute, then bring her back to why we're here. "So . . . you made a tape."

Anna Groszek's eyes narrow. "My security camera makes the tape. When my husband leaves, I start my own cleaning company. I hire four girls to work for me, all from Poland. I put flyers in doors where the wealthy people live. I make sure my girls work hard, do a good job. Word of mouth, and I have more business than I can handle. So I hire more girls, and more again. Over the years, I save my money. I buy a big house. Four stories. A dump. So I put in new plumbing, new electric, new roof, new kitchen, bathrooms. Good carpet, expensive drapes. It's very nice."

"On Pine Street, this house?"

Anna glances at me, annoyed, but doesn't deny it. "Two years ago, I am robbed. Thieves break in through the back door, take all my sterling silver. A hundred years old. My grandmother's. I bring it over from Poland. They also take a pendant my mother gave me when I was sixteen." Anna shakes her head, then continues. "So I call the police. After a very long time, one policeman shows up at my house. He takes a statement, tells me to call my insurance company. And that's it. I never hear nothing more from the police. The next month, I am robbed again. I come home and my TV is gone. I go upstairs, where the rest of my jewelry is. It should be there because after last robbery I buy heavy safe and hide it in the closet. Except now I find the safe is gone, too!

"So. Another call to the police. Another long wait. The same policeman shows up and takes a statement. I ask him what has been done on the first robbery. He looks at me like I'm crazy. He says they almost never arrest someone for burglary because the burglars come when no one's home to see them. He says they can't arrest someone if they don't know what he looks like. That's when I know I am going to have to do police job for them. I buy cameras for the backyard. Good ones, too, weatherproof, can see in complete darkness. They come with digital video recorder and DVD burner."

"You had the cameras pointing at Jennifer Yamura's house?"

"No. One camera I point into my yard, the other in the alley. But that second one, something hit it, lifted it a bit, so it shows back of girl's house. Lucky for me," Anna adds, and smiles. Then shrugs. "Not so lucky for others."

"Why haven't you gone to the police with the video?" I know the answer already, of course, but I have to go through the motions.

Anna sighs. "I am tired, Mr. McFarland. And I'm getting old. I want to go home."

"And you want to fly first class."

Anna smiles. "At the front of the plane, in one of those seats you can lie down in. And when I land, I take suite at the City Park Residence Hotel. Call Emeryk, talk to his bovine wife, tell her I'm back, and rich."

"Your house on Pine Street must be worth a pretty penny."

"It's like *Titanic*," says Anna Groszek. "Underwater. I refinance to make the repairs. Now is worth less than balance on mortgage."

I look across the park, my eyes taking in Rouge, the upscale restaurant on Eighteenth Street. I say nothing more, wait for Anna to say what she's really here to tell me. It doesn't take long.

"Three million. For the videotape. Tell your Mr. Hanson."

"What?" I start to jump up but catch myself, sit back down, look directly at Anna Groszek. "That's crazy. He'll never agree to that."

Anna looks back at me, her blue eyes cold, matter-of-fact. "I know all about your client, Mr. McFarland. He's a very rich man. Crazy for him not to pay. I know all about you, too, Mr. Criminal Attorney. And that prosecutor—the one who wears the fancy suits, wants to be the next DA, then mayor—how happy do you think he would be if I were to call him instead of you? Ach. The three of you. Moe, Larry, Curly. One, two, three. Three million."

For the first time, I wonder whether Anna might be slightly unhinged. But her eyes appear lucid, and her tone couldn't be more serious.

"Still, you didn't go to the DA . . ." I study her face for confirmation.

She shrugs. "He has no money."

I nod. This is a business deal to her, pure and simple. She has an asset to sell, and she's peddling it to the highest bidder. David Hanson.

"And what if my client says no? What if he'd rather take his chances facing that tape than giving in to blackmail?"

Anna Groszek shakes her head. "I put my faith in you. Your client will not like the amount, but you will persuade him. You *must* persuade him. You know this. He must pay, or all is lost."

I look down at the ground. Of course she's right. "Where will you want the money wired?"

"Ha!" Anna blurts loudly. "*Wired.* I want cash, Attorney McFarland. I want to see the money, have it in my hands. It will be for me to deposit it in a bank and wire it to Poland. Then I give other copy of video."

"What assurance do I have that you won't give a copy of the video to the police once you get the money?"

Anna Groszek stands up and looks down at me, her icy eyes flaring. "You have my word. That is your assurance." She turns away.

"Wait," I say, standing. "Where . . . when . . . ?"

"Two weeks from today," she answers, turning back to me. "Bring it to my house. Use the front door."

And with that, Anna Groszek turns again and walks away.

17

MONDAY, OCTOBER 1

The following Monday, at two o'clock, I'm standing by the reception desk going over some phone calls with Angie when Vaughn walks up.

"I'm ready when you are," he says. I look at him, uncomprehending. "The Hanson case . . . it's all laid out in the war room."

"Right. Good," I say. A couple of days ago, I told Vaughn to lay the case out on the table in the small interior conference room that we call the "war room." I do this with every case, a month or so before the trial. Vaughn and I review everything in detail, figure out the prosecution's strengths and weaknesses. Then we turn to our case, decide the best order to present our witnesses and evidence, and put our own case under a microscope. "I'll be there in a minute."

Angie watches Vaughn walk away, then turns back to me. "Do you feel all right? You don't seem yourself. Are you sick?"

"Maybe a little," I say. "Change of seasons."

Half an hour later, I'm sitting in the war room, and Vaughn is in the midst of his presentation. The way he sees it, Devlin Walker will open up with Matthew Stone, the leader of the crime-scene unit. "They start by showing the body pictures to get the jury hating Hanson right away.

Stone will also testify that David's hair and prints are all over Jennifer Yamura's house. After the CSU witness, Devlin will . . ."

Vaughn talks on, but his voice fades into the background as I stare at the crime-scene photos. Jennifer Yamura, faceup on the stairs. Her white cotton T-shirt and tan shorts. The red strawberry bruising to her knees, caused when she crawled across the rough concrete floor. And the blood. Everywhere. Blood on Jennifer's hair and clothes. Blood on the steps. Blood covering the concrete block at the bottom and all over the floor near the steps. And, though it doesn't show in the photos, blood leading away from the steps on the basement floor, as revealed by the CSU's luminol.

I now know from the video that David was the last of the men who visited Yamura's house that day and who therefore had to be the one who happened upon her after she'd been pushed down the stairs and managed to start crawling away. He wasn't the one who pushed her, but he was the one who dragged her back to the steps to bleed out. I wonder what David's reaction was when he found her, how much time it took him before he decided to finish her off. It couldn't have taken long; he was only in the house for five minutes.

"Mick? Mick?"

I look up and see Vaughn staring at me. "I'm sorry," I say. "Can we finish this tomorrow? I don't feel great. I think I'm coming down with something."

Vaughn says sure, no problem, but I can tell he's wondering what's going on. He gathers a few of the papers and leaves the room.

I look back down at the table, reach for the manila envelope containing the autopsy pictures. Now I see Jennifer Yamura's face, empty of expression, eyes flat. The eyes of the dead. I have seen thousands of photographs like these. Pictures of dead men and women. Young, middle-aged, old. Stabbed, shot, strangled, even hacked to pieces. I long ago became desensitized to them. Just more evidence, to present to juries when I was a prosecutor, to argue against once I became a defense attorney. But the pictures of Jennifer Yamura jar me. I close the folder and slide it away. I close my eyes, take deep breaths, one after another. *Christ, this is awful. So fucking awful.*

I get home around seven. Piper is pacing the kitchen, talking on her cell phone. Gabby is at the table, a piece of construction paper in front of her. Gabby's crayon drawing is a tangle of yellow and green and brown, with jagged lines of black. Gabby sits with her left elbow on the table, her head in her hand. A familiar pose of frustration.

"Dad, can you tell Mom to get off the phone? She's been on it forever."

I look over at Piper, who turns away from me, then leaves the kitchen for the deck. Ten minutes later, she's back. By now I am sitting with Gabby, helping her to finish her masterpiece, hearing why each color I choose and each stroke I make is wrong. Piper walks to the refrigerator, pulls out a casserole dish containing the leftover chicken soufflé from last night.

"Tommy wants you to call him," she says.

"Is that who you were talking to?"

"I'm just going to reheat this, since you weren't here last night."

"What did Tommy want?"

"I told you, he wants you to call him."

"I mean, what was he talking about with you for so long?"

She turns her back to me. "Just call him. Please." She slides the leftovers into the oven. Closes the oven door, then walks past the table. "The timer's set for thirty minutes. Set the table just for you and Gabby. I'm going upstairs. I'm not hungry."

Gabby glances at me and purses her lips, then resumes drawing. "I don't want chicken again," she tells me. "Can you make spaghetti instead?"

I muss her thick, black hair. "Sure, why not?"

I start to stand, and Gabrielle asks me, "Daddy, why does Mommy cry all the time?"

I'm taken aback but try not to show it. I sit back down. "What do you mean, all the time?"

"Last night. Mommy made me go to bed early, and I heard her crying in your room."

"Well, maybe her tummy hurt."

"The night before, too."

I look down, try to process what my daughter is telling me.

"No, honey. Mommy's just not feeling well, that's all. She'll be better soon."

But will she? Piper knows more, much more, than she's told me. And in the end it's all going to come out.

"Daddy? Daddy?" I hear Gabby's voice in the distance and refocus my attention on her.

"What's the matter, sweetheart?" I ask.

"Are you sick like Mommy?"

"No, why?"

"Because now you're crying, too."

It startles me. But she's right. Tears are sliding down the side of my face.

An hour or so later, Gabby has been fed, and she's planted in front of the television watching one of her favorite videos. I lift my iPhone from the kitchen counter and tell Siri to call Tommy. He answers in just two rings.

"What's up?" I ask. "Piper says you want to talk to me."

"I want us to go see Mom and Dad." Tommy and I have a tradition of visiting our parents' graves every year, usually on Father's Day. We didn't make it this year because I was so wrapped up in the Hanson case.

"Sure," I say. "As soon as the Hanson trial is over, we can—"

"I don't want to wait," Tommy interrupts me. "Let's go this weekend."

"Tommy, I'm getting ready for the trial. I can't just . . ." I stop in midsentence. "All right. Saturday morning. I'll pick you up; we'll drive together."

"If it's all the same, I'm going to ride my bike," Tommy says, referring to his beloved Harley.

"No problem. I'll see you at the cemetery. How's ten o'clock sound?"

Tommy says that'll be fine.

"Hey . . . ," I say before hanging up. "What's going on with Piper? Gabby just told me she cries all the time."

There's silence on the other end of the line.

"And what gives with the two of you? I feel like you're both keeping something from me, and I don't like it."

Tommy pauses. "We're helping each other through some things."

"What things?"

Another pause. "I'll see you Saturday."

"I don't like secrets."

But the phone's gone dead.

18

WEDNESDAY, OCTOBER 3

It's just after four in the afternoon. Vaughn and I are in the war room, finishing up our strategy session on the Hanson case. The table is cluttered with files, legal pads, photographs; the trash can overfilled with the remains of the lunch we ordered in from Marathon Grill. In the far corners of the room stand two aluminum easels supporting thirty-six-by-forty-two-inch pads of paper, on which are scribbled in black marker the names of each side's potential witnesses. For the prosecution: arresting officers Tim Kujowski and Nicholas Pancetti; John Tredesco, lead detective; Ari Weintraub, medical examiner; Matthew Stone, CSU; Barbara King, David's secretary; Albert Mays, manager of David's garage.

For the defense, I've written the name Lonnie Gorman, a twice-convicted second-story man recently arrested for a burglary just two blocks from Jennifer Yamura's house. David Hanson's name is also listed on the board—with a big question mark next to it. Finally, though it's doubtful I could compel testimony by any of them, I've listed every one of the seventeen officers of the Thirteenth and Fifteenth Districts the grand jury recommended be charged, along with Lawrence Washington and Terrance Johnson, the two surviving officers who testified before the grand jury in return for immunity.

Vaughn and I go around and around about our defense. We've agreed that we must present a plausible alternative to David Hanson as the murderer of Jennifer Yamura. We have two choices. On the one hand, Jennifer's missing laptop, iPhone, watch, and money support the argument that she was killed as part of a robbery. That's where Lonnie Gorman comes in. On the other hand, we have the grand-jury angle. The crooked cops clearly had a motive to kill her. And in slaying Stanley Lipinski, who'd turned state's evidence against them, we know at least one bad cop was willing to take a life.

Vaughn and I argue back and forth for a while about which of our two alternative-killer theories to press. We could offer both theories up to the jury, let them bite on whichever seems the more appetizing. But then we would lose the force of conviction, the persuasive power carried by the message that *this is what we believe.*

I stand up, walk to the credenza, lift a bottle of Fiji water from a silver serving tray. "Let's turn to David," I say.

"Yes, let's," says Susan, who's appeared in the doorway. "What are we going to say about the fact that Hanson stayed in the house for who knows how many hours with the bloody, murdered body of his lover? How do we address the coldness of the soul of a man who could do that?"

"Dissociative state," I answer immediately. "A person of normal mental health like David Hanson happens upon the murdered body of his girlfriend. He's desperate not to have their affair revealed and irrationally latches onto the hope that he can clean up the house, remove all traces of himself. But he's never seen a murder victim before, let alone the body of someone he's had an intimate relationship with. So his mind splits. The part of his consciousness that holds his humanity—his compassion, his love, his morality—numbs itself completely, while the other part of him—his practical side, the lizard brain—takes over and starts cleaning."

Susan smirks. "I don't think they'll buy it, not with David. I think the jury is going to see him as a cold fish. A rich, calculating prick perfectly willing to do whatever it takes to protect himself."

"Which brings us," Vaughn says, "to the big question. Do we try to change the jury's view of David by putting him on the stand? Let him talk to the jury, look in their eyes, and tell them he didn't do it?"

Now that I know David had to be the one who dragged Jennifer back to the stairs to die, I can't ethically put him on the stand to perjure himself by denying his involvement. Not that ethics would stop me. Indeed, as I've charted it out in my head, my literally "criminal" defense of David Hanson will necessitate a heaping dose of perjury. But I can't share that with Vaughn or Susan, or anyone. Not yet.

"Think about it," Vaughn continues. "We could have David testify about sponsoring those three foreign musicians in New York. Humanize him."

Susan flinches at the idea of perpetuating that sham.

"If we put him on the stand," I say, "he's going to have to tell the jury where he was."

"And his fairy tale about the long walk isn't going to fly," adds Susan. "Which brings me to what *I* think the big question is. If David didn't kill Yamura, where was he, really, at the time she was murdered? What could he have been doing that is so terrible he wouldn't disclose it to save himself from a murder conviction?"

"Even if there comes a point when we want David to disclose his alibi, we have a Rule 567 problem," Vaughn says.

He's referring to the rule of criminal procedure that requires the defendant to notify the court and prosecutor within thirty days after the arraignment of the defendant's intent to offer an alibi defense, specifying the details as to where the defendant claims he was and whom he claims he was with. That window, of course, has come and gone.

"So we're in agreement," I say. "We keep David off the stand if at all possible." I look at Vaughn and Susan, and both nod. "Which brings us to heart of the matter. Reasonable doubt. Does the prosecution have enough to convict? Let's start with the evidence of motive. There is none. Sure, Devlin can speculate that David and Jennifer had a falling-out. But that's all it will be: speculation. And David's prints and hair and DNA being all over the house? Of course they were, he owned the place and had been there a hundred times. And as for David getting caught in the house, it was more than nine hours *after* the murder. Walker hasn't identified a single eyewitness who can put David there at the time of the crime. Bottom line is that the prosecution may have the goods to make the jury pretty sure David killed Yamura. But it doesn't have the evidence to prove it beyond a reasonable doubt."

"Nice closing, Mick," Susan says. "But David is tainted in the eyes of the jury pool, the whole city. *Pretty sure* may be enough for a conviction in this case."

"Okay. I think we've done enough for today," I say, ignoring her take. "Nice job, Vaughn. We'll press on with this tomorrow."

That's his signal to leave. Then I look at Susan and ask her to stay in the room with me. When Vaughn's gone, I close the door and sit next to my partner. I put my elbows on the table, rub my eyes with my hands, and blow out some air. "Susan—"

"Look," she interrupts, "I know this case must be hard for you, with David being your friend. Are you sure you even want to be first chair? I can step up if you need me to."

"Thanks. But I can push through it. And I think I better do it alone. That's what I want to talk about. I know I promised you I could play it straight. But there are things going on in this case that you don't know about, and that I can't tell you. The fact is, I may have to go completely cowboy once we get to court. And the whole thing might blow up in my face. If that happens, I don't want you anywhere near the fallout."

Susan leans back in her chair, crosses her arms. "What exactly are you telling me here? Or *not* telling me? Did David confess to you? Are you looking to get rid of me so you'll have a free hand to put him on the stand, help him perjure himself? I mean, what the hell? That's not the type of law practice I want to be a part of. I used to be a United States attorney. I can't have you helping clients lie on the stand." She emphasizes the point by nailing the conference-room table with her index finger.

"It's not that. I'm not going to help David lie under oath."

"Then tell me what's going on."

"I *can't* tell you," I say too loudly. "And that, too, is to protect you. All I can say is that you don't want to get too close to this one."

Susan exhales, waits for a minute before saying anything. "Is this the only thing that has you so on edge? Or is there more? Is it the firm's financial problems? Things at home?"

Though I've not gone into any great detail, I've confided to Susan that things between Piper and me could be better.

"None of that helps," I say. "But, look, the firm's been short of cash before, and we've gotten through it. And Piper and I . . ." I shrug. "What can I say? It is what it is."

"So it's just the case, then?"

I nod.

"And you're going to handle it the way Marcie told you? *Whatever it takes?*"

"Whatever it takes. That's exactly how it's going to be. How it has to be."

Susan studies me, then stands and pats me on the shoulder. "I hope you know what you're doing," she says. "For everyone's sake."

"So do I," I answer.

For everyone's sake.

◆ ◆ ◆

It's 7:30 p.m., and I'm alone in the office except for the cleaning lady, who's finishing up our suite. My phone rings. It's the night-shift security guard, calling from the front desk. "I have a visitor—Mr. Hanson. Is it okay to send him up?"

A minute later, I hear the elevator door ding and see David turn the corner, walk down the hall. He's wearing an Italian black-leather jacket that likely cost as much as I make in a month. His jacket hangs over a light-blue, herringbone, button-down shirt that David probably had made in London. His wool trousers are sharply pleated and break perfectly over his shoes. I remember David telling me once that he had all his dress shoes made for him in Argentina, that he flew down once a year to meet his shoemaker, pick out the leathers, have his feet remeasured.

David's face shows me he's still basking in his victory at the gag-order hearing. He's all smiles. He won't be for long.

I open the door for David, shake his hand perfunctorily. I offer few words. All business. I lead David into my office, close the door, and lock it. David sits on one of the chairs across from my desk. He's sensed my tension.

"Is everything all right? With the case?"

"Turn your chair around," I say. "I have to show you something." David turns his chair so he's facing the large TV screen, which is linked with my computer. I pull the DVD out of its plastic container, slide it into the computer.

Five minutes later, David is slumped in the chair, his expression that of a man standing before a firing squad. It is so quiet now that I can hear the second hand of my watch. I let it tick for a full minute.

"I didn't do it, Mick. I didn't kill Jennifer."

I stare at David, wait a beat. "Sure you didn't—just like you never went to her house that day. That is what you told me, right?"

David lowers his head, closes his eyes. More time passes. "I'm sorry for lying to you. But she was dead when I got there. I swear it."

"Then why didn't you call the police?"

"I froze. I panicked. I thought about calling the police; I really did. But I knew it would all come out. I was on the verge of some big things with the company. A scandal would have ruined it. Years of work down the drain."

Years of plotting and scheming, I think.

"So you just left her there, a woman you'd been intimate with who-knows-how-many times? Someone you laughed with, played with, maybe even bared your soul to? You left her lying on the basement steps?"

David closes his eyes again. "It was an awful thing to do. A cowardly thing. If I could go back, do it again, I'd call the authorities."

"Why go back at all, if you knew what was in there? Why expose yourself to getting caught in the house with a body? How could you even dream that you could sanitize a crime scene so well that the CSU guys wouldn't pick anything up?"

David's jaw tightens. I get the impression he's asked himself the same question a hundred times. "It was a stupid thing to do," he says. "Idiotic." We sit for a minute as David stews. Then he considers what he's seen on the tape and asks, "Was I the only one on the video?"

"Yes," I answer. A lie. I can't tell David who else was on the original video, which I edited down to the much shorter version that I just shared with David.

David clenches his jaw. "Fucking Devlin Walker must be dancing in the streets over this."

"Devlin Walker has no idea this video exists," I say. "And it's my intention to keep it that way."

David is puzzled.

I answer him before he asks. "This tape was delivered to me as part of a blackmail attempt."

"Blackmail?" David literally shouts the word, and I almost laugh out loud at his indignation. After everything he's done, he's upset at mere extortion? David steams for a few seconds, until his practical side kicks in. "Who? How much?"

"It's better you not know who," I say. "As for how much . . ." I tell David the figure, and he shouts again.

"No way! That's insane. I want to know who's behind this."

I sit calmly, my elbows and forearms on my desk, hands together. "I'm not sharing that with you. And as for 'insane,' I think it would be crazy of you not to pay."

"Let Walker have the video. I'm not afraid of what's on it. I'll explain to the jury that Jennifer was dead when I got there, and you'll argue that someone else killed her before I arrived."

"Was she dead when you first got there? Or only by the time you left?"

"Fuck you, Mick! Fuck you. I did not kill Jennifer. I told you—"

"You told me a lot of things!" Now it's my turn to yell. I shoot out of my seat, point my finger at David. "You told me you weren't at Jennifer's house anywhere near the time of murder, and that was a lie. You told me you'd only been seeing her a few weeks, and that was a lie. And you've been feeding me and my staff that fairy tale about spending the whole afternoon taking a thirteen-mile walk in your suit and custom-made shoes. So stop telling me you didn't kill that woman and insisting that I believe you. I'm not accepting anything you say at face value anymore. As a matter of principle."

David's face is purple now. The veins in his temples are throbbing. His teeth are showing. Something flashes across his eyes. Glee, a cruel glee, is what I see. David is itching to tell me something. But he pulls back. He closes his eyes, takes a deep breath, then another. He sits down, puts his elbows on the chair arms, steeples his fingertips. I use the pause in our fight to remove the DVD from the computer, walk it to my wall safe, lock it inside. Then I return to my chair and address my antagonist in as calm a voice as possible.

"I'm going out on a limb here. It's against everything I believe in to give you this advice. It's unethical—in fact, *illegal*—for me to say this, but here it is. You have no choice. You must pay the money."

David stares at me, matches the control in my voice, and tells me, "I'll think about it. That's all I can promise." Without saying more, he stands and walks out.

I wait until I hear him leave our suite, hear the door click behind him. Then I pick up my phone, dial the number, and wait for her to answer.

"Hello, Marcie," I say. "It's Mick. Remember what you told me when Susan and I came to your house? Whatever it takes?" I pause. Marcie waits quietly at the other end, wondering what I'm going to say, calculating. "David's just left my office. He's very upset. I've told him to do something he doesn't want to do. He's going to ask your opinion. When he does, you will advise him to pay the money."

I close my eyes and sit still in my chair, let the silence wash over me. For the first time in a long while, I feel I've managed to get some control over things. David Hanson will pay the money; I have no doubt. Marcie will make him. That will ensure that the video does not reach Devlin Walker until I decide it's time to show him the parts of the tape he needs to see. I smile as I envision the look on Devlin's face when that time comes. David, of course, will still have to unveil his real alibi. And in the end, if all goes well, David will walk. Jennifer's other killer will stay hidden. And my family will be preserved.

19

It's almost midnight, and I am still awake. Gabby is in her room, asleep. Piper is probably on Amtrak, heading toward 30th Street Station, returning from yet another trip with her girlfriends to New York City.

I sigh and open my eyes. I'm not going to fall asleep anytime soon. The neon-blue numbers on my alarm clock change to 12:00 midnight exactly, and I begin to wonder what all the important people in my life are doing right now.

I see David and Marcie Hanson sitting in David's study, surrounded by priceless art, drinking tea or sake out of dainty Japanese cups, plotting their next move, some bold gambit designed to direct public attention away from David's apparent guilt, portray him as a pawn in the ambition-driven plans of the district attorney's office.

I envision Anna Groszek, dreaming of returning in triumph to her hometown of Poznan, showing up at the home of her ex-husband in a chauffeur-driven limousine. Anna sends the driver to knock on the door and watches from the car as Emeryk Groszek and his cow-faced second wife walk out onto the porch, peer at the limo, try to figure out what great and important person has come to visit them. Anna rolls down her tinted window, takes in the shock on Emeryk's and Agneska's faces as they realize who it is. She laughs, leans out the window, and spits on the road in front of their house.

Finally, my mind lands on Tommy. I see him with terminally ill Lawrence Washington, the two of them sitting at the picnic table outside Tommy's trailer in Jim Thorpe, bundled in heavy sweaters against the chill of the fall night air. Tommy gets up to fetch them each a bottle of Bud. He sits back down, and the two of them stare at each other and take turns swigging their beers. Again, I wonder why Tommy's putting himself through the same passion play he shared with our father. And, for the first time, I think I might know the answer: Tommy's using Lawrence to punish himself. The cop's slow death is another thing to feel guilty about. To beat himself up over.

I sit up in bed, swing around so that my feet are resting on the floor. I'm terrified that Tommy is going to wander off the straight and narrow again, disappear back into his netherworld of dive bars, fleabag hotels, and impulsive violence. I've been afraid of it since the day he was released from prison, and my fears deepened when Lawrence Washington told me about Tommy working for the cop drug ring to pay off his gambling debts.

"Damn, Tommy." I say the words out loud. What can I do to help him? Why must he punish himself like this?

I sit for a long time. I can hear the ticktock of the grandfather clock in the living room downstairs. Across the hall, Gabby murmurs in her sleep. I stand up, walk to her room, sit on the bed next to her. Gabby's mop of dark hair is spread all over the pillow. Her tiger, Toby, has fallen onto the floor, and I reach down, pick him up, and put him into her arms.

As if on cue, Gabby flips onto her stomach. I shiver as the image of Jennifer Yamura, faceup on her basement steps, flashes through my mind. I think of Jennifer's parents. I'd read in the *Inquirer* that their names were John and Margaret Yamura. That John was a longtime IT specialist with the University of Southern California, and Margaret a stay-at-home mom. The article said John and Margaret's own parents had been rounded up during World War II and held in the internment camps. After the war, of course, they were all released—to pay their taxes and raise children who could serve the country in later wars. Jennifer's father served two tours in Vietnam, and her uncle died there.

I cannot imagine what they've been going through these past five months. Every moment, every milestone Piper and I have experienced with Gabby, the Yamuras enjoyed with Jennifer. And they had twenty more years' worth of memories. Lacrosse and basketball—sports Jennifer played in high school, according to the *Inquirer*. Prom night. High school graduation, college graduation, the first job, the big move to the East Coast to take a job with a major-market TV station. And, I imagine, adult conversations. Late-night telephone calls to Mom or Dad when Jennifer was lonely or had suffered a setback, in need of a small slice of the comforts of home.

And, finally, the call that ended it all. Some police officer telephoning from three thousand miles away to tell John and Margaret Yamura that their daughter had been murdered and asking would they mind flying to Philadelphia to identify her body. They did, of course, right away; their pictures were in the paper. With them was their son and Jennifer's fraternal twin, Brian, a computer guy like his father, who'd gotten in early at MyFace, the social networking site, and made $1 billion when the company went public. Brian Yamura, the American dream, brother of Jennifer Yamura, the American nightmare.

I lean over and kiss Gabby on the cheek, whispering, "I will never let anyone hurt you." I sigh and leave the room, climb back into my bed.

About an hour later, I hear the automatic garage door open for Piper's car. I hear her high heels on the wood floor as she walks around the kitchen. She pulls something out of the refrigerator, probably a cold bottle of Smartwater. Before long, Piper is in the bathroom, brushing her teeth, then in our bedroom and taking off her clothes. I don't open my eyes, don't stir, wanting her to think I'm asleep. Piper climbs into bed next to me. I can tell she's lying on her side, her elbow on the bed, her hand holding up her head. I can't see her, but I can tell she's looking at me. Studying me.

Piper stays this way for what seems like a long time, and I begin to get the sense that she wants to say something. Emotion surges suddenly through my chest. Is this the night she's going to confess? Is she ready to tell me? Am I ready to hear it? I hold my breath, start to count. One thousand one. One thousand two. One thousand three. Piper turns on her back, exhales. Tonight is not the night. I exhale, too.

I wake up to the smell of bacon. Sunlight washes through the front bedroom windows. The alarm clock reads 8:00—the latest I've slept in a long time.

"Look, Daddy!" I turn to see Gabby standing in the doorway, a white porcelain mug in her hand. "Mommy made you coffee. You can drink it in bed!" Taking her time so as not to spill, Gabby delivers the mug to me. I take the mug, inhale the rich aroma of freshly brewed Starbucks French roast. Gabby climbs into bed with me and tells me how she's been helping her mother cook our breakfast. "We're having eggs and pancakes and bacon, and you're going to read the Sunday paper, and me and Mommy are not allowed to bother you, and that's an order."

I smile, tousle Gabby's hair. "You can bother me all you want."

What is Piper up to? Watching me sleep last night, coffee in bed, and a big breakfast this morning? I search my memory of the past few days, searching for some reason for Piper's apparent warming, but can find none. In earlier years, such solicitousness was typically a prelude to request to make a major purchase. But Piper no longer seeks my approval before buying big-ticket items. She now prefers to spring them on me and coil for the counterattack she knows she'll launch in response to my protestations.

Our breakfast proves to be the most pleasant meal I've had with Piper in years. She tells me all about the show she saw last night, and how she and her friends reacted to it. Gabby pipes in that she wants to go to a play, and Piper says she'll find one the three of us will enjoy. I say what great fun it would be to go to a show with Piper and Gabby, and we all agree we'll see one before Thanksgiving.

After breakfast, I move into my home office, crank up the computer, and work on an appellate brief that's due to be filed with the superior court. Piper knocks on the door's frame and asks if I want a sandwich before I leave to meet Tommy. Still full from breakfast, I beg off but thank her for asking.

An hour later I'm in the car, heading to Lancaster. I wonder why Tommy was so insistent on visiting our parents' graves this weekend, why it couldn't wait until after the Hanson trial. I let my thoughts drift to the period after Mom died, when it was just Dad and Tommy and me, groping our way through it. The memory that comes to mind is of Tommy and me hiding behind the trunk of the big tree in our backyard one December evening as our dad grilled us all some steak; Dad was awful with the oven and cooked most of our meals on the grill, even in the winter. Tommy and I waited until Dad opened the grill lid to flip the steaks, turning his back on the tree. We sprang from our hiding place and pelted him with snowballs. He dropped his spatula into the grill and engaged us in a snowball fight that took us from the backyard to the front. All of us forgot about dinner, and the meat and the plastic handle of the spatula were burned to a crisp. Dad ended up taking Tommy and me to Burger King, the three of us laughing our heads off over the mess we'd made.

I suddenly can't wait to see Tommy, smile with him over the snowball fight. As I turn into the cemetery parking lot, I'm in the best mood I've been in for months. This is exactly what I needed. I'm glad Tommy persuaded me to do this. I get out of the car, walk past Tommy's black-and-silver Harley. It's a chilly day, overcast and in the low fifties. I'm surprised Tommy rode his bike. He's told me before how cold it can get riding on a day like this, even with leathers.

I walk through the arbor leading into the cemetery and make my way down the path to my parents' graves. In the distance, I see Tommy in front of the big marble headstone that marks their final resting place. Tommy is kneeling, and it seems to me he's talking to them. He sees me approach and stands up. His solid, 210-pound frame is covered in black leather from collar to foot—a guy you wouldn't want to meet in an alley. I smile and wave to my brother. Tommy waves back. I step up beside him, and we shake hands. I'm still smiling, feeling light.

"Drive by the old house after this?" I ask, something we often do after visiting the grave site.

Tommy looks at the headstone without answering. He kneels back down, adjusts the fresh flowers he brought with him. I never remember to do that. Tommy never forgets.

I kneel beside Tommy, brush my fingers across our parents' names. "Thanks for suggesting this," I say. "I needed to do this more than I thought." After a minute, I remind Tommy of a time that all four of us went together to Long's Park for a picnic. How pretty Mom looked. How strong Dad was, how far he could throw a football. How young we all were.

Tommy nods but keeps staring at the tombstone.

After a while, we both stand up, and I ask Tommy how he's doing. Whether Lawrence Washington is still hiding out at his trailer and if he is, how he's holding up.

"Still there," Tommy answers. "How's he doing? He's dying. He's down about forty pounds."

"He should be in a hospital."

"He doesn't want to be in a hospital. Hooked up to all that equipment. Nurses in and out all day and night, sticking needles in him. Maybe have some roommate who can't stop talking. Where he wants to be is home, but he can't go there. The DA would be all over him for taking off. And his former buddies might smoke him before he's ready to go."

"Tough situation," I say.

This isn't going like I'd planned. Tommy has only smiled once since I arrived. Hasn't volunteered a single good memory of Mom or Dad. *Okay, so it's up to me.*

"Do you remember that big snowball fight we had with Dad by the grill?"

Tommy stares at me, then looks down at the marker. A raindrop smacks against the top of the tombstone. Then another, and another. I'm thinking that I wish I'd bought a baseball cap when Tommy says, still looking down, "He didn't just die."

Tommy waits for the words to sink in, but they don't. I stand there, uncomprehending. Tommy looks up at me, and I see his eyes are wet—and not with rain. "He was in so much pain," he says.

Now I get it.

"Jesus, Tommy. What did you do?"

"I kept asking the doctors to give me more morphine to take to him; I begged them for it. But they said no, he'd get addicted. Can you believe that? He's lying on his fucking deathbed, in agony, and they're holding back on the painkillers 'cause he might become an addict. I almost punched that one doctor, the young one. I did take him by the collar. But I stopped myself, before . . ."

Tommy is rambling now. I step back, trying to comprehend what I'm hearing. "Are you saying you—"

"I couldn't take it anymore. He kept moaning and crying. I begged him to let me call the ambulance, take him to the hospital, but he told me no way, no way. He wanted to go in the house. He told me he could see Mom, sometimes, by the bed, waiting for him. Oh, Christ . . ."

The tears are streaming down the sides of Tommy's face now, mixing with the rain. My own eyes are filling now, too. "Did he ask you? To do it?"

Tommy shakes his head. "He never would've put something like that on me. Never. But I had to do it. I had to. It was the only way." Tommy keeps talking, and by the time I hear the word *pillow*, my mind is completely dazed. I try to free myself from what Tommy is saying. I look down at my father's name carved in the marble, then at my mother's. I look at the flowers, purple and pink. I gaze up at the sky, try to find a bird to fly away with. But the gravity of my brother's pain keeps pulling me back to him, to his shaking hands, his stinging eyes, his twisted face. Tommy is literally drowning in front of me. I want to reach out, grab him. Save him, somehow. But I am frozen in place.

My brother and I stand there, facing each other in silence as the seconds drag on. Tommy is looking to me—for something. But I have nothing to give.

Finally, I lower my head. "My God," I say.

And that's the end of it. Tommy looks at me another minute, his eyes filled with sorrow, disappointment, anger. Then he turns away. I watch him walk down the path to the parking lot and disappear through the arbor. I hear the engine of his motorcycle, loud as he starts the bike and revs it, then fading as he rides away.

20

Sunday, October 7, Continued; Monday, October 8

I am soaking wet. I have no idea how long I've been in the car or how long I stood at the grave site after Tommy left. I can't see out the windshield, it's raining so hard now. The car isn't running, and I realize suddenly that I'm cold and have been for some time. I turn the key, start the engine, adjust the heat. The radio is on, a female pop singer. Against the backdrop of what's just happened, it feels obscene to listen to the upbeat music. I turn it off, close my eyes, relive the scene at the grave site. Tommy, state wrestling champ, the unbreakable slab of marble, tattooed survivor of the prison system, leather-clad Harley rider, crying like a two-year-old. Spilling his guts to his older brother, reaching out for . . . what? Something I failed to give him. So he had to ride away, alone.

I back up, make a three-point turn, and pull out of the parking lot. I'm almost at the turnpike, twenty-some miles from the cemetery, when I realize the radio is on again. I must've turned it on, but I don't remember doing so. It's four o'clock when I pass through the tolls for Highway 76. Next thing I know, it's thirty minutes later, and I'm close to home. But I don't want to go home, so after I exit the turnpike, I make my way to the Stadium 16 movieplex at King of Prussia, across from the mall. In a daze, I buy a ticket and make my way through the crowded lobby, past the ticket taker, down the hall to the theater, where I take a seat in the back row. The lights go down, the noise level rockets, and I sit numb and motionless through ninety minutes of explosions, computer-generated images, and adolescent dialogue.

I remain utterly disengaged from the movie until, toward the end, one of the characters, the lead, I think, if there is a lead in this jumble of science-fiction action scenes, asks something that strikes me.

"Why now?"

Why have the big robots chosen this precise moment in human history to attack the earth, wipe out humanity? The world is already on the brink of war, the superpowers poised to annihilate one another with nuclear bombs. All the robot invasion seems to have accomplished is to forge mankind into a band of brothers fighting together against a common enemy.

Why now?

And I ask myself the same question about my brother. Why has Tommy chosen this precise point in time to tell me he killed our father? Tommy's had twenty years to unburden himself of his secret. Why didn't he tell me sooner? Why not wait a little longer?

After the movie, I drive to Minella's Diner on Lancaster Avenue, take a seat at the counter. I order meat loaf with mashed, and when the waitress asks what other sides I want, I tell her to surprise me. My iPhone, on the counter, buzzes. I must've turned it to silent mode at the movie theater. I lift the phone and see that Piper is calling. I click the power button to turn off the phone, send Piper to voice mail. Then I turn the phone back on and see that she has called me three times already. After a while, I notice the waitress has delivered my food. It gets cold as I pick at it and order refills on my coffee.

Sometime around eight o'clock, I make it home. I know Piper will be pissed at me for not answering the phone, and I expect a scene as soon as I walk in the kitchen. She's waiting for me, but it's concern, not anger, that etches her face. Dense as I am, I figure out why. Tommy must've told her ahead of time what he had in store. Which can only mean one thing.

"You knew?" I say. "You knew!"

Piper keeps her cool, keeps her voice steady, quiet. "You wanted Tommy to open up to me, Mick," she says. "You said he was closed off. That he needed someone he could talk to. And you were right. He carried it all inside, for years. The grief. The pain. And the guilt. Monstrous guilt. It's why Tommy threw his life into the trash heap. Why, when he faced hard time, he didn't even fight the charges. Tommy is as good as they get, at his core. In his heart. And he knew that, however good his intentions, he had to be punished for what he'd done to your father."

I am dumbstruck. I stare at Piper. "He told you all that?"

"He didn't have to. It was obvious to me, once he told me about the euthanasia."

"Euthanasia?" I repeat the clinical term. "Patricide."

Piper's eyes turn to steel, and she speaks slowly, with visible restraint. "You have no right to judge. You left him there, by himself, to deal with your father's failing health. You went off to college while Tommy stayed home and put his life on hold. You took your classes, played tennis, and went to frat parties while Tommy struggled at a job he hated just to pay the bills." She holds up a hand to stop my protest. "Yes, you offered to stay home and help. But Tommy knew, and your father knew, where your heart really was. So they told you to go back to school, finish up. While Tommy watched the man he idolized, his hero, waste away. In the end, Tommy was bathing him, helping him on and off the toilet. Feeding him. Listening to him moan and cry out, so delirious with pain he imagined he saw your mother in the room with him." Piper is crying now. "Think about it. How could Tommy feel anything other than that you'd abandoned him and your father both?"

I bend over, put my hand on the marble top of the island in the middle of our kitchen, lean into it as I lower my head, close my eyes. My voice is quiet when I ask, "Why didn't he tell me . . . about Dad? Why did he hold it back all these years?"

"I asked him that when he first told me. Tommy said he didn't want to lay that at your feet. He thought it would mess you up. And make things worse between the two of you."

"But now he *has* laid it at my feet. Why? And why *now*?"

Piper shakes her head. She doesn't know why any more than I do. She stares at me, searching, it seems, or wanting to say something more. But the air goes out of her. She turns and walks toward the stairs. She pauses at the threshold, closes her eyes, takes a deep breath. After a moment, she opens her eyes again and walks up the steps.

I stay where I'm standing for a long time, watching the space at the bottom of the landing. I am spent, wiped out. I'm also still confused, unable to figure out Tommy's motivation for suddenly telling me what he did. And I'm pissed because Piper has known all along. I'm feeling like the odd man out in my own marriage, the schmuck left standing without a chair when the music stops. Then again, I've been feeling that way for a long time.

A few minutes later, I'm in my home office, throwing back a glass of eighteen-year-old Macallan, the thick liquid burning the back of my throat.

Much later, the bottle sits half-empty on my desk. My head aches. My stomach is churning. I haven't eaten since breakfast. Tommy's revelation has unhinged me. Piper's indictment has cut me to the quick. I see my brother, twenty years old, no one around to help him, looking down at our pain-racked father. I see him crying as Dad's face disappears under the pillow. I feel Tommy's strong, resolute hands hold down the pillow as our father goes through his death throes. And when it's over, I hear Tommy wailing as he cradles Dad, begs his forgiveness.

I pour another glass of the Macallan, seeing it all clearly now. I've spent my entire life leaving the people I love. First, I disassociated myself from my mother's death. Then I abandoned Tommy and our dad. The DA's office was another example. Everyone was stunned by my announcement. It was sudden, and I'd done nothing to prepare my team for my leaving, for the onslaught they expected would come from Devlin and his allies. No chance to mend the political fences they'd broken in my name. It was lucky for them that Devlin turned out to be a good leader and welcomed them to his own team.

And what had it done to Piper? During my years with the prosecutor's office, Piper and I had done a lot of socializing with my colleagues. Not just the ADAs, but with the detectives who worked side by side with us to build our cases. There were backyard barbeques, picnics, and pickup baseball games in Fairmount Park. Kids' birthday parties, more than a few weddings. Piper became close with many of my colleagues and their spouses. And yet—inexcusably, I now see—I never considered what my leaving the DA's office would do to Piper. Looking back, I realize that my abruptly switching sides to become a criminal-defense attorney must've been awful for her. Her many friends in law enforcement must surely have given her the cold shoulder. I envision Piper leaving messages on answering machines and getting no return calls. I see the invitations to parties and girls' nights out drying up. But Piper kept it from me, never once complaining.

And to bookend the evaporation of Piper's social life, I gave her less of myself as a private practitioner than I had as a prosecutor. I stayed later at the office, worked every weekend. And when I was home, I wasn't engaged. As she told me recently, *Even when you're here, you're not here.* Piper had been sitting across from me at the dinner table, helping Gabby relate a funny story about something that had happened at school. I wasn't reacting, and Piper flipped out. "You may as well go back to the office," she snarled. "You just pretend to be at home with us." Piper slammed her fork onto her plate and left the table. Gabby started crying. I looked back and forth at the two of them, oblivious.

"You idiot." I say it out loud. "You prick."

And with that, something inside me, something that's been lurking for a long, long time, reaches up and pulls me down from the sky and throws me through the window, into the kitchen, where Mom lies dead and Dad weeps over her body. I sit across the table from my little brother, so small, racked with pain and incomprehension, staring at our parents and then looking to me for help. And this time, there is no escape for me. The window is closed; the birds fly past without me. Sorrow slices my heart.

But this time, I do what I should have done before. I walk Tommy to the floor, where we hug and hold on to our broken father, showing Dad and our departed mother that our love lives on.

My mind leaps ahead to the summer after my freshman year in college. Tommy and I are sitting in the backyard, watching our father cooking on the grill and coughing. I tell Tommy I'm transferring to Millersville, the local state college, so I can help care for Dad. For the next three years, I live at home, and Tommy and I together share the burden of caring for our father. We are both there when he passes, without our help. Then Tommy enlists in the military, becomes a Navy SEAL. He serves heroically, risking his life in one dangerous black-ops mission after another. When he accepts his discharge, the other men in his unit lament the loss of their best man. Tommy comes home, and I take a few weeks off from my job as an assistant district attorney to vacation with him somewhere hot and hopping with other young people. Then Tommy heads off to the federal law-enforcement training center to become a federal agent. He falls in love with a woman he meets undercover, a frank-talking Italian with a crooked smile and a black belt in kickboxing. They get married, have three boys—roughnecks like their father.

I meet and marry Piper Gray. She supports me in my career as an assistant district attorney. The years roll by, and I advance in the prosecutor's office. Gabby does well in school, and Piper and I share a strong and happy marriage. We go on long vacations, have date nights, talk in bed after we make love. I eventually jump ship to the defense side, but I give my staff plenty of warning to prepare themselves. And I make sure to preserve plenty of time for Gabby and for Piper.

On the straight and narrow, Tommy never becomes a mule for the crooked policemen. Never meets Jennifer Yamura to tell her about the drug ring. And Jennifer herself, having no story to print, never winds up at the center of a storm, never has need of a slick criminal-defense attorney, and never ends up dead on the stairs.

These visions from an alternate life only double my anguish over what I have done. I plant my elbows on my desk, bury my face in my hands. My eyes flood.

"I can't believe it. I just can't believe it."

Sometime later, I pass out. In the morning I awaken, still at my desk, to the distinct feeling that I'm being watched. I lift my throbbing head, look around. The light stinging my eyes, I bring Piper into focus. She's standing in the doorway, a cup of coffee in her hands. She studies me, then moves into the room, sits down across the desk, tentatively slides the cup to me. "Here," she says.

I shake my head slowly. *I'm sorry*—that's what I want to say, but my throat is so raw and dry I can't push the words out. So I cough, reach for the cup, and take a sip of coffee.

"I can only imagine what you're feeling," Piper says. "But try to remember . . . Tommy was so young. He did what he felt was the right thing to do. And it broke him. It shattered him into pieces."

I look across the desk at Piper and then down at my cup of coffee, nodding. "I know."

"You have to forgive him, Mick."

My eyes begin to tear up again. "There's nothing to forgive. He did the right thing."

"Then you tell him so."

I slide my hand across the desk, reaching for Piper. She takes it in her own.

"Mick," she says, her eyes filled with what seems to me to be sadness, bottomless sadness. I push myself off my chair, walk around the desk to meet my wife. Piper stands, reaches around me as I kiss her forehead, caress her hair, more tenderness between us than we've shared for years.

"Tommy's going to be all right," I promise. "*We're* all going to be all right."

Piper looks up at me, forces a smile. She lowers her head against my chest, and I feel a shiver run through her.

"Daddy, you look awful!"

"Gabby!" Piper and I shout in unison, and Piper adds, "How many times have I told you not to sneak up?" Gabby's face contorts like she's going to cry until she sees Piper smiling, and we all begin to laugh.

Seeing that she's brought the house down, Gabrielle goes on. "You smell really bad, too. You should go get a shower."

I look at Piper, who says, "Yeah, you really should."

So I do. And when I'm done, I join my wife and daughter in the kitchen, and we eat a big breakfast and tell stories and laugh, and I do something I haven't done in years. I take a weekday off from work.

21

Thursday, October 11

The clock on my dashboard reads 7:15 p.m. Tomorrow, I am meeting Anna Groszek. Tonight, I visit David Hanson to pick up the money. One of the doors to his four-car garage opens, and I pull inside. Once my car is stopped, I hear the garage door close behind me. I get out, look around. To my right is David's black BMW 760Li and, beyond it, a gray two-door Bentley Continental GT. To my left is a red Porsche 911 Turbo S Cabriolet. I know there's another garage on the property where David keeps his super-high-end cars.

What I don't see is David. Instead, to my surprise, I spot Marcie at the back of the garage. "Something came up at the last minute, and David had to leave," she says. "You'll be happy to know he's driving my Audi A6," she adds. "It's white and small. He hates it."

She's referring to the warning I gave David about not driving any of his sportier or more luxurious cars. I don't want potential jurors to see a picture of him in the newspaper climbing out of a Lamborghini.

I remain standing next to my car, unsure what to do, until Marcie taps one of the two black Tumi suitcases sitting on the floor next to her. "I think these are what you came for." With that, Marcie extends the handle and pulls one of the two wheeled bags to the back of my car. I walk over and get the other suitcase, then join her by the trunk. I press the button on my electronic key, and the trunk opens. I lower the handles on the two bags and deposit them into the trunk, then close the lid.

"Just so you know," Marcie says. "Coming up with this much cash isn't as easy as you'd think. David had to take the company jet so he could secretly leave the country and fly to the Caribbean and Mexico. He pulled the first two million from numbered accounts in Grand Cayman. The second half he 'borrowed' from some HWI slush fund in Mexico." Marcie smiles at the last part, probably thinking that David's withdrawal in some way put the screws to Edwin.

I don't know what to say to this. I've seen it speculated that David's net worth is close to $100 million. The amount I told David he had to turn over is a small fraction of that. Still, I guess it would be a chore to convert millions of dollars from entries on a balance sheet into cash.

Marcie and I stand face-to-face for a long minute. Then she smiles and asks if I can stay for a bit. I hesitate, but she says, "Come on. I just gave you two suitcases full of money; the least you can do is share a drink with me." She turns, and I follow her out the door and across the roofed pathway leading to the large mudroom at the back of the house. Marcie takes off her jacket, hangs it on a hook, and slips off her shoes. "Come on," she says again and leads me down a long hall to the great staircase by the front door.

We ascend the steps to the second floor, walk down another long hallway. Marcie opens a door to what she tells me is her personal sitting room. "Luxurious" doesn't do the space justice—it's like a beige-and-tan fantasy out of the *Arabian Nights*: plush wall-to-wall carpet; low-to-the-ground, U-shaped Roche Bobois sofa; six-foot candle stands; walls adorned with pastel paintings.

"I designed it myself."

I tell her I like it. "There's something comforting about it. Soothing."

Marcie nods. "I had it built out after my recurrence, when I found out the surgeons would have to carve me up like a turkey. I knew I would need a space where I could take care of myself. A healing space. Something very different than the rest of this Gothic rock pile." Marcie looks around the room, a faint smile touching her lips. "There was a time when I holed up here for a full month. There's a small bedroom with its own bath behind that door," she says, nodding to a door on the far wall. "I actually took my chemotherapy in this room. My oncologist came himself, sat with me through the IV. You can get pretty good service if you donate enough money to the right hospitals."

I glance at the floor-to-ceiling windows making up most of the back wall. "I imagine during the day this room is awash in sunlight."

"Yes," Marcie says. "And through the windows, I can take in most of the grounds." Then she frowns and stands up. "Though at night, the windows tend to darken the room." With that, she moves to the rear wall, presses a button, and blinds descend over the windows. Marcie motions for me to sit, and I lower myself onto the couch. She sits next to me, close enough that our knees are almost touching.

Before us sits a glass cocktail table on chrome legs. A silver serving tray is positioned in the middle. An open bottle of red wine and two stemmed glasses stand on the tray. Marcie leans forward and pours herself a glass, and then a second one for me. "You like pinot noir?"

I decline, and we sit in silence until Marcie starts up again. "My hair had fallen out, my breasts were gone, my skin was sallow. I became severely depressed, had no appetite. I lost so much weight I looked like a concentration-camp survivor." Marcie takes a sip, gives me a chance to let it all sink in.

"Eventually, my hair began to grow back, though I had to wear a wig for more than a year. There's a guy in New Jersey who does brilliant work, actually specializes in wigs for chemo patients. I started to eat again, gained some weight. When I was strong enough, I flew the boys to my sister's house in California to get away. That's where I was when David was arrested, when I got his call. A most unwelcome surprise."

Marcie shares all this with no trace of bitterness or sorrow in her voice. Her tone is frank, matter-of-fact, as though she were teaching a tennis lesson. I admire her for it. I also admire how she has turned herself around physically. Three weeks ago, when Susan and I came by, I saw how healthy Marcie looked. What I notice now is how fit she really is. Her sleeveless red-silk blouse and thin black skirt reveal her arms and long legs to be firm, even sculpted. And her chest, as I'd noticed before, is full.

"You've been through a lot," I say. "And it's probably of small consolation, but you look great."

Marcie smiles. "Thank you for saying so. I'm always open to a compliment. It makes all the hard work—the weight training, the running, the yoga, the reconstruction—worthwhile." She reaches out, touches my hand, her own very warm. Then she does something that completely stuns me. She reaches toward the cocktail table, picks up a gold case, opens it, and withdraws a cigarette. She lights it with a sleek ceramic lighter lying next to it.

You're kidding me. That's what I want to say to Marcie. *You just survived breast cancer, and now you're smoking?*

Marcie leans back and laughs. "Oh, Mick! The look on your face!" She takes a deep drag of the cigarette. "I was never a smoker," she says. "Not really. Oh, I would bum a cigarette or two when I was drinking, at a party, before my boys came along. But I never craved nicotine. Now, though, I smoke exactly one cigarette a day. It's my way of looking cancer in the eye and saying, 'Fuck you. You owned me for a while. You stole my body; you took my health. But now I'm back. I'm in control. And if you show up again, I'll set fire to your sorry ass just like I'm burning your little pet here.'" With that, Marcie takes another drag and forcefully expels the smoke. Then she leans forward, toward me, and crosses her lean, tan legs. She says, "And one thing you have to admit about smoking: if it's done right, it's sexy as hell."

Instead of agreeing, I steer the conversation in another direction. "How is David holding up?"

Marcie waits a beat, licks her lips, studies me. "He's worried," she says. "We both are. Of course. Our little ploy with the house in New York buoyed us for a while, but this whole videotape thing has us shaken." I nod my head several times, unsure what to say. Then Marcie asks me the same question David had asked. "What guarantee do we have that the blackmailer won't take our money and disclose the video anyway?"

"Guarantee? There is none. But it wouldn't make any sense to do so, because then David would have no reason not to tell the authorities that he'd been blackmailed, which would cause the police to hunt down the blackmailer. The smarter play for him," I say, pretending the blackmailer is a male, "is to take the money and run. And that is exactly what the blackmailer's told me he's going to do. Take the money and leave the country."

"And when he blows through the money in a year or two?"

"I don't think that's going to happen," I say. "My read on the blackmailer is that he's not the type to squander it. And even if he did and came back for more, David will already have been acquitted. And with double jeopardy—"

"Or convicted," Marcie says, interrupting me. "In which case, disclosure of the video would destroy any chance of a successful appeal. And even if David's acquitted, we'll face an uphill battle convincing everyone that he really is innocent. If the tape came out then, it'd be a disaster. So, no matter what happens, the blackmailer would be in a position to come back for more—and expect it."

I have to nod. Marcie's right.

"I don't suppose you want to share the identity of the blackmailer?" she asks.

"I can't. Along with the money, that's part of the deal."

Marcie looks away for a quick second, then looks back at me and changes the subject. "How is Piper? How are things between the two of you?"

The question stops me. I blink before answering. "Piper is good."

"And things are good?" Marcie leans into me as she asks, puts her hand on my thigh. Again, I feel her warmth. Now I'm really taken aback. Marcie is making a play, and she's not trying to disguise it.

"Marcie . . ." I close my leg, slide away from her.

Marcie purses her lips, repositions herself a little farther down the sofa. Then she laughs. "Mick, you can't be serious!" She's covering herself, backtracking now that I've rebuffed her. "I expect that you've seen couples driven apart by what David and I are going through. But I'd have thought that you could see by now that David and I are working together on this thing. That we're a team."

"You certainly seemed to be on the same page when you pulled that stunt with the New York geisha house."

Marcie takes a last drag on her cigarette, long and slow. Then she leans forward, stubs it out in the ashtray. "The last time you were here, I told you that David and I have had some long talks since his arrest. And we have. Long and difficult. David has told me many things. Things I'd rather not have learned. One thing David *didn't* tell me was that he killed Jennifer Yamura, and I can assure you, I asked him point-blank. He swears he didn't, and I believe him."

I let this hang in the air for a moment, then ask something I wish was unnecessary. "In these talks you had, did David happen to let you in on his alibi? Where he was when Jennifer was being killed? Not that BS about walking a marathon up and down the sunny banks of the Schuylkill River, but where he really was?"

Marcie hesitates, looks away, and I realize instantly that David has told her. And I also know why Marcie made a play for me.

"Tell me," I say, "was it a *team* decision that David had to be somewhere else tonight?"

Now it's Marcie's turn to stare at me. "David didn't kill that girl, Mick. And he can't go to prison."

"Whatever it takes?" I ask.

Marcie picks up her glass, takes a sip, and looks away.

"You tell me David insists he didn't kill Jennifer Yamura. What if he'd told you he did kill her?"

Marcie doesn't miss a beat. "I'd lie through my teeth and say otherwise. But that's not the case."

"I believe you," I say.

"That David's innocent?"

"That you'd lie through your teeth."

Ten uncomfortable minutes later, I'm back in my car. The exchange with Marcie Hanson has left me nonplussed. The whole thing was a setup. The plan was for Marcie to seduce me. Maybe go through with it, or maybe stop it just in time. Either way, Marcie and David would have something on me, something they could hang over my head. A secondary goal was to convince me, once and for all, of David's innocence. Looking back on the whole weird scene, I know Marcie was honest about one thing: she and David continue to work as a team.

22

FRIDAY, OCTOBER 12

"Daddy, I think we should play hockey again," Gabby says. "I want to go back and see the tigers."

Gabrielle, Piper, and I are sitting around the island in our kitchen, finishing breakfast.

Piper rolls her eyes. "I think we've created a monster."

Gabby means hooky. The day I took off from work, Piper called Gabby's school and told them our daughter wasn't feeling well and was staying home. I'd told Gabby, "We're all playing hooky today, and we're going to the zoo." You'd have thought I'd just told Gabrielle that it was Christmas.

Gabby loved the zoo, running from one set of animals to another, eager to drink them all in. Watching our daughter so happy filled me with joy, and I promised both Piper and Gabby that there would be lots more trips like that from then on.

That night, after dinner, we watched a Disney flick and cozied up together on the sofa. When the movie was over, I carried Gabrielle up to her bed, dressed her in her pajamas, and tucked her in. While Piper got ready for bed herself, I came back downstairs, ran the dishwasher, let Franklin out one last time, and turned off all the lights. When I climbed into bed next to Piper, I thought she was asleep. I turned onto my side, spooned her, and to my surprise, Piper backed into me. And things took a course they hadn't taken in a long, long time.

"It's not 'hockey,' peanut," I tell Gabby. "It's 'hooky.' And if you do it more than once, the principal gets wise and makes you stay after school." Gabby slumps in her seat, turns away as I try to kiss her good-bye. A quick tickle changes her mood, and she gives me a full-on hug around the neck as I bend over her. "I'm on my way," I tell Piper, kissing her as I pick my car keys off the counter. "I won't be home late tonight. Maybe 7:30."

Plodding along with the heavy traffic on the Schuylkill Expressway, I'm nervous as hell. My trunk has two suitcases stuffed with money, and I'm petrified of getting into an accident. I envision a fender bender sending a cloud of green paper exploding out the back of my car, the highway jam-packed by a mile-long pile up of cars, trucks, and thousands of people streaming through it to pick up the money and run.

I reach town and park the car on the north side of Pine Street, across from Anna Groszek's house. I look up and down the street as I lift the suitcases out of the trunk. I roll the bags across the street and lift them up the white marble steps and onto the small marble stoop by the front door. My heart pounding, I ring the bell. I hear footsteps on the other side of the heavy door. When the door opens, it isn't Anna Groszek, but an enormous young man in black pants and a red golf shirt stretched across his broad chest. He's six three, at least, and must weigh 250 pounds. The man's eyes are ice blue like Anna's, his jaw chiseled like the rest of his rock-solid physique. He looks to be in his midtwenties. Without a word, he leans down and grabs both of the suitcases and turns around. I follow him inside.

We take a few steps down the center hallway, then turn left through sliding pocket doors and into a large sitting room. In the center of the room, across from the doors are two antique couches facing each other across a coffee table. Anna Groszek, sitting forward in one of the couches, motions for me to sit in the other. Her friend remains standing and takes a position behind Anna.

Anna sees me looking at her friend and says, "My nephew, Boris." I nod and glance up again at him. His eyes narrow as he returns the look.

Anna pours coffee from a white porcelain pot into a pair of dainty porcelain cups. She asks me if I would like cream or milk. I start to say neither, that I've had my morning ration of coffee, but Boris stiffens. I tell her milk will be fine. Anna pours the milk, then lifts my cup and hands it to me across the coffee table. I thank Anna, take a sip of the coffee. It's very good, and I say so.

Anna nods, and we sit quietly and, from my end, uncomfortably. All I want to do is get the video and tell Anna to get away before the Hansons come after her. But the old woman is stretching this out deliberately. She knows I'm ill at ease, and she's having fun watching me squirm. Finally, Anna decides it's time to move things along.

"It's all there? The amount we agreed to? Yes?"

"Yes," I say. "I've counted it myself."

Anna looks back at Boris, who walks to the suitcases, lays them on their sides, and opens them. His eyes widen when he sees the money. Anna remains impassive. "Very good," she says. "Of course, we will count it ourselves, once you've left."

I exhale, relieved. "Of course."

Anna waves to Boris to zip up the suitcases. She watches him do so. We both do. Then the old woman turns to me and asks, "Your client, he was good with this?"

"Not hardly," I say. "But I convinced him that he had no choice."

"As I knew you would." With that, Anna reaches into a white leather handbag and removes a mustard-colored nine-by-seven-inch envelope. "As we agreed," she says, handing me the envelope. "Two copies."

I reach out for the envelope, take it, and bring it to my lap. I hesitate. "These are all the copies of the video? There are no others?"

Anna Groszek casts me a cold look. I have offended her. "Your client is safe. You have honored your end of the bargain, and now so do I."

Anna stands and I follow her lead. "Look," I say, "there's something you should know. I'm pretty sure Mr. Hanson has figured out you're the source of the video. The angle of the video is straight on and down, and yours is the house directly behind Jennifer Yamura's house. My client is a powerful man, Mrs. Groszek. And recent events indicate to me that he's more cunning than I'd given him credit for. And more dangerous. I'm not sure when you're planning on leaving the country, but I'm thinking the sooner the better."

The old woman processes what I've just told her. She looks once at Boris, then back at me. "Do not worry about me, Mr. McFarland. This money will be deposited this morning into my bank and wired immediately to my other bank in Poland. Tomorrow, Boris and I fly on US Air to Frankfurt, then to Warsaw."

"Envoy class, of course."

Anna Groszek smiles.

23

SATURDAY, OCTOBER 20; SUNDAY, OCTOBER 21

It's been a week since I met Anna Groszek, and Piper and I are in our room at the Park Hyatt at the Bellevue. We checked in an hour ago, enough time to change and get ready before heading down to the ballroom and this year's American Way charity gala.

I watch Piper pull on the strapless black Romona Keveza gown she bought at Latrice, a pricey boutique in Bryn Mawr. The dress looks great against her shoulder-length blonde hair, and I say so. I put on my jacket, and we leave the room, take the elevator down to the hotel lobby, and walk toward the elliptical marble-and-iron stairwell that leads up one flight to the grand ballroom. The ballroom is vast. Almost a hundred feet long and eighty feet wide, with thirty-foot ceilings, the space can comfortably accommodate eight hundred people. Tonight it holds seventy-five tables set for ten. Each is fitted out in white linen, white china, sterling silver, and glistening crystal stemware—appropriate for the annual blue-chip charity affair. I lead Piper into the room, toward our table near the front. I spot Kimberly Baldwin, who, apparently, will be sitting with us. Next to Kimberly is a good-looking man who appears to be twenty years her senior. The imprisonment of Kimberly's husband, Phillip, doesn't seem to have stunted her social life.

"Hello, Mick. Piper, you look smashing!" Kimberly gushes as she leans in to kiss me and Piper. Kimberly introduces us to her date. "My dear, dear friend, Allen Cohen. He's been such a godsend to me through the nightmare of the past two years."

Piper praises Kimberly's gown and hair, and Kimberly makes Piper promise to give Kimberly the name of her stylist. Allen and I are exchanging small talk about the Eagles when I spot my partner, Susan, coming up to the table. Piper and I stand to greet her.

Just as Susan joins us, I hear Piper say, "Uh-oh." I turn my head in time to see Devlin Walker approaching us. With him is his wife, Leisha, wearing a blue sequined gown altered to accommodate her condition. She's visibly pregnant, her abdomen sticking out, though you probably couldn't tell if you were standing behind her. Leisha is apparently one of those lucky women who carries her pregnancy only in the front. "Basketball on a stick," Piper once described it.

"Hello, Mick, Piper," Devlin says, extending his hand. "Leisha, you remember Mick and Piper McFarland from Mick's days at the DA's office. This is Mick's law partner, Susan Klein."

"So, when are you due?" Piper asks Leisha.

"If I stuck myself with one of those temperature thingies turkeys come with nowadays," Leisha says, "it would pop."

We all smile, then Leisha says to Devlin, "Come on, honey, I need to sit down." Devlin takes Leisha's arm, and they walk away.

We take our seats, and I scan the room. Our table is one row back from the stage. The front line of tables includes three containing the American Way of Eastern Pennsylvania officers and directors and their spouses. Another table is filled with local politicians. I see the president of the city council and his wife. Seated with him is the chairman of the Philadelphia Democratic City Committee and his wife, and the president judge of the court of common pleas and her husband.

The fifth table in the front row was purchased, as it is every year, by Hanson World Industries. David's half brother, Edwin, sits facing the stage. The physical differences between Edwin and David are striking. Where David is tall and lean, Edwin is a fireplug, maybe five foot seven, and thick and solid as rock. In contrast to David's fair complexion and sandy-blond hair, Edwin is olive-skinned and has dark hair. There is something striking about David's older brother, though. He radiates strength, energy. Not the charismatic Kennedy type that wins instant affection, but the subdued, smoldering kind that commands respect, even fear. Contributing greatly to this are Edwin's eyes: wide set on his large face and deep and dark, almost black. They give the impression that they front a keen and calculating intelligence.

To Edwin's left is a dour woman who appears to be in her late forties and who I assume is Edwin's date. To Edwin's right are Kevin Kratz, David's law-school lackey, and Kevin's wife, Loretta. After we graduated, David made sure to enlist Kevin to follow him to HWI's general counsel's office. Based on what I've learned recently about David, my guess is that he knew that in order to seize the general-counsel position, he would need a loyal lieutenant by his side at HWI, just as he did in college and law school. Ironically, when David stepped down, Edwin tapped Kevin Kratz to succeed him. I'm sure this galls David, and I'm equally sure that was a big part of why Edwin did it. To the left of Edwin's date sits Brandon Landis, the president of HWI's North American operations. Next to Brandon is his trophy wife, Lauren. The last two seats at the HWI table are empty. I wonder who had the audacity to stand up Edwin Hanson by no-showing.

Edwin looks tense. Even more tense is Kevin Kratz, whose facial tic, a twitching of the right side of his mouth, is running on overdrive.

One row back from us, in the third row, is Devlin's table. He and Leisha are seated there with three other couples. I recognize two of the men and one of the women as assistant district attorneys. Among them is one of my closest allies in the turf war Devlin and I waged before I left the prosecutor's office. From what I hear, he's now Devlin's best friend. I think of the many bridges I burned with the thoughtless manner of my departure. A wave of sadness sweeps through me.

After a moment, I feel Piper's hand on my own. She leans toward me and whispers in my ear, "Are you all right?"

Before I can answer, a sudden silence seizes the room. For some reason, my eye alights on Kevin Kratz. His twitching has stopped. His face is frozen marble. Then he says something to Edwin, and I see Edwin's left hand form into a fist.

I feel Piper's hand on my own, pressing down hard. I turn to her and see that she's facing the back of the room, the central door, where David and Marcie stand smiling, poised to enter.

"What the hell is he doing here?" Susan says. "What is he thinking?" Piper continues to press my hand.

Then Kimberly Baldwin puts her two cents in. "Ooh la la. This is going to get interesting."

David and Marcie glide across the room. David's custom-made tuxedo is perfectly tailored to fit his broad shoulders. His diamond studs and cuff links sparkle in the light cast by the massive chandeliers. Marcie is stunning. She's wearing a strapless, ombré, floral-print gown in hues of green and silver. Formfitting, the dress highlights her trim figure and generous bosom. Her lustrous raven hair kisses her bare collarbones.

"Would you look at that ice . . ." Kimberly says, referring to Marcie's necklace, a five-strand beaded creation of emeralds accented with round brilliant diamonds that would put Harry Winston to shame. I glance at the necklace, but I'm more captivated by Marcie's green eyes, which seem to gather in the emerald light of the stones; her irises have an almost otherworldly glow.

"Like they were the king and queen," says Allen Cohen.

Susan and I exchange uncomfortable glances, shake our heads. I know she's thinking the same thing I am: *Bad move. Bad freaking move.*

I notice now that Piper no longer has her hand on mine. Instead, both of her hands are under the table. I'm guessing she's rubbing them furiously, something she does when she's especially nervous.

David and Marcie reach the HWI table, where no one rises to meet them. David leans down to Edwin and offers his hand. Edwin accepts it, reluctantly, his eyes filled with fury. Then Marcie leans down and pecks Edwin on the cheek, and she and David move around the table. Edwin's date smiles nervously, and Brandon and Lauren Landis are cold but polite. Kevin Kratz's wife certainly understands what's happening but looks too bored and miserable to care. Then David and Marcie reach Kratz himself. David hovers over Kratz, staring down at him, without offering his hand. Kratz glances at Edwin, then, drawn by the force of David's will, stands up and extends his own hand. David waits before accepting, then leans in and whispers something in our classmate's ear. Kratz turns positively white.

The whole room has watched this little play unfold, and everyone is talking about what they've seen. At our own table, Kimberly Baldwin expresses her distaste for Edwin and her hope that David's clever lawyers help him beat the charges, forgetting, it seems, that those clever lawyers are sitting with her. Susan gapes openly at Kimberly when she says this. Piper continues to lean forward in her seat, her hands beneath the table. From a table behind me, I hear references to Cain and Abel and Romulus and Remus. For my part, I'm still flummoxed as to why David, soon to face a jury likely composed of blue-collar workers struggling to make ends meet, would show up at a black-tie gala. He's smarter than this. So is Marcie.

A few minutes later, just after our salads are delivered, the band stops. I notice Candace Stengel, the American Way chairperson, up on the stage. She gives the typical introductory remarks, naming the other officers and directors with her tonight, thanks everyone for donating their time and money, and makes a fuss over the politicians sitting in the front row. Then she says something about tonight being "especially special" thanks to a pair of exceptionally generous gifts made by two of our fellow attendees. "I first want to thank Kimberly Baldwin, who has reached out to the American Way during a tragically painful time in her life. It would have been easy for Kimberly, whom I count as one of my dearest friends, to have become cynical. But Kimberly, as we all know, is the eternal optimist and never one to be kept down. And she's shown it to the American Way tonight by donating a hundred thousand dollars."

Kimberly basks in the praise. But I know the reason behind her generosity isn't to get accolades or do good—she simply wants everyone to know she's still rich. Still in the game.

When the clapping dies down, Candace continues with a short speech about the American Way's philosophy of focusing on the community, working with neighborhood groups to empower individual citizens through education, employment, and financial assistance. "American Way really defines what it means to be a grass-roots organization," she says. "And here in Philadelphia, there is one company that has kept its boots on the ground and marched right beside us for more than a quarter century. That company, as most of you know, is Hanson World Industries, Philadelphia's own homegrown Fortune 500 company. And I am proud—no, breathless—to announce that in addition to HWI's annual corporate gift, one of its directors has today donated the unprecedented sum of one million dollars to our Educational Impact Fund."

The room falls completely silent. All eyes move to the HWI table just below Candace at the front of the room. All eyes, that is, but mine and Susan's. We've both figured it out, and we're looking at each other.

Candace spends the next five minutes gushing about the generosity of David and Marcie Hanson. I study her face for some sly signal to her guests that her praise is tongue in cheek. But she betrays no crack in the apparent sincerity with which she sings tribute to my clever client and his Machiavellian wife. It can't be easy for Candace, I'm sure. David has been charged with a young woman's murder. But $1 million is $1 million. And Candace will put that money to good use.

As for the crowd, it is a squirming millipede. Legs crossing and uncrossing. Hands wringing, fingers fiddling. Pained, even cringing, faces. Most everyone clearly wants to stand up and shout: *Candace! The guy's a murderer! Take his money, okay. But shut up, already!*

And then comes something even harder to bear. Candace calls David Hanson up to the stage to say a few words, accept the organization's thanks.

David kisses Marcie, then stands and glides to the steps that lead him up to the stage. Candace hugs him, hands him the microphone, then steps aside. David starts his speech by lamenting the high school dropout rate in Philly's poor inner-city neighborhoods. African American neighborhoods are particularly hard hit by this plague, he tells us. The very children who most need education to raise themselves out of the poverty into which they've been unfairly cast by birth and circumstance have the hardest time staying in school. And that is why, he says, he felt compelled to donate a million dollars to the American Way's Educational Impact Fund. Real money to address a real problem.

Somewhere in the middle of David's speech, I glance back a couple of rows, to where Devlin Walker is sitting. I see my adversary staring at my client, utterly motionless. What I also see is the smile on Devlin's lips. It's there because Devlin, like Susan and I, knows that this is all going to come back to bite David in the ass. Perhaps sensing me, Devlin turns in my direction. His smile grows just a little wider, and he raises his glass ever so slightly. I turn away.

Later, after dinner, Piper visits the ladies' room while Susan and I take up positions near one of the two small bars set up in the foyer. I spot David and Marcie in the back of the ballroom, talking with two couples. The men I recognize as senior partners in a big defense firm that handles a lot of HWI's legal work. Both lawyers are visibly uncomfortable. They cannot afford to irritate Edwin Hanson, who could pull their assignments on a moment's notice. On the other hand, they can't disrespect David, either, because if he wins an acquittal and returns as general counsel at HWI, he'll be the one holding their purse strings.

Susan is more interested in Marcie Hanson than in David. "She's like Madame Defarge in *A Tale of Two Cities*." The comparison to the female revolutionary who knits the names of the people she wants killed when the revolution finally comes strikes me as apt. "She's taking notes on how people are treating her husband. Those who treat David well will be taken care of when he returns to power. Those who don't will lose their heads."

"*When* he returns? Not *if*?"

"Look at them," Susan says of David and Marcie. "They're acting like there's no doubt in their minds. I think they're absolutely certain David is going to beat the charges."

"He has great lawyers," I say, trying to sound carefree myself, though I am far less certain of David's fate, even given the things I know that David doesn't. A moment later, I watch David and Marcie take their leave of the corporate attorneys and walk toward us. "Give me a minute with them," I ask of Susan. I walk to meet the Hansons.

"I need to speak with you—both of you," I say. Then I lead them to an unoccupied corner of the foyer. "What the hell are you two doing at a gala? Tuxedo and ball gown? An emerald necklace that costs more than most people's houses? Diamond cuff links? Seriously, what the hell?"

David and Marcie look at each other, smile. "There's nothing to worry about," Marcie says.

"We have a plan," David pipes in.

"A plan? *You* have a plan? Hey, guys, I'm your lawyer. The show is run according to *my* plan."

David casts me a cool look. "Once we're in court, Mick, it's all you. Your speeches. Your questions. Your choice of witnesses. Your strategy. But we're not in court yet. We're still out here, in the real world. And

Marcie and I are taking measures of our own to win the proverbial hearts and minds."

"But you're not winning over anyone. Didn't you see how everyone reacted to your donation? Your speech? They couldn't have turned their noses away any faster if they'd walked into a room full of dead skunks."

"The donation and speech weren't for the people at this party," David answers. "They were for my jurors. The people who will actually decide whether I spend the rest of my life in prison. The Philadelphians who live in shithole neighborhoods, whose kids have the highest drop-out rates in the country. The people whose kids I've just given a million dollars to help."

Now I'm steamed. "First of all, most Philadelphians do not live in 'shithole' neighborhoods. They live in working-class neighborhoods, with decent schools. Second, even the truly poor in the city will see your gesture as transparent. People will feel like you're trying to buy them off. Tomorrow morning there's going to be a big story in the *Inquirer* portraying this gambit of yours as nothing more than a bribe. How do you think the jury pool will feel about you then?"

"We've taken care of the *Inquirer*," Marcie says. And with that, she takes David by the arm and leads him away.

Seeing them leave, Susan joins me. "That looked like it got pretty heated. You better ratchet yourself down a little. This place is full of photographers. You don't want to see some nasty picture in the paper tomorrow of you arguing with our clients."

Piper approaches Susan and me at the bar, and I excuse myself to go to the men's room. As I'm walking, Devlin Walker comes up next to me, asks me how my brother's doing. My hackles go up instantly.

"Speaking of Tommy," Devlin says, "how's his buddy Lawrence Washington? I hear they're close."

"How would Tommy even know Lawrence?"

"You think if we brought Tommy in, he could give us some insight as to where Lawrence is holed up?"

"You're not bringing Tommy in," I say. "Ever."

Devlin shrugs. "Well, he could just come in voluntarily. Answer a few questions."

"Back off, Devlin," I say, then turn to leave. Walking away, I make up my mind that of all the people who will have to pay to save my family from the Jennifer Yamura fiasco, Devlin Fucking Walker is going to suffer the most.

Later, in the hotel room after Piper falls asleep, I toss and turn. At four, I sit up in a cold sweat. I get off the bed, walk to the bathroom, close the door. I turn on the cold water, cup it in my hands, and splash my face. For a long time, I stare at myself in the mirror.

"Mick?" It's Piper calling me from the bed. "Are you all right?"

I tell her I'm fine, that something I ate must have disagreed with me.

I climb back into bed. I lie on my back, and Piper puts her arm around me, her face on my chest. We're both quiet but awake.

After a while, Piper says, "Marcie looked great. Didn't she?"

"Stunning."

Another minute passes, then I hear Piper's voice, small and hesitant. "What's going to happen, Mick?"

The question hangs in the darkness until I answer. "It'll work out. I promise. It'll all work out."

Piper hugs me tighter. She doesn't believe me.

Later that morning, Sunday, Piper and I enjoy breakfast in the restaurant on the top floor of the hotel. The restaurant is a grand space, composed of two large rotundas with thirty-six-foot domes and floor-to-ceiling windows. We sit at a table for two next to one of the windows, drink mimosas, and gorge ourselves on Sunday brunch. We start with smoked Scottish salmon, cheeses, and salads from the café table. Then Piper has a Belgian waffle and I have the crab-cake Benedict. We finish off with mini cakes and parfaits. All the while, we gossip like schoolgirls about the dramas of the night before.

When we're finished, I pick up an *Inquirer* from the front desk and carry it back to the room. While Piper packs, I open the paper and look for the article reporting David and Marcie Hanson's extravagant gift to the American Way. It doesn't take long to find it; the article is on page two, above the fold. The reporter, a name unfamiliar to me, gushes even more about the Hansons than Candace Stengel had the night before. And not just about last night's gift. To the contrary, the article laundry-lists a dozen other sizable donations David and Marcie have made in the last decade to organizations as diverse as breastcancer.org, the Jewish Defense League, the United Negro College Fund, the Human Rights Campaign, Catholic Charities USA, Planned Parenthood, the Police Athletic League, Greenpeace, and the SPCA.

"What are you reading?" Piper asks me as she packs away her gown.

"The biographies of Saints David and Marcie," I answer. Then I return to the article and the photographs of the Hansons. The editors have chosen two plain head shots. The pictures taken last night of David and Marcie in their formal wear and jewels have been deep-sixed.

I sit back and wonder what they're planning next. And worry.

24

WEDNESDAY, OCTOBER 24

It's the Wednesday after the gala, just before five o'clock. I'm sitting in my office in front of my computer. Jury selection in the Hanson trial begins in three weeks, and I'm working around the clock getting the case ready. I've begun writing cross-examinations of the prosecution's likely witnesses and direct examinations of my own witnesses. I'm satisfied that I can poke some serious holes in the prosecution's case. Not enough to guarantee reasonable doubt, but that won't matter if everything goes as I'm hoping and the jury never gets the chance to reach a verdict.

A loud knock at the door, and Vaughn rushes in.

"You're not going to believe this." He hands me what appears to be a legal brief, then drops into a visitor's chair.

"What is it?"

"Devlin's filed a motion seeking to disqualify you as David's lawyer."

"You're fucking kidding me. On what grounds?"

"The phone calls from Jennifer Yamura's cell phone to our office. Walker is claiming that they were from David, that they prove he was at Yamura's house, using her cell, within the time period of her death."

"That's ridiculous," I say. "Those calls were from Jennifer herself. And even if they had been from David, they'd be privileged as attorney-client communications."

Vaughn shakes his head. "Not if they were part of an effort to conceal a crime."

"You're not telling me—"

Vaughn answers before I can complete my question. "Walker's posturing to set you up as an accessory after the fact."

"I don't believe this," I say, bolting from my chair. "Wait a minute." I move over to my phone and hit "0" for Angie. "The day Jennifer Yamura was killed," I tell my secretary, "do you remember her calling here and asking for me? And you put her through?" Angie says of course she does. "There!" I say to Vaughn. "Devlin's motion is bullshit, and we can prove it."

But Vaughn, who has read Devlin's motion, leans into the speaker and asks, "Both times?"

There's a pause on the other end of the line. "Both times what?" Angie asks. "She called here once. I put her through to you, Mick, and you took the call. Tommy was in your office with you; he knows, too."

"Shit," I say. "Angie was at lunch the second time she called. I picked up the line myself. And Tommy had left by then."

Vaughn frowns.

"When is the hearing set for?"

"Two days."

I exhale. "I can't believe Devlin is pulling this kind of crap. He knows Judge Henry isn't going to buy into this. He's up to something."

I work with Vaughn for several hours on our answer to the prosecution's motion to disqualify me. Once Vaughn's gone, I start in on a mound of other work and don't lift my head until the City Hall clock outside my window strikes midnight. On the way home, I stop at a Wawa. Piper had called me around ten, saying we had no skim milk for her coffee in the morning. An *Inquirer* deliveryman drops off the next day's papers as I enter the store, and I take a look at the front page to find that David and Marcie continue to move full steam ahead on the PR campaign. The new article is just below the fold on the right-hand side. It's a one-column article that carries over to the business section, where it takes up half the page. Its headline reads, "Hanson's Quest for Philly Jobs," and it tells how David's singular focus at HWI has been to leverage the company's burgeoning relationships in Asia to build Philadelphia's own manufacturing base.

"There's been too much foreign outsourcing of jobs," David is quoted as saying. "My mission at HWI was, and will be again, to reverse that tide and bring jobs back home."

The article's author explains a convoluted business deal David had been working on before he began his "temporary leave of absence" to "address his present personal difficulties." The deal involved Kimozuma Unryu, a Japanese shipping company, along with Yokahama Tokai, a Japanese manufacturer of sophisticated navigation equipment, and the Chinese steel giant Angong Steel. The way David had negotiated it, HWI would purchase navigation equipment from Yokahama Tokai and steel from Angong Steel and use both in the building of a fleet of container ships that HWI would assemble in Philadelphia, in partnership with the Aker Philadelphia Shipyard. Yokahama would buy the ships. It was to have been a two-decade, multi-billion-dollar deal that, in David's words, "would have added three thousand jobs in Philadelphia, forever." Continuing, the article outlines two other similarly complicated deals that would have added thousands more jobs to the local community.

"The linchpin of all of these deals," the article concludes, "was David Hanson himself. Although technically employed in HWI's legal department as general counsel, Mr. Hanson was the executive within the company who had forged the personal relationships on which all the

Asian deals were built. According to sources at HWI, until Mr. Hanson returns, these deals will remain on hold. 'Which is why,' Mr. Hanson says, 'I have pushed so hard for a quick trial date on my own matter, to ensure these deals are consummated and the jobs are brought to Philadelphia.'"

I drop the paper back onto the pile. How many more stories have David and Marcie Hanson planted to appear between now and the time of David's trial? Will their plotting be limited to stories in the news, or will it involve more grandiose gestures as we get closer to the courthouse steps?

Of course, the Hansons' plans are not the only thing I have to contend with. Now Devlin Walker is trying to get me booted from the case. And nothing could be worse for anyone on our side than that.

25

Friday, October 26

At 1:00 p.m. sharp, Angie buzzes me in my office to tell me that David and Marcie Hanson are here to discuss Devlin's attempt to cut me out of the case. I ask Angie to bring them back. The first thing David says to me when Angie leads them into my office is, "Did you see the article?" I wait for him and Marcie to sit before I respond.

"Yes," I answer coolly. "And it was a bad idea. If it ever comes out that you were the one behind the story, that you planted it to prejudice the jury pool, the press itself will hang you."

"Nothing's going to come out," Marcie says. "There's no way to trace the story to David, or to me."

"There's always a way," I say. "But we really don't have time to be arguing this. Right now we have to get ready for this hearing."

"Hey, just put me on the stand," David says, "and I'll deny I was the one who called you. With your testimony that should be enough, shouldn't it?"

"But I can't put you on the stand, David, because that would subject you to cross-examination. And the first thing Devlin Walker will ask is where you were at the time of the murders. You'd have to disclose your alibi, tell the court where you really were."

David leans into my desk. "I don't need an alibi to create reasonable doubt. I've reviewed the so-called evidence over and over in my mind. They don't have enough to convict. There's no evidence of motive. None whatsoever. Because I *had* no motive to kill Jennifer," he adds quickly. "And with that video safely tucked away, they have no evidence that I was at the house anywhere near the time she was killed."

"And your attempt to clean up the murder scene?" I ask. "And running away when the cops showed up?"

"I did all that out of panic," he says. "I was worried that my affair with Jennifer would be revealed and that the scandal would derail HWI's deals with Japan and China."

"The deals that would have created so many jobs here," Marcie adds, smiling. "At least, that's what I read in the paper."

I sigh. There's no getting through to these two. All the initial terror David had displayed when he was first arraigned has vanished. He is now fully—and foolishly—confident that he will be acquitted at trial.

By two o'clock, we're all in Courtroom 1007 on the tenth floor of the Criminal Justice Center. David sits next to me at the counsel table, Marcie right behind us. At the prosecution table, Devlin is accompanied by ADA Christina Wesley, a short, thick woman whose face remains locked in a perpetual frown. The courtroom is nothing like the vast, grand courtrooms in the movies. It is a small space: spectators' benches, counsel tables, jury box, court reporter's box, deputies' and law clerks' desks crammed into a sixty-by-forty-foot room. It's the courthouse equivalent of an office cubicle. A close, cramped space when populated only by parties and lawyers, it's positively claustrophobic when packed with spectators. Like today.

The Honorable William Henry sits on the bench, his robe hanging loosely over his shoulders. He's not happy about the prosecution's motion, and he's clearly livid about the circus of reporters in his courtroom.

"Mr. Walker," Henry starts in on Devlin, "are you really serious about this? You really think defense counsel helped Mr. Hanson cover up the crime?"

"If there's another explanation," Walker responds, "the people are ready to hear it."

This is my cue to shoot to my feet.

"The state *has* already heard it," I exclaim. "Back at the end of August, Detectives Tredesco and Cook came to my office asking about the calls. I told them then, and I'm telling the court now, that those calls were placed to me by Jennifer Yamura herself. And I have in the courtroom with me Mrs. Angela Toscano, my secretary, who took the first call, and who can testify that it was Jennifer Yamura and not Mr. Hanson on the other end." At the mention of her name, Angie stands. "I also have present in the courtroom my brother and the firm's investigator, Mr. Thomas McFarland, who was present when I took the first call and to whom I described the call once it was over." Tommy is standing now, too. My heart has been breaking for him since his gravesite confession. As soon as the Hanson case is over, I'm going to sit down with him and throw open the floodgates of my guilt and shame at having abandoned him.

Judge Henry looks from Tommy to Angie to Devlin Walker. "If these two witnesses take the stand and testify, as defense counsel has represented they will, will that be enough for you?"

Devlin hesitates, so the judge waves him off and tells me to call my witnesses and be done with this. So I call Angie to the stand and then Tommy. Devlin's questioning of each is cursory. With Angie, he simply makes a point of confirming what I've already told the judge, that Angie took only the first call. When Tommy takes the stand, he tells the court he was in my office for the first call, and that afterward, I told him it had been Jennifer Yamura on the line. There had been no mention of David

Hanson, and I didn't seem the least bit upset after I'd hung up. Devlin limits his cross-examination to two questions, the first one establishing that Tommy is indeed my own brother, the second one establishing that Tommy is a convicted felon. Judge Henry rolls his eyes at the first question and looks visibly annoyed with Devlin over the second.

"So, Mr. Walker," the judge says, "you've established that, one, Thomas McFarland is biased, and two, he should be ashamed of himself. How much farther do we have to go with this?"

Before Devlin can answer, I hear a commotion behind me. I turn to see that the reporters are all facing the back doors. Detective John Tredesco, Edwin Hanson, and Kevin Kratz, along with two men and two women I've never seen before, have entered the courtroom. With them is Caroline Robb, an assistant district attorney with the DA's financial-crimes unit.

David Hanson leans into me and asks, "What the hell is this?"

I tell him I have no idea, although I now understand what this hearing was really all about. Inwardly, I smile.

Very clever, Devlin.

This is actually what I was hoping for.

"Your Honor," Devlin Walker addresses the judge, "I apologize and ask the court's indulgence for one minute. This could be very important."

Bill Henry is now officially pissed off. "One minute, counselor. And it better be important."

Devlin and Christina Wesley confer with Caroline Robb, who hands Devlin some papers. Every now and then, Devlin or Christina looks to the back of the courtroom at Edwin, the two men, or the two women. This is an act—the whole thing. Devlin Walker knows exactly who everyone is and what they're there for.

"Your Honor," Devlin begins, "in light of the testimony by defense counsel's secretary and brother, the people are willing to withdraw, for now, our petition to remove Mr. McFarland as defense counsel."

"The motion is withdrawn—and not just for now." Judge Henry leans forward. "Now, who are all these people?"

Devlin takes a deep breath, as though he's upset by what he has to tell the court. "Your Honor, I didn't want to raise it with the court until I was absolutely certain, but now I am. The people have received strong evidence that Mr. Hanson is planning to flee the jurisdiction."

This stops everyone in the courtroom cold.

"This is bullshit," I say, shooting to my feet.

"Your Honor," Devlin continues, his voice soft and matter-of-fact, "the people have learned that Mr. Hanson has been siphoning cash from personal and corporate accounts, and—"

"How much money?" William Henry interrupts.

Devlin waits before answering, allowing the drama to build. "Four. Million. Dollars."

I hear several of the reporters gasp. The court stenographer's eyes bulge, and the judge's courtroom deputy does a double take. David slumps in his seat. He's screwed, and he knows it. Judge Henry stares down at me, then looks at David. We have nothing, so the judge looks back at Walker, who resumes.

"I have the CEO and the general counsel of Hanson World Industries, who will testify to the defendant's embezzlement of two million dollars from HWI. Also here is Detective Caroline Robb, from our financial-crimes unit, to testify that the defendant withdrew an equal amount from a personal account in the Cayman Islands."

"And how did you know to go to Hanson World Industries?" asks the judge.

Walker pauses before answering. "We received an anonymous call," he says, causing Bill Henry to narrow his eyes. "I know, Your Honor. I know. At first, we didn't give the call any credence. It seemed too far-fetched to believe that the defendant would do something so transparent as withdrawing vast sums of money on the eve of his trial. Still, we had to follow up the lead. So I called our financial-crimes unit and asked Ms. Robb to call HWI and see if there was anything to it. She reached Mr. Kratz, who said the claim was insane but that he'd check into it. He got back to us two days later and said that, in fact, Mr. Hanson had personally taken two million dollars in cash from the vault of a corporate subsidiary near Mexico City. We also learned that, from Mexico, the defendant had the company jet fly him to the city of George Town on Grand Cayman Island, where he withdrew two million more from a numbered account in a private bank."

I know already how this is going to turn out for David. The Philadelphia criminal-court system has been plagued by defendants failing to appear for trial since the 1960s, when the court abolished commercial bail as a result of scandals involving private bail bondsmen, leaving it to the court itself to handle pretrial releases. In 2010, the *Inquirer* presented an investigative series showing that massive numbers of arrestees ducked hearings after posting 10 percent of the bail amount. Philadelphia's FTA, or failure-to-appear rate, was the highest in the nation. Forty-seven thousand defendants were long-term fugitives from the court, which was owed more than $1 billion in forfeited bail. To address this problem, the state supreme court enacted changes in 2012 to help private bail firms finance bail, based on studies showing that defendants are more likely to show up for hearings if bail is posted through private bail bondsmen as opposed to being posted by the defendants themselves. Taking their cue from the state supreme court, the Philly trial judges have taken a hard line on defendants who skip out before trial.

Devlin's first witness is Brad Collins, an HWI pilot. Collins testifies that he and a copilot flew David on a company Gulfstream V from Philadelphia International Airport to a small private airstrip outside of Mexico City.

"Excuse me?" It's Judge Henry. He's fully engaged now. "Are you telling the court that the defendant has recently left the country? Since the time of his arrest and arraignment?"

David had to surrender his passport and agree not to leave the country as a condition of bail.

The pilot looks up at the judge. "Well, sure. Mr. Hanson had us fly him abroad a few times, but that was to Japan. This was the first time he had us go to Mexico."

The judge glares at me and David both, then tells the witness to continue.

Moving forward with his tale, Collins explains that David boarded the plane with two suitcases. "He took one of the suitcases with him, when he left the plane in Mexico, while we refueled and waited for him." Two hours later, when Hanson returned, "he carried the suitcase like it was heavy." The pilots then flew David to George Town on Grand Cayman Island. "This time he took the second suitcase. When he left, it looked empty. When he came back, it was definitely full."

Then Devlin gives us the money shot. "Do you know what was in the suitcases?"

Collins hesitates, then lays it out. "Well, Jake the copilot and I got to talking about what was in that first suitcase while we were waiting for Mr. Hanson in George Town. We didn't want to be a part of anything illegal, like drugs or who knows what. So we decided to check and see what was in that suitcase. There was no lock on it," he adds. "So we went back onto the plane, and we unzipped the suitcase. And it was filled with money. Hundred-dollar bills."

Devlin pauses for this to sink in, then sits.

I hit back at once with the only answer I can think of to the pilot's testimony. "But the important part is that you, Mr. Collins, don't know what Mr. Hanson was going to use the money for, do you?"

"Well, no. It was none of my business."

At this, I practically shout. "None of your *business*? Well, that didn't stop you from violating Mr. Hanson's privacy by riffling through his personal luggage in the first place, did it?"

Collins squirms. I stop here, hoping that Devlin comes back with the obvious rejoinder. He doesn't disappoint me.

"One more question, Mr. Collins," Walker begins on redirect. "Since you don't know what Mr. Hanson planned to use the money for, would you object to him telling us all now?"

I object, as Devlin knew I would. But he wasn't asking the question to get an answer. He was making a point for Judge Henry. If David wasn't going to use the money for a nest egg once he fled the jurisdiction, he needs to explain what he was going to do with it.

Devlin's second witness is Kevin Kratz. My old classmate is even more nervous than he was sitting across from David Hanson at the American Way gala. Throughout his direct examination, Kevin uses his handkerchief to wipe sweat from his face. I can see him fighting the urge to glance at David, but he can't help himself. He locks eyes with David half a dozen times. Three questions into direct examination, everyone in the courtroom can see that Kratz is absolutely petrified of David Hanson.

Devlin finishes up with Kevin's position at HWI and has Kratz explain to the judge how he received the call from the police department's financial-crimes officer about whether David had taken a large amount of company cash. "I told her it was impossible," Kevin explains. "That David was no longer with the company. And that even if he were still employed at HWI, he wouldn't have cause to be handling company cash. Still, I promised to check it out. The officer told me that she thought the cash may have been taken out of a subsidiary in Mexico, so I began making calls. That's when I found out about the trip to Mexico City, where he absconded with two million dollars in cash from one of our subsidiaries there, Azoteca Comercial."

"Objection," I say. "Anything that Mr. Kratz is claiming to have learned from a third party not present in the courtroom is hearsay."

Judge Henry thinks for a moment. "Overruled. I'll hear the testimony. If I decide we need a representative from Azoteca Comercial here to testify, I'll order it, and we'll have a second day of hearings." The judge then directs Kevin to continue.

"Of course, I took this information to Mr. Hanson, Edwin Hanson, our CEO," Kevin says. "He was as shocked as I was. He asked me if I knew of any other money David might have made off with."

I make a mental note of "made off with" and "absconded." Kevin is peppering his speech with words and phrases from a 1940s film-noir screenplay. And this is when I realize that Kevin Kratz has made a decision to see that David, now down, stays down.

"The only other money I knew about," Kratz continues, "is the money he parked in the numbered accounts in the Caymans. Years ago, David had asked me to find out how to set up overseas accounts there. He said he wanted to hide . . . that is, *place* . . . some of his money offshore. So I contacted some banks and set up some accounts for David. Then I helped David wire money a number of times from accounts here in the United States. A few times, David asked me to transfer money from one of the Cayman accounts to the other. That's when he gave me the passwords to the accounts. So, when Edwin asked me about other money, I told him about the accounts, and I contacted the banks and used the passwords to have them e-mail me activity statements. I learned that the same day he withdrew the money from Azoteca Comercial, David withdrew two million more from one of his Cayman accounts. I reported this all back to Edwin Hanson, who told me to share it with the police."

Devlin has Kevin Kratz describe his meetings with Caroline Robb, the financial-crimes detective, to lay the foundation for Robb's own testimony. Then he turns my old classmate over to me for cross-examination. I start to stand, but David puts his hand on my arm. I sit back down, and David whispers in my ear, "Leave it." I look at him, puzzled. I'm about to ask why, but then I figure it out. Kevin Kratz has a lot more dirt than just this on David. Additional questioning only risks opening a Pandora's box.

"No questions," I say.

Judge Henry raises his eyebrows, then tells Devlin to call his next witness.

Edwin Hanson takes the stand. Walker has him identify himself as the CEO of Hanson World Industries. Then he asks Edwin if David is his brother.

"My half brother," Edwin says.

Devlin then gets down to business. He has Edwin identify the account in question as one belonging to Azoteca Comercial, an HWI subsidiary headquartered in Mexico City. From there it gets a little dicey for Edwin, who variously characterizes the money sitting in Azoteca Comercial as a "discretionary spending fund," "nonallocated short-term capital," and the "corporate equivalent of a petty-cash account." By this point, everyone in the courtroom has figured out that HWI likely set up the account as a slush fund to hold money HWI needed to grease the gears of the Mexican bureaucracy—in violation of the Foreign Corrupt Practices Act.

"Is there any conceivable corporate purpose for the defendant, your half brother, to have withdrawn two million dollars in cash since his leave of absence from the company?" Devlin asks.

"None whatsoever."

"Was the defendant traveling for a corporate purpose when he flew to Mexico City to withdraw the cash?"

"None whatsoever," Edwin repeats. "He had no business using that plane."

My cross-examination of Edwin is short. I can't play up the dubious nature of the account David plundered because connecting David to a fund set up for an illegal purpose would hurt him as much as Edwin and HWI. Instead, I try to undercut Edwin's testimony that David did not travel to Mexico for a company purpose. It doesn't work.

"You've testified that my client took a leave of absence pending his trial," I begin.

"It was that or be fired," Edwin answers before I can complete the sentence.

"Yet your brother remains on the company's board of directors," I continue, ignoring Edwin. "He is still therefore technically performing corporate functions."

Edwin leans forward and bores into me with his dark wide-set eyes. "Mr. McFarland, let me make this clear. David Hanson was not—*not*—on company business when he had our jet fly him to Mexico. It was *not* for any company purpose that he looted that corporate account. None whatsoever. As for his position on the board of directors: it won't be for long. I've called an emergency meeting of the board for tomorrow morning, and I can assure you that, his inherited stock in our company notwithstanding, my half brother is going to lose his position. My family is a large one, and we are all very different people. But we will not have our company used for disreputable purposes. And we will not have it run by disreputable people."

In my peripheral vision, I can see David's clenched jaw and fisted hands. I feel the heat radiating from his face and head. It is everything he can do not to spring from his seat and throttle Edwin.

"Easy," I lean in to him and whisper. Then I stand to counter Edwin's speech with one of my own.

"Objection," I say. "I move to strike the witness's testimony in its entirety. It was nothing more than a gratuitous slur by a jealous brother. Jealous that his younger sibling has managed to do in just a few years what the witness himself failed to do at the company's helm in almost two decades. Namely, to build solid relationships throughout Asia, and to engineer deals that would have—and, if justice is done in this case, still may—bring thousands of jobs and billions of dollars to our local economy. Edwin Hanson may be CEO of his family's company, for now, but he's in no position to deny my client's efforts, even under the stress of an impending trial, to further the company's interests and the interests of our entire community."

Now it's Devlin's turn to object. He demands that my own speech be stricken from the record, complaining that I'm trying to poison the jury pool, just as my client has been doing by planting stories in the media. Walker and I shout at each other, until finally Judge Henry brings us all to order with the smashing of his gavel—something entirely out of character for him. Behind me, the press is having a field day. I hear at least a dozen newsmen tap, tap, tapping the screens of their iPads, writing down everything that's going on. I'm certain that others are recording the whole clusterfuck on their smartphones.

William Henry sits back in his chair and closes his eyes. After a long minute, he opens them and leans forward. "All right, let's cut to the chase. We're going to assume that the witness from the DA's financial-crimes unit will testify the way Mr. Walker says she will. Is that okay with you, Mr. McFarland, or do you need it all played out in detail and on the record?"

"For the purposes of this hearing, Your Honor, and only this hearing, the defense will stipulate that the witnesses will so testify."

"All right, then." William Henry looks at me. He opens his hands and waits. After a minute, still looking at me, he says, "Well?"

I look up at the bench. "Your Honor?"

"Come on, Mr. McFarland. You can't figure out what I'm looking for? Your client has smashed the proverbial piggy bank on the eve of trial. He's withdrawn four million dollars in cash. My question should be obvious. If he didn't take the money to help him flee, what did he take it for?"

"Your Honor," I say, "if Mr. Hanson were planning to flee, he wouldn't withdraw a bunch of cash. He'd just wire the money to another account in a bank located where he planned to go."

"Maybe he did that, too, and we just haven't found out about it yet," Devlin Walker pipes in.

"I'm still waiting, Mr. McFarland," says the judge, ignoring Devlin.

"Your Honor, I'd like a minute to speak with my client in private."

The court calls for a break and lets me take David to a small conference room just outside the courtroom. As soon I close the door, David starts in on me. "You've killed me! You've fucking killed me! What the hell are we going to say? What's our answer? That I needed the money to pay off a blackmailer who had a DVD of me at Jennifer's house right around the time she was killed?"

"David—"

"You know what? Fuck it! That's exactly what we're going to do. We'll go back into the courtroom and tell everyone about that fucking recording. It doesn't prove I killed her. It doesn't prove anything. Come on!" David brushes past me toward the door, but I reach out and grab him by the arm.

"Are you out of your mind? That video will hang you. No one can *ever* know anything about it. *No one* can find out you were at Jennifer's house at the time of the murder."

"Find out? Everyone out there, everyone in the whole city, already thinks that's exactly where I was when Jennifer was killed."

"But they don't *know*. Some of them think it. Some believe it. But no one *knows* for a fact that you were there that afternoon. And it has to stay that way for you to have any chance of staying out of prison."

"But that's what this whole hearing is all about. If we don't come up with some answer for the money's purpose, that judge is going to have me carted me off to county lockup. Today. Right now. Right? Right?"

I lower myself to one of the scratched metal seats around the scratched metal conference table. "Sit down, David. Please. We have to think this through."

David remains standing, rubs his hands through his hair, then sits at the end of the table. "I can't believe this is happening," he says. "I just can't believe it."

Thirty minutes after he called the break, Judge Henry is back on the bench. David and I are at the defense table. Devlin Walker and Christina Wesley are seated at the prosecution table, their witnesses and a smiling John Tredesco behind them. On my side of the courtroom, Marcie Hanson sits in the first row of seats behind the bar. Tommy and Angie are a few rows behind her. Only two things are different. First, there are even more reporters than were here before the break. Apparently, the word is out that blood's being spilled. Second, two sheriff's deputies have appeared and are standing by the doors in the back of the courtroom.

"Have you had a chance to consult with your client?" the judge asks me.

"I have, Your Honor. And all I can say is that Mr. Hanson is well known around the world as a philanthropist. He's also a man of his word, and he has no intention of betraying the uses to which he donated that money."

Devlin springs to his feet. "Objection! Counsel is testifying. He doesn't dare put his client on the stand, so he's blowing a smoke screen."

Judge Henry, now visibly spent, interrupts. "Mr. McFarland, is your client going to take the stand or not?"

Evading the question, I stay on message. "Your Honor, Mr. Hanson had no intention, *has* no intention, of fleeing the jurisdiction. He very much wants his day in court, he wants the chance to be here to dispute the specious charges brought against him."

Bill Henry doesn't skip a beat. "Then let's make sure he gets his wish. I am revoking the defendant's bail and remanding him to the county prison, to remain there until and through the duration of his trial." With that he nods to the two deputies, who walk to the front of the courtroom, cuff David, and lead him out the side door, their destination the holding cells in the subbasement. David will stay there until five o'clock, at which time he will be loaded into the sheriff's bus and transported to the Curran-Fromhold Correctional Facility in Northeast Philadelphia.

I watch David's exit, watch him hold his head high, keep his back straight, trying to retain as much dignity as he can. Before the deputies close the door behind them, David glances back into the courtroom. I've seen the "last glance" from dozens of defendants, seen the guilt, sorrow, regret, fear, numbed disbelief plastered all over their faces as they take in a final look at the loved ones they're leaving behind, sometimes for good. But David isn't looking back in sadness or distress. And he isn't looking at Marcie. His eyes hold only hatred for his real enemy. For Edwin. According to David, it was Edwin who placed the anonymous call to the DA's office. Somehow, his half brother had found out about his taking the money from the Mexican subsidiary and tipped off the prosecution.

I look from one brother to the other. Then, in my peripheral vision, I see two other people watching David. The first is Marcie. Her eyes are narrowed, her lips turned down, but her head, like David's, is held high. Resolve. The second person whose eyes I see locked on David surprises me. It's Tommy. He's standing in the back of the courtroom, legs spread apart, arms crossed. Tommy's lips are turned up in a smirk.

"Chambers in ten minutes," the judge announces from the bench, summoning counsel for both sides into his private office.

When I arrive at the judge's chambers on the twelfth floor, I find only Devlin Walker in the waiting area. He must've sent Christina Wesley and Caroline Robb back to the DA's office. Bill Henry nods to his law clerk as soon as we sit, and she hands Devlin and me a sheaf of papers.

"I've ruled on your omnibus motion, Mr. McFarland," the judge begins before I have a chance to scan his order.

The Pennsylvania Rules of Criminal Procedure require defense attorneys to put all their requests for relief into one all-encompassing, or "omnibus," motion. I submitted ours weeks ago, as did Devlin.

Among Devlin's requests was that the court exclude the evidence of the burglaries in Jennifer Yamura's neighborhood during the weeks before and after her murder. Judge Henry tells us he's reserving his ruling on that motion, that he will wait and see how strong the other evidence is supporting the defense theory that Jennifer may have been murdered as part of a burglary gone bad.

The judge then turns to my requests and announces his decision to exclude any evidence of the calls to my office from Jennifer Yamura's cell phone during the time period within which she was murdered. "There is no proof that Mr. Hanson made those calls," he explains. "In fact, we know from Ms. Toscano's testimony that the first call was definitely not from Mr. Hanson. As to the second call, any probative value is outweighed by the unfair prejudice to the defense should the calls be allowed into evidence."

In my omnibus motion, I also asked the court to exclude all of David's clothing, collected upon his arrest, on the grounds that the police had lacked probable cause to arrest him. My argument was that although David was caught fleeing Jennifer's apartment, it was hours after her death. And, I contended, the police had no business being there in the first place because the 911 phone call tipping them off—in which the caller claimed he'd heard sounds of a struggle—had to have been a ruse, because by that time, Yamura had been dead for hours. I also asked the court to exclude David's statement at the police station that he'd been at work all afternoon, also on the grounds that the police had no probable cause to arrest my client. Finally, I asked for a change of venue to Pittsburgh or Williamsport, arguing that the pretrial publicity had irredeemably poisoned the jury pool against him.

I expected the court to deny my first two requests. Our appellate courts have found probable cause to arrest on far less evidence than the defendant fleeing the scene of the murder after being caught red-handed trying to clean it up. I am a bit surprised, however, when the judge announces that he's denying my change-of-venue request, until he explains himself.

"I was all but ready to move this case out of Philadelphia," Judge Henry says, looking at me, "until I saw all those well-placed articles in the newspaper about your client's wonderful gifts to charity and his personal mission to bring jobs back to the city. How could any reader think ill of Mr. Hanson after reading those articles? In my mind, those stories more than made up for the prosecution's anonymous tip to the newspapers about Mr. Hanson's love nest in New York."

"That was not us, Your Honor," Devlin interjects.

"Even so," I interrupt, ignoring Walker, "the court must surely recognize that it will be impossible for Mr. Hanson to find an unbiased jury given the prosecution's latest motion and Mr. Hanson's imprisonment on the eve of trial."

"Oh, no, no, Mr. McFarland." Bill Henry shakes his head and smiles. "Your client brought that on himself. Violating his bail terms by jet-setting all over the globe. Withdrawing millions of dollars just weeks before a trial that might wind him up in prison for the rest of his life. No, counsel, this case is here to stay. And Mr. Hanson will be here, too. Of that we can now be sure."

"He can always plead," Devlin says. "I've told defense counsel we'll accept voluntary manslaughter if Mr. Hanson admits to accidentally killing the victim. Of course, he'd have to produce the victim's laptop and other missing items."

The judge thinks for a minute, then asks Devlin, "You think he got into a fight with the decedent? Lost control and pushed her down the stairs?"

"I think it was premeditated, and he should go away for first-degree murder. But if the defendant can convince me I'm wrong, I'll let him plead to the lower charge."

"Can we leave now, Your Honor?" I ask. I don't like this little exchange about my client's guilt between the prosecutor and the judge.

Bill Henry appraises me, then turns to Devlin. "I'm not so sure the defendant is guilty of anything, Mr. Walker." Devlin blinks at this and is about to chime in when the judge stops him. "I'm bothered by all these anonymous phone calls. The one that tipped you off that Mr. Hanson was hoarding cash. The one about the New York love nest. And, most of all, the 911 call on the night of the murder. Everyone in this room knows that there couldn't have been yelling and sounds of a struggle when the victim had been dead for hours. Obviously, there's another person involved in all of this. And whoever that person is, they're out to get Mr. Hanson. They made sure the police showed up to catch him trying to destroy evidence. They made sure the whole world knew about his penchant for Asian mistresses—don't think for one minute, Mr. McFarland, that I was fooled by that dog-and-pony show your client put on about sponsoring gifted foreign-exchange students—and, finally, they blew the whistle on his jet-setting money junket."

"All of which I'm planning to highlight in my opening statement," I say, which causes Devlin to squirm in his seat.

"Well?" The judge looks at Walker, meaning, *What's your answer to all that?*

"With all due respect, Your Honor," Devlin says, "I don't think this is the appropriate forum to get into trial strategy."

This makes Bill Henry smile. Then he leans forward and looks from Walker to me. "I want to make something very clear to both of you. There has been more posturing in this case, both in court and in the public, than I can remember for a long time. That posturing is now over. Do you hear me? Mr. McFarland? Mr. Walker?" We both say yes. "Good. Because whatever happens in this case, whatever result the jury reaches, I will not have it said that the defendant did not receive a fair trial." With that, William Henry shoos Devlin Walker and me out of his office.

My adversary and I walk to the elevators in silence. We descend without a word. Devlin, I can tell, is waiting for me to start in on him, harangue him about throwing my client in jail on the eve of trial, tainting the jury pool. Instead, I wait for the doors to open, turn to the prosecutor, and smile. "That hearing, the whole money thing," I say. "Brilliantly played, Devlin. Brilliantly played."

Devlin's mouth drops, and his eyes fill with confusion.

I tell him to have a nice day and leave the elevator ahead of him, the smile still on my face.

David and Marcie Hanson aren't the only ones who can place anonymous calls.

26

MONDAY, NOVEMBER 12

David Hanson has been stewing in jail for more than two weeks. Today, the trial begins. Courtroom 1007 is packed. All four of the hard, black benches in the spectator's gallery are filled. At the prosecution table, Devlin Walker sits motionless, eyes closed, elbows on the table, hands together and formed into a steeple, his two index fingers touching his lips. To his left lies the jury box, where the jurors will enjoy an unobstructed view of the prosecutor throughout the trial. To his right sits Christina Wesley, doing her best to look as thoughtful as her boss, not quite pulling it off.

On the first row of benches behind the bar on the prosecution's side are John and Margaret Yamura and her brother, Brian. Mr. and Mrs. Yamura sit ramrod straight in their seats, eyes locked forward. I've read that both are in their early sixties, but the shock of their daughter's violent death and the months of grief have taken a toll, and they look older. Brian Yamura caught me glancing at him and his parents when I first came into the courtroom. I saw at once the intelligence in his eyes—and the hostility. Brian recognized me for what I am to him and his family: the enemy. The man working to ensure that his sister's killer escapes justice.

David and I are at the defense table, across the aisle from the prosecutors. I am closest to the jurors; David is to my right. Susan, at my request, is absent from the courtroom. I don't want her anywhere near this trial. Yet. Her time will come, I hope. If not, it will be because this whole spectacle imploded like a black hole. To ensure that doesn't happen, I have secured the presence of the iconic attorney Alexander Ginsberg. I've told David and Marcie that I hired him to watch the trial and give me his daily read on how things are going for us. Alexander's real mission is quite different.

Ginsberg sits right behind the defense table, next to Marcie Hanson. On Marcie's other side, Vaughn Coburn sits; he will take notes and discuss the progress of the case with me every day after trial. Before the jury comes in, I glance back at my team. Ginsberg smiles at me. Marcie nods imperceptibly. I've told her never to smile anywhere in the courthouse, or in public. No one—not the jury, not the press, not the public, not the judge—must perceive her as anything but serious and respectful. She and David both must display the crushing burden the charges have placed on their shoulders. What they must not display, I've told them, is their wealth. Gone from David's finger and wrist are his gold signet ring and Rolex watch. Missing from Marcie is her five-carat Tiffany diamond engagement ring. Her visible jewelry consists only of her gold wedding band and a pair of modest pearl earrings. She is dressed at my instruction in a conservative gray pantsuit with a vest and white shirt buttoned at the collar. I will have no female jurors envious of Marcie's legs or bust. David is wearing a blue off-the-rack Brooks Brothers suit with a white shirt, maroon tie, and black wingtips. The type of suit you see but don't notice.

There is one more person whose presence in the courtroom has special importance. Sitting in the second row of benches, behind Marcie, Vaughn, and Alexander Ginsberg, is Piper. It's been years since she's attended one of my trials. But I made a point of asking her to attend David's trial. I told her it would mean a lot to me. I didn't tell Piper I needed her there to witness the case crashing down around us.

David's imprisonment three weeks before the trial had caused a feeding frenzy in the press. The headlines in the *Inquirer* and *Daily News* screamed: "Hanson Imprisoned: DA Claims Millionaire Preparing to Flee" and "Hanson Withdrew Millions in Cash on Eve of Trial" and "Accused Geisha Killer Readies Corporate Jet to Flee." None of the articles reported my insinuation at the hearing that David had used the money to fund charities. All of them played up his plane flight to Mexico, where he landed at the same private airstrip employed by cartel drug runners. One story colorfully painted a picture of David's Learjet escaping Philadelphia late at night in a driving rainstorm. It used terms like "lurking" and "dodging" and "absconding," and referred to David as a "fugitive."

It took four days to pick the jury. Our panel of twelve jurors and four alternates are from all parts of the city, all walks of life. Kensington, South Philly, West Philly, the Northeast, Rittenhouse Square, the art-museum area, and Old City. A schoolteacher, a nurse, an aerobics instructor, a college track coach, a car salesman, the manager of a Wawa, a college student, a retired businessman, a FedEx driver, a building security guard, a retired insurance salesman, a hairstylist, a retired accountant, an unemployed truck driver, an unemployed factory worker, and a reporter for the *Daily News*. Ten men, six women. Five whites, nine blacks, two Hispanics. No Asian Americans—I made sure of that.

Judge Henry used Friday afternoon to hear arguments and rule on my motion to prohibit the prosecutor from presenting Edwin and the HWI pilots to testify to David's withdrawal of money on the eve of trial. I argued that the issue of David's supposed plans to flee was a straw man that would serve only to poison the jury against him. But the court bought Devlin's argument that David's actions evidenced a consciousness of guilt. "If you feel that strongly that the evidence is misleading," Bill Henry told me, "you can present your client to explain to the jury what his actual intentions were for the money."

Judge Henry enters through a door at the rear of the courtroom and takes his seat on the bench. Framing him on the back wall are the American flag on his right and the state flag on his left. Directly behind and above the judge hangs the blue-and-gold seal of the Commonwealth of Pennsylvania.

"Please bring in the jury," Judge Henry says to his deputy, Mike Holleran. "Everyone remain seated while the jury enters the courtroom," he tells the rest of us. Holleran knocks on a door on the back wall of the courtroom, to the left of the bench. The door opens and, one by one, our special sixteen file into the courtroom and take their seats. Once they're in position, most of them glance at Devlin and me. All of them look at David. The juror sitting in the first seat in the first row, our presumptive foreman, is the retired businessman. His name is Peter Drummond. He's seventy-one years old and a former member of the Philadelphia Chamber of Commerce. Drummond has a full head of silver hair and has come to court dressed in a button-down shirt under a deep-blue blazer over charcoal slacks. His face is square and distinguished looking, reminiscent of John Forsythe of the old TV series *Dynasty*.

"Good morning, ladies and gentlemen," Judge Henry greets the jury. The jurors say "Good morning" or nod and smile. His Honor spends about half an hour giving the jury preliminary instructions, telling them what our daily schedule will be: 9:00 a.m. sharp to 5:00 p.m., with an hour for lunch, a fifteen-minute break in the morning, and a fifteen-minute break in the afternoon. And Bill Henry means it. He tries a full day, every day.

"And now we will start the trial with the attorneys' opening statements. The statements themselves are not evidence, and you are not to consider them as evidence. Rather, these statements are counsel's explications of what they expect the evidence will show." Judge Henry speaks for another few minutes and then turns to Devlin. "Is the prosecution ready?" Walker states that he is, and the court nods for him to begin.

The prosecutor rises from his seat and buttons his jacket. Dressed in a three-button black suit, white herringbone dress shirt, black-and-white-striped tie, black-and-white porcelain cuff links, and gleaming black loafers, Devlin has an American flag pin on his lapel and his hair freshly cut close to his head. He moves slowly to the center of the courtroom, pauses for a moment before the bench, and says, "May it please the court." Judge Henry nods, and Devlin turns to his left and walks up to the jury box. Careful not to invade the jurors' space, he plants himself four feet from the box. A portable lectern is available, but Devlin has chosen not to use it. He has no notes. He's going to be speaking from the heart.

Devlin sighs, showing the jurors there's no joy in what he has to do on behalf of the people, but that he's still going to see it through, for all of our sakes.

"Good morning, ladies and gentlemen," Devlin says, then pauses. The jurors respond to him. Most of the women smile. Most of the men nod. "I come before you today to obtain justice for a murdered young woman. Jennifer Yamura, a bright woman with a promising future, whose parents worked hard to raise and educate her." Devlin pauses again, turns toward the Yamura family, gives the jury the chance to see who they're really fighting for. "Jennifer Yamura, whose life was stolen from her by a man who would have you see him as some sort of public benefactor." I want to object here, but I know Devlin is baiting me to do it, hoping to get the jury to see me as disruptive. Devlin makes a few more gratuitous remarks about David's wealth and privilege, then moves to the heart of the case.

"Thursday, May thirty-first, at 11:30 p.m., Officer Tim Kujowski and Officer Nicholas Pancetti are traveling south in their patrol car on

Pine Street when they get a call from dispatch to go to 1792 Addison Street, on a report of a disturbance. They get out of the car, see the lights are on, hear someone inside running a vacuum cleaner. Officer Kujowski knocks on the door, and the vacuum stops. From inside, someone tells them to hold on, but he never answers the door. Officer Kujowski knocks on the door again. Still, no one appears, so Kujowski runs around back. He gets to the back of Jennifer Yamura's house just in time to see a tall, well-built man running out the back door. The defendant. David Hanson. Officer Kujowski tells him to stop, but the defendant keeps on running. But Kujowski was a track star in high school, and the defendant doesn't get far.

"Called by his partner, Officer Pancetti checks to make sure that Officer Kujowski has secured the defendant, then walks inside the open kitchen door, calling out to anyone who might still be inside. In the kitchen, Officer Pancetti sees that the dishwasher is running and the sink is full of water, suds, and dishes. Moving into the living room, Officer Pancetti sees the vacuum cleaner. On the coffee table he sees a can of lemon Pledge, a bottle of Windex, and some rags. By now it's obvious to Officer Pancetti that Mr. Hanson had been trying to clean the place. Officer Pancetti searches the rest of the house. He starts with the second floor. Then he looks for the basement. The doorway is covered by a curtain of yellow glass beads. Officer Pancetti pushes the beads aside, and he sees Jennifer Yamura lying faceup on the steps. Her eyes are open. Blood has drained from the back of her head, down the steps, and pooled onto the floor.

"Officer Pancetti calls Officer Kujowski on the radio, tells him what he's found, then calls dispatch for backup. He asks dispatch to send the detectives and the crime-scene investigation unit.

"Within thirty minutes, Detectives John Tredesco and Ed Cook arrive at the house. They make a cursory examination of the premises, being careful not to disturb it—at least not to disturb it any more than the defendant already has. Then they turn the scene over to the

CSU team, take the defendant into custody, and transport him to the station house. There, the defendant does two things. First, he lies and says he was at his office all day. You'll hear from his secretary that that isn't true. Second, he demands to speak to his attorney and clams up until Mr. McFarland arrives.

"Fast-forward four months. The trial in this case is less than a month away. The defendant has been out on bail since the murder. A main condition of bail was that he forfeit his passport and promise not to leave the country. But the defendant is about to face you folks, and he knows it. A Learjet lands on a private airstrip outside of Mexico City. The plane's door opens. David Hanson descends the stairs to the tarmac, takes a limo to a company known as Azoteca Comercial, where he enters the corporate vault and physically makes off with two million dollars in cash. Then he has the pilots fly him to the Cayman Islands, where he withdraws another two million dollars from his own personal offshore accounts."

David Hanson fleeing from the scene of the murder after getting caught trying to disinfect it of every trace of himself.

David Hanson lying to the police about where he'd been at the time of Jennifer's murder.

David Hanson preparing to flee from the jury on the eve of trial.

Damning stuff. And now that he's grabbed the jurors' hearts, Devlin lays it out for their minds, methodically previewing each witness he intends to present, and what each witness will say. Finally, sixty minutes after he began, Devlin concludes by lifting onto an easel a large color photograph of Jennifer Yamura. The picture depicts the young woman in her college cap and gown, standing between her proud parents.

"Jennifer Yamura had the whole world open to her that day she graduated," Devlin says. "She could have gone anywhere to pursue her dream of becoming a journalist. She chose to come here, to Philadelphia. Our city, yours and mine. The City of Brotherly Love. The city Jennifer Yamura came to love. The city she came to fight for as a journalist, exposing crime and corruption, working for the betterment of our schools, the integrity of our government, the safety of our streets. In the short time she was with us, Jennifer never let this city down, and this city isn't going to let her down." Devlin pauses, takes the time to look each and every juror in the eyes, then turns and walks slowly back to his seat.

I want to give my opening right away, not allow Devlin's speech to congeal in the jurors' minds, but Judge Henry lets the jury take a fifteen-minute midmorning break.

When we come back, we repeat the same routine. The judge takes the bench, has Mike Holleran summon the jury to take their seats. Like Devlin, I walk slowly, pay my respects to the court, then take my place before the jury. No notes. "Good morning," I say. I pause to see how they respond. No one smiles. A few say, "Good morning." A few nod. Most look down, or over at Devlin.

I inhale, wait a beat, then begin. "Ladies and gentlemen, it was my privilege for twelve years to work as a Philadelphia district attorney."

I pause and let my words sink in. I want the jury to see from the start that, like my opponent, I was the people's servant—*their* servant—for many years. I want them to see me as one of the good guys. And, importantly, I want them to know that I know what I'm talking about when it comes to how the police should investigate crimes, because that's going to be a major theme of my defense.

"As a prosecutor, I was privileged to work with some of the finest police officers ever to serve our city. And what made those officers so good, every one of them, was this: They never stopped short. They never took the easy way out of an investigation by latching on to the first possible suspect. They turned over every stone, questioned every potential witness, took the time to investigate and rule out every possible perpetrator, to make sure they didn't bring an innocent man to trial. Didn't destroy his reputation. Didn't force him to suffer through the hell of living with the threat of false imprisonment hanging over his head. Didn't—"

"Objection." Devlin is on his feet. We both know I've crossed the line into improper argument, and Walker's own opening has won him more than enough political capital with the jury to object during my opening—one of the advantages of going first. The judge sustains the objection, and I continue.

"Without belaboring the point," I say, my voice now quiet, "the police officers I served with did exactly what the officers who *investigated*"—I use my fingers to make air quotes around the term— "Jennifer Yamura's tragic death failed to do. Detective John Tredesco, the detective in charge, in particular, latched on to David Hanson to the exclusion of all other possible suspects. And the evidence will be clear that there were many very dangerous people who had reason to both hate and fear Jennifer Yamura. The prosecutor made reference to Jennifer's work as a reporter who exposed corruption and tried to make our streets safer. And many in this city know, as you will hear witnesses testify, about Jennifer Yamura's work as a reporter in exposing a ring of crooked police officers, men who violated their sacred duty to protect us by banding together with drug dealers to flood the city's streets with drugs. One of those officers, Stanley Lipinski, testified before the grand jury against his fellow conspirators, publicly dared his criminal friends to come and get him, and they did, gunning him down on the street."

I have no proof that Lipinski was killed by any of the crooked cops, and Devlin knows it. He has the right to object, but he's holding back, not wanting to look obstreperous to the jury.

"As the prosecutor has told you, Detective Tredesco is going to testify that he didn't need to consider other potential defendants because the police caught Mr. Hanson, quote, 'red-handed' running out of Jennifer Yamura's house. The prosecution's theory is that Mr. Hanson's running away—and his trying to clean up the murder scene itself— shows consciousness of guilt. But you're going to hear the detectives themselves admit that Ms. Yamura had been dead for at least eight hours by the time they discovered Mr. Hanson at her house.

"The prosecution will also concede that Mr. Hanson had a strong motive to cover up his involvement with Ms. Yamura that had nothing to do with murder. Mr. Hanson, a married man, was having an affair with Ms. Yamura. Now, I'm not going to ask you to excuse or forgive Mr. Hanson for his affair. Only his wife, Marcie, can do that. And she has, which is why she's here today, supporting her husband."

This is an important point for me to make to the jurors, especially the women. David was a rake. But he's a good enough man that his wife was willing to forgive him for the affair and stand by his side.

"And although an affair is not and has never been proof of murder," I continue, "it provides a man a powerful motive to hide evidence of his involvement with a woman." I pause to let this sink in. "But Mr. Hanson also had a *second* reason to try to cover up his affair with Ms. Yamura, and you'll hear this from one of the prosecution's own witnesses, Edwin Hanson, the CEO of Hanson World Industries. Now, Edwin Hanson has no love for his half brother, but he will admit that at the time David Hanson discovered Jennifer's body, David was on the verge of sewing up one of the largest international business deals in HWI's history. A deal that would have brought thousands of jobs and countless millions of dollars to our city. A deal that would have propelled David into a position of high leadership at Hanson World Industries, despite the hatred of his jealous brother, Edwin. And Edwin Hanson will admit that any threat of scandal might have put the deal on ice. And, indeed, it has. This very complex, very fragile business arrangement that would have brought vast benefits to our city was stopped in its tracks the minute the district attorney jumped the gun and charged David Hanson with the murder of Jennifer Yamura.

"So it's no wonder that David Hanson tried to clean the Addison Street house after he discovered his lover's long-dead body, or that he tried to flee once the police arrived. But there is something at the very heart of this case that should—and will—cause every one of you to wonder. A gaping hole at the center of the prosecution's theory that David Hanson was the one who killed Jennifer Yamura. I'm speaking of the 911 phone call. The call placed from a disposable, untraceable phone, a burner phone of the type used by drug dealers and other career criminals.

"The prosecutor glossed over it in his opening. He said that the police showed up at 1792 Addison Street in response to a call about a 'disturbance.' What Mr. Walker failed to tell you was that this phone call—and you will hear it for yourself on tape—demonstrates that someone other than David Hanson knew that David was in Jennifer's house that night. That Jennifer Yamura was dead. And that someone was out to make very, very sure that the police arrived to catch David in the house with Jennifer's body."

Here I take some time to explain how the anonymous caller claimed to have heard people shouting and the sounds of things crashing—all of which was impossible, as Jennifer had been dead for hours.

"Who was this caller? And why was he so determined to have the police seize David as the prime suspect? Was it the real murderer? Or someone who knew the real murderer and sought to protect them by misdirecting the police? One of the corrupt police officers who wanted Yamura dead to stop her investigation? One of David Hanson's many powerful enemies in the business world? Or was it a burglar Jennifer caught in the act of breaking into her home—maybe the same burglar who'd recently broken into other homes in her neighborhood? We'll never know, because the police never followed up to find out. But he almost certainly was watching the house after killing Jennifer Yamura, which gave him the opportunity to blame it on David Hanson."

I'm pouring it on thick now. And Devlin Walker could properly have objected at any number of points. But Devlin believes he's holding all the cards. He's letting me grandstand the way a tolerant parent lets a child throw a temper tantrum, knowing it will come to nothing.

"And then there's the other gaping hole in the prosecution's case. The complete absence of motive. I waited throughout the prosecutor's opening statement to hear what the state had conjured up as Mr. Hanson's supposed motive for killing Ms. Yamura. But it never came. There will be no witnesses testifying that Mr. Hanson and Ms. Yamura had a falling-out. No witnesses testifying that they were seen fighting or arguing, that their relationship was a volatile one rather than a smooth relationship of convenience. If the prosecutor's opening speech accurately laid out the case he intends to prove, you will not hear one word speaking to any reason that Mr. Hanson would have wanted to kill Ms. Yamura.

"In the end, what you will be left with is this. First, that Jennifer Yamura was murdered. Everyone agrees to this. Second, that Mr. Hanson was having an affair with Ms. Yamura. Everyone agrees to this. And third, that Mr. Hanson's attempt to clean the Addison Street house of all evidence of his presence and his attempt to flee when the police arrived was consistent with his wanting to hide the evidence of his affair with the victim.

"The prosecution has a heavy burden. But it's their burden. Never lose sight of that. Equally important, know that only your acquittal of David Hanson will allow the police to find the real killer of Jennifer Yamura." I turn toward the Yamura family. "And that her family will get the justice they deserve."

Jennifer's father looks into my eyes, his own eyes filled with turmoil and pain. I hold Mr. Yamura's gaze for a moment, then turn back to the jury, say thank you, and take my seat.

I don't think I've ever felt worse about myself than I do right now.

27

Monday, November 12, Continued

Judge Henry recesses for lunch. During the break, my team and I gather around the defense table.

"I think you gave the jury some things to think about," Alexander Ginsberg says. "But it's going to be an uphill battle."

"It was a good opening, Mick. Thank you." Marcie's smiling, but her eyes remain sharp, steely.

She's watching me like a hawk. Me and everyone else. I was right to plant Ginsberg next to her, to whisper doubts in her ear as the case moves forward. Worry her.

An hour later, everyone is back in their seats. Devlin's first witness is Tim Kujowski. With only three years on the force, Kujowski is the youngest of the officers involved in the investigation. He looks sharp in his crisp blue uniform and buzz-cut blond hair. A Boy Scout.

Devlin quickly runs Kujowski through the preliminaries—how long he's been on the force, what district he works out of, what time he reported to duty. Then he gets to the meat.

A Criminal Defense

"Did there come a time that night when you received a call from dispatch telling you and your partner to investigate a possible disturbance at 1792 Addison Street?"

"It was about 11:30. Officer Pancetti and I were close by, so it only took a couple of minutes to get to the address."

"And what did you observe when you got out of the patrol car? What did you and Officer Pancetti do?"

"The lights were on. I could hear a vacuum cleaner running. I went up the steps and knocked on the door. The vacuum kept going, so I knocked harder. The vacuum stopped, and whoever was inside told us to hold on. We waited a minute, and the door still didn't open, so Officer Pancetti told me to go around back. I jogged to Eighteenth, took a right, and then took a right down Waverly, which is the little street behind Addison. I got to 1792 just in time to see a tall man bolt out the back door. He saw me and sped up as he ran down Waverly. He was pretty fast, but I caught up and tackled him."

Devlin pauses to let the jury take in the picture painted by Kujowski. "And is the man you saw running out the back door here in the courtroom?"

"Yes, sir. He's sitting right there." The patrolman looks at our table and points at David.

"Let the record reflect," Walker says, "that the witness has identified the defendant."

"No doubt about it," says Kujowski.

"Please tell us what happened next," Devlin asks.

"Well, I cuffed him. Then I helped him up and took him to the back of the house. As I was walking the defendant, I called Officer Pancetti on my radio and told him to come to the back. So I'm standing there with the defendant, and he says, 'This isn't what it looks like,' and I say, 'Yeah? What does it look like?' and he just kind of looks away and clams up. Officer Pancetti arrives and sees the door is open, so he goes inside. He comes out a minute later, tells me there's a dead girl in the house and I should call for backup. Then he goes back inside."

At the first mention of the "dead girl," I see some of the jurors glance at David and me. They're looking to see how he reacts to the testimony, see if they can spot signs of guilt or innocence. I've instructed David to keep a poker face throughout the trial. Even the slightest reaction can be misread by a juror as proof of guilt.

Devlin continues with Kujowski for another forty minutes, going from the arrival of backup to secure the house to the handoff of David Hanson to Detectives Tredesco and Cook.

Now it's my turn.

"So, if I heard you right, Officer Kujowski, the very first thing Mr. Hanson said to you was that it wasn't what it looked like?"

"That's correct."

"Nothing that would have amounted to any sort of admission?"

"Uh . . ."

"He didn't say 'I couldn't help myself,' or 'She came at me,' or 'I can't believe I did it,' or anything like that?"

"He didn't choose to incriminate himself, that's correct."

I smile. Devlin has coached the young patrolman well.

"I'm sorry, what did you say? That he didn't *choose* to incriminate himself?"

"That's correct."

"Come on, Officer Kujowski. This isn't the first time you've arrested someone at a crime scene, is it?"

"No, sir."

"And doesn't it often happen that the person is upset and blurts out whatever it is that's happened?"

"Well . . ."

"The person will say exactly the type of thing I asked you about earlier. He'll say he couldn't help it. He can't believe he did it. Even that he's sorry. You've heard all of those things, haven't you?"

"I guess so."

"But Mr. Hanson's message to you, at the crime scene, before he spoke with any lawyers, was that it wasn't what it looked like. Meaning that he didn't kill her, correct?"

"After he ran out of the house, yes, that's what he said. Or wanted me to believe."

I ask a few more questions, then return to the defense table.

Devlin stands. "Officer, the defense counsel asked you questions about how other suspects reacted when caught immediately after a crime. But this wasn't immediately after the murder, was it?"

"As it turned out, no, sir."

"Ms. Yamura had been dead for quite some time. Time enough for the defendant's emotions to cool, to think, to plan. To speak with an attorney, perhaps?"

I object. Judge Henry sustains the objection, but the damage has been done. Some of the jurors are now looking at me, probably wondering whether David called me between the time of Jennifer's murder and the time he was caught by the police at her house.

"And one more question, Officer. Since defense counsel brought up this notion of suspects being distraught and upset, what was Mr. Hanson's emotional state at the scene of the crime?"

Kujowski looks directly at the jury. "He was cool as a cucumber."

Walker's next witness is Officer Pancetti, whose testimony overlaps and corroborates Kujowski's. Pancetti is the one who went inside the house, and Walker has him testify about the vacuum cleaner sitting in the middle of the floor, the running dishwasher, the lemon Pledge and Windex sitting on the coffee table.

When Pancetti is finished, Walker asks him, "Did you reach any preliminary conclusions?"

"Well, yeah. He was tampering with evidence, trying to wipe the place clean of prints, hair, and everything else."

I object, but the judge overrules me. *It is what it is,* his face tells me.

Walker wraps up by having Pancetti describe where he found Jennifer's body. Then Devlin obtains the court's permission, walks up to the witness box, and hands Pancetti a photograph.

"Does this photograph, Commonwealth Exhibit 1, accurately depict the location, position, and condition of Ms. Yamura's body when you first observed it?"

Pancetti says it does, and the photograph is admitted into evidence. Devlin has his trial technicians pull up the photograph on the large screen they've set up in the courtroom. This is the first of the many gruesome dead-body photographs the jury will see, and it impacts them. Some of the jurors stare at the picture, transfixed. Some look away immediately, gather their courage, and then look back at it again.

Devlin lets the moment hang in the air until the judge presses him to move forward. "Do you have a question, Mr. Walker?"

"Yes, Your Honor. Thank you." Devlin turns back to the witness. "Was her body exposed like this when you arrived?"

Jennifer Yamura is fully clothed in the picture. But there's something very private, almost obscene, about her dead body. No person would want themselves to be seen by others splayed out like she is on the steps.

"That's how she was," Pancetti answers.

Devlin pauses, then looks at the jury. "He didn't even bother to cover her up? Put a blanket over her? This woman he'd made love to—how many times?"

I object, and the judge sustains me. But the point has been made, and I see fury in some of the jurors' eyes.

And this is how the first day of trial ends.

David is allowed to lean over the bar and kiss Marcie before the deputy escorts him out of the courtroom. Marcie, Vaughn, Alexander Ginsberg, and I wait for him to leave. We stand together quietly as the press and other spectators make their way out of the courtroom. I wait for Devlin and Christina Wesley to pack up and leave. Then I turn to Ginsberg.

"Good luck," he says, shaking his head. "I'll call you in a little while, after you get back to the office. We'll talk in more detail." He turns and leaves the courtroom.

"I think you did well with the crosses of Kujowski and Pancetti," Vaughn says. "But Devlin's getting his below-the-belt punches in over your objections. It's close, but all they've proven so far is what we already admitted: that Jennifer was murdered and that the police found David at her house hours afterward."

Marcie looks from Vaughn to me, then takes her leave.

"I'll see you back at the office," I tell Vaughn, hinting that it's time for him to go, too.

I leave the courtroom and walk over to Piper, who's been waiting at the end of the hallway. I reach out for her hands, take them in my own. I sigh, and we stand there looking at each other.

Then she breaks the silence. "I think you did great," she says with a smile, but I see the fear in her eyes.

"This is all going to turn out okay," I say. Just like I promised her in the hotel on the night of the charity gala.

Piper moves into me, and we hug, tightly. I walk her out of the building and down into the underground Love Park garage. Piper climbs in her car, opens the window. I lean through it and kiss her.

"You'll be late, I know," she says. "I'll have some leftovers in the fridge in case you're hungry." And with that, she drives away.

Half an hour later, I'm back in my office. Vaughn has filled Susan in on what happened at trial. Now she sits in one of the chairs across from my desk. We talk a little about the two cop witnesses, and about what Devlin is likely to do tomorrow.

Then I ask, "Have you seen Tommy? Is he planning to watch any of the trial?"

Susan tells me that Angie said he's up at the trailer.

Our conversation ends abruptly, and I get to work. The hours pass quickly as I finish my cross-examination prep for Devlin's witnesses. I turn to the window behind my desk. The tower clock at City Hall reads 9:45. My eyes take me past City Hall and down a few blocks on Market Street to the tall building whose roof still holds the red, neon PSFS sign. I stare at the sign. Then the letters fade, and I see my own eyes staring back at me.

A tidal wave rises inside me, threatening to wash me away, drown me . . . the same way I felt when Tommy told me about killing our father. But this time I do not surrender to the pain. I cannot. I must, must, must hold myself together, see this thing through, make it work out, for everyone's sake. Everyone, that is, except Jennifer Yamura and her shattered family.

28

TUESDAY, NOVEMBER 13

Day two starts with my cross-examination of Officer Pancetti. "Yesterday, your testimony and that of Officer Kujowski seemed to cover everything—except why you were there."

Pancetti sets his jaw. He knows where I'm going and why.

"The prosecutor asked if you were directed by dispatch to go to Addison Street to follow up on a report of a possible disturbance. You remember that?"

"Sure."

"But you chose not to go into the details of what was reported to dispatch."

"I just answered the questions. I didn't choose anything."

"Fair point. It was Mr. Walker who chose not to play the audio of the 911 call."

Devlin objects, and the judge sustains him.

"You've heard the tape, haven't you?"

"Sure."

I nod to Vaughn, who moves up to the counsel table and pushes some buttons on the laptop hooked into the courtroom's audiovisual system. I tell the judge we're going to play the audiotape for the jury, subject to later authentication by the dispatcher during our own case-in-chief. Judge Henry asks Devlin if there is any dispute as to the tape's authenticity. Devlin says no, so Vaughn plays the tape.

The first words the jury hears are, "911, what's your emergency?" The dispatcher's voice is clear, but the caller's voice sounds muffled, as if he's trying to disguise it. I listen carefully, as I have every time I've listened to the tape. There's something vaguely familiar about the caller's voice.

"Something's going on in a house in my neighborhood," the caller says. "I think maybe someone is getting hurt. There's a lot of shouting and screaming coming from the house. And it sounds like things are crashing and getting smashed up. Lotsa rockin' and rollin'."

"What's the address?" the dispatcher asks.

"It's 1792 Addison Street."

"I'll send someone over."

"You better hurry. They're shouting and screaming at each other. And it sounds like someone is getting hurt real bad." Then there's a click.

When the tape is finished, I refocus on the witness. "But when you went into the house, you found the oddest thing, didn't you?"

"I don't understand."

"Well, the caller said he heard people shouting, but there was only one person in the house, and that was Mr. Hanson, right?"

"Maybe he was shouting to himself."

"But the caller said 'they' were shouting 'at each other,' didn't he?"

"I guess."

"And all that crashing the caller heard. When you went inside— nothing was broken, was it?"

"No."

"No smashed vases?"

"No."

"No broken glasses or windows or shattered glass from picture frames?"

"No."

"You didn't find a single broken item, did you?"

"No, sir."

I pause and let this sink in. Then I make my point.

"Someone knew Mr. Hanson was in that house and wanted very much for the police to catch him there, didn't they?"

Devlin objects that my question calls for the witness to speculate. The judge sustains him, but the point's been made. To nail it home, I press forward.

"As a police officer at a murder scene, did you ask yourself why someone would call the police and say things that couldn't possibly be true—like the voices shouting and all the crashing?"

"I didn't know the details of the call when we first got there."

"But you heard the tape later. Didn't you ask yourself then?"

Pancetti hedges.

I've made my point. Before he can think something up, I end my examination. "Nothing further."

Devlin, still on his feet, asks one follow-up question. "Regardless of what was said on the call, when you got to the house, you found that it turned out to be the scene of a murder?"

"Yes, it did."

Devlin's next witness is Barbara King, David's executive assistant at HWI. Barbara is a tall, attractive woman in her early sixties with perfectly coiffed white hair. Barbara walks with authority to the jury box and looks directly at the jurors as she puts her hand on the Bible and promises to tell the truth. Although some businessmen enjoy having a young bimbo as their assistant, the smart move for someone as highly placed as David is to have a mature, no-nonsense woman running his office. That Barbara King is such a woman comes across quickly.

"Ms. King, by whom are you employed?" Devlin asks.

"Hanson World Industries," Barbara answers crisply.

"Until June of this year, what was your title, and who was your immediate superior?"

"My title was executive assistant to the general counsel. I worked directly under David Hanson."

"And since June?"

"When Mr. Hanson took a leave of absence, I kept my title but began reporting to Mr. Kratz."

"How long had you been Mr. Hanson's executive assistant?"

"For ten years, since our previous general counsel retired."

"Over the course of the decade during which you worked for Mr. Hanson, did you become familiar with his routines and procedures?"

"Yes."

"Did you manage his schedule?"

"Yes."

"Do you remember Thursday, May the thirty-first, of this year?"

"With the help of my calendar, yes."

Devlin has a printout of the calendar marked as an exhibit. He hands it to Barbara King. He has her testify to David's schedule. It was a busy day that started at 8:00 a.m. He had three back-to-back meetings, followed by a long phone call to outside counsel and a shorter call to Edwin. At 11:15, David had a light snack brought into his office from the executive dining room. He placed two more calls while he ate, then left the office at 11:50.

"It sounds like Mr. Hanson's days were tightly scheduled," Devlin says.

"That's correct."

"And as his executive assistant, you knew with whom he was meeting, and when, and who he was talking to on the phone?"

"Correct."

"But he left his afternoon open?"

"Correct."

"Did he tell you where he was going?"

For the first time, Barbara shifts in her seat, glances at David.

"No."

"Did he always take off in the afternoons without telling you where he was going, like he did the afternoon Jennifer Yamura was murdered?"

"No."

"Did he often do that?"

"No."

"This was not a typical occurrence, then?"

"Correct."

"Mrs. King, let me ask you directly. Was David Hanson in the office any time after 11:50 on May the thirty-first of this year?"

"No."

"And if he told the police who arrested him that he was in the office all afternoon, that would have been a lie?"

Barbara pauses before answering. "It would have been incorrect."

"Would it have been a lie? Since he had to have known where he was, and since he wasn't in the office, his telling the police that he was in the office had to have been a lie, correct?"

I object, and the judge sustains me. Devlin is beating a dead horse. Everyone in the courtroom knows David lied to the police about where he was at the time of Jennifer Yamura's death.

When my time comes to question Barbara King, I walk toward the witness box with a smile. "Good morning," I begin. Mrs. King wishes me a good morning in return. "It seems like the prosecution was trying to make the point that it was unusual for Mr. Hanson to leave the office in the afternoon without telling you where he was going." Walker could object to my statement, but he's clearly reluctant to do so on my very first question. "Although it wasn't Mr. Hanson's everyday practice to do this, did he in fact clear out of the office from time to time?"

"Yes."

"And when he did this, would he tell you where he was going?"

"No."

"Did you ask?"

At this, Barbara King pauses for only the second time in her testimony. "No."

"Let me ask you frankly. Did you, as Mr. Hanson's executive assistant for ten years, suspect he was having an affair?"

"Of course."

"So when he left the office that day and didn't return, it didn't surprise you?"

"No."

"And the other times he was out of the office, a woman who turned out to be his lover didn't end up dead?"

"Certainly not."

I ask whether David is the only high-ranking executive she's worked for at HWI over the years who performed this disappearing trick. Devlin's objection is sustained, but my point is made. Lots of alpha businessmen have calendars with empty afternoons.

Devlin is on his feet the instant I'm seated. "Mrs. King, the defense is claiming that Mr. Hanson was *not* with Ms. Yamura the afternoon she died. If he wasn't at the office, where else could he have been? Who else would he be with but with his lover, Jennifer Yamura?"

At this, Barbara King blanches. She looks quickly at David, then me, then past both of us into the spectator benches. Devlin doesn't catch this because he is facing the jury with a smug look plastered on his face. He doesn't see whom Barbara King glances at in the gallery. I don't need to see. I know who it is.

Devlin's next witness is Albert Mays, one of the managers of the garage in David's office building. As he did with Barbara King, Devlin moves quickly through Mays's testimony, establishing that David pulled into the garage at 7:45 a.m. the day Jennifer was killed and didn't leave until 6:20 that night. He returned to the garage four-plus hours later, at 10:40 p.m., and his car remained there until the next afternoon. I pretend to pay little attention to his testimony, again trying to convey to the jury that I think it's unimportant. When Devlin is finished with direct, I act as though I'm unsure whether even to bother with any cross. Then I turn to the jury, shrug, and ask the witness just two questions.

"So if I understand the import of your testimony, Mr. Hanson was likely somewhere in the city of Philadelphia at the time of Ms. Yamura's murder?"

"Uh, I suppose so."

"Just like a million other people?"

Walker objects, and I withdraw the question.

Judge Henry dismisses Albert Mays and signals it's time to take our midmorning break. After the break, the court refills, and Devlin puts Kevin Kratz on the stand. Kratz's testimony is pretty much a replay of what he'd said at the hearing that caused Judge Henry to revoke David's bail and send him to jail pending the outcome at trial. This time, however, Kratz doesn't seem afraid so much as resigned. He says what Devlin wants him to but comes across as listless, almost lifeless. This frustrates Devlin, who glances back periodically to Christina Wesley. Given Kratz's complete lack of enthusiasm for what he's saying, I decide to limit my cross to a single, vital point.

"When my client went on a leave of absence, you're the one who took his job as general counsel of HWI, isn't that right?"

"Yes."

"A big raise in pay?"

Kevin takes a deep breath. "Substantial. Commensurate with the additional responsibilities."

"You took over his office?"

"Yes."

"His secretary?"

"Yes."

"David's brother, Edwin Hanson, made all that happen for you, didn't he?"

"Well, yes. He's the CEO. It's his decision who serves as general counsel."

"Edwin Hanson hates David Hanson, doesn't he?"

Kevin hesitates.

"You're under oath," I say.

"There is enmity between them."

"David Hanson lives in the family home, rather than Edwin—isn't that right? Because their father granted David's mother a life estate in the property. She's letting David, not Edwin, live there."

"Yes."

"Has Edwin complained bitterly about that?"

"He has expressed his displeasure."

"Is Edwin also jealous that David, before his arrest, was on the verge of securing a huge deal for HWI—and for our entire region? Edwin was upset because he knew he was going to have to make David an executive vice president once it went through and bring him into the operations side of the business, isn't that right?"

Devlin is on his feet. His anger has gotten the better of him. "Objection! There are about five questions in there. Not even questions. Statements. Five of them."

Bill Henry smiles. "I think there are only two questions, counselor. Would the witness answer the first one first and the second one second?" The judge directs the court reporter to read my questions back.

"David was on the cusp of a very large deal, yes. And Edwin was going to have to promote him."

I pause for a moment, then turn to the jury. "Cain and Abel," I say.

Devlin objects, but the jury gets the picture. "Nothing further," I tell the judge.

Devlin decides he wants Kratz off the stand as soon as possible and tells the court he has no redirect.

Despite the late start, Judge Henry breaks for lunch at 12:30, as usual. I speak for a few minutes with my team, telling Vaughn to walk Marcie and Alexander Ginsberg back to the office, where Angie will have lunch already set up for everyone.

The trial resumes at two o'clock. Devlin puts on the pilots, who regurgitate their testimony from the motion hearing. The jury hears all about David's trip on the Learjet to Mexico and the Cayman Islands. The pilots' testimony is sensational and makes an impact on the jury. Equally damning is the testimony of Caroline Robb, the assistant district attorney from the financial-crimes unit. She's good on the stand, telling a story that transforms the jurors into fellow travelers on David's cash-gathering journey. By the time she's finished, each juror feels exhilarated by their jet-setting adventure. And dirty. Because it was a dirty business.

Cross-examining Caroline Robb, I know, is not going to be easy. She's a pro. She has the evidence. She believes what she's saying. Still, I have to try.

"All that flying around from one country to another . . . ," I begin. "Seems like a lot of work to accomplish what you could do with a phone call or few keystrokes on a computer."

Devlin objects, says that's not a question. The judge sustains him.

"Ms. Robb, isn't it true that Mr. Hanson simply could have called his bank in the Caymans and directed them to wire the money to an account here in Philadelphia and then have withdrawn the money here?"

"That would have left a paper trail. An American bank would have been required to report a withdrawal of that size to the government."

"To the federal government, not the district attorney's office?"

"He couldn't have just told Azoteca Comercial to wire money to an account here," Robb continues. "That money was cash, to begin with. The employees in Mexico would have had to deposit the money into a bank and then wire it here. It seems likely that someone would have called the home office before doing that, and your client would have been foiled before he could get the money."

"But there's an even larger problem with your theory," I press. "If Mr. Hanson was planning to flee, there would never have been a need to wire money into the United States to begin with, would there?"

"I don't follow."

"Mr. Hanson has millions of dollars already in the United States that he could have wired to whatever country he was planning to flee *to*, right?"

Robb doesn't skip a beat. "Except that wiring the money would, again, have created a paper trail that tipped the government off to his intended destination. Which is precisely why it was necessary to collect a bunch of cash and take it with him."

"But there was no reason for him to forward money to his so-called destination in the first place, was there?"

"I don't follow."

"Mr. Hanson has accounts around the world. There's money already waiting for him wherever he'd want to go, isn't there?"

This stops Robb. She hasn't thought of this. Or maybe she has thought of it but hasn't figured out an answer. Still, she's good on her feet and comes back with an answer. "Once your client fled the country, Mr. McFarland, he would have been a fugitive. There aren't many countries without reciprocal extradition treaties. He couldn't have gone to Europe. Or Canada. Or Australia or New Zealand. Or the Scandinavian countries. Even Iceland and Greenland would have shipped him back. I doubt that he had his money parked in any of the places that are left. He'd have needed cash."

"So, you're saying he had it all planned out? That he was acting rationally and that his plan all along was to get out of the United States and stay out?"

"I have no doubt of it."

"Then why did he do it?"

"Do what?"

"Do what?" I repeat Robb's question, my voice loud, my arms spread, looking straight at the jury. "Do the one thing that puts the lie to your whole theory."

Robb rolls her eyes. "I have no idea what you're talking about."

"Come back!"

Caroline gets it now. "Well . . ."

"Mr. Hanson was already in two foreign countries, but he came back to the United States, correct?"

"Yes."

"To Philadelphia?"

"It would seem so."

"He was in the Caymans! With a jet! And four million in cash! He was scot-free!"

"Objection!" Devlin is on his feet.

I ignore him. "But *he came back here* on the eve of his trial. Two weeks before jury selection. To prepare his defense!"

"The objection is sustained!" Now the judge's voice is raised. Bill Henry's upset with me. "Counsel will limit himself to questions, not speeches."

The jury can see that I've crossed the line. But the point is clear. The last thing a rat trying to flee a trap will do once he gets out is to climb right back in.

◆ ◆ ◆

Now it's Edwin's turn. Devlin wants to wrap up the afternoon having David's own brother indict him. He moves quickly through the background questions about Edwin's and David's roles at HWI. He has Edwin repeat what Kevin Kratz told the jury about being asked by the DA's financial-crimes unit to look into the possibility that David had misappropriated corporate cash. But when Devlin gets to the "money shot," things go wrong for him.

"Was there any possible corporate purpose," Walker asks, "for your brother's taking two million dollars in cash from Azoteca Comercial?"

At the motion hearing, Edwin had answered, "None whatsoever." The answer he gives today, however, is different.

"None that I was apprised of at the time."

Devlin tries to hide his surprise. He stands behind his table, pretends to look through his notes. He's trying to decide whether to remind Edwin of his prior testimony or leave it alone. He glances over at me and realizes I've caught the twist in Edwin's testimony and that I'll jump all over it if he doesn't nail Edwin down first. "Mr. Hanson, do you recall that in previous testimony before this court, you stated that there was *no* corporate purpose for your brother's using the company jet and taking the money from Azoteca Comercial?"

"I believe I said 'none whatsoever.' And there wasn't that I was aware of at the time of my earlier testimony."

"Well, as CEO of Hanson World Industries, you certainly would be aware of the use of the company jet and the withdrawal of large sums of cash."

At this, Edwin's tone turns nasty. "Mr. Walker, my company employs forty thousand people in two dozen countries. We have countless executives, and I don't know how many airplanes. I assure you that I do not keep track of it all."

Devlin is incredulous. "But this was your own brother, taking a jet out of Philadelphia and looting a subsidiary."

"Objection," I say. "The prosecutor is arguing with the witness. *His own* witness," I add.

"Sustained," the judge says. Then he looks to Devlin. "Is it your intention to impeach your own witness? You certainly may. But you have to ask permission first."

Devlin is completely flustered at this turn of events. He pretends to look down at his notes again. I use the time to glance at David and Marcie, both of whom have very slight smiles on their faces. And I can guess why. They've gotten to Edwin, threatened him with something. It's causing Edwin to throw Devlin a major curveball on direct and, if I'm guessing correctly, follow my lead on cross. So when Devlin mumbles that he has no further questions, I stand and lead Edwin down the primrose path. The path that I'd started to clear during the motion hearing.

"I understand that Hanson World Industries is involved in many humanitarian efforts around the globe," I begin.

"Yes. That's right. We're very proud of our charitable work, particularly in Central America and the African nations."

"I expect that your company would prefer to work through the governments of the countries in which you give aid. But some of those governments are less than trustworthy."

"Yes."

"So you've found it prudent to pay for food, clothing, services, and medical care directly. With cash."

"Correct."

"Do you require receipts?"

"Of course not."

"And which executives at HWI oversee the company's charitable efforts?"

Edwin pauses, but answers as I expect him to. "We have a department that runs all of our overseas aid. That department reports to the general counsel's office."

"And before your brother took his leave of absence, did he, as general counsel, fill you in on all the operational details of those efforts?"

"No."

"So when you said that your brother's use of the corporate funds from Azoteca Comercial was not for any purpose *that you knew of,* is it possible he took the money to use as part of HWI's charitable work?"

Edwin clenches his jaw. "Yes."

I thank Edwin for his candor and turn to take my seat. I can't resist sneaking a peek at Devlin and Christina Wesley, both of whom are struggling to remain impassive. But there is someone in the courtroom even more upset by Edwin's testimony than the two prosecutors. As David's brother passes by the defense table, facing away from the jurors, he lets the mask he's worn fall away. Edwin's face remains fixed in stone, but his eyes are filled with hate.

29

Tuesday, November 13, Continued

Judge Henry waits for Edwin to exit the bar, then calls counsel up to the bench. "It's 4:30," he says, looking at the clock on the wall. "I'm going to send the jurors to their hotel. Then I want to meet with you in my chambers. We have some housekeeping matters."

The judge tells the jury their trial day is over and reminds them not to talk about the case.

The jurors nod to show the judge they understand and will heed him. I know better, of course. By now the jury will have broken into smaller cliques of two or three. Could be along racial lines, gender lines, age lines, politics, or education. Or based on nothing more than how close some of the jurors are sitting together in the box. The members of these small groups will discuss the evidence. They'll also exchange snide remarks about the witnesses, the lawyers, the judge, the people sitting in the spectator benches. Or other jurors. Sometimes the court's deputy will overhear them and laugh along or mildly scold them. The bottom line is that opinions about every facet of the case have already begun to form in the jurors' minds. These opinions will congeal over the next few days; in fact, some jurors will have already made up their minds long before the attorneys' closing arguments.

Once the jurors and spectators have cleared the courtroom, I take my troops into the hallway for our daily debriefing. "Henry never should have let in all that stuff about David traveling abroad to gather money," Alexander Ginsberg says. "I'm surprised he did."

I thank Ginsberg, then turn to Marcie. "I'd like to meet with you after the conference with the judge," I tell her. "Vaughn, will you walk Marcie to the office?" I watch them make their way down the hall toward the elevators. Piper has been hanging back a few feet away. I tell her I'll be there in a minute.

"Mr. Walker was one unhappy pup in there," Ginsberg says. "Any idea why his man Edwin turned coat?"

"An idea? Yes."

"You know, Mick, you're really not doing all that poorly. This may be a case to take to the jury, after all."

I take a deep breath. I haven't told Ginsberg about the tape. He doesn't know, as I do from the video, that *three* men met with Jennifer Yamura in her house the day she was killed. That the second man pushed her down the stairs. And that it must have been the third man, David Hanson, who finished her off. And Ginsberg doesn't know why I must ensure that David gets away with it. Or why, to make that happen, I need to see to it that this case never goes to verdict.

"I can't have this case get anywhere near the jury," I tell him. "And David and Marcie have to be plenty scared when the defense rests its case. That's why you're here."

"I remember."

Ginsberg leaves me, and I go over to Piper.

"I forgot how good you are," she says. "And how interesting trials can be."

"Interesting is a good word for it."

"Ancient Chinese curse, I know," Piper says, referring to the famous line: May you live in interesting times. "Seriously, though, I felt like I was on a roller coaster in there. The morning was bad for David, but in the afternoon things seemed to turn around. What did Mr. Ginsberg think?"

"He said that we can't let this case get anywhere near a jury." Piper's face falls dramatically. "Hey, don't worry. The prosecution's case is full of holes, and I'm going to rip them wide open for the jury. Then comes our turn."

"Will David have to testify?"

I take a deep breath. "I'm hoping not. Devlin would crush him. Unless David chooses to disclose his alibi for where he was at the time of the murder."

"How long does he have to decide to do that?"

"We were supposed to notify the court and prosecution of a potential alibi defense a long time ago. Still, if David came forward even now with a credible alibi, I don't think Bill Henry would exclude it." I pause. Piper seems not to realize that I have stopped talking. "Hey? You okay?"

"Yeah." She checks her watch. "Oops. I've got to get to my parents' house and pick up Gabby."

I walk Piper to the elevators and press the "Down" button for her. "I'm not going to be too late tonight," I say. "I have to meet Marcie for a few minutes, discuss strategy, then tighten up my cross-examinations on some of the prosecution witnesses. Shouldn't take more than a few hours. I'll be home by nine." Piper's elevator arrives and she starts to enter. Then she turns to face me, holding open the doors.

"Is Marcie involved in the strategy?" Piper asks.

I nod. "Sometimes I think she's more involved in it than I am."

Piper stares at me for a moment, then smiles wanly and lets the elevator doors close. I take the next elevator to the twelfth floor and the judge's chambers. The judge, Devlin Walker, Christina Wesley, and the judge's law clerk are all waiting for me.

"Glad you could join us, Mr. McFarland," the judge says. There's a sharpness to his voice, and I decide not to make light of my tardiness. "All right," he says, "now that we're all here, let me get to it. This whole money thing is bothering me. I think I may have made a mistake in letting it in." This causes Devlin to shift in his seat. Christina Wesley's jaw drops. The judge goes on, addressing himself to me. "That's why I gave you broad latitude in asking about all that charity stuff. Do you have a fair basis for that line of questioning? Some evidence to support it? It's one thing to imply that your client used the money for a worthy goal in a motion hearing. It's another entirely to use your questions to send a false message to the jury during trial."

I look the judge in the eye and answer, "I do have a fair basis for my questions. Whether I decide to have my client take the stand and disclose that information is up in the air."

Devlin is halfway out of his seat by now. "Your Honor, I would strongly object to the court's reversing itself on this issue, particularly now that the Commonwealth has presented evidence on it. The jury would think we tried to get away with something and Your Honor shut us down."

"Relax, counselor," the judge says. "I haven't made up my mind what I'm going to do yet. But from this point on, I don't want any more testimony on it. I want you to focus on the elements of the charges."

"Edwin Hanson was our last witness on the flight issue," Devlin says.

The judge nods, then turns back to me. "I'm going to let in the evidence of the neighborhood robberies. This is a murder case, and it seems to me that other break-ins close in time and place to the murder are probative of the issue of whether there may have been someone other than the defendant with the motive and opportunity to kill the decedent."

Devlin protests. "Your Honor, there are burglaries and petty crimes in every neighborhood in the city. Are we going to conduct mini trials on every neighborhood transgression in all of our murder cases? It would be unworkable!"

Then it's Christina Wesley's turn to vent. "This is ridiculous! We don't even know who committed those burglaries. How can we investigate a crime if we don't know who the criminal is?"

The judge, Devlin Walker, and I all look at the young prosecutor. After a moment, I offer, "Well, gee, Ms. Wesley, I thought that part of the investigation process is finding out the identity of the criminal."

Christina's face turns crimson. I can't tell whether she's more embarrassed at herself or livid with me.

"Is there any talk of a plea here?" Bill Henry asks, out of the blue. "I know your client isn't going to cop to first degree," he continues, looking at me. "But what about voluntary manslaughter? Or even involuntary manslaughter?"

Devlin says he has little interest in a plea but will consider it if approached by the defense.

The judge shrugs and tells me to talk to my client, see if he'll agree to plead to a lesser charge.

"I'll run it by him, Your Honor," I say, without enthusiasm.

The judge dismisses us until tomorrow, and I leave chambers ahead of Devlin and Christina. I'm walking toward the elevators when Walker comes up behind me.

"A minute, Mick," he says.

I turn and wait.

"Early on," Devlin says, "I offered to let your client save himself from life imprisonment by pleading to voluntary manslaughter. I'm making that offer again, for the last time, but only if—"

I put up a hand to stop him. "I know. I know it chapter and verse. How about you tell *me* something."

Devlin stares at me, waiting.

"What's the big secret?" I ask.

He looks at me, confused.

"Come on, Devlin. You've zeroed in on that computer from the get-go. What about it is so important that you're willing to let go of the biggest murder conviction of your career? A conviction that would make you a shoo-in for DA when you-know-who decides it's time to step down?"

"You know why I want that computer. Yamura had more information on the police drug ring. More names—maybe a lot more. I want those names and whatever additional evidence she had. I've never made a secret of that."

I stare hard at Walker, let the corner of my mouth curl up just a little. "There's more to it than that. You would never trade a David Hanson just to rope in a few more crooked cops." Now it's Devlin's turn to stare. "It's something close to home, is what I'm betting. The hard-on you have for that laptop isn't because *you* want to see what's on it. It's because you don't want *someone else* to see it."

Devlin's jaw stiffens. I've struck a nerve, as intended, but he still thinks I'm only guessing. "One last chance, Mick. Your client can plead to voluntary manslaughter tomorrow morning, before we start the day's testimony. But that offer goes away the minute my first witness is sworn in. Forever." With that, he turns and walks away.

It's close to six o'clock by the time I get back to the office. I go right to the conference room, where Marcie is waiting for me. Seated at the far end of the table, she watches me as I enter and close the door behind me.

"There's fresh coffee," she says, nodding to the white porcelain pitcher sitting in front of her. "I assume you're planning on a late night."

"I'll get some later," I say, taking a corner seat closest to Marcie. For someone who's spent all day sitting in a crowded courtroom, she looks remarkably fresh. Her conservative blue pantsuit doesn't have a wrinkle, and not a hair is out of place on her head. The faintest wisp of perfume dances across my face, and I wonder whether Marcie just spritzed herself in the ladies' room or if she's wearing some immorally expensive fragrance that has a time-release element built in.

Marcie and I sit for a moment, looking at each other, until I split the silence with a single word. "Edwin."

Marcie smiles. "Yes, Edwin," she says, her eyes alight. "He and I had a little sit-down this morning at his office. The sun wasn't even up, but he was already at work, as I knew he would be. He thought he'd have a fun day in the courtroom, hanging my husband out to dry. I convinced him otherwise, made him see that he hadn't thought things through."

"What exactly did you threaten him with?"

"David was general counsel at HWI for close to ten years. His job was to manage all of the company's legal problems. Manage as in keep secret. Hide. Sweep under the rug. David told me to convey to his brother that if Edwin hurt him with the jury, the phones would begin ringing in every major news outlet in the country as well as in dozens of state and federal regulatory agencies. Payoffs to politicians, here and abroad. Environmental violations, big and bigger. Cover-ups of discrimination claims. Falsified drug-test results. Weapons technology sold secretly to certain unsavory governments. Violations of international trade agreements. And the paperwork to back it all up. By the time David and I finished with him, poor Edwin would have to spend the next decade testifying before congressional subcommittees. And then, of course, the United States attorney would take his turn."

I sit back in my chair and take all this in. What Marcie is telling me without shame or hesitation is that her husband, along with his brother and their henchmen, engaged in corporate villainy on a titanic scale.

"What about Kevin Kratz?"

"What about him?"

"You're going to lop off his head," I say.

"As soon as the verdict comes down, no matter what that verdict is. Same with that worthless enabler, Barbara King. I made Edwin promise."

"But what if Kratz makes the same threat to Edwin you have? Demands to be kept on or given some huge golden parachute?"

Marcie laughs outright at this. "Come now, Mick. Do you really think that little weasel has it in him?"

She's right, of course. Kevin wouldn't dare take on David or Edwin Hanson.

I tell Marcie what Judge Henry said after court about possibly reconsidering his admission of David's gathering $4 million on the eve of trial. Marcie smiles and says, "I think after tomorrow, the judge will do just that."

Her remark instantly fills me with worry. "What are you talking about?"

"Do you know how many people have been starving in South Sudan? How many have been displaced around the world by civil war?"

I can feel the blood draining from my face. "What have you and David done this time?"

Marcie pulls out a cigarette and lights it up. She stares at me as she takes a deep drag. Then a second. "David didn't kill that tart. And I'm not going to let him go to prison for her death."

"How can you be so sure he didn't do it? Maybe they got into a fight. Maybe he lost control."

"David doesn't lose control," Marcie said.

"Everyone loses control! You didn't see David the morning of his arrest, sitting in that prison cell. That was not a man in control."

Marcie glares at me.

"And what's your answer to the video?"

"All it shows is David going in and out of the house."

"During the time period Jennifer Yamura was killed. David would be sunk if that film ever got out."

"Oh, knock it off. This isn't just about you protecting David. If it ever *got out* about that video and your role in keeping it under wraps, you'd be charged with obstruction of justice. You're protecting your own ass as much as you're looking out for David."

I grit my teeth but say nothing. Marcie's right. That video would damn me, too.

Marcie stands, puts her coat on, wraps the strap of her handbag around her shoulder. I watch her walk to the door, thinking she's going to leave without saying good-bye. But she turns.

"I know this case has been rough on you. And that it'll probably get rougher—for a whole lot of reasons. David and I aren't making it any easier. I know that, too. But we can't just sit back and hope the legal system works the way it's supposed to. David and I have assets—relationships and avenues not open to most people. We're going to take advantage of them. You disagree, but we think our efforts will help. But even if they don't, at least David and I won't look back with the regret that comes from not doing everything one could have." Marcie looks at me for a long moment, then turns and walks out the door.

When she's gone, I stare at the empty conference room for a long time.

I know all about regret.

30

Wednesday, November 14

Devlin Walker, Christina Wesley, and I are seated before Judge Henry in his small office adjoining the courtroom.

"Well?" the judge asks. "Have you considered my request for a plea deal?"

Devlin jumps in before I can answer. "We offered Man One, Your Honor. As sweet a deal as this defendant could ever hope to get."

The judge considers this, then looks at me.

"I met with Mr. Hanson this morning, and we talked at length." I pause and withdraw a piece of lined yellow legal paper from my breast pocket. "My client paid close attention to everything I told him. Then he asked me for a pen and something to write on. He said he wanted to make sure Your Honor heard his message in his words. What he wrote is this: 'I did not kill Jennifer Yamura. Not deliberately. Not accidentally. Not in a fit of passion. Not by reason of insanity or whatever other loophole could lessen the sentence. I did not kill Jennifer Yamura, and I will not plead guilty to any crime that implies that I did, even if it would keep me from spending a thousand years in prison. As to the lesser charges pertaining to altering the crime scene, I ask Your Honor to understand that the murder charges wrongfully brought against me by the jump-the-gun prosecutor have destroyed my reputation, left my career in ruins, and derailed a business deal that could have benefited every man, woman, and child living in Philadelphia. Like any innocent man, I shudder at the prospect of imprisonment. But I am not going to enter into any deal, on any charge, proposed by this wrongful prosecution.'"

I fold the piece of paper, place it back into my jacket, and look at the judge.

"So," the judge says, "even if the DA offered Man Two . . ."

"Not even jaywalking."

At this, Walker actually snorts his contempt. The judge casts him a disapproving glance and then orders us to go back to the courtroom. I pause at the doorway while Christina Wesley and Devlin leave. Then, before I cross the threshold, I glance back. Bill Henry is staring at me, and I can see he's gotten the message——David Hanson is innocent and will cop to nothing.

Which will play perfectly into my endgame.

I watch the jury file in and take their seats.

"The Commonwealth calls Detective John Tredesco to the stand," Devlin announces.

Tredesco enters the well through the gate on the left of the courtroom, the prosecution side, passing between the prosecutor's table and the jury box. His thinning black hair is freshly cut, but it still looks greasy on his small head. He has his suit jacket buttoned as he walks past the jury, so they can't see his gut sticking over his belt. Tredesco turns to face the jury and can't help hard-staring them as he takes the stand.

Devlin begins with the usual questioning, about Tredesco's having been raised in Philadelphia, his time at the academy, and his fifteen-year tenure as a detective, the last eight with homicide. Those boxes all checked, Walker takes Tredesco to the night of Jennifer Yamura's murder.

"Officers Pancetti and Kujowski handed the defendant over to Detective Cook and me, and we drove him to the station house," Tredesco begins. "He was processed and brought to an interview room. Detective Cook offered him coffee. He said no, at first, then after a while said okay. So we brought him the coffee and some milk, too, but he said he had to have skim milk. Detective Cook went and checked the fridge and brought back two percent milk, and the defendant said, 'No. I said skim. Not two percent.' So Detective Cook found some skim. But by then the defendant said the coffee wasn't hot enough and asked could we nuke it."

This is vintage Tredesco bullshit. Fabricated details to make a defendant look bad. Tredesco has been offering this stuff up on the witness stand as long as I can remember. When I was a prosecutor, I had to tell him to knock it off more than once.

"Did you question the defendant before he asked for a lawyer?" Devlin asks.

"Before, yes. Not after." Tredesco knows to emphasize that anything he's going to attribute to the defendant was said before the invocation of Miranda rights. "We asked him why he killed the girl, Jennifer Yamura. Was there a fight? Did she want to break things off? Did she catch him with someone else?"

"What did he say?"

"He denied everything."

"Did you ask him where he was when the victim was murdered?"

"Yes."

"Did he answer?"

"He said he was at work all afternoon, which I found a little odd."

"Why did that strike you as odd?"

"I never told him when she'd been killed. So how did he know that it was that afternoon?" Devlin lets this hang in the air for a while. I see a couple of jurors raise their eyebrows. A few look toward the defense table to see how David and I react to this.

"So, he told you he was at work all afternoon," Devlin follows up. "Did you come to learn whether that was true or not?"

Before Tredesco can answer, I stand. "Your Honor, we'll stipulate that Mr. Hanson wasn't at work all day. Ms. King testified to that, and we've never disputed it." The judge casts me a cold look. David's lying is an important point for the prosecutor, and Bill Henry isn't going to let me pretend otherwise by offering to stipulate to it.

"Overruled."

"We found out from his secretary," Tredesco starts in, "that it wasn't true that he was at his office. She told us that he took off without telling her where he was going and never showed up again."

Devlin says, "I'm not going to ask you about fingerprints and DNA found around the house. That will be for the CSU witness to describe for the jury. But did you learn anything important about the house itself?"

"Absolutely. We learned that Mr. Hanson arranged for the purchase of the house about six years ago through a subsidiary of Hanson World Industries."

"How do you know it was the defendant who was responsible for the purchase and not someone else at HWI?"

"His name was on the agreement of sale. He signed it as general counsel."

Devlin requests permission to approach the witness, then walks to the stand and has Tredesco identify the sales agreement.

Devlin moves the exhibit into evidence, then asks Tredesco if he learned anything else about the house at 1792 Addison Street.

"The whole place had just been remodeled," the detective answers. "New carpets, new furniture, new TV. A brand-new bed. I figured the defendant was planning to get a new girlfriend, too."

I object, and the judge strikes the remark from the record, tells the jury to pretend they didn't hear it.

Devlin asks Tredesco whether he considered any potential suspects other than David.

"Of course," Tredesco lies. "I do that in every investigation. Even where it's clear from the start who committed the crime, I try to play devil's advocate, ask myself who else might have done it. If another lead does appear, I follow it wherever it takes me. That's what criminal investigation is all about."

Devlin spends another half hour with Tredesco, having him recount to the jury his and Detective Cook's investigation, step by step. Their interviews with all the neighbors, giving their names and the dates and times they were interviewed. Their interviews with Edwin Hanson, Kevin Kratz, the garage manager, and then Barbara King and half a dozen of David's other colleagues at work. Reviewing the evidence with the CSU team and the medical examiner. Interviews with Jennifer Yamura's coworkers, friends, and even her parents and brother. Late nights and early mornings. Meals skipped. Even an anniversary missed. Devlin's message to the jury: the police conducted a thorough investigation and followed the evidence to David Hanson.

"Did you find anyone who could place the defendant anywhere other than at Jennifer Yamura's house on the afternoon of her death?" Walker asks.

"No one placed him anywhere else."

"Did you find anyone who had information that Mr. Hanson put, or intended to put, the four million dollars to any use other than as seed money for an attempt to flee the jurisdiction?"

"No one came forward with any other reason for the money."

"One final area of questioning, Detective," Walker says. "And it's an important one. Did you find any other credible leads, any other suspects in Jennifer Yamura's murder, that weren't speculative?"

"That weren't speculative, no. I mean, we knew Ms. Yamura wasn't exactly liked by the police officers charged in the drug ring. But none of them were caught running out of her house. And the CSU team didn't find any prints of those particular officers in the house. So we marked them off the list. After due consideration, of course."

"Had Ms. Yamura received any death threats from any of the officers?" Devlin asks.

"There was no evidence of that."

"Any phone calls to her house made from the numbers of any of those officers? Or calls from her to them?"

I'm ready to spring now. The court has made clear that Jennifer's calls to me are out of bounds, but I can imagine Tredesco trying to slip them in.

He plays it straight. "No."

"Other than her relationship with the defendant, did you learn of any romantic relationship that would give someone a motive to kill Ms. Yamura?"

"No one," Tredesco answers.

"Thank you, Detective," Walker says. "Your Honor, that's all I have on direct."

The court gives everyone a ten-minute midmorning break to stretch and use the bathroom. I wait for the deputy to take David through the side door to the holding cell. Then I turn to Ginsberg and Vaughn. Marcie is leaving the courtroom through the door on the left, Piper through the door on the right.

Ginsberg rolls his eyes. "Tredesco." He knows the detective as well as I do.

Thirty minutes after the ten-minute break has begun, the jurors are back in their seats. Judge Henry gives me the nod, and I'm on my feet in a flash, going right at John Tredesco.

"You would have this jury believe that you conducted an exhaustive investigation?"

"Very exhaustive."

"That you left no stone unturned? That you looked into every possible suspect?"

"Every credible suspect."

"List for the jury the names of the drug-pushing cops you looked into. Tell the jury every step you took to investigate each of them."

"Like I said, their prints weren't at the scene. There was no evidence they even tried to contact the victim before she was killed."

"List their names, Detective. The names of the drug-pushing cops indicted by the grand jury." Tredesco pauses, glances at Devlin, who merely opens his hands.

"I don't remember their names," Tredesco says, so I hand him the list.

"Does that refresh your recollection?"

Tredesco hems and haws, but I eventually get him to list the officers' names.

"What was that phrase you used on direct examination?" I ask. "That Ms. Yamura 'wasn't exactly liked' by the crooked cops? Did you really say that?" Tredesco stares at me. "Those crooked cops *hated* her, isn't that true? Her story on them instantly destroyed their reputations, cost them their jobs, and sped up their prosecution. Isn't all of that true?"

"Like I said, there was no evidence they even tried to contact the victim before she was killed."

"Really? They didn't *call her* to warn her they were coming? Is that what you're saying?"

Tredesco's eyes bore into me. "There was no contact between any of those officers and the victim. And none of their fingerprints were found at her house."

"Did you consider the fact that experienced police officers might have *heard about* fingerprint evidence and decided to *wear gloves?*"

"We found no gloves at the scene."

"Because the police would know better than to leave gloves at the crime scene. Gloves that would have their prints and DNA all over them."

Tredesco sits rock-still in his chair. "The police didn't kill her."

"They killed one of their fellow officers who testified against them, Stanley Lipinski. Shot him down like a dog in the street."

Devlin is on his feet, objecting, as he should. "Your Honor, there is not one shred of evidence that Officer Lipinski was killed by other police officers, let alone the ones implicated in the drug ring. I move to strike counsel's remarks and ask the court to stop this absolutely improper line of questioning."

The court sustains the objection, and I move on.

"Let's change direction for a minute," I say. "You told the jury that you couldn't find any witnesses who placed Mr. Hanson somewhere other than the murder scene at the time Ms. Yamura was killed."

"Not one."

"What about the other half of the equation, the half that you forgot to tell the jury?" Tredesco squints. He knows where I'm going. "In all your exhaustive efforts, with all those people you interviewed, all those stones you turned, you didn't find a single witness who *placed* Mr. Hanson at the murder scene that afternoon, either. Isn't that true?"

"I guess nobody was looking out their window when he came in and out of the house."

I'm about to move the court to strike the snide answer, but Judge Henry beats me to the punch, leaning over the bench toward the witness. "Answer the question squarely, Detective. Did you find any witnesses who placed the defendant at the scene of the murder at the time of the murder?"

Tredesco answers grudgingly. "No."

Tredesco and I dance a little more around the lack of evidence placing David at the scene when Yamura was killed, then I move on to another subject. "I understand there was a rash of break-ins in Ms. Yamura's neighborhood around the time she was murdered."

Tredesco shrugs. "It's Philadelphia."

A couple of the jurors smile.

"Two break-ins before the murder and one afterward, all within a couple blocks of the house on Addison Street?"

"I looked into it, thoroughly. There was nothing to connect the burglaries to the murder."

"One of the burglars was caught. He was booked and charged and is sitting in prison. Damian Sheetz. Did you go to the prison and interview him, try to get a confession out of him?"

"I was aware of Mr. Sheetz. I looked at his rap sheet. There was no history of violence. Just break-ins. And a bunch of shoplifting charges. Possession of stolen goods."

"So he was stealing money and valuables from people's homes and from stores, to pay for a drug habit. Tell me, Detective, what happens when a drug addict, desperate for a fix, breaks into someone's house to steal something and is surprised to find the resident inside? Do they have a nice conversation? A cup of tea?"

"He would have run, not attacked her."

"Because running away would be the smarter thing to do and, being a hard-up junkie, he'd have been thinking rationally, right?" Devlin objects, so I withdraw the question. "Speaking of drug addicts looking for money and things to pawn," I continue, "please tell the jury what you did *not* find at the murder scene."

"I don't know what you mean."

"I'm talking about Ms. Yamura's jewelry. And the money from her wallet. Did you think Mr. Hanson was strapped for cash? And what about Ms. Yamura's laptop? That was gone, too. Did you think Mr. Hanson couldn't afford a new computer?" I fire these questions so fast I'm out of breath by the time Walker stands and objects.

The judge sustains the objection. "One question at a time, counselor," he scolds me, though I can see by the smile in his eyes that he's enjoying my cross.

I turn back to Tredesco. "You can certainly see that Mr. Hanson has no need to steal a laptop computer."

Tredesco smiles. "I'm sure your client could afford to buy a computer for every room in his mansion," he says. "For every stateroom on his yacht. He didn't steal the computer for its cash value. Our theory is that he wanted the computer for what was *on it*. Your client had a long-term relationship with the victim. Maybe they sent each other naughty e-mails. Or sex videos."

I steal a glance at Devlin Walker. He smiles. I turn back to the witness stand. "And the money? The jewelry? Did you think Mr. Hanson was short of cash?"

Again, Tredesco is ready for me. "This is why we believe the crime was premeditated. He took the money and jewelry to make it look like a robbery gone bad. To use as a defense, like you're doing for him now."

I turn to the judge and object. "This whole theory should be stricken from the record. It's all just so much speculation."

Even before Devlin can answer me, Tredesco butts in. "It's not speculation, Your Honor," he says, lifting his finger up to the side of his nose. "It's fifteen years investigating crimes."

"The objection is overruled," says Judge Henry.

I look back at the witness. "You testified that it struck you as odd that, when you asked Mr. Hanson where he was when Ms. Yamura was killed, he said he'd been in the office all afternoon. Do you remember that?" Tredesco says that he recalls the testimony. "You said his answer made you conclude he had to have known when she was killed, yet you hadn't told him."

"Exactly."

"But Mr. Hanson had spent some time in the house before the police came. He'd have seen the body and seen that her blood was dried. He'd have known she'd been dead for a while."

"I don't know about that. Your client's not a medical examiner. Or a police officer."

I spend the next ten minutes grilling Tredesco about the 911 call, retracing my questioning of the uniformed officers. "So there's no doubt that someone *other* than David Hanson knew about the goings-on at 1792 Addison Street and deliberately lied to the police to get them to show up when Mr. Hanson was still in the house."

"I can't say he lied. Maybe there was crashing, but nothing got broke."

"Things were crashing but nothing got broke? Did you really just say that?"

Tredesco doesn't answer.

"How can that happen? The same way two people can be shouting at each other when one of them has been dead for eight hours?"

"Objection," Devlin says, an edge to his voice. "Hounding the witness."

Judge Henry sustains the objection. "We get it, Mr. McFarland. Move on."

"So we have this other person making the call. What efforts did you make to find out who it was and why he lied to the police?"

"We tried to trace the call, but it was made from a disposable cell phone."

"A disposable cell phone? Like the ones drug dealers use?"

Tredesco leans over the stand at me. "Like the phones thousands of people use. Like maybe someone who wants to report a crime but doesn't want any blowback."

"Blowback?"

"Witness intimidation! It happens all the time in this city. Everyone knows about it. It's all over the papers. It's the biggest problem we have in making arrests. No one wants to come forward because they're afraid." Tredesco has scored a point with the jury, and he knows it. He leans back, satisfied with himself.

I quickly change the subject and trade punches with Tredesco for another few rounds, winning points, losing points. Finished with the detective, I turn toward counsel table. Then, as though I've just remembered something, I turn back to the witness. "Oh, one more thing. Your testimony about Mr. Hanson wanting his coffee heated up and asking for skim milk?"

"Yes."

"Why do you suppose Mr. Hanson would ask for milk at all? Given that he's lactose-intolerant and always drinks his coffee black?"

Tredesco blinks. He knows I "gotcha'd" him. So do the jurors, several of whom cross their arms and smirk. Devlin's probably stewing. Like most by-the-book prosecutors, he doesn't like Tredesco's tricks. He'll have a little talk with the detective, I'm sure, after trial.

It's 12:30, and Judge Henry dismisses the jury for lunch.

"He hurt us," Vaughn says.

"Yep. For all his smarminess, Tredesco gave the jury two things it lacked up to now. A reason for taking the computer and an explanation for why David would have stolen the cash and jewelry, too."

Half an hour later, I'm sitting at the defense table, going over my questions for the next witness, Matthew Stone, the CSU team leader. I hear the door behind me and turn to see Vaughn racing for me, out of breath.

"You're not going to believe what's all over the news!" Vaughn exclaims. "Foreign-aid workers are coming forward claiming they've received millions in under-the-table humanitarian donations from Hanson World Industries. They say it's been going on for years. The stories came out first on YouTube, but now they're being picked up by the mainstream news outlets. And get this, two donations of two million apiece supposedly showed up in—"

"Let me guess," I interject. "South Sudan."

Vaughn stares at me.

"Marcie warned me last night that something like this was going to break."

The clock on the wall reaches 1:45, then 2:00, then 2:15, but the trial does not resume. Mike Holleran tells Devlin and me that the judge is holed up in his office, watching TV.

I glance at Devlin.

"Another stunt." He sits and murmurs something to Christina Wesley.

"This is tremendous," Vaughn whispers next to me at counsel table. Once David is brought into the courtroom, he'll move to his usual seat next to Marcie. "I think we should demand a mistrial. And if the judge doesn't go for it, we should ask for a week's adjournment to fly those foreign-aid workers here, have them testify."

I purse my lips, say nothing. Vaughn can see I'm displeased, and he's confused. Vaughn has no idea that the case isn't about the case. I look back at Alexander Ginsberg, who seems confused himself. He knows that Bill Henry is not one to be late to court. Piper, too, casts me a look that says, "What's happening?" The only person who appears at ease is Marcie, who smiles when I glance her way.

At 2:30, Holleran ushers David into the courtroom. A few minutes later, the judge strides onto the bench, buttoning his robe on the fly. He begins talking even before he's seated. "We have a problem," he says. "I'm going to want to talk to counsel in my chambers. First, though, I'm going to call in the jury and dismiss them for the day." Judge Henry nods to Holleran, who brings in the jury. He smiles at the jury, tells them he has good news, they're getting a break. Something's come up—an administrative matter, nothing to do with the case—and the trial day is being cut short. "So go back to the hotel, relax. Don't talk about the case. And, most important, as always, do not, under any circumstance, listen to the news or read the papers."

The jurors look from the judge to Devlin and me, and then to one another. They're all thinking the same thing. Something big about the case has broken in the media.

Fifteen minutes later Vaughn and I, along with Devlin Walker and Christina Wesley, are seated in Judge Henry's chambers. The judge begins by saying, "I'm now convinced that I made a mistake letting in the evidence about the money and the trips to Mexico and the Caymans. I've been in my chambers for the past two hours watching news stories about millions of dollars in under-the-table humanitarian aid spread around the world by Hanson World Industries. It's been going on for years. And, apparently, it was all being run by the defendant."

With that, the judge uses his remote to turn on the television in his office. CNN comes on with a video clip of David in some remote, war-torn village. He's sitting with a group of villagers. On his lap is a dark-skinned boy, maybe four or five years old. David smiles at the boy, tousles his hair, talks to the camera about the desperate plight of the villagers. A second video clip shows David in jeans and a short-sleeved white shirt leading a group of adults and children along a path in some other remote village. David himself looks to be about five years younger than he is now.

The judge turns down the sound and turns back to us.

"Your Honor, please. This has to be some kind of—" Devlin begins, but the judge interrupts.

"Let me finish. This does not appear to be fabricated. The foreign-aid workers themselves are coming forward with the information. And there are video clips purportedly showing Mr. Hanson meeting with these same workers in a number of villages over a period of time going back at least five years."

This part floors me. I'd assumed that Marcie's plants were going to come forward only with claims of recent donations, money tendered after David withdrew the $4 million. I imagined that Marcie could get her hands on another $4 million and fly it abroad fast enough to cover

David's tracks. But if the judge is right, David has been dumping cash for years.

Why?

Devlin pipes up again, and he and the judge begin arguing. Their voices fade into the background as my mind locks on to what David has been up to. I remember Marcie's threat to Edwin to disclose HWI's rampant criminality should he hurt David in court. Criminality that included illegal payoffs to foreign officials. And just that fast, I get it: David has been secreting millions in humanitarian aid as potential cover should HWI ever be accused of foreign bribery and need to account for vast sums of money disappearing from the company's coffers. Any congressional subcommittee poring over HWI's books would find a paper trail carefully left by David showing millions of dollars in HWI funds making their way to the hands of happy foreign-aid workers ready to testify to their receipt of the money, which they then used to feed, clothe, and educate the world's poor and downtrodden. All of which has turned out to be a massive stroke of luck for David, who can use the same planted millions as cover for the money he stole to pay off the blackmailer. Absolutely brilliant. Absolutely sinister. Absolutely David Fucking Hanson.

"Mr. McFarland?" It's the judge. "What are your thoughts? A limiting instruction telling the jury to disregard everything they've heard about the four million dollars? Or an outright mistrial?"

I pause a moment to let the question sink in, bring myself up to speed.

"Your Honor," I answer, "I'd like some time to think about it. To talk about it with my client. Certainly a mistrial would not be unwarranted. But perhaps a limiting instruction would be enough. I'd like to talk to Mr. Ginsberg as well. Your Honor may have noticed that he's been sitting with Mrs. Hanson throughout the trial."

"Yes, of course. Talk to your client. Talk to Mr. Ginsberg. Think it through. Just tell me tomorrow."

"Your Honor, I really must protest." Devlin's voice is thick with desperation. "As I said before, a limiting instruction will poison my credibility with the jury. You'd be telling them that I've been spouting nonsense. A mistrial would be . . . would be . . . it's just not warranted."

Bill Henry turns to me. "I'm assuming that your client, or someone from HWI, would be able to testify that the four million was in fact used for humanitarian aid. As part of this larger program. Is that right?"

"I'm sure that's exactly what Mr. Hanson would say. But, of course, I haven't decided to call him as a witness. Your Honor isn't suggesting that I *must* call Mr. Hanson to the stand to rebut the testimony about the four million?"

The judge sighs. "At this point, I'm not sure what I'm suggesting. Let's everyone sleep on this, and we'll revisit it tomorrow."

Half an hour later, I'm sitting across from David in his holding cell.

"Let me guess," David begins. "The news of my philanthropic ways has His Honor out of sorts."

I want to rip David a new one for this latest ploy. Tell him he'll never get away with it, at least not in the long run. But, of course, for David there will be no long run unless he beats the murder charge. Almost any risk is worth taking. So I limit myself to a question of tactics: "Why wait? Why rot in prison for three weeks before springing the news?"

"I wanted the prosecution to commit itself at trial. I wanted them to stake their credibility on it."

"But the jury's sequestered," I say. "They're not going to know about your humanitarian efforts."

David laughs. "Come on, Mick, you can't be serious. Do you really believe that the jurors aren't going to get wind of the story? That they won't spy the headlines at the newsstands between here and their hotel? That they won't channel surf in their rooms, looking for what the six or ten or eleven o'clock news is saying about the trial? That their family members won't text them a heads-up? Really?"

David is right, of course. One would have to be insanely naive to think that the news of HWI's humanitarian program won't make its way to the jury.

"And once the judge tells the jury to disregard the prosecution's evidence regarding my supposed plan to flee before trial, the jury will think the prosecution has been caught trying to pull one over on them. It will taint Devlin Walker's entire case." David smiles, and I see behind his blue eyes the same coal-black intelligence that flares inside Marcie's.

"I told you the judge was thinking of a limiting instruction *or* a mistrial."

"*No* mistrial," David says instantly. "I won't go through this again." Then he smiles, sits back, and switches gears with ease. "Thank you for taking care of Marcie," he says. "For explaining everything to her, letting her explain things to you. I know I've told you this before, but my wife has proven to be a tremendous asset."

31

THURSDAY, NOVEMBER 15

Nine a.m. and we're all back in the judge's chambers. His Honor has decided to postpone his decision between granting a mistrial and giving the jury a limiting instruction to disregard the evidence regarding David's cash-gathering flights. The judge did this at my request. On the one hand, like David, I do not want a mistrial; this odyssey has to end quickly for my plan to come to fruition. On the other hand, I'm afraid that a jury instruction will give David and Marcie too much confidence. I need them afraid.

For his part, Devlin has fought mightily against either a mistrial or a limiting instruction. Now, with the judge's decision to put the issue on hold, Devlin is fit to be tied. He's clutching the armrests of his chair so hard his knuckles are white.

"All right, then," the judge says. "I'll see everyone in court at 9:30. And from here on out, I want things to run fast—and smoothly."

Thirty minutes later, the trial resumes and Devlin calls Matthew Stone, the lead investigator for the Crime Scene Unit. Stone is the polar opposite of John Tredesco. He's pushing forty but looks ten years younger. He has large eyes, short-but-stylish blond hair, and an open face. Self-deprecating and quick to smile, Stone is someone most people find instantly likable. I know from experience that he's also a completely honest cop.

After some preliminary questions about Stone's background, Devlin gets down to business.

Stone explains what was done to secure the premises and preserve the integrity of the crime scene. Then, with the court's permission, he steps down from the witness stand, positions himself next to the big screen, and addresses the jury.

I have stipulated to the admissibility of diagrams of the house, so Devlin has Stone pull them up on the screen. The first diagram depicts the first floor—the kitchen and living room and the short hallway between them containing the door to the powder room and the doorway to the basement behind the curtain of glass beads. The second diagram shows the basement, including the steps.

Then comes the emotional evidence. At Devlin's request, Stone pulls up the first picture, showing Jennifer's body lying on the steps. It is an overhead picture, taken from the top of the steps. As they did during Devlin's opening, some of the jurors look away. They take a few seconds to steel themselves, then look directly at the photo as Matthew Stone tells them what they're seeing.

Stone describes what the photo depicts, then pulls up another shot, a close-up taken just inches below Jennifer's battered head. Dried blood is caked all over her matted hair. The jurors stare at the image, some of their faces turning gray.

Devlin has Stone describe the hair and bloodstains on the fifth and sixth stairs, which are consistent with having been stricken by the back of Jennifer's head when she fell. Then he pulls up a photograph of Jennifer's knees, and Stone describes the fresh scrape injuries.

"Did you form any conclusions as to how she sustained the injuries to her knees, given that she fell backward down the stairs?"

Stone nods and pulls up a photograph of the basement floor. "When we began to study the basement, I saw what I thought may have been blood traces on the concrete floor. The floor also smelled of household cleanser. So we sprayed luminol to see if there was more latent blood on the floor than could be seen with the naked eye. Sure enough, there was a trail of blood along the floor, starting at the bottom of the stairs and continuing for about five feet. The injuries to the victim's knees were consistent with her having crawled along the rough cement of the floor."

Devlin pauses to let the testimony sink in with the jurors. Then he asks Stone to tie it all together. "Please explain to the jury what this physical evidence led you to conclude about the nature of the crime and how it was committed."

Stone inhales, then looks at the jurors. "The victim was pushed through the beaded curtain. She fell backward. The back of her head struck the fifth step with great force, and it struck the sixth step as well. The steps were old wooden steps with rough, splintered edges, and we found remnants of hair, skin, and bone on each of these two steps. The victim lay there for some indeterminate minutes, then managed to get off the steps and crawl along the basement floor, trailing blood the whole way."

Here, Devlin stops Stone. "But the victim was found *on* the steps, her head lying on the concrete floor at the bottom of the steps, feet toward the top. Having left the stairs, why would she have gone back?"

"She didn't. Someone dragged her back to the stairs and positioned her head down, on her back. And, there, she bled out and died."

Devlin pauses to give the jury time to chew on the image of this lovely young woman, desperately crawling on hands and knees trying to get away from her assailant, who pursues her and finishes the job he started when he pushed her down the stairs. I turn slightly to the left, just enough to glimpse Jennifer's mother weeping.

Devlin starts up again, switches gears. "Did you find any evidence of a break-in? Jimmied locks on the doors, broken windowpanes?"

"There was nothing like that."

"What did that tell you?"

"That the perpetrator either had his own key, or he was let into the house by the victim. If the latter was the case, there's a strong chance she knew him." Stone's final words cause several of the jurors to look at David.

Devlin asks a series of questions establishing David's presence in the house. Stone testifies that David's fingerprints were found throughout the house, as were strands of his hair. Stone also describes the items of David's clothing found in the master bedroom closet: a suit, some shirts, shoes, boxers—all in David's sizes—along with some ties and a belt.

Devlin concludes his questioning, and Judge Henry orders a fifteen-minute break for everyone to stretch their legs.

As soon as the jury returns, I start in on Matthew Stone. "You began by telling the jury that part of crime-scene processing is to secure and control the area—did I hear that right?"

"Yes."

"And this idea of securing the crime scene is a fundamental principle of crime-scene processing, isn't that true? A golden rule, so to speak?"

"I think that's fair to say."

"And a key part of securing the crime scene is restricting access?"

"Yes."

"The integrity of the crime scene must be maintained, and that means you don't allow people to come in and drop hairs and prints and dirt all over your crime scene, right?"

"Absolutely."

"But it didn't quite work out that way for you in this case, did it?" My question takes Stone aback.

"I don't know what you're talking about."

"Your crime scene was invaded and contaminated by someone who had no business being there." Stone doesn't answer, just stares at me. He has no idea where I'm going with this. I press forward, saying, "You hadn't even been at that crime scene for an hour when someone came in—not wearing booties, not wearing gloves, not wearing a plastic cap on his hair—and traipsed all over that house. Isn't that so?"

Stone gets it now and turns to Devlin.

I follow his eyes and say, "Yes, it was Mr. Walker himself." I'd learned about Devlin's intrusion onto the crime scene from Tommy, who found out about it from an acquaintance on Stone's CSU team.

Devlin shoots to his feet, objects, and demands a sidebar. Judge Henry overrules the objection and refuses the sidebar but tells me to get to the point.

"How long was he there before you knew he was there?" I ask Stone.

"I don't know."

"Because he didn't sign in?" I don't wait for Stone to answer. "He just waved his DA credentials, and your officers let him in, isn't that right?"

"I spoke to my team about that afterward. I do remember that now."

"Their letting him in and his presence in the house upset you at the time?"

Stone exhales loudly. "I wasn't happy."

"When your men dusted the house for prints, did you find Mr. Walker's prints?"

"Well, yes. As we just discussed, he came to the house."

"Did you find hair samples belonging to an African American?"

Stone's eyes bore into me now. "Yes. Along with your client's prints."

"Did Mr. Walker go into the basement after he entered the house?"

"I believe so, at some point."

"Is it possible Mr. Walker tracked some of the victim's blood across the basement floor?"

Devlin's on his feet again. "Objection! This is ridiculous!"

The idea that Devlin tracked Jennifer's blood all over the basement floor is, indeed, absurd. I've gone too far, and the judge sustains the objection and tells me to move on to another subject. I don't mind that I'm being shut down at this point. This entire line of questioning isn't for the jury anyway—it's for Walker himself. He'll know why soon enough.

I ask whether, in addition to David's and Devlin's prints, the CSU team found other prints. Stone says yes, a number of prints. "Then there's no question that Mr. Hanson and Mr. Walker were not the only men to have been in that house prior to Ms. Yamura's death?"

"No."

I pause and switch tracks. "Earlier, you'd said there was no evidence of a break-in, and you based that on the lack of broken windows or jimmied locks. You said that indicated to you that the perpetrator either had his own key or was let in by Ms. Yamura. But there's a third option, isn't there?"

Stone takes the question seriously and considers it. Before he can answer, I say, "The doors, or at least one of them, could simply have been unlocked."

"Uh . . ."

"If a door was unlocked, anyone—a neighbor, burglar, thief—could have walked into the house without the need to jimmy locks or break windows, right?"

"Well, yes."

"And isn't that the first thing a burglar does when he's trying to get into someone's house to rob it? Check to see if a door is unlocked so he won't have to pry his way in?"

"I suppose."

"And had the door been unlocked, so that the burglar gained entry without a sound, he could have suddenly happened upon Ms. Yamura and attacked her once she saw him, before she had a chance to scream, right?"

"That's possible," Stone concedes, "though, in my experience, most burglars don't commit violent crimes, especially murder. Even under duress."

"Unless they're two-time losers, and one more strike will get them life," I say.

Devlin objects and the court sustains him, but my point has been made.

"So, now that we're talking about a home invasion, let's discuss all the things that your crime-scene investigation found to be missing. Would you pull up one of the photographs showing Ms. Yamura's wallet?" The witness does so. "That's it? Lying open on the kitchen counter?"

"Yes."

"Had it been emptied of all the cash?"

"There was no money in it."

"Please pull up one of your pictures of Ms. Yamura's bureau, in her bedroom." Again, the witness complies. "The drawers have all been opened?"

"Yes."

"You found them that way when you arrived?"

"Yes."

"But her clothing was inside, including her underwear?"

"Uh, yes." Stone sounds confused.

"So the perpetrator wasn't a pervert looking for women's undergarments?"

"Ah, no."

"As to what he was looking for, is that a jewelry box sitting on top of the bureau?"

"Yes."

"Also with all its drawers opened?"

"Yes."

"Any jewelry inside?"

"No."

"Did you find Ms. Yamura's laptop computer?"

"There was no laptop."

"How hard did you look?"

At this question, Matthew Stone glances at Devlin. "We did a thorough search."

"Because the prosecutor, who wasn't supposed to be there, told you to scour the house for the laptop?"

"He didn't say laptop. He just said to look for any computers. We would have done that anyway," Matthew adds indignantly.

"Was he upset when you told him you couldn't find the laptop?"

"Objection." Devlin is on his feet. "This is nothing more than grandstanding, Your Honor."

"Sustained. Mr. McFarland, this case is not about Mr. Walker. I instruct you to stop with this line of questioning."

"Yes, Your Honor." I glance at Devlin. He's pissed at me, but there's something more in his eyes than mere annoyance. I'm hitting a nerve, as I knew I would.

"And in addition to Ms. Yamura's expensive laptop, her cash and jewelry, is it true that you also didn't find her iPhone?"

"No, we didn't. We learned of the calls to your office from subpoenaing the records from her carrier, Verizon."

I stare at Matthew Stone. He's looking back at me guilelessly. He's just made a huge mistake, but he doesn't know it. The jury was not supposed to hear that calls were made to my office from Yamura's phone. I know Stone well enough to know that he would never intentionally mention evidence excluded by the court. He's too straight a shooter. This was a mistake on Devlin's part. He'd told Tredesco not to mention the calls. Probably had to tell the detective ten times. But he forgot to tell Stone.

But now the jury has learned about the calls, and they don't know the background. I glance at the panel, and I know what they're thinking:

Calls from the victim's phone to the defendant's lawyer? What calls? Why haven't we heard about them? The jurors appear to be confused. All of them—except for their foreman, Mr. Peter Drummond. I look at him and see that he is looking at me, having inferred the message that Devlin wanted to send all along. That David, in a panic over having killed Jennifer Yamura, used her cell phone to call me, his law-school classmate and chum. In the foreman's mind, David and I have now been in this thing together from the beginning.

All these thoughts go through my own mind in a split second. When I recover, I see Judge Henry looking down at me from the bench, expecting that I'll object, ask the court to strike the testimony about the phone calls. But all that would do is highlight the point, so I keep quiet.

I smile at Matthew Stone and plow ahead. "So. Stolen cash, stolen jewelry, stolen computer, stolen phone. And maybe the victim left the door unlocked? Does that pretty much summarize what we've just gone over?"

The witness shrugs. "I guess. In part."

"Nothing surprising to you as a police officer, given that the invasion at Ms. Yamura's home happened in the midst of a crime spree in her neighborhood."

Stone admits that he'd heard of the break-ins near Jennifer's house but says he hadn't been briefed on the details.

I tell the court I have no more questions for the witness, and Judge Henry turns to Devlin. But Devlin doesn't even bother to redirect. He doesn't need to. The damage has been done. The image of Jennifer—wounded, bleeding, and desperate, crawling along her basement floor trying in vain to escape the murderer—is seared into the jurors' minds. I'm also certain that no one has forgotten about the phone calls placed from Jennifer's cell phone to David Hanson's attorney—to me.

◆　◆　◆

Judge Henry calls the lunch break, and I watch the jurors file out of the box and out of the courtroom. For the most part, they keep their eyes on the floor. Except for the foreman, Drummond, who looks directly at the defense table as he exits the box. He holds my eyes for a long time.

After the jury is gone, David is taken away and the courtroom empties. Piper smiles wanly at me, then follows the others out the door. The only ones left other than my team and me are Devlin, Christina Wesley, and John Tredesco, who hovers by the back door. The detective sees me looking at him and slowly stretches his thin, bloodless lips into a predatory smile. I keep my face blank of emotion, then turn away, catching Devlin Walker staring at me. Though not as blatant about it as Tredesco, he's smiling, too.

Back at the firm for lunch, I spend a few minutes at my desk, then go directly into the conference room. Marcie sits before an untouched salad. I fix myself a sandwich, pick up a bottle of Fiji water, take a seat across the table from her. Marcie stares at me, her eyes flat.

"So," she says, "tell me about these phone calls."

I take a swig of water and explain the calls in detail. Jennifer's first call to the office, placed through Angie, during which she asked me to represent her and we set up a meeting. "The second call went directly to my phone because Angie was at lunch. Yamura sounded panicked and asked to move up our meeting."

"Why was she panicked?" Marcie asks.

"I don't know. I never got the chance to ask her."

"Do you think someone was with her when she called that second time?"

"She didn't say so."

"When did she want to meet?"

I pause. "The first time she called, I scheduled a meeting for four o'clock the next day, Friday. She called the second time because she wanted to meet earlier, Friday morning. I checked my calendar. It was clear, so I said okay."

"And that was all you two talked about?"

"She hung up. I got the impression she didn't want to discuss any details over the phone."

Marcie studies me, much like our jury foreman had. Then she turns and leaves without looking back.

I sit by myself for a couple of minutes, take a few bites of my sandwich, and finish the water. Then I pick up my notes, stop in Vaughn's office, and tell him I'm heading back to court. When I get to the tenth floor of the courthouse, I spot Piper sitting on a long bench by the window. She smiles when she sees me but doesn't get up, waits for me to reach the bench and sit beside her.

"You never came back to the office for lunch," I say.

"I'm too nervous to eat," she says. "It's been so long. I'd forgotten how tense your trials are."

"Someone's freedom is on the line," I say. "Their whole life, really."

Piper and I sit quietly for a while. Then I pat her gently on her leg, lean over, and kiss her on the forehead. "Once more into the fray."

Devlin's first witness of the afternoon is Ari Weintraub, the deputy chief medical examiner. As he did with Matthew Stone, Devlin has the medical examiner pull up photographs of Jennifer's body. Unlike the CSU officer, Ari doesn't leave the stand. He uses a laser pointer to direct the jurors' attention to specific parts of the photographs. He begins the meat of his testimony with a detailed discussion of the autopsy. Reading off the postmortem reports, he begins with the personal data: thirty-one-year-old female, Asian, single; address 1792 Addison Street,

Philadelphia, Pennsylvania. "She was pronounced dead at the scene and taken to the medical examiner's office. The following day, I performed the postmortem examination myself," Ari says, and begins by describing the clothing he removed from Jennifer's body. Continuing to his external examination, Weintraub describes Jennifer's body as "measuring sixty-two inches and weighing one hundred and five pounds." He continues in this clinical vein as he describes the reporter's hair color and length, the color and clarity of her eyes, and other routine details.

Then Ari gets to the head wounds, and the picture show begins. The first photo he chooses is a middle-distance shot of the back of Jennifer's head, to give the jurors an idea of what they're looking at. He pauses for a moment, then switches to a much closer shot, showing a tangle of matted black hair and dried blood littered with bloodied particles of gray and white. Again, reading from his report, Weintraub states, "There were two overlapping wounds to the parietal area of the skull, right of center. The first wound was the big one. It consisted of a visibly depressed, comminuted fracture measuring five-point-two centimeters by four-point-four centimeters, with extrusion of bone. The wound extended through the skull bone and dura and into the subdural space. The second was a one-centimeter fracture just below the first wound."

"Would you explain to the jury what it was about these wounds that caused the massive blood loss?"

"Yes. The first blow severed the right occipital artery. That's a branch of the external carotid artery, responsible for supplying blood to a good portion of the posterior scalp, along with some muscles in the neck and back."

"And what does the force of that first blow tell you about what caused the wounds?" Devlin asks.

"The first wound, the large one, is consistent with the victim's head-strike to the steps after she'd been pushed."

I object. "There's no direct evidence the victim was pushed, as opposed to having fallen."

Devlin smiles. "Dr. Weintraub, please address Mr. McFarland's remark."

Ari pulls up an autopsy photograph of Yamura's upper torso. The photograph depicts two large brownish marks just below each shoulder and above each breast. "What you're seeing here are two large bruises. They would not, could not, have been caused by the fall, as she landed on her back. They must have been caused before she fell, and they are consistent with someone using the palms of their hands to push the victim, hard. Very hard."

Devlin pauses to let this sink in. "Would it have been possible, with the victim's blood loss, for her to have retained sufficient consciousness to get herself off the steps and crawl along the floor?"

"She likely would have been unconscious for some period of time after the first blow. But given her youth and fitness, it is entirely possible that she regained some level of consciousness, appreciated her predicament, and sought to save herself."

The jurors take this in and exchange glances among themselves.

Weintraub takes the jury through the scenario of Jennifer, spilling blood from the back of her head, crawling across the basement floor, scraping her knees as she moved. Then Devlin asks if it was possible that Jennifer herself crawled back onto the steps in an attempt to get upstairs but didn't make it and fell down again.

"Highly unlikely," Ari says, "given that she ended up head down, on her back. If she'd tried to crawl up the stairs and lost consciousness while doing so, she would simply have stopped moving and ended up lying facedown with her head at the top and her feet at the bottom."

"Dr. Weintraub, would the blood loss from the fall have killed the victim had she not been placed back onto the step, head down?"

Ari takes a minute to think about this. "Eventually, perhaps. As I said, the first wound severed the occipital artery. But what's certain is that her death was guaranteed when she was placed back onto the steps, head down, and allowed to bleed out."

Devlin pauses, pours himself a glass of water, drinks. Then, as if he'd just thought about it, he asks, "Given that the victim was sufficiently conscious to crawl off the steps and to appreciate what was happening to her, could she have had the presence of mind to have been pleading for her life at this point?"

I object immediately.

The judge correctly sustains my objection, and Devlin continues. But Jennifer's mother is sobbing again, and the jurors are looking at her. The jurors are also looking at David, and they're not hiding how they feel about him. I know now for certain that we've lost the jury. The image of the bloodied young woman, crawling across the floor in a desperate attempt to flee, probably begging for her life while David drags her back to the steps and positions her there to die is simply too much.

"And finally, Doctor, would you tell the jury your opinion as to the time of death?"

"Yes, certainly. Based upon the victim's weight and the temperature of the liver taken at the scene, and the advanced degree of rigor mortis, the ambient air temperatures in the house are consistent with a time of death between noon and two o'clock on the day the victim was found."

"So, then," Devlin asks, "if the defendant left his office at 11:50 and it took him fifteen minutes to walk to 1792 Addison Street, his arrival time of 12:05 would be within the time of death?"

"Yes."

Devlin asks a few more questions, then thanks the witness and turns him over to me.

I rise, walk around the defense table, and move to within a few feet of the jury. I turn to face the witness so that the jury is now on my left. In a quiet voice, I begin. "So, Doctor, we're all agreed—both the prosecution and the defense—as to how this young woman died. She died of massive blood loss from the artery severed as a result of blunt-force trauma to the back of her head."

"That's what I testified to, yes."

"But this trial isn't about *how* the victim died—we all agree on that—it's about who killed her, true?"

"It's about both."

"And the only thing the physical evidence tells us about the killer," I say, ignoring his answer, "is that, if your theory is right, the person had to be strong enough to carry or drag the victim from the basement floor back to the stairs."

"I would agree that the perpetrator was strong enough to do that."

"But that could be virtually any man in the city, couldn't it?"

"I don't know about that."

"Virtually all of the men and at least some of the women, right?"

"Well . . ."

"Mr. Hanson would certainly be strong enough, right?"

"I'd expect."

"But so would a former high school basketball star, like Mr. Walker."

"Objection!" Devlin's on his feet. "Again, Your Honor, this is beyond inappropriate. It's offensive to the dignity of the court."

The judge calls counsel to the bench for a sidebar and launches into me as soon as we get there.

"Mr. McFarland, this really is quite enough," the judge says.

"This is a murder trial," I answer. "I'm entitled to some leeway."

"Leeway?" Devlin spits the word.

"Go down this road one more time," Bill Henry says, "and I'll sanction you in the presence of the jury. Do you understand me?"

I say I do, and Devlin and I move back to our places.

"Thank you, Your Honor," I say, the old trial lawyer's trick to make the jury think the judge came out on my side.

"What are you thanking me for?" the judge says, not letting me get away with my ruse. "Your behavior was out of line, and I told you so."

Now would be a perfect time to stop, sit, and bury my head in my legal pad. But I have to press on. There's one final point that Devlin snuck in on direct that I must address, a point I anticipated from my reading of the autopsy findings. Devlin didn't ask it directly, and I suspect it's because he left it for my cross—a little bomb to go off all over me. A bomb that I, too, want to detonate. "Dr. Weintraub, you were asked a question about whether the victim could have been pleading as she crawled along the basement floor. You didn't find any physical evidence as to that. And, in fact, the head wounds and blood loss would have left the victim in an impaired state of consciousness. So impaired that she really didn't understand what was happening to her, isn't that right?"

"No, I think that's wrong," the medical examiner says, pulling up a close-up photograph of Jennifer's face. "These dried salt deposits track down from the victim's eye ducts."

I stare at Ari as though I don't understand.

"She was crying, Mr. McFarland. The victim was crying."

32

THURSDAY, NOVEMBER 15, CONTINUED

Jennifer Yamura's mother's quiet sobs intensify into all-out weeping. Her husband and son lean in from both sides to comfort her, but it does no good. There is no other sound in the courtroom until the judge directs me to continue.

I run through a few more questions, vanilla stuff, then pass the witness. Turning to take my seat next to David, I catch Marcie glaring at me. The other person whose face I'm drawn to is Piper. She has the dazed look of someone who's just been kicked by a horse.

As was the case with Matthew Stone, Devlin doesn't bother to redirect. I expect, at this point, that Devlin will rest. I would were I in his place.

Instead, he stands and announces, "As our last witness, the Commonwealth will present Brian Yamura." And just that fast, the courtroom is electrified.

The victim's twin brother.

I feel David stiffen next to me as he picks up a pen and draws a big question mark on the legal pad between us. I quietly tell him I don't know what Brian Yamura is going to say. He's on the prosecution's witness list, but there was never a chance we were going to get a statement from him.

Everyone in the courtroom follows Jennifer's brother in his slow procession through the gate, past the jury box, and onto the stand. He's a good-looking young man, thirty-one, like his sister. Thin and athletic and insanely wealthy, he walks poised, shoulders back and head up.

Devlin asks a few background questions, then gets right down to why Brian has been called as a witness.

"Were you close with your sister?"

"We were twins," Brian says. "We knew each other before we were born."

"Of course," Devlin nods. "And you remained close throughout your lives?"

"We were best friends. Jen was more of a people person than I am. I was the tech nerd, so I turned to her for advice about how to handle personal situations. She was always helping me out with my girlfriends. Lord knows," he adds, shaking his head, "I needed it."

"And on the other side of the coin," Devlin asks, "did you help your sister with her relationships?"

"Like I said, Jen was good with people. And she had a good head on her shoulders. She never needed my help with men, as a rule."

"Were there any exceptions to that rule?"

Brian Yamura inhales. "Just one. Her relationship with . . . him." Brian turns toward David, and the jurors' eyes follow him. "She'd told me that she'd met someone very special. An important man. Someone powerful and rich. But there was a problem. The man was married." Here, Brian closes his eyes, lowers his head. "I told her she was crazy to get involved with a married man, especially some rich, older guy," he says, opening his eyes and looking at the jury. "I told her guys like that only want to use younger women like toys. She told me not to worry, she could take care of herself. She said that this guy wasn't like those others. He really cared about her."

Devlin pauses to let the first chapter of the story sink in. "So what happened as time went on?"

"For a long time, nothing. I mean, nothing bad. Jen and I would call each other, and she always sounded happy, told me it was going great with him."

"And then?"

Jennifer's brother pauses again, looks at Devlin, then past him to the seats in the back of the courtroom. This puzzles me, so I turn to see who Brian is looking for. I spot him instantly: John Tredesco. And now I know what's going on—and what's coming. Brian is acting out a story fed to him by Tredesco. I can easily envision how it unfolded. Tredesco probably approached the young man in the hallway, expressed his condolences, told Jennifer's brother how badly Tredesco and the whole prosecution team wants to see David Hanson convicted. Unfortunately, though, the prosecution has no evidence of a motive. "Like if Hanson had wanted to break up with your sister, but she loved him and didn't want to." In my mind, I can hear Tredesco spoon-feeding the story to the angry, devastated brother. Peppering it with the threat that, absent a motive, the jury will be forced to find David Hanson not guilty, even if they believe he did it.

Tredesco catches me staring at him and nods.

I turn back toward the front of the courtroom, where Devlin is asking Brian Yamura to tell the jury what his sister told him toward the end.

"The last couple times we spoke, Jen told me the defendant was showing a side of himself he hadn't shown before. Like he was Jekyll and Hyde. He tried to kick her out of the house on a moment's notice."

I could object to all this as hearsay. But I want this damning testimony in. It will scare David and Marcie and move me closer to my endgame.

"Jennifer was afraid," Brian continues. "She told me so, and I could hear it in her voice. But the thing was, she loved him. And she said she believed he really loved her, too, deep down. But he had a wife he felt he couldn't get away from. So Jen was going to do something about it."

"Do what?"

"She was going to tell his wife. About them."

"When was this, exactly?"

Brian inhales, looks up at the ceiling, then back at the jurors. "The night before the police found her. It was 6:00 p.m. my time, so it had to be nine here on the East Coast. I called to see how she was doing. We talked for a long time. That's when she told me she was going to come clean with his wife. She said she'd warn the defendant first. Give him a chance to get ready for whatever his wife might do. Then she was going to call their house and lay the cards on the table."

And just like that, Devlin has motive. A cheating husband's lover threatens to disclose the affair to his wife. He freaks out, pushes her down the stairs.

I can already hear Devlin Walker replay it in his closing argument. I can see the jurors leaning forward in their seats as Devlin's oratory sweeps them into the final, terrible moments of Jennifer Yamura's life. Except that Devlin will never get that chance; I have to make sure of it.

Devlin thanks Brian Yamura for his testimony, and the judge turns the witness over to me. Instead of walking to center court, seizing control of a hostile witness, I remain seated. My message to the jury: I will question the victim's brother, but I will not bully him.

"Mr. Yamura, let me begin by expressing my heartfelt sorrow for your loss." I've never begun a cross like this, and my words are not a ploy. My heart is truly breaking for Brian Yamura, his mother, his father. Jennifer Yamura didn't deserve to be killed, and her family doesn't deserve to suffer as they are. "You shared with all of us that you and your sister were close and spoke often. I assume Jennifer told you about the trouble she was in with Mr. Walker and the crooked cops?"

Brian Yamura stares at me, and I can tell I've hit home. Behind me, Devlin is undoubtedly squirming in his seat, because I'm opening a part of the narrative that he chose not to share with Brian Yamura—or the jury.

"Did your sister tell you that she'd broken a story on a ring of crooked police officers in Philadelphia?"

"Yes."

"Did she tell you that, in doing so, she made public a grand jury whose very existence was being kept secret by Mr. Walker, the prosecutor here?"

"She told me about the grand jury."

"Did she tell you that Mr. Walker subpoenaed her to a grand jury, then personally threatened her with contempt and imprisonment if she didn't show up and disclose the source of her information?"

"That was *him?*" Brian Yamura looks at Devlin as he answers. He's wondering why the same guy who was threatening his sister is the one now seeking to avenge her death.

"Yes, it was," I say. "Did your sister share with you that she was afraid of the crooked cops whose names she revealed?"

Brian hesitates but answers honestly, to a point. "Maybe a little afraid."

"Are you aware that one of the police officers who ratted on the others was gunned down on a city street?"

Devlin objects, but this time the judge overrules him.

"I think I heard something about that." Brian Yamura answers my question, but he's not looking at me or the jury. He's looking at Devlin Walker.

"Thank you, Mr. Yamura. I know this is difficult for you."

As I expected would be the case, my cross has done nothing to undermine Brian Yamura's testimony, and Devlin knows it.

"No questions, Your Honor," Devlin says. "The Commonwealth rests."

The judge calls us to the bench. Once we're in position, he says, "I'm going to tell the jury to disregard everything they've heard about the defendant's trips to Mexico and Grand Cayman, and the four million dollars." Devlin begins to protest, but the judge puts up his hand, telling Devlin, "If you want me to reconsider, file a motion. I'll consider it carefully, but I have to tell you now that I'm not likely to change my mind. And there's not going to be a mistrial," he adds, looking at me.

Ten minutes later, I'm standing in the spectator benches with my team—Vaughn, Marcie, and Alexander Ginsberg. This is the first time Piper hasn't left the courtroom as soon as the trial day is over. She stands one row behind us.

"Alexander, your thoughts?" I ask.

"You've been doing a great job," he says. "But today . . ." Here he turns to Marcie. "I don't mean to be insensitive, Mrs. Hanson, but I have to be candid—today has been a train wreck for the defense. The brutality of the crime, the picture of the victim crawling away, maybe begging for her life, crying, really got the jury. The methodical way the killer retrieved her, took her back to the steps to bleed out . . . That speaks to premeditation. And Brian Yamura gave the prosecution the only thing it lacked: motive."

I look to Vaughn, who nods in agreement. I glance back at Piper. She's frozen in place. I nod, then look back at Ginsberg, who continues. "You have one chance here, Mick. This jury is absolutely convinced that, at the time Jennifer Yamura was murdered, your client was right there with her. You have to present the jury with a compelling alibi. Your client has to take the stand, convince them he was somewhere else. Convince them beyond a reasonable doubt."

"But it's the prosecution's burden to prove . . ." Piper's voice startles us all.

Ginsberg, Vaughn, and Marcie pivot around to look at her.

"You're quite right," Ginsberg says. "In theory. But when the prosecution has put on a case as emotionally compelling as the one presented here, to the point that the jury *wants* to convict, it becomes the burden of the defense—in fact, if not in law—to come forward with irrefutable evidence showing the prosecution's view to be frankly false. To put it simply, you have to put the lie to the prosecution's entire case."

I look at Marcie and, in a voice loud enough for everyone to hear and strong enough to bring home my point, I say, "David's going to have to testify to where he was at the time of the murder. And he'll need to give the jury something more than his word. He'll need corroboration."

I let my little speech hang in the air. Then I tell everyone to go home and get a good night's sleep. I walk Piper into the hallway and tell her I'll be home by eight or nine. "I've got to meet with David in his holding cell now, then get ready for tomorrow."

Piper asks me who my first witness is going to be.

"David," I answer. "I have to get his alibi before the jury. I hate to have to put him on the stand because Devlin will eat him alive. But I just don't see any other way."

Piper looks away, looks through the window to the sky outside. For a second, I wonder whether, mentally, she's flying through that window, leaving this sad scene behind, like I did the morning my mother fell dead on the floor.

"I'll see you when you get home," she says.

My meeting with David is brief. He expresses his distress over the day's events, reserving special scorn for Brian Yamura. "Everything he said was a goddamned lie. I never told Jennifer that I was going to break up with her. And Jennifer never said she was going to Marcie. We never fought. It was a relationship of convenience, and we were both happy with it."

I sit with my arms crossed, watch David pace his cell, whining as though he were the victim in all this. I don't think I have ever hated someone as much as I hate David Hanson. I curtly take my leave of him and walk into the hall, where I spot Piper exiting the ladies' room. In a few seconds, Marcie exits behind her. Both women seem taken aback when they see me but do their best to recover quickly. We ride the elevator down to the first floor, no one saying anything. Marcie bolts out ahead of Piper and me. I walk Piper to an entrance to the underground garage. Then I head back to the firm.

When I get to my office, I close the door, sink into my chair, put my elbows on the desk, and bury my face in my hands. I think of Jennifer Yamura and am suddenly overwhelmed by the picture painted by the prosecution of the young woman, her head already bloodied, crawling on the basement floor in a vain attempt to save her life. My thoughts then skip to Gabby and Piper. There is nothing I wouldn't do to protect my own little family. I shiver, and think again how weary I am. But, of course, I must press forward. The major battles lie ahead.

Everything will be won or lost in the next twenty-four hours.

I work late, ensuring that Gabby will be long in bed before I get home. Because if I've done my work as well as I think I have, I know what awaits me with Piper.

An hour later, I turn into my driveway, press the button that opens the garage door, and pull inside. The kitchen light is off. Piper's car is here, so she must be, too, though I see no evidence of her presence. The house is soundless. The television is not on. There is no music coming from the Sonos sound system. "Hello?" I call out. "Piper? Gabby?" No one answers. Even Franklin seems to be gone. I make my way through the kitchen, down the hall, and into the living room, which is also dark. But once there, I see a dim light. I follow it from the living room and down the short hallway leading to my office.

And there sits Piper, in the shadows, on the leather couch. She's wearing the same outfit she had on in court, except that her shoes are on the floor next to her. An open bottle of wine and an empty glass sit on the coffee table in front of the couch. The only light is provided by the green banker's lamp sitting on my desk, across the room.

"Piper? Are you all right?"

For a long moment, Piper's face remains hidden in shadow. Then she slowly looks up at me, her face contorted with pain. "It was me."

33

THURSDAY, NOVEMBER 15, CONTINUED

"I was with David. I'm his alibi."

Piper returns her gaze to the floor as I lower myself into the chair facing her. I let Piper's confession hang in the air between us.

This is it. Every step I've taken, every move I've made since Jennifer Yamura's death, was designed to bring Piper and me to this moment. And I know as I cross the threshold that everything hangs in the balance. I have to keep focus, keep my emotions locked down, as I have for so long.

The grandfather clock's pendulum slowly strokes the seconds. Piper gently rocks her body, almost to the beat of the clock. She's weeping softly now.

"We didn't plan it. It just happened."

I've done my best to ready myself for this. But I still feel my body stiffen in my chair as she speaks.

"I was at the mall one day. David happened to be there, too. He came up to me, and we started talking. He suggested we walk to the Starbucks, have some coffee. We talked for a long time. He was funny. And sweet. And sad over what was happening to Marcie. The cancer. We finished our coffee, left the mall, and said good-bye. A couple weeks later, David called me, said he was out at the mall again, asked me if I wanted to join him for another coffee. It was close to five o'clock when I got there, so we decided to get a drink. You were in Pittsburgh, speaking at some legal conference."

My stomach is churning, but I control my breathing, remain expressionless.

"Gabby was with my parents." Here, Piper pauses, fills her glass, takes a sip of wine. "That was the first time." She takes a bigger sip, then starts to fill in the blanks. The initial guilt over what she'd done. Followed quickly by a second time, then a third, until she and David had a standing date every other week at one luxury hotel or another, until . . .

My face burns with shame and anger, but I don't interrupt.

"That day, the day . . . she died. David and I were going to meet at the Rittenhouse. I checked in to the hotel, ordered up some lunch. Then I left the hotel to shop a little."

"That's when I saw you on the street. You were carrying a Lululemon bag. It was stuffed."

Piper nods. "I went to the Holt's Cigar store. David told me they were getting in some special type of cigar, so I bought him a box."

So he could have a smoke after you were done screwing? I want to shout the words, but I hold back.

"I put it in the big Lululemon bag, under the clothes I'd bought. I went back to the hotel, and David called me later, just before two o'clock. He was upset, said something awful had happened but that he'd be there soon."

I put up a hand to stop her. "The police subpoenaed his cell-phone records. There was no record of any calls after he left the office that day."

"Oh, God . . . this is so hard. We both had disposable cell phones. David insisted."

And the camel's back is broken. I leap to my feet.

"You had *burner* phones? Just so you could screw around on me? Fuck David, buy him cigars, and use burner phones so I wouldn't find out?" I pause to take a breath, and my chest hurts. "Lying to me through your teeth then, and since David's arrest. Forcing me to look at your lying face, hold down my anger, and make sure we all aren't brought down by this goddamned disaster."

My pulse feels white-hot, deafening in my ears. The rage I've held back for so long finally overtakes me. I don't know how long my rant lasts, but when I finally stop and gather myself, I see the wine bottle missing from the coffee table and the TV screen in shards. And a deep red stain dripping down the wall beneath it. Dripping like blood. Like the blood running out of the back of . . .

Oh, Jesus.

I drop to the couch, close my eyes. I am spent, and I am lost. It's all lost.

The grandfather clock begins to chime.

When finally I open my eyes, I see Piper staring at me, studying me. "You knew."

I stare back.

"How long?" she asks.

I desperately want to escape this moment. But there will be no flying away this time. I lock eyes with Piper, take a deep breath, and say the words that I know will seal my fate. Turn Piper against me forever.

"I've known since she threw it in my face. Jennifer Yamura. The day I pushed her down the stairs."

Piper's eyes widen. Her lips part. I see confusion, then terror. She blinks once, twice.

"It was the second call," I begin. "The one Jennifer made to me when Angie was at lunch. She wanted to move up our meeting. But not for earlier the next day. She said she had to see me right away. She asked me to come to her house."

I see the terrifying image of myself at Jennifer's back door on Anna Groszek's videotape, forty-three minutes before David Hanson's own appearance on camera. The image that forced my decision to make David pay the blackmail, no matter what . . . to protect my own sorry ass.

Piper is gaping at me now, and I realize that I have stopped talking. I inhale and continue recounting, step by step, the horror of that day.

"She let me in the back door, led me to the living room, and told me that she didn't trust the TV station's lawyers to protect her. She said she wanted someone whose loyalty wasn't divided. I told her that if she retained me, I would work only for her. We talked some more, and she said there was someone involved in the investigation we could blackmail. Someone important. But before she could tell me who it was, I stopped her. I said I wasn't blackmailing anyone. We argued the point, and she became extremely angry. Started shouting at me. Berating me, calling me a coward. I shouted back, and that's when she told me about you and David. She said you'd been having an affair for months, and the whole world would find out about it if I didn't back her blackmail plan. She said I most certainly *would* blackmail whoever she told me to, that I'd get her out of testifying in front of the grand jury and beat back any contempt charges. These weren't requests," I emphasize. "These were orders."

"I don't—" Piper begins, but I raise a hand to stop her.

"I told her I was done listening to her. I said I couldn't have a professional relationship with a client who said terrible things about my wife, who spoke to me like that. I headed for the back door, but she cornered me in the hallway, where the doorway to the basement is, and she threatened me again."

Piper questions me with her eyes, pleading silently for a reason that will justify what she knows is coming. And she finds one. "Tommy."

I nod. "Jennifer said if I didn't get her out of her jam, she'd tell the grand jury all about Tommy. That he was part of the drug ring. That it was he who first tipped her to the grand-jury investigation."

"But—" Piper begins.

"She and Tommy had been lovers."

Piper puts a hand to her mouth.

"I told her to leave Tommy out of it. But she kept screaming that she'd have him sent back to prison. I lost it. I pushed her. She fell through the curtain of glass beads."

This isn't exactly how it happened. I've changed the order of things, for Piper's sake. Yamura did corner me in the hallway, but it was after she'd made her threats against Tommy, not before. She sneered at me, bared her teeth, and told me about Piper and David. She told me how David loved to brag about his other conquests. She told me some of the things David had shared with her about his encounters with Piper. Personal and private things. My stomach turns even now at the memory.

"David and I laughed about her, actually," Jennifer had said. "For all her good looks and that bitching little body, your wife's a bit of a prude. Or she was at first. But she came around." Then Jennifer stepped into me, said, "One of the things David taught her was to cradle his balls," and with that she cupped her own hand around my testicles, "like this, when she sucked—"

That's when I snapped. I shouted something and, as I told Piper, shoved Yamura backward, shoved her hard, and watched her disappear through the curtain of glass beads.

"I heard her hit the steps," I tell Piper. "I pushed the beads aside and saw her lying there, on her back, halfway down the stairs." This is why I was surprised when I first saw the crime-scene photos showing her all the way at the bottom, with her head on the concrete block.

"Her eyes were closed. She wasn't moving. Blood was spilling out of her head onto the steps. I took a couple steps down, called her name. She didn't respond. I waited, but she didn't move. I was certain she was dead."

"So, when I saw you on the street . . . ," says Piper.

"I was coming from her house."

Piper winces. "You had your leather satchel. It looked full, but I didn't think anything of it."

"I had her computer and jewelry. The money from her wallet."

"To make it look like a robbery."

What I'm expecting from Piper is revulsion and a stream of questions. How could I push a young woman down the stairs? What kind of man am I that I could callously strategize even as I stood over what I believed was her dead body? How could I calmly traipse around her house, stealing things to cover my tracks by making it look like a robbery? And how could I contain the knowledge of Piper's affair with David—and with it, the rage—all this time? These rhetorical questions will be the mallet Piper uses to shatter the already-cracked crystal that is our marriage. And then she'll call Devlin Walker.

But the questions do not come.

"From the beginning, you invited me in," she says, so quietly at first that I can barely hear her. "You had me come to your trials. You practiced your openings and closings on me, ran ideas past me. You brought me to the victory dinners with your colleagues, the political events. Even when we socialized with the other DAs and the cops, we went as a couple. From the start, it was always *us*. Mick and Piper. I jumped onto your bandwagon, and it became *our* bandwagon. And on top of that, what we were doing was important. We were fighting the good fight, sending the bad guys away, making the streets safer. And when Gabby came along and we had a child to protect, that made our crusade even more important to me.

"And then, out of the blue, you said you wanted to leave the prosecutor's office and jump to the other side. I couldn't believe it when you told me. But I thought, okay, I can do that with you. We'd fight for guys like Tommy. Good people who'd done some bad things. People who just needed a second chance. And then you joined up with Lou Mastardi," she says of the partner who'd formed the firm Susan and I inherited. "And that was the end of it—of all of it—for us. It was the end of us. Our circle of friends excluded us. You worked even longer hours than before. When you got home, you were too tired to talk about your cases, let alone ask me what I thought. I went to your trials at first, but it was all I could do to get you to acknowledge me. All my ideas about fighting for worthy defendants . . ." She shakes her head. "I was naive, I know." Piper pauses. "All that was left of *our* great mission was *your* job. Mick and Piper became Mick. Mick in the office, Mick in the courtroom, Mick across the state at some legal seminar. Piper at home, with Gabby."

Piper stops, looks at me, and I hang my head. Piper isn't telling me anything that I hadn't already figured out. Still, to hear her tell it cuts me to the quick.

"I understand why you went to David. I really do. And I have no excuses. Any more than I have for what I'd done to Tommy. But it still hurts to hear it. God, it hurts." I double over, my arms around my belly. But Piper has already delivered the blows.

After a long while, I sit up, look at Piper. "So what now?" I ask. "Is there a chance? Can we get back to *us*, or is it over?"

Piper stands. She leaves the room. I sit in the semidarkness, in fear. For all I know, she's packing her bags. Or calling the police from the kitchen. After what seems like forever, she comes back. In her left hand is another bottle of wine, in her right two fresh glasses. She pours the wine and hands me a glass.

"*Us* is all I've ever wanted, Mick. And *us* is more imperative now than ever, because of the most important mission of all."

I smile through my tears. "Gabby."

Piper nods. "Gabby."

We raise our glasses, clink them, and drink.

And then, with a self-possession that amazes me, Piper returns to her narrative.

"When David got to the hotel, he was in a panic. He told me everything—about Jennifer Yamura, their arrangement. He said he'd gone to the house on Addison Street to give Jennifer something or pick something up, I can't remember. He told me she was dead, that he'd found her on the cellar stairs. That her blood was everywhere. He said someone had obviously killed her.

"I was furious when I found out I was just part of a larger harem. But I believed him, and I didn't want his life to be ruined for something he didn't do. So I decided to help him." Piper pauses here, and I can tell she's thinking about how to finish the story. "So we worked out a plan. David agreed to go back to the house that night, try to clean it all up. Remove his fingerprints. Clear out all of his clothes and belongings. He said there was no way the house could be traced to him."

I watch Piper closely. Part of her story doesn't ring true to me. If David "agreed" to go back to Yamura's house, that means the suggestion had to come from Piper, and I just can't see her suggesting something like that.

Piper sees me studying her and looks away.

I take a moment to gather my own thoughts. Then I continue recounting my side of the story. How I believed I had killed Jennifer until I received the prosecution's evidence and learned that she hadn't died from the fall down the stairs. That she'd crawled away from the steps and been found by someone else, who dragged her back to the stairs and left her to bleed out.

I tell Piper all about Anna Groszek's blackmail scheme and explain that the reason David was caught flying to Mexico and Grand Cayman was to fetch the money to pay the blackmail. "I didn't know for sure whether it was David who dragged Jennifer back to the steps until I received the blackmailer's surveillance tape and saw him entering the house after I left." I let this last part hang in the air.

Piper nods, her gaze distant. "There was blood on his shirtsleeves. He said he went down the stairs to where she was lying. He said he tried to rouse her, and that's how he got the blood on him. But he was lying, wasn't he? He really *did* kill her. And lied to me afterward." Piper suddenly looks faint. "Jesus, what are we going to do?"

I reach over and take her hands. "We're going to finish the plan," I say. Then I explain who, besides David and me, appears on the videotape. Last, I tell Piper the part she'll have to play. How she must lie under oath and testify that David was with her at the time of the murder, not afterward.

"But why can't I just repeat the lie David told me when he came to the hotel about Jennifer being already dead when he found her? The jury would find him not guilty."

I shake my head. "The jury would hang him. Think about it. David came to the hotel room *after* Yamura was murdered, admitting that he'd *just come from her house.* Your testimony would place him at the scene of the murder precisely within the time frame fixed by the medical examiner. And the plan you two worked out to have him go back to the house to clean up the crime scene? That would make you an accessory after the fact." I pause. "There's only one way to get us all out of this. One way to make sure that David isn't convicted so that he never needs to hire appellate counsel or tell them about the video."

"But so what if he does tell some other lawyers about the video? You only showed him the part with him on it. He has no idea you were in the house before him, that it was you who pushed Jennifer down the steps."

I explain to Piper that David and his blue-chip appellate team would have no problem finding out who lived in the house behind Yamura's, and little difficulty tracking down Anna Groszek. Once they found her, they'd pressure her—or, more likely, bribe her—to turn over the original copy of the video. Once they had it, I'd be done for.

"Your alibi testimony ends the trial," I say. "It's our only hope."

Piper sits quietly for a moment, then asks, "What if I hadn't caved? What if I hadn't admitted to you that it was me who was with David? What would you have done?"

I don't answer. I don't know. Instead, I stand and pull Piper up with me. I put my arms around her and hug her as tightly as I can. "I love you," I say quietly. "And I'm sorry I left you and Gabby like I did. I'm never going to do that again." I loosen my grip, kiss Piper on the lips, and tell her to go upstairs. "I'll be up in a few minutes."

After she leaves, I move to my desk and mull over what has happened. My mind fixes on Piper's statement about perjuring herself. And just that fast, it hits me. I'd been wondering why David Hanson chose me to be the lawyer to defend him, given that he was having an affair with my wife. That's a lot of power to give someone who, sooner or later, will find out he has good reason to hate you. To justify taking such a risk, there had to be a reason. And now I get it. As distraught as David was when he was first arrested, he realized that Piper was the key to his salvation. He knew that Piper would have to lie for him, have to swear under oath that she was with him *while* Jennifer Yamura was being murdered, not only afterward. And David knew there was only one person in the world who could persuade Piper to perjure herself for him: me.

That's why David hired me. He had it all figured out from the get-go. He knew my endgame long before I puzzled it out myself. And he also knew that the timing of the disclosure of Piper as his *faux* alibi would be critical. Piper's claim to have been with David from the time she checked into the hotel could be undermined by her receipts from the cigar store and Lululemon. So, the disclosure of her as David's alibi was something that had to be sprung on the prosecution at the last moment, during the trial itself, before Devlin and his detectives could vet Piper's story.

All of this means that I never had to hire Alexander Ginsberg to sit with our team at trial to lament how poorly it was going for us in order to frighten Piper into admitting her affair with David, and scare David and Marcie into putting pressure on Piper to do so. David had been planning to strong-arm Piper into coming clean all along; he was just waiting for the right time.

Still, David was taking a monumental risk. His entire strategy depended on my being motivated to persuade Piper to perjure herself for him. Given that I would be livid over the affair, there could only be one reason I'd ever agree to suborn perjury to help David: if I was convinced of his innocence. But why would David think I'd believe he didn't do it? He was, after all, caught trying to clean up the murder scene. He ran when the police came. Then he lied to the police and to me. Many times. And he certainly didn't know I was the one who pushed Jennifer down the stairs, so he couldn't have held that over my head. Unless . . . *Jesus.* Did Jennifer tell him, injured on the basement floor, that I pushed her? Had David known all along? If so, why not threaten me directly, from the outset? Order me to have Piper lie to the police, tell them she was with him at the time of the murder? Why wait until Piper disclosed the affair and take the chance I'd have her lie for him on my own? The questions make my head spin.

I turn my chair around to look out the big bay window behind me. It's a clear night. The moon is almost full. The stars are shining. But I still feel like a blind man walking in the dark.

After a while, I turn off the desk lamp, leave the darkened office, and walk upstairs. I enter Gabby's room, sit on her bed, and watch her breathe. The sleep of the innocent. I look to the nightstand and pick up the book I've been reading to her at night. Another Dr. Seuss book: *Oh, the Places You'll Go!*

"Congratulations! Today is your day. You're off to Great Places! You're off and away!" I lean in to Gabby and whisper the words. She stirs a little. Good; she can hear me at some level. Maybe she's even dreaming the story as I read it. Dreaming she's *in* the story. I hope so. I read slowly, with the same emphasis I use when Gabby's awake. It's not long before I hear paws on the hardwood floor. Franklin has shown up. He watches me finish the book, return it to the nightstand, and gently ruffle Gabby's hair. He watches me lower my head as I remember that somewhere in Center City, in a hotel room, are the loving parents of another girl, a girl who will never again go to great places, never look up and down streets, look them over with care, her shoes full of feet.

"My God." The tears slide down my face. I shake my head slowly. I can't believe it. What I did. What I'm doing.

What am I? What have I become?

A shiver runs through me. I wipe my face, sit up straight, then stand. I look down at Gabby, tell myself to carry on. *Just get through this! Get it done. For her sake. For Piper's. For . . .*

I don't let myself finish the thought.

34

FRIDAY, NOVEMBER 16

It's 5:30 in the morning, and I'm at the office. I reach over my desk, pick up the phone. I call Devlin Walker. As early as it is, I know he'll be working.

"It's Mick," I say, my voice flat. "I need you in my office in twenty minutes."

Devlin snorts. "The time for your client to plead has come and gone. I was very clear the last time we spoke. So I won't be coming to your office today—or any other time. Now, if you don't mind, I have a lot of work to—"

"There's a video," I say, interrupting him. "It shows the back of Jennifer Yamura's house on the day she was murdered. It shows who went in and out of the house, just before and after she was killed." I let the news hang, and start counting. *A thousand one, a thousand two, a thousand three, a thousand four . . .* But no sound comes from the other end of the line. So I say, "Twenty minutes." Then I hang up.

At six o'clock, the guard rings me, says there's someone here to see me. I tell the guard to send him up. I'm standing by the front door to our suite when I hear the *ding* as the elevator doors open. After a minute, Devlin Walker turns the corner and moves toward me down the hallway. Even from a distance, I can see that he hasn't slept a wink. When Devlin approaches, I hold open the door for him, then lock it behind us. Neither of us says a word as I lead Devlin to my office, nod to one of the visitors' chairs, which I've faced toward the TV. As soon as he's seated and I'm behind my desk, I press the "Play" button, and the image of Jennifer's back door appears on the screen.

The clock at the bottom right-hand corner of the screen reads 11:50 a.m. when someone appears on the screen: Devlin Walker, the first of the three men who visited Jennifer Yamura that day. He moves around Jennifer's car, approaches the door, and knocks. Jennifer opens the door and lets him in. After a few seconds, the screen turns to fuzz. In another second, the image of Jennifer's backyard reappears. Devlin is halfway through the back door on his way out of the house, the motion of the door opening having triggered the camera to begin recording again. The clock reads 12:25 p.m., meaning that thirty-five minutes have elapsed between Devlin's entering and leaving the house. Devlin walks away, and a few seconds later, the camera turns to fuzz, then black. Thirty-two minutes later, the camera captured me appearing at Jennifer's back door, but of course I don't show that part of the video to Devlin. Nor do I show Devlin the portions of the video showing David Hanson arriving thirty minutes after I left.

"The rest of the tape shows what everyone in the courtroom already knows happened," I say. "It shows David arriving that night. After about an hour, he runs out the back door. From that point on, the tape plays almost without a break until sunrise, what with all the patrolmen and CSU guys."

Devlin stares at me, his eyes betraying a mind in the grip of panic.

I wait a moment, then lean across my desk. "You prick. You murdered that poor girl. And then you did everything in your power to frame an innocent man."

"No," Devlin says, his voice almost a whisper.

"Here's my guess. You slept with her, maybe even had a full-blown affair. You let it slip about the grand-jury investigation. You tipped off a young reporter to a story that could make her career. Somehow, she got on your computer, copied your files to her laptop. That's how she knew so many of the details—which cops had spilled the beans, and what they'd said. Then one morning you open the paper and there it is, laid out in black and white—details that only someone close to the investigation could know."

Devlin's head is down now, his eyes closed, his jaw clenched. His arms are wrapped around his chest. My words are body blows, and he knows there's nothing he can do to deflect them.

I go on. "Now comes the ironic part. As the DA running the grand jury, you're professionally obligated to subpoena Yamura to appear and testify, disclose her source—*you*—and testify to what else she knows. But her doing so would ruin you. So you're caught between a rock and a hard place. You issue the subpoena, and you know that, sooner or later, she's going to have to show up or face a contempt charge. So you go to her house and beg her to lie under oath and not reveal you as her source. She laughs in your face, tells you that she won't go to prison to protect you. It's all too much for you, so you throw her down the stairs. When you see she isn't dead, that she's able to crawl off the steps, you follow her down, carry her back to the stairs to bleed out and die. Then you search the house for the laptop but can't find it. So you take a few minutes, try to clear your head, figure out what to do. That's when you come up with the idea of taking the money out of her wallet and her jewelry and phone, to make it look like a burglary gone bad. I have to hand it to you, Devlin, you were always good on your feet."

Devlin shakes his head. "No, no, no," he moans.

"You left the house without the laptop, but you knew you had to get it somehow. With Jennifer dead, the copies of your files on her computer were the only things that could link you to her story. That's why you pressed me again and again for the laptop. Why you stressed that my turning it over was a condition of David's getting a plea deal. It's also why you warned me not to open the files on the computer."

Devlin puts up his hands to stop me. "What you're saying doesn't make sense. Why would I think David Hanson had the computer, if I, not he, was the one who killed Jennifer?"

"Because during your affair, Jennifer told you that David owned the house. You figured there was a hiding place in the house, maybe a secret safe that the police didn't find, and that's where Jennifer had put the laptop. You decided that David opened the safe and took it after you murdered Yamura."

Devlin closes his eyes.

"Tell me, Devlin, was she crying like the medical examiner said? Did she beg you for her life as she crawled away—like you insinuated to the jury? Is that how you came up with that question—because you saw it play out in real life?"

"I didn't kill her."

"How did you hold yourself together all these months? Did you lock it away in some remote dungeon in your brain? Did the memory of it all fade over time until it all seemed like just a bad dream? They could write whole psychology books on you, man."

Now it's Devlin's turn to lean across the desk. "I did *not* kill that woman! I did not!"

I return Devlin's stare, my eyes cold with accusation and contempt. "You were going to take everything from David. His reputation, his life's work. His freedom. Well, now I'm going to take everything from *you*. This morning, when the judge asks me to call my first witness, guess who I'm going to name? *You*. And when Bill Henry calls us both up to sidebar, I'm going to tell him I have a videotape that shows you were the one who killed Jennifer Yamura. And just like that, your career will be over. Your marriage will be over. *You* will be over." I sit back and wait.

Devlin shrinks in his seat. After a minute, he lays it all out. "It was months ago, and only a few times," he starts. "She came on to me at some political function when my wife was out of town. She was so good-looking, and I was long past sober. So I followed her back from the hotel, the Warwick, to her house. An hour of drunken, sloppy sex, then I was out of there and swearing I'd never go back. But the next day, I couldn't stop thinking about her. And the day after that and the day after that. I called her one morning, asked if she wanted to meet me for a cup of coffee. I was thinking Starbucks. But she suggested I come to her place, said she'd make a fresh pot. That was the second time. After we were done, lying in bed, we got to talking. I asked her about her family, where she came from, what her goals were. She asked me what I was working on. And like an idiot, I told her. The grand jury, the police drug ring. I made her promise not to share it with anyone, and she did."

"The laptop," I say.

A bitter smile forms on Devlin's lips. "A couple of times when I went to Jennifer's house, I brought my own laptop with me. I'd shower before I went home. I think she took that time to copy my files. I was supposed to put a password on the computer, but I never got around to it." Devlin shakes his head. "And then, like you said, one day I woke up, went outside my house to get my paper, and there it was in black and white—the story about the grand jury and the crooked cops. I knew I was fucked. I made a big show of subpoenaing Jennifer to appear before the grand jury to disclose her sources. But privately I was pleading with her to fight the subpoena. That's why I went to her house the day she was killed. I told her not to testify. And I begged her not to implicate me."

"And she admitted what she'd done? Copied the files from your laptop?"

"She didn't even apologize for it."

"And that's when you threw her down the stairs," I say.

"No. That's not what happened. I cooled down, and we talked. I convinced her that she needed to hire her own lawyer. Someone other than the TV station's hacks." Here, he pauses, looks at me, and says,

"I gave her the same name I'd given her before. *Your* name," he says bitterly, and the irony slaps me in the face. "The next time I saw her was after the murder, at the crime scene, that night."

I sit back in my chair. I understand the timing now. Jennifer called me at my office, having earlier been given my name by Devlin. Devlin then went to her house and pressured her again, and she called me a second time, telling me she needed to see me right away. So I went to her house. Later, when Devlin got the call that Jennifer had been killed, he knew the CSU guys would be at her house.

"So," I continue, "you got a call from one of your contacts in the police department that David had been busted at Jennifer's house, and you hightailed it over to Addison Street. You barged in and made sure to pollute the crime scene, including the basement, with your hair and skin and fingerprints—because you knew the CSU team was going to find all that stuff anyway. You'd been in the house during your affair. Hell, earlier that day."

Devlin says nothing.

"I wonder whether it was in the back of your mind to kill her even before she opened the door for you."

"Goddamn it! Why aren't you listening to me?" Devlin's voice is thick with exasperation. "I did *not* kill her! I thought we could find a way to make it all work out."

"With my help?"

"You're the best in the city, Mick. The slickest. And, quite frankly, the most ruthless. If there was anyone who could get her out of having to testify, I knew it would be you."

I think back to Jennifer Yamura telling me there was someone we could blackmail—meaning Devlin. But that doesn't make sense. Devlin didn't want Jennifer to testify any more than she did, so blackmailing him wouldn't have accomplished anything more than Devlin would have readily done on his own if he could've managed it. As for Devlin's hope that I could figure out some way to rescue Yamura from the grand jury, it was a pipe dream. No lawyer was going to beat Devlin's subpoena. Devlin and Jennifer were both so desperate, it clouded their judgment.

Devlin laughs bitterly, shakes his head. "Christ, what a fuckup. What a massive fuckup. One mistake. One fucking mistake, and everything down the drain."

The words are a punch to the gut. It takes all my effort not to double over from the same sense of desperation that's driving Devlin.

"I never should have let her lure me in, never given her the chance to trick me."

I laugh. "Is that how you see it? She was the clever fox, and you were her witless prey?"

Devlin steels himself, looks at me. "I think she knew about the grand jury before I told her."

"How could that be?"

"Your brother. He's friends with Lawrence Washington. Lawrence probably told Tommy about his testimony. Or maybe," and here Devlin leans toward me, "Tommy was a part of it all. Lawrence brought him into the scheme, and Tommy gave Jennifer the initial heads-up, when he was taking his turn with her."

"You have a rich imagination."

"How is Tommy doing these days? I haven't seen him in court. Doesn't he usually sit in?" I glower at Devlin, who glares back. "Whatever happens to me, to David Hanson, Tommy's going down, and I think you know it."

"The only person going down is you. And it's going to happen *today*. I'm going to stop you from sending an innocent man to prison to cover for your own crime, and I'm going to destroy you in the process."

Devlin's shoulders slump, every ounce of bravado draining from his body. There's no way out for him, and he knows it. I sit back in my chair for a long moment and enjoy it. Then I say the word that saves his life.

"Or . . ."

For the next twenty minutes, Devlin sits perfectly still, staring out the window behind me as I lay it out for him. When I'm done, he fixes on me, his face incredulous. "You expect me to let a murderer walk out of that courtroom, scot-free?"

"But it was always your plan to walk out of that courtroom. Now David—the man you set up to take the fall for you—is going to walk out, too."

"Listen to me: I did not—"

"Stop it! Just stop it. No more trying to bullshit me into thinking you're innocent. I'm giving you one chance to avoid the catastrophe you've brought on yourself. Take it or leave it. Either way, David Hanson's going to walk."

Devlin exhales, nods. He lifts himself out of his seat, as deflated as I've ever seen him, as spent as I feel myself. When he gets to the door, I call after him.

"We're not done," I say.

He turns, opens his arms: *What else?*

"One more thing," I say. "Tommy. He gets a pass. You leave him alone. And you make sure everyone else does, too. Including Tredesco."

Devlin glares at me. "You're a prick, McFarland. You know that?" And he's gone.

Vaughn gets in an hour later. I hear him greet Susan fifteen minutes after that. I give Susan a chance to situate herself in her office, then I go in and close the door. "I'm going to need your help this morning."

"Sure, anything."

"I need you to question our first witness."

"This morning? Is he already prepped? Do you have a list of questions for me?"

"The witness is fully prepped." Then I tell Susan who the witness will be and why I need her to be the questioning attorney. When I'm done, she stares at me, her jaw hanging. "Jesus Christ."

Half an hour later, just before 9:30, Susan and I enter the courtroom. Susan heads for counsel table while I have the guard let me through the side door leading to David's holding cell. I walk down the narrow hallway, the guard in front of me. He goes to open the door, and I say, "Don't bother. Just give us some room." The guard walks away, and I look through the bars at David, who stands up, wondering how this is going to play out. He knows with my first words.

"Piper told me everything," I say. "You piece of shit."

"Mick, I'm sorry. We never—"

"There will be an accounting, David. As soon as this is over, there will be an accounting." With that, I turn and leave.

Minutes later, the jury is in the box, the judge on the bench, the spectators in their seats, everyone waiting for the show to begin. Judge Henry nods toward me and asks if the defense is ready to present our case.

When Susan rises instead of me, expressions of surprise echo from behind us, everyone wondering what she's doing there. Her voice strong and clear, Susan declares, "The defense calls Piper McFarland."

And the courtroom is instantly abuzz. I look across to the prosecution table, where Devlin is already on his feet.

"Objection," Devlin says. "This witness wasn't named on the defendant's witness list."

He's sticking to the script. Good. He has to fight it on the record, at least at first.

"Sidebar," says the judge, and Susan and I, Devlin and Christina, make our way toward the bench. "What's going on here, Mr. McFarland?" the judge asks me. "Is this witness related to you? What are you offering her for?"

"The witness is my co-counsel's wife, Your Honor," Susan interjects.

Judge Henry looks at me. "Your *wife?*"

"Yes," Susan answers. "The defense is presenting her as our alibi witness. She was with the defendant at the time of the murder."

The court reporter raises her eyebrows.

"I object," Devlin repeats. "The time has long past for the defense to identify alibi witnesses."

"Your Honor," Susan chimes in, "Mr. McFarland only learned last night that the witness was an alibi witness, and—"

Devlin interrupts and speaks over Susan. "The rules require the defendant to disclose any alibi witnesses at the time they file their omnibus motion."

"Your Honor," Susan cuts in, "the defendant was prepared to go to prison for a crime he did not commit to protect the reputation of his alibi witness. But she decided she could not let that happen. Exceptional circumstances are present here."

"I demand an offer of proof," Devlin says, following my script. "I want to hear what this witness is going to say before she's allowed to go anywhere near the jury."

Bill Henry leans back in his chair. He gets it now. And despite his decades as a trial attorney and judge, seeing and hearing it all, he can't quite keep the *Holy shit* from his face. "Very well, Mr. Walker, you'll get your offer of proof. I want counsel, the defendant, and the witness in my chambers in ten minutes. You, too," he says to the court reporter, whose vigorous nodding makes clear that wild horses couldn't keep her away.

Ten minutes later, we are all assembled in chambers. The judge is behind his desk, the court reporter sits next to the desk, to the judge's right. Four chairs sit in front of the desk, and seated in them, left to right, are Piper, Susan, Devlin, and Christina. Behind the four chairs is a long sofa. I am on the far left side of the sofa; David is on the right. David's face, like mine, is set in stone.

Susan begins. "Your Honor, the witness is prepared to testify that on the day of the murder—"

"No," says the judge. "You're not going to summarize her testimony. She's going to testify here, under oath, before me. I'm going to hear what she has to say and how she says it before I decide whether to let her take the stand."

This is what I expected—and hoped for. I told Susan not to protest this if the judge required it. If he did not, Devlin was to demand it and Susan was to agree.

The court reporter administers the oath to Piper, who says "I do" in a barely audible voice. The judge tells her to keep her voice up, and Piper says, "Yes, Your Honor. I'm sorry." Susan questions Piper briefly about her background, establishing that she is, indeed, my wife. Then Susan gets down to business.

"Please tell the court where you were on Thursday, May thirty-first, of this year, from 11:00 a.m. until 4:00 p.m."

Piper glances from Susan to the judge. "I was in room 703 of the Rittenhouse Hotel."

"Were you alone?"

"No."

"Who was with you?"

I watch Piper lower her head and hear her say . . . nothing.

Jesus Christ—she's changed her mind.

I stop breathing. But then Piper lifts her head, looks at the judge, and says, "David Hanson was with me."

"The whole time?" asks Susan.

"He arrived right at noon. But after that, yes, he was with me the whole time."

"When he arrived, did he have any blood on him? Did he appear disheveled in any way?"

"Blood? No. He was dressed in his suit. He looked normal. Buttoned and tucked."

"When did you first tell defense counsel about all this?"

"I told my husband last night."

"Why didn't you come forward sooner?"

Piper looks away from Susan, fixes her gaze on some invisible spot on the wall behind the judge. Of course, everyone in the room knows why she didn't fess up earlier. Tell her husband that she was sleeping with his old friend.

"I just couldn't face . . ." Piper's voice trails off.

"Then why are you coming forward now?"

Piper looks squarely at the judge. "Because David Hanson didn't kill that woman. I can't let an innocent man go to jail. No matter what, I just couldn't."

Susan waits for the words to sink in, then says, "Thank you. Your Honor, nothing further."

Devlin jumps right in with his cross. "Mrs. McFarland, what were you and Mr. Hanson doing all this time, in room 703 of the Rittenhouse Hotel?"

Piper stiffens. "We were . . . we were having relations."

"You mean you were having sex."

Susan is about to answer when Bill Henry interjects, "The court already understands what the witness meant. The follow-up remark is stricken."

Devlin pauses, then asks a question I prepped him for. "Do you have any proof you were at the Rittenhouse Hotel that day?"

"Yes," Piper says, and then she pulls out the hotel receipt showing the charge for the room. "David gave me money to pay the bill in cash so there wouldn't be a credit-card record. But the hotel still gave me a receipt when I checked out."

Devlin studies the bill and asks Piper to state what it is for the record. Then he turns to the judge and says, "Your Honor, I don't want to be indelicate here, but I think I'm entitled to some more background.

I need it to weigh what the witness is now telling us. And, quite frankly, I think the court is entitled to that as well."

"I agree," says the judge. Then he looks at Piper and says, in a kindly voice, "In requesting the court to let you testify at this late date, defense counsel is asking quite a lot. Normally, an alibi witness is identified well in advance of trial, giving the prosecution the chance to investigate the veracity of the alibi. Here, unless I were willing to suspend trial for some period to allow the prosecution to check out what you're saying—which is not something I want to do—the prosecution will not have had that chance. So I'm going to allow Mr. Walker an opportunity to question you, at length, about the circumstances surrounding your alleged meeting with the defendant on the day of the murder. Do you understand?"

Piper nods. "Yes."

"Does defense counsel have any objection to this?" Judge Henry asks Susan, who says she does not. "Very well, Mr. Walker. The witness is yours."

Devlin spends the next twenty minutes excavating the details of Piper's affair with David Hanson. When it began and how. How often they met and where. How they arranged their meetings so their spouses wouldn't find out about them. It's an agonizing interchange. It feels as though Devlin is taking a long sword and slowly pushing it through my heart, inch by inch. From time to time, he glances back at me. I can tell he's enjoying my torment. And then comes the final plunge of the blade.

"One more question, Mrs. McFarland. And here I cannot help but be indelicate. To corroborate that you were in fact engaging in *relations*, can you describe any sort of mark or scar on Mr. Hanson's body that wouldn't be visible unless he were disrobed?"

Piper swallows hard. Her shoulders slouch. She averts her eyes from Devlin, then closes them. "He has a mole. On his upper thigh, the left one."

Fury fills me as pictures of my wife and David Hanson flash across the movie screen inside my mind. It takes every ounce of my strength not to attack David right there in chambers, batter his face into pulp. Instead, I close my own eyes, take deep breaths. After what seems like an hour, but which can't have been more than a few seconds, the judge asks Susan if the client will acknowledge that this is the case. But Devlin has a better idea.

"Your Honor," my adversary interjects, "the Commonwealth needs more."

It takes a moment for Bill Henry to figure out what Devlin is asking, but when he does, he sighs and nods. He asks Devlin if he's done with the witness, and if there's any need for Piper to remain while the defendant disrobes.

Devlin glances at me, and I glare at him. "The prosecution has no more questions for the witness at this time. We have no objection to her leaving chambers during the examination."

I stand as Piper leaves the chair. "With the court's permission," I say, "I'd like to be allowed to leave for this part as well." Judge Henry grants me leave, and I accompany Piper out of chambers. I escort her past the secretarial well and out the door into the hallway. We walk quietly to the long bench by the windows at the end of the hall and sit. Piper leans into me. I wrap my arms around her and promise her, again, that this is all going to turn out okay.

After a few minutes, one of the judge's law clerks walks into the hallway and summons me back to chambers. Judge Henry looks at me, concern and pity in his eyes. "The inspection corroborated the witness's testimony," he says. Then he turns to Devlin. "Does the Commonwealth still object to the defense's presenting the witness?"

Devlin looks at the judge, then leans forward in his seat, places his elbows on the armrests, steeples his pointer fingers, and puts them to his lips. He closes his eyes for a long minute. Then he opens them again, leans back in his seat. "The Commonwealth is satisfied that the witness is telling the truth." Then, as though he were thinking out loud, Devlin continues. "If the earliest the murder occurred was noon, as the pathologist testified, and if the defendant left his office at eleven fifty, it would be impossible for him to have traveled to Addison Street, even by cab, pushed the victim down the stairs, dragged her back to the stairs, cleaned off all the blood that would've gotten onto him, and made it to the hotel by noon." Devlin pauses, sighs, and says the words that stun everyone present—except me. "We're ready to drop the charges."

"*What?*" Christina Wesley almost falls out of her chair.

"Excuse me?" the judge says.

Susan jerks her head back to where I'm sitting on the couch. Her eyes are filled with disbelief.

"Your Honor," Devlin begins, his voice low and calm, "in all my years as a prosecutor, I have never once knowingly sent a man to prison whom I believed was not guilty. I've never even brought charges against someone where I wasn't personally convinced of their guilt."

"That's not the standard for bringing a defendant to trial, Mr. Walker," Judge Henry says. "If there's sufficient evidence to support the charges, a prosecutor may properly bring those charges, regardless of his personal beliefs. That's the standard."

Devlin lifts his head. "Respectfully, Your Honor, I hold myself to a higher standard."

I can't help but smile. Devlin's being clever. He knows this transcript will be made public, just as he knows he's going to have to justify his heretical decision to drop the charges against David. And there is only one acceptable justification: actual innocence. Devlin has to take the position that he believes David Hanson is not the one who murdered Jennifer Yamura. He is doing so now, and is painting himself as a prosecutor who takes the moral high ground.

"Would you like some time to talk with your boss?" the judge asks Devlin.

"This is my call, Your Honor."

There's no way Devlin is going to call the DA. The district attorney would yank Devlin from the case, appoint Christina Wesley first chair, and tell her to press vigorously for a conviction.

"I don't need to tell you that if you drop the charges, double jeopardy will attach, and there can be no retrial for homicide," the judge says.

Devlin doesn't answer, just stares at the judge. Beside him, Christina Wesley sits frozen in her chair.

"And what about the lesser charges?" Bill Henry asks. "Tampering with evidence, interfering with a crime scene, and so forth?"

Devlin considers this. "The Commonwealth will drop those as well."

Back in the courtroom, David, Susan, and I take our seats at the defense table. After a good five minutes, Devlin and Christina enter the courtroom. They were arguing outside the judge's chambers when we left them. The judge takes the bench, and Holleran opens the door for the jurors. They walk fast, with purpose, their heads up, eyes bright. The rest of the courtroom is electrified as well. By now everyone knows that the defense's first witness is going to be the wife of the lead defense attorney. Sparks of one type or another are going to fly.

Bill Henry looks out at the courtroom, scans the faces of the parties, their counsel, the reporters, the onlookers, his staff, and finally, the jury. He smiles at them, and they smile back. Then, without preamble, he says, "The charges against the defendant are dropped."

A collective "Huh?" reverberates in the courtroom.

"Ladies and gentlemen," the judge continues, looking at the bewildered jurors, "I thank you for your service. You have been most patient and most attentive. The parties, the Commonwealth, and I personally, are grateful to you." Then he looks to defense table and says, "Mr. Hanson, you are free to go. Court is adjourned."

A loud bang of the gavel, and Bill Henry is gone from the bench. And the courtroom falls into mayhem.

I turn away from David to avoid shaking his hand. I nod to Vaughn and Alex Ginsberg, signaling for them to follow me out of the courtroom. The press is on me even before I get to the door. I swat them away. "No comment. No comment." As I pass the rows of spectators, I cannot help but glance at Jennifer Yamura's parents and brother. Her mother is weeping openly, her father trying in vain to console her. Brian Yamura glares at me. And one row behind them, I see John Tredesco, his face etched with rage.

I bolt from the courtroom, the floor, and the courthouse. I sprint back to the firm. After a while, Vaughn, Susan, and Alexander Ginsberg arrive and set themselves up in the conference room. By now Susan will have told Ginsberg and Vaughn what went down in Judge Henry's chambers. I hear them talking as I approach the conference-room door. They all quiet down when I walk into the room. Susan is the first to say what they're all thinking: "Devlin dropping the charges? What the hell was that?"

I shake my head, take a seat at the table. "Devlin obviously believed Piper's testimony."

Vaughn opens his mouth to say something but decides better of it. Anything to be said about Piper is going to have to come from me.

"The important thing," I continue, "is that it's over. The client has been completely exonerated and will get on with his life. Chalk up another win for the good guys." I force a smile, then ask Vaughn and Susan to give me a few minutes with Alexander Ginsberg. As soon as I close the door, the legendary lawyer is on me.

"You knew," he says. "You knew it was going to go down just like it did."

"I hoped. I didn't know."

Ginsberg studies me like he's studied a thousand witnesses on the stand. "Give me the backstory," he says. "Tell me why you wanted to make sure this case never reached a verdict. Why you hired me to sit in court every day just so I could tell your client that his defense was a sinking ship unless he came forward with the alibi."

I don't answer.

Ginsberg studies me some more, then says, "What I also don't get is why Walker dismissed the charges once Piper claimed to be his alibi. Devlin could have crucified her on the stand. Slapped her with her obvious bias as your wife and painted the two of you as conspirators in perjury."

Again, I don't answer.

Ginsberg nods his head slowly. He reaches out and shakes my hand, pats me on the shoulder. "Tell me one thing. Was justice done here today?"

The question evokes in my mind the Yamura family sitting, broken, in the courtroom.

"Not even close."

35

FRIDAY, NOVEMBER 16, CONTINUED

After Ginsberg leaves, I walk to my office and close the door. "No calls," I tell Angie on the phone. "No visitors." I flop into my chair, feeling physically and mentally spent. And morally bankrupt. I betrayed every professional principle I hold dear. I misled my legal team every step of the way. I helped blackmail my own client, even engineered his being tossed into prison. I perpetrated a fraud on the court. I worked the system to deal a dreadful injustice to the family of a murdered young woman. And then there's what I did to my own family: deceiving Tommy and Piper and subjecting Piper to crushing pressure until she broke down and allowed herself to be manipulated into perjury.

I tell myself I did it all to save my family. But there's no nobility in my deeds. Because everything I did, I also did to save myself from the consequences of my own terrible act. An act that splits my gut every time I think about it. An act for which I will never forgive myself.

I look at the beautifully framed admission certificate to the Pennsylvania Supreme Court hanging on the wall.

How do I face another jury, another judge, after what I've done? What right do I have to fight for another man's freedom?

I sit numbly for a long time. My eyes closing, opening, searching for something to help me go on.

And then I spot the envelope from the Pennsylvania Supreme Court. I lurch forward, grab the envelope, rip it open, and read. It's the decision in the Justin Bauer case. I skip to the end, and tears begin to trickle down my face. The court is giving Justin a second chance. I take a deep breath and lift the phone.

"Celine, it's me. Good news. *Great* news."

36

SATURDAY, NOVEMBER 24; MONDAY, NOVEMBER 26

Piper, Gabby, and I are wolfing down a big meal at Godmother's, Gabby's favorite restaurant in Cape May. We've been here a week, and I don't think any of us have ever had a lovelier time at the shore. Piper and I took Gabby on long morning walks on the beach, which was deserted except for the three of us. We collected shells, chased the gulls, and watched the sandpipers dart back and forth at the water's edge. We rode bikes along the back roads, visited the pigs at Beach Plum Farm. At night—every night—once Gabby was asleep, Piper and I made love. It was tender and real. The coupling of two people who'd been swept away from each other by an angry tide, then, miraculously, washed ashore a century later on a deserted island. At least that's how it feels to me.

But, of course, civilization is only a headline away. The hotel carries the Jersey Shore edition of the *Inquirer*, so I couldn't escape the aftermath of the Hanson case. The initial press reports damned and derided me. Half the accounts accused me of using my own wife in a scheme to dupe the judge and prosecutor. The other half painted me the fool. Depending on which reporter you followed, I was either a cuckold or the most calculating son of a bitch ever to practice law, and Piper was either an unfaithful wife or a perjurer.

It was all too much for Thatcher Gray. The day after Piper and I left for the beach, Sir Thatcher ordered his wife, Helen, to pack their bags, and they took a late-night flight to London. Helen called to tell us that Thatcher was nursing his rage at their hotel bar.

The reportage on Devlin has followed an interesting arc. Early articles skewered him for letting a millionaire off the hook. But Devlin went on the offensive, making appearances on all the local TV stations. He had two themes. The first: the moral high road. He recognized that his decision was politically unpopular. "But," he was quoted as saying, "I cannot claim to apply the laws evenly regardless of social status and then send an innocent man to prison simply because he's wealthy." And that led into Devlin's second theme: David Hanson was innocent. Devlin espoused the view that Jennifer Yamura was likely murdered during a burglary gone bad, the killer having gained entry to her house through an unlocked door. It must have galled Devlin to declare David innocent, convinced as he is of David's guilt. But it's the road he has to take.

Devlin's new spin was manna from heaven for David Hanson. It sent the message that David hadn't gone free due to high-priced legal trickery but because he deserved it. Like Devlin, David Hanson was making the TV news circuit. The *Inquirer* quoted an interview on Channel Six's Sunday-morning news magazine. Anchorman Jim asked David whether he intended to bring a wrongful-prosecution case. David said no. "The city is financially strapped as it is. And my mission isn't to take—it's to bring money to the citizens and taxpayers of this town by cementing the business relationships that will pull jobs into our region."

Now David is well placed to complete those Asian deals, having been grudgingly reinstated by Edwin at Hanson World Industries and promoted to president of HWI-Asia.

◆ ◆ ◆

It's Monday, and I'm back at the office now, refreshed and renewed by my time at the shore with Piper and Gabby, hoping I'm strong enough to face the ordeal ahead: the "accounting" I promised David Hanson. He's been waiting in the conference room for thirty minutes. I had Angie park him there because I can't abide his presence in my personal office. I've had him wait so long because . . . well, because I want to make him wait.

When finally I enter the conference room and close the door, David looks up at me. I can see his mind spinning, trying to figure out how to play his part so that the scene between us resolves to his advantage. Should he be contrite, beg my forgiveness? Or go on the offensive, use whatever ammunition Piper had given him to justify her betrayal? He elects to open with a question.

"Why did Devlin fold like he did?"

"You heard him. He believed Piper was telling the truth."

"He could have cross-examined her in open court. Let the jury decide."

I shrug. "He was convinced you're innocent."

David studies me for a minute. "Marcie thinks there's more to it."

I shrug. "Occam's razor. Sometimes the simplest explanation is the truth." I hold David's gaze as I lift a water bottle from the silver tray on the table, open it, take a sip. "So, why did you do it?"

David looks away, but only for a second. "It began by chance. Piper and I ran into each other at the mall and . . ."

I put my hand up to stop him. "Not that. I know why you did *that*. You're a self-serving narcissist who can't keep your dick in your pants. No, what I want to know, now that you can never be retried for it, is why you murdered Jennifer Yamura."

David stares at me. I can feel the heat rising in him. He leans ever so slightly into the table, toward me. "I didn't kill her, Mick."

"Did Jennifer really threaten to tell Marcie," I ask, "like her brother said? I know Tredesco put him up to saying that on the stand. But did it really happen? Did you see the scandal of it playing out in the newspapers? Were you terrified Marcie would leave you, take the boys and a bunch of your money? Or was it that you'd never get to the top at HWI?"

"I did not kill Jennifer," David repeats, a little more strain in his voice.

"And here's another question. What *were* you doing between 11:50, when you left your office, and 1:45, when you showed up at Jennifer's house?"

"Piper asked me to come to the hotel in the afternoon. It was a nice day, though, and I wanted to leave the office earlier. I knew the arts festival was happening on Rittenhouse Square, so I decided to take it in. I did just that. And in answer to your next question, no, there's no one who can vouch for me being there."

I snort. "I don't buy it. My guess is you paid a visit to another *special friend*. Jennifer and Piper weren't enough for you. You had a third one in the mix. You really are a piece of—"

"Enough," David interrupts. "What am I here for? Because it's sure as hell not to take shit from you."

"You have quite a temper," I say. "I never picked up on it when we were in law school. Then again, everything was going so swimmingly for you back then. You were surrounded by friends—admirers, really. Kevin Kratz got you on the *Law Review*, then abdicated the editor-in-chief position to you. You were getting laid left and right. You were the star of the show."

"You have no idea of the pressures I was under, then or since. The expectations placed on me . . ." David's voice trails off, and we sit in silence for a moment. "Just send me the bill. I'll pay it as soon as I open the envelope."

I pin him with my stare. "Yes, you will pay. I also told you there'd be an accounting between *us*." I pull the DVD from my desk drawer, set it on the table.

David knows where I'm headed. "You don't dare leak that," he says, "or Piper will go to prison for perjury."

I smile. "Oh, I doubt that. She has a good attorney. He could probably get her off. He found a way to keep *you* out of jail, and you're a murderer."

"Fuck you." David sighs. "What's your endgame here?"

"I just want you to pay your legal bill. And to show a little gratitude for the exceptional job that I've done, I think a five-million-dollar bonus would do it."

"That's highway robbery!"

"No, that's blackmail. You should recognize it; we've both been down this road before."

This would be the perfect time for me to disclose to David that Anna Groszek had demanded only $3 million, and not the $4 million I'd made David come up with. But I hold my tongue.

David glares, perhaps seeing this side of me for the first time.

"There's one thing I just don't get," I say. "You hired me because you knew that Piper would have to lie for you on the stand, and you figured I was the only person who could get her to do that. But what made you so sure I'd be confident enough in your innocence to persuade her?"

David's face lights up, and he laughs a bitter, full-hearted laugh. "Your confidence in my innocence? Oh, Mick, you really are a crack-up. I wasn't counting on your believing I didn't kill Jennifer. The truth is that I didn't know what I'd be able to hook you with once you found out about Piper and me. But you're right that I figured you'd be the only person who could get Piper to perjure herself. So I hired you with the hope that somewhere down the line, I'd find something to use as leverage against you."

I hold my breath. If the dying Jennifer Yamura told David I pushed her down the steps, this is where he'll spring it.

He shrugs. "I never did, but you convinced Piper to perjure herself anyway. And I'm torn as to why. The idealistic part of me says that, even knowing what I did with Piper, you helped me because, deep inside, you know I didn't kill Jennifer. But my gut says that you offered up your wife because that's what it took to carry the day. When Marcie told me she ordered you to do whatever it would take to win, I laughed and told her she needn't have wasted her breath. She might as well have been telling a fish it had to swim."

I'm about to launch into David when I hear a knock at the door. It opens, and Susan peeks her head in. "Everything okay in here?"

"Peachy," I answer. "David's just told me that he's so happy with the job we did that he's paying us a five-million-dollar bonus!"

Susan's jaw drops. She looks from me to David, back to me. "Holy shit" is all she can get out.

Before I can say anything else, David stands. He walks away but pauses and turns in the doorway.

"You know what, Mick? I'm happy to pay you the five million. Teaching your wife how to fuck was worth every penny." And with that, he brushes past Susan, leaving her to witness the humiliation in my burning face.

An hour later, I still feel raw as I speed up the 476 toward Jim Thorpe—and Tommy. I take deep breaths, steel myself. I've resolved to fix things. The chasm between us, opened by Tommy's euthanizing our father, has to be closed.

I turn onto the dirt road leading to his trailer and see Tommy open the door and come outside to meet me. He knew I was coming; I called before leaving the city. I park the car, walk to Tommy, shake his hand. It's chilly this November afternoon in Jim Thorpe, and Tommy is wearing a long-sleeved red-flannel shirt, the tail hanging outside his worn jeans. His black-leather biker's boots crunch the gravel beneath his feet. I feel out of place in my business suit and wingtips.

"I guess I'm supposed to say congratulations," Tommy says.

I shrug. "Why don't you just get us some beer?" I say, then I sit at the picnic table while he goes inside to fetch a couple of Buds.

When he returns, Tommy sits across the table, hands me a bottle. "So," he says, "Devlin rolled over. He quit the fight. Now he's going around telling everyone he believes David is innocent. How'd you manage that?"

I look at Tommy, throw back my beer. "Devlin was on the tape."

I tell Tommy how I confronted Devlin, strong-armed him into making our deal. Tommy works to keep his face neutral as I tell the story, but I see judgment in his eyes. He thinks I wronged Devlin Walker. I feel the urge to defend myself, but I didn't come here to talk about Devlin Walker or David Hanson.

"There's something I need to say to you."

My brother puts down his beer, puts his hands on the table, and waits. I take a deep breath and continue.

"You did the right thing," I say. "For Dad. Ending his pain. It was the right thing to do," I repeat. "Noble, and loving. And you paid a terrible price for it. A price you never should have had to pay, not by yourself. I should have been there with you. And not just to help Dad at the end, but for all the time leading up to it." I pause, lock eyes with my brother, make sure he hears me. "Tommy, I'm sorry. For everything. For abandoning you and Dad. For not doing more to help you later."

"What could—?"

"I should have come after you. Brought you home. Not let you wander the country drinking yourself to death, trying to get thrown into prison. If I had, you would have told me what you'd done, instead of carrying it around inside you all those years. I can't imagine what it was like for you, living with that kind of secret." I shake my head, look down.

When again I look at Tommy, he has an odd look on his face. I can't read it, but I find it unsettling.

Tommy takes a breath, then says, "You can't blame yourself for my taking off. There was nothing you could've done about that. But you're right about keeping what I'd done inside. That was the worst part of it, after the guilt." Here, he pauses, looks hard at me. "You keep a secret like that, it eats away at you. Some things, no matter how bad they are—*because* of how bad they are—just need to be talked about."

Tommy takes a swig of his beer, his eyes locked on me the whole time. I begin to feel a queasiness in my stomach. Tommy's clearly fishing for something.

"How's Lawrence doing?" I ask, nodding toward Tommy's trailer.

"Not good. In and out. More out these past couple weeks. But he's not in my trailer. He's over there." Tommy nods toward another trailer sitting across the gravel road from his own. "Guy who owns it is a friend of mine. He's in Florida, so he's letting me use it for Lawrence. I keep tabs on him with a baby monitor. Can you believe that?" He shakes his head. "You want to see him?"

Tommy is out of his seat and walking toward the trailer before I can answer. I stand and follow.

Lawrence Washington is lying in a bed in the back room of the trailer. The bed is just about the width of the room and is pushed up against the window that takes up most of the far wall. There are windows by the head and foot of the bed as well, so Lawrence lies awash in light. The trailer stinks—of sweat, urine, stale breath, and Lawrence's dying.

"Up until last week," Tommy says, "I could get him to the toilet, most times. These past few days haven't been so good." He smiles wanly. "I never raised kids, but I bet I've seen more diapers than you."

"Jesus," I say, my voice barely above a whisper.

"Hey, Lawrence," Tommy announces. "Look who's here to visit you."

Lawrence slowly opens his eyes. It takes some time for it to register with him who I am. When it does, he smiles. "Hey," Lawrence says weakly. He lifts his right hand a few inches off his stomach.

I take it. "Sorry it took so long for me to come up again," I say. "Better late than never, right?"

Lawrence smiles. "Pretty soon," he says, "I'll be both. The late, and never." Then he coughs, his face contorted in pain.

"You want some morphine?" Tommy asks, but Lawrence waves him off.

"You have morphine?"

"A good buddy of mine is a hospice worker. I called him, told him about Lawrence. He drove me up some drugs on the sly, for when it gets bad."

Tommy pulls up a plastic chair for me to sit on next to Lawrence's bed while Tommy fixes something for Lawrence to eat. I sit quietly with Lawrence for a few minutes. Then Lawrence looks over at me. "So, I hear you beat the pants off Devlin. He's a wily one. But you were always clever, too. I liked working with you." Lawrence coughs again.

"You sure you don't want some medicine?" I ask as Tommy comes back carrying a plastic tray with a plate of what appears to be baby food and a juice box.

I stand to make room for Tommy, and Lawrence answers me. "No. I'm used to the pain by now, except when it gets real bad. Mostly, though, it's just lotsa rockin' and rollin'. I can take it."

My vision blurs, then clears as I stare at Lawrence Washington in disbelief. It feels as if someone's just whacked me with a two-by-four. *Lotsa rockin' and rollin'.* The same words the caller used when he phoned 911 to report the imaginary fight at 1792 Addison. I repeat the words out loud. "Lotsa rockin' and rollin'."

I back away from the bed, and Tommy turns to look at me. He's puzzled at first. But after a second, he gets it. "Mick." I hear my brother behind me, but I'm already out the door.

"Mick!" Tommy shouts after me as I make my way across the gravel road. I stop and turn toward him.

"It was Lawrence who made that call," I say. "And you who put him up to it."

"Let's sit down," Tommy says.

"You knew David was in the house! You wanted the police to catch him!"

"Mick! Please. Sit down."

I hesitate but follow my brother to the picnic table. It's getting on to dusk now. The sun is behind the trees, and it's starting to get colder. Tommy takes a deep breath. "They called me from the hotel. Piper and David. Piper told me everything, about the affair and about David finding Jennifer Yamura dead on the stairs. They were both in a panic."

"It was *your* idea," I say. "To have David go back and clean up." Tommy nods. "But you had to know there was no way he could clean all the . . ." My voice trails off as all the pieces click into place. From start to finish, Tommy had set David up.

"Why?"

"It was a betrayal!" Tommy practically shouts the words. "Piper with that prick."

I stare at my brother. It's clear that Piper's betrayal hit him hard. But her betrayal of whom?

"So you told them that David needed to go back and clean up the place."

Tommy nods. "Lawrence was ready to make the call as soon as I signaled him. I waited for David to get deep into the cleanup job, then I rang Lawrence and he made the 911 call on a burner."

"After David's arrest, I caught you and Piper fighting on our back patio. That's what it was about, wasn't it?"

Tommy nods. "Piper figured out that I was the one who'd fingered David. It drove a wedge between us."

"Why did she decide to call you in the first place?"

Tommy smiles, but there's bitterness in his eyes. "When I got out of prison, Piper was my biggest fan. She'd been writing to me while I was inside, encouraging me, and she kept it up once I was released. She told me I was no worse than anyone else, that I'd just had some bad breaks. But when this thing with David happened and she needed advice on how to deal with a crime, I was the one she called. For all her talk, Piper still sees me as a criminal."

My mouth starts to open, but I close it. Piper's call must have hurt Tommy.

Tommy looks away, and we sit in silence for a long while. I chew on what Tommy has told me. I get that he hated David Hanson because of his affair with Piper. But there has to be more. Tommy wouldn't frame an innocent man just because he was pissed.

"That day," Tommy says, "when I was in your office and Jennifer called, I realized she was in a bad spot with the grand jury and was looking for a way out. I figured she might try to save herself by selling me out as her source. So I decided to go see her. I was mad and a little scared, and I didn't want to show up half-cocked and say something stupid, make things worse. So I decided to stop for something to eat, to cool off and think things through. I went to a sandwich shop on Walnut Street for a while, then walked down Seventeenth, took a right, toward her house. When I got to Waverly, I looked down the alley."

Tommy's words hit me like a sledgehammer. "You saw me leaving," I say, almost a whisper.

"You were walking down the alley, away from me. I started to call out after you, but something stopped me. I waited until you turned the corner on Eighteenth. Then I kept walking down Seventeenth and turned onto Addison. Jennifer said she made everyone—which I figured meant the men she was screwing behind Hanson's back—come through the back door. But I told her no way. I wasn't sneaking through anybody's backyard. So I always came to the front, and I did that day, too. I rang the bell and I knocked. But there was no answer. So I opened the door; it was unlocked."

Tommy and I sit in silence until the full horror of what must have happened floods my head. I'd thought David Hanson was the only one who'd entered the house after I left. But he wasn't. Tommy got there before David, but he didn't appear on Anna Groszek's video.

"Oh, God, Tommy," I say as my heart breaks one more time for my brother. For one more terrible thing that he'll have to carry around inside him. "You went into the house and found Jennifer." Tommy looks at me but says nothing. "But she wasn't dead."

Tommy shivers. "She was lying on the steps. Her eyes were closed. Then she opened them and looked up at me. She was confused at first. Then it was like she figured out where she was and what had happened, and she got a scared look in her eyes. She kind of lifted her back, let herself slide down the steps. At the bottom, she rolled over and started to crawl away. Left a trail of blood. I stood there trying to wrap my head around the thought that you—*you*—had pushed her down the steps."

"I thought I'd killed her," I whisper.

Tommy considers this. "I went down and tried to help her up. But she didn't want me near her. She was half out of it. More than half. She thought I was you. Started mumbling how she was going to nail you for attacking her. Going to get 'your brother'—me—too. Tell the cops all about me and the drug ring." Tommy stops talking, clearly struggling with the memory of what happened next.

"She fought a little when I carried her back to the steps, laid her down. But then she became very still. After a bit, she talked some more—mumbled more than talked. Then she laughed. And then tears started flowing, like she was crying, but she didn't make a sound. She was slipping away. I knelt next to her, held her hand. I told her it was going to be okay. Toward the end, she opened her eyes, looked up at me. But she wasn't really seeing me. It was like when a baby looks up at you. Its eyes can't focus. She mumbled something again. I think it was her brother's name—Brian. Then her body went limp, like a balloon with the air drained out of it. I sat with her for a while more. Then I panicked. Started cleaning up the basement, as though I could wipe away all that blood. But I knew there was no way to make it look like an accident, make the police think she'd just fallen and stayed on the steps. I did my best to wipe my prints off everything in the basement, including her. I took off all my clothes so as not to track blood, went upstairs, got one of Hanson's shirts, a pair of his pants, a pair of his sneakers. Put them on, put my own stuff and the rags I'd used to try to clean up the blood in a trash bag, wiped off everything I'd touched, and left."

Tears are streaming down Tommy's face now. His lip is quivering.

"You have to let it go," I say.

Tommy's eyes snap to mine. "Just like that, huh?"

I'm good at pushing down my emotions. I'd done exactly what I'd accused Devlin of. I'd locked this terrible thing in my private dungeon, hidden it from myself. I'm telling Tommy to do the same. But Tommy isn't me. He can't hide from his demons.

"So, what then?" I ask. "You were going to keep this to yourself? Even though you just told me that keeping something like this hidden is the worst part?"

"*You* were going to keep it to *yourself*," Tommy says.

And I realize, now, why, after so many years, Tommy suddenly chose to open up to me about what he'd done to our father. It wasn't to unburden himself. Tommy was giving *me* an opening to clear my own conscience, to confess what I'd done to Jennifer Yamura.

Tommy and I sit in silence for a long moment. "She would have bled out," I say. "Whether you'd shown up or not."

"Her cell phone was in her shorts. If I hadn't gone in, she might've remembered it, called for help. She might have, but I made sure that didn't happen."

"She would have destroyed us both," I say.

"But I'm the one who killed her."

"No, Tommy. You didn't kill Jennifer. We both did."

37

TUESDAY, NOVEMBER 27

I awake the next morning inside Tommy's trailer; I'm curled up on the worn leather couch. My head is pounding from the bottle of bourbon Tommy and I polished off last night. The light is painfully bright to my eyes. I force myself to stand and walk outside. The late-November morning air is cold and thick and carries the smoky scent of burning wood. I inhale deeply.

Tommy exits Lawrence Washington's trailer, and we stand facing each other for a while.

"I meant what I said last night. About Dad. You did the right thing."

Tommy stares at me. "And Jennifer? Was that the right thing?"

"She would have wrecked our family, Tommy. Not just you and me, but Piper and Gabby, too."

Tommy looks away. My words aren't enough, won't ever be enough. And how could they be? Words are just words. I wasn't there with Tommy, helping him to tend our father. Nor was I with him when he cleaned up the awful mess I'd made with Jennifer Yamura. Once again, I wasn't there for Tommy when he needed me most.

"Will you be able to come for Christmas?" I ask.

Tommy shrugs, tilts his head toward Lawrence's trailer.

"Stupid question," I say.

Tommy and I shake hands, and I get into the car. He watches as I drive off. I wave, but he doesn't wave back. I'm abandoning him again, and the chasm between us will widen with every mile I drive down the pike.

I'm twenty minutes away when it finally dawns on me. "You idiot," I say. "Neanderthal."

I call Piper on my cell phone and tell her what I'm going to do. There's a long pause at the other end of the line, then, "Yes," she says. "Yes. That's exactly what you need to do."

"And then, for us, it'll be Paris and London," I say. "You and me and Gabby. We'll stop in New York first so we can take Gabby to see *The Lion King*." Piper and I talk for a few more minutes, then I hang up.

At the next exit, I turn the car around and head north, back toward Jim Thorpe. That's where I'll stay until it's over. Whether it takes a week or a month, I'll help Tommy care for Lawrence Washington. I'll hold Lawrence's hand and talk to him. I'll feed Lawrence, medicate him, turn him so he doesn't get bedsores. I'll be there until Lawrence passes in the trailer, or until the pain gets to be so bad that we have to take him to a hospital. I'll stand beside my brother every step of the way, as I should have done once before. And in doing so, I will begin the process of mending the wound I opened so long ago.

As for what Tommy and I did to Jennifer Yamura, there will never be peace for either of us. Her killing will be a burden we carry for the rest of our lives. But we will carry it together.

ACKNOWLEDGMENTS

This book is the result of the generous effort and contributions of many great people. First and foremost is my wife, Lisa, who believed in me and the book even when I had my doubts. Her reassurances kept me moving forward, and her editorial suggestions were inspired. I also want to thank my early readers, Kelly McFarland, Alan Sandman, and Jill and Neil Reiff.

For teaching me how the industry works, and pointing me to Ed Stackler, I extend my special thanks to my fellow attorney and author Anderson Harp. Thanks, too, to Bill Lashner, whose own books I have thoroughly enjoyed over the years and who schooled me in the many benefits of publishing with Amazon.

I extend huge thanks to Ed Stackler, my editor, who laboriously chiseled away until he found the statue inside the marble slab. Ed, your artistry was transformative.

To Cynthia Manson, my agent, I give my heartfelt gratitude for your critical structural suggestions, for getting the book into the hands of Nancee Taylor-Adams, who did a really wonderful job of fine-tuning the book, and for getting the book to Gracie Doyle.

And, finally, to Gracie Doyle herself. Your suggestions about the protagonist were exactly what the story needed. Thank you for that, and for taking a chance on an old trial dog like me.

ABOUT THE AUTHOR

Photo © Todd Rothstein

William L. Myers, Jr. was born into a proud, working-class family in Lancaster, Pennsylvania. He attended college at Clarion University and law school at the University of Pennsylvania. For the past thirty years, he has fought for his clients in state and federal courtrooms up and down the East Coast and has had the honor of arguing before the United States Supreme Court. Bill lives with his wife, Lisa, in the western suburbs of Philadelphia.